Hey Jude

Kathleen Stone

Copyright © 2021 Kathleen Stone

All rights reserved. No part of this book may be reproduced or transmitted in any form or by any means, graphic, electronic, or mechanical, including photocopying, recording, taping, or by any information storage retrieval system, without the permission in writing from the publisher.

Any resemblance to actual people and events is purely coincidental. This is a work of fiction.

Cover design by Ken E. Kirk

Paperback: 9798466586251

Hard Cover: 9798467748962

"Deaf people can do anything, except hear."
~ Marlee Matlin

For Sammi and Sophi

Chapter 1

"Do you believe in love at first sight?"

Without even looking at him I threw back the fiery liquid from the shot glass and slammed it back on the bar.

"Nope," I answered.

As Huey Lewis sang "Do You Believe In Love?" overhead I heard him say, "Do you believe in love?"

Could this guy be more cliché? Then who was I kidding… sitting in a club on New Year's Eve wearing a cheetah patterned miniskirt with a matching bra top, more makeup than a prostitute, and bleached-blonde hair that was so big it could've been four cats sleeping on my head. I was the biggest cliché in the place.

"No, I certainly don't," I finally answered, still refusing to look at the stranger. I hadn't believed in love in a very long time. Love of any type.

"Do you like to party?"

I swiveled on my stool to face him, dramatically crossing one leg over the other, my silver studded ankle boots sparkling under the club lights. "Now you're talking," I replied, looking him up and down exaggeratedly, taking him in with my suspicious brown eyes.

He looked to be about my height, maybe five foot eight, and he was dressed all in black with a pair of ripped up jeans, button down shirt, leather jacket and boots. More clichés. His long dark hair fell to his shoulders, curling up once it touched down, topped off by a middle part that didn't seem to know which path it wanted to take, crooked like a bolt of lightning.

I watched his face as he ordered a shot for both of us then smiled at me. In the dim lighting of the club it was difficult to discern his facial features clearly, but he was cute, and all I really cared about was the party he was offering.

"Happy New Year!" he cheered, clinking his shot glass against mine.

We threw back the liquid and slammed our glasses on the bar. I stood up and Carl, the bartender, said, "Take it easy, Marla. If you're not in that cage by eleven-thirty you're gonna get fired. And you're already drunk."

The stranger gawked at me and chuckled, "You're one of those dancers? In the cage?"

"Is that a problem?" I snarled.

He grinned. "Not at all. What're you drinking?"

"Marla...," Carl warned.

I waggled my fingers at Carl without even glancing his way. "Martini. Extra olives."

"Make that two," the stranger told Carl.

I could hear Carl grumbling as he made our drinks and when he was finished the stranger gave him a wad of cash, handed me my drink, and I led the way through the crowd into the club's front foyer to an elevator where I punched in a code before we stepped in and I got a much better look at him. He looked much younger in the light than he did inside the club, but it didn't matter. I didn't even want to know his name.

"So where are we going, Marla?" he asked, grinning at me.

I was mesmerized as I looked deep into his hazel eyes that at the moment were flecked with sparks of green and blue, like a kaleidoscope pulling me under his spell.

"Top floor. VIP," I answered.

I watched as he plucked the toothpick out of his drink with his long, slender fingers and ate one of the olives. He looked at his watch and said, "It's a shame you have to be in a cage at midnight."

"How much time do I have?"

"One hour."

As the elevators opened I stepped into the foyer then grabbed his hand and pulled him into the VIP club which was very dimly lit, the music was more subdued and everyone up there was interested in privacy, therefore paid no attention to anyone else. I chose a comfy couch in the farthest corner of the massive space and sat down, pulling him next to me.

"So Marla," he said, gazing at me as he sipped his drink. "If that's your real name."

I laughed. "Hardly. All the girls here have fake names because of stalkers."

"It's an old church turned into a dance club… it's not like you're strippers or something."

"You'd be surprised," I scoffed, my head feeling a little dizzy.

"So what's your real name?" he asked.

I finished my drink and set the glass on the table. "Look, you wanna party, let's party. I'm not interested in getting to know you."

He feigned sadness as he placed a hand over his heart. He leaned closer and I saw that he was looking at the "P" charm dangling from my necklace.

"P," he said. "I guess it's as good a name as any."

I was getting impatient, crossing one leg over the other and nervously kicking my foot up and down. "Why is it a shame I'll be in a cage at midnight?"

He set his drink down, throwing his right foot atop his left knee. "It's New Year's Eve and you'll be spending midnight locked in a cage instead of getting kissed by some handsome guy you just met."

I had to cover my mouth to keep my laughter from exploding out of me. He was awfully presumptuous! And yes, on that evening, I preferred to be locked in a cage than locking lips with *anyone*. For me, love didn't exist unless it was a one-time fling where I didn't have to see the man again.

"I'd rather be in a cage," I chortled. "Men don't know the first thing about kissing."

He pulled a face, looking like I'd just stabbed him with one of my dangerously long fingernails. "Who do you kiss then?" He grinned, taking another sip of his martini but never taking his eyes off of me.

"No one if I can avoid it." My answer was short, but sincere. "Kissing is for teenagers."

"Hold that thought."

I watched as he got up and went to the bar for more drinks. I fanned myself, feeling the heat of the alcohol making its way to my face like a thermometer from my belly. The stranger returned quickly and set two martinis on the table, full of olives.

"Are we going to party or what?" I hissed. "I don't have much time left."

"Yeah, but I have rules."

I pouted and rolled my eyes. "I don't play by the rules."

"Good," he replied, leaning close to my face. I leaned far away from him and he said, "Trust me."

What the hell was this? Was he going to drug my drink so he could drive me to some isolated wooded area to kill me then bury me where I'd never be found?

"I don't even know you," my voice croaked.

He leaned back and spread his arms along the back of the couch, then smiled. "Look, its New Year's Eve… I'm lonely and I was just looking for a pretty girl to party with tonight. And seeing as you don't have much time left until you're up in a cage, we're wasting a lot of party time."

He was winning me over and he was far too cute to turn away. "Okay fine," I conceded. "What do you want me to do?"

"All you have to do is sit there. Close your eyes and don't move."

He's going to kill me.

I sat up straight with both feet on the floor and closed my eyes, my hands clasped together and resting nervously on my lap. He shifted his position on the couch, sensing him very close to me, then both of his hands were holding mine and my eyes flew open. He smiled at me and for some reason I believed I could trust him; I felt safe and closed my eyes again. My heart raced for two reasons — one, it was getting closer to eleven-thirty and two, I could feel his warm breath on my hands as he brushed his lips against the top of them. His lips were slowly leaving soft air kisses up my arm until he reached my neck where I felt the wetness of his tongue. He placed his hands gently against either side of my neck and I could feel my chest heaving as I tried to stay in control, wondering what he was going to do next. I felt his breath against one cheek, then the other, but his lips never touched my skin. I tried to calm my breathing but he was really getting under my skin and I was afraid of letting him get too close. His thumbs caressed my neck as his hands remained there, and I soon felt his mouth hovering close to mine, but never touching it. I opened my mouth slightly and he did the same, touching his lips gently to mine but doing nothing else. My entire body was on pins and needles waiting for what he'd do next but all he did was breathe. I opened my eyes to see that his were closed and his long eyelashes fluttered as his breath warmed my mouth like a summer breeze.

"I can turn you on without ever taking your clothes off."

I broke the spell by pushing him away from me, then grabbed his hand and dragged him out of the room, down several flights of stairs and outside into the bitter cold.

"Where are we going?" he asked.

"My car."

I pulled him along until we reached the parking garage next door and when we reached my beat up old yellow Chevy Chevette hatchback, I fished the key out of my cleavage and opened the door, telling him to get in the back seat. It was a struggle, but we managed to force ourselves into the cramped area with him sitting on the seat and me straddling his lap.

"You better be a good kisser," I said breathily, the excitement of this stranger almost too much to take.

"What about the party?"

"Kiss me first."

I watched his glorious Adam's apple wiggle as he chuckled nervously, as if he weren't as confident about his kissing abilities now that we were alone in the back seat of my car. He was probably a liar and a fraud just like all the rest of them but I wanted to give him the benefit of the doubt, so I waited for him to make the first move. He cupped my cheeks with his hands and pulled my face to his, gently touching my mouth with his, then slowly, almost agonizingly, he tilted his head and introduced his warm tongue to the inside of my mouth. It wasn't the usual animalistic, wide open-mouthed kiss, or even the snake-tongue sliding down the back of my throat that most guys were guilty of, but a kiss so sensual the enormity of its affect on me traveled from my tongue through the rest of my body until it reached it's intended target… the throbbing sensation between my legs.

His kisses were soft and sexy, not hard and hurried, which is something I'd never experienced before. Most guys were more interested in eating your face off while they tried to get in your pants, and I was always a willing participant, but I'd gotten to the point where I barely allowed kissing at all, almost like a prostitute. This guy… this *stranger*… kissed me like he cared, like he was actually a pretty decent guy who wasn't a douchebag. But if he was coming after me for a party, he most certainly *must* have been a douchebag. I never attracted decent guys, and that was okay because I never wanted to stick around anyway. I was all about the party and the quick exit. Time to get this one moving along.

As his kisses continued pulling me under his spell, my fingers quickly opened the buttons of his shirt as his hands slid down and landed firmly on my backside where he squeezed. Without ever separating my lips from his I deftly unbuttoned his jeans then slid down the zipper, and as he struggled in the cramped space to wiggle them down, I told him to hold on.

I managed to turn around and stuff myself between the two front seats, leaning over the emergency brake and stretching to open the glovebox. As I succeeded in opening it and grabbing the condom I was searching for, I felt him slide my miniskirt up and my panties down. I tried to reach back and hand him the condom but I was stuck and there was no way he was putting that thing in me without covering it up.

I was frantically trying to loosen myself when I felt him tapping lightly and the next thing I knew he was snorting blow off my ass. Not just one cheek, but both. This pissed me off because we were supposed to have that party *together* and he was cheating because I was bare-assed and wedged between the front seats of my old, broken down car.

"Hey!" I shouted. "That's not fair!"

He began laughing hysterically and offered to help me, and as we both maneuvered my body back to him, which caused him to get a face full of ass with each movement, he managed to pull my panties away from my ankles and placed me back on his lap, where I felt his full arousal underneath me.

I watched as he lightly tapped my portion of the party onto the top of his hand and I eagerly inhaled it, squeezing my nostrils tightly closed with my fingers until the burning sensation subsided. I saw him gazing at me with those kaleidoscope eyes and dove forward, covering his neck in hot, wet kisses until he brought my face back to his. He kissed me urgently as he expertly slipped on the condom and I wasted no time filling myself with everything he had to offer.

By the time we finished my windows were steamed to perfection and we were both panting like we'd just run a marathon neither of us was prepared to take part in. I pushed his sweaty hair away from his face then playfully nibbled on his neck before leaning back to open the car door. I managed to push my miniskirt down to cover my naughty bits before stumbling out of the car as I waited for him to pull up his pants and fall out after me.

"What time is it?" I asked.

He struggled to read what his watch said, then replied, "Twelve-thirty."

Shit.

He pinned me against the car and kissed me. "Happy New Year," he whispered with a grin.

"You go back inside and find us a table. I just need to freshen my makeup."

"Don't be too long."

I watched as he jogged away and as soon as he disappeared from sight I got back in my car, started the engine and sped off. It didn't matter that I couldn't see two feet in front of me with the foggy windows; I knew the streets of Chicago with my eyes closed and I wasn't stopping until I made it home.

ॐ

I felt the rain splashing my face, gently at first, then a cold, torrential downpour pelting my skin so hard it felt like needles stinging me. I gasped for breath as I struggled to open my eyes, then saw my mom standing over me with the shower head in her hand, hosing me down like a car needing washing.

"Oh good," she grumbled. "You're awake."

As she turned off the water and placed the shower head back in its holder on the wall, I tried to remember how I got into the bathtub.

"Dinner in an hour."

"Dinner?" I groaned. "What time is it?"

"Four o'clock. Before you make yourself presentable, you need to come downstairs." She grabbed my towel off the rack and held it out to me but I never moved from my fetal position at the bottom of the tub. "Don't make this more embarrassing for yourself than it already is. Get up. *Now*."

She threw the towel at me then stormed out of my bathroom and down the stairs, her thunderous footsteps echoing in my painfully throbbing head. I gingerly stretched my limbs and unraveled myself from myself, slowly standing up. I didn't have to see my reflection in the mirror clearly to know I looked like a drowned, deranged clown covered in skimpy cheetah skin. I dried myself off as well as I could, clothes and all, wrapped the towel around me and headed down to the kitchen where my mom ordered me to put on shoes.

I slipped on my boots and reluctantly followed her outside to the front yard. I shivered in the bitter cold, my teeth chattering so loudly I thought they'd crack into tiny little pieces. My breath caught in my throat as I saw the front of my car smashed into a pine tree with mass destruction all around. A flattened mailbox, winter-dead rose bushes uprooted and lying on the ground, and one of the porch handrails ripped from its cement foundation. I could see the neighbor's window curtains moving as I realized they were watching us from inside.

"So this is how you celebrate your sister's memory?"

"I was working," I mumbled.

She grabbed my arm forcefully and dragged me closer to the car where she opened the driver's side door and flung the front seat forward. I peered into the back seat and immediately shrunk next to my mom, her judgmental glare burning fire into my cold skin. I spotted the used condom on the floor next to my panties… I clenched my butt cheeks together and yep, I apparently never put them back on. I was horrified as my mom picked something off the back seat and shoved it in front of my face.

"And what kind of work do you do exactly?"

I stared at the small vial and knew instantly it must have fallen out of the stranger's pocket as he exited my car.

I squirmed as I quietly answered, "You know I'm a bartender."

My dad came out of the house to meet the tow truck that arrived as my mom grabbed my arm and dragged me back into the house. I headed for the stairs to go back up to my bathroom, but she ordered me to sit down in the kitchen. As I opened my mouth to protest she started screaming at me like a lunatic and I could only catch bits and pieces of what she was trying to say.

"The last straw… rehab… trashy behavior… embarrassment to our family… we raised you better… your sister…."

As soon as she mentioned my sister, I went upstairs and locked myself in the bathroom. Nobody missed Prude more than I did, and every day I wished it had been me, not her. She was the sweet sister, the kind sister, the one everybody looked up to and adored because, unlike me, she was worthy of such adoration.

I stared at my hideous reflection in the mirror as my mom's cringeworthy screaming got closer, reminding me what a disappointment I was.

Hello, 1990.

꩜

The first week of the new year brought about an ultimatum — I go to rehab or my parents kick me out of their house. I argued that I didn't *need* rehab; I partied for fun, not because it was something I couldn't control. I wasn't an *addict* or an *alcoholic* or a *whore*. Well maybe a little bit of a whore, but only because I needed to feel wanted without getting emotionally attached. I started to pack a suitcase, having no idea where I was going to go, but I couldn't stand living under my parents' roof any longer. I was twenty-two years old, my twin sister and best friend was dead, and I needed to start over somewhere new. My parents had a change of heart when they realized I was going to leave and never return, giving me one other option — change my image and get a real job. I didn't even know what that meant!

My mom dragged me to her hairdresser to have my bleached-blonde hair obliterated, trimming the dead ends and coloring it a light brown shade, which was close to the color of my natural hair. I loved being blonde; it was true that blondes had more fun. I sat in my mom's car fuming afterward and she had the audacity to think taking me for ice cream would heal the wounds inflicted on me.

"You looked like a stripper!" she yelled. "Your sister was blonde and you're *not*!"

I wanted to hurt her and the only weapon I had was words. "I thought you'd love me more if I was blonde."

"You're being ridiculous!"

My parents were hoping for a girl and a boy so there would be no competition, and while my sister was the blonde, blue-eyed princess, she was also deaf. This somehow became my fault, simply for being the hearing child.

"I know how disappointed you were that I was a girl," I continued as she drove. "And that I could hear."

Taking one hand off the steering wheel my mom lashed out at me, barely clipping my cheek with her fingers.

"You may try to look like your sister, but you will *never* be anything like her. It's time you grew up and took control of your own life instead of trying to be something that's impossible!"

"You're right. Expecting to be someone my parents love is impossible."

My mom's voice shook as she replied, "You're being completely unfair."

"She was my best friend! The only one who ever understood me! It's not my fault she's gone… you think I don't wish every day that it was me instead of her?"

It was true, yet I shed no tears. I had no tears left because I was full of anger and wanted everyone to just leave me alone. My mom careened into the driveway, narrowly missing my dad's car, then parked and marched into the house. I sat there staring into my lap, wondering what I had to do to be accepted by my parents. Become a doctor? A lawyer? A memory?

When I had composed myself well enough that I wouldn't verbally attack my mom, I got out of the car and went inside. My mom had just hung up the phone and met me in the hallway, pushing me toward the staircase.

"Hurry up!" she shouted. "You have an interview in one hour!"

I had no idea what she was talking about.

"You have an interview with a job agency in one hour!" she yelled, as if I didn't hear her the first time. "Get changed, get presentable! Dad was able to pull some strings to get you in!"

"How did Dad—"

"Someone he knows at the bank. Now go!" As I reached the top of the stairs she made sure to add, "And make sure your makeup is subtle!"

Subtle makeup was not in my realm of understanding. My hair was already freshly cut and blown out, so I didn't have to do anything with that other than brush all the tiny, itchy hairs off my face and neck. I turned on the cassette player sitting on top of my toilet tank and pressed play. As Y&T's "Lipstick and Leather" filled the air I stared at myself in the mirror. I hated what my hair looked like; it was no longer fun and playful but drab and boring, just like someone twice my age would wear. My hair was parted down the middle and blown completely straight, falling just below my shoulders. I hated that I didn't even look like myself anymore. I had my own look, my own identity, and now I looked just like everybody else. Since I never left the house without makeup, my face was already done to the hilt, so my task was deciding what to *remove* in order to be considered presentable.

I must have been taking too long for my mom's liking because I soon heard her footsteps on the stairs and she positioned herself in the doorway with her arms folded across her chest.

"You haven't done a thing!" she shouted. She snapped the cassette player off and forced me to sit on the toilet as she rummaged through the vanity drawers for makeup remover and cotton balls. My protests were ignored as she held my face tightly with one hand while rubbing my mouth and eyelids roughly with a soaked cotton ball.

"Mom, I can—"

"Be quiet. You don't know the first thing about makeup. You're worse than a clown."

"And you do?" my voice squealed as I eyed the woman who never wore a stitch of makeup.

By the time I wrestled myself away from her and stood in front of the mirror, the only makeup left on my face was mascara, and there wasn't much of that either.

"Why can't you just accept me for who I am?" I asked, my voice shaking.

"Of course we accept you. Don't be ridiculous." As I opened my mouth to retort she pushed me out of the bathroom toward my room to choose my outfit for the interview.

I watched as she sifted through the clothes hanging in my closet, grumbled, then started from the beginning to do it all over again. She eventually pulled out a black skirt and black blouse covered in large, white polkadots.

"I hate that outfit," I protested.

"This isn't a party," she snapped. "It's the only thing you have that's decent enough for an interview. Put it on."

She went back downstairs to give me some privacy and as soon as I was dressed I went into the bathroom to look at myself one last time. If my mom wasn't going to let me wear my makeup the way I liked, I decided to wear my mask a different way. I grabbed a pair of scissors out of the drawer and gave myself a set of bangs. Bangs that were so long they nearly covered my eyes.

It'll have to do.

I slipped on a pair of black shoes and headed downstairs with my purse. "How am I getting there?" I asked.

My mom gasped when she saw what I did to my hair; you'd have thought I shaved half my head. "Well since you totaled your car, I guess I'll have to take you, won't I?"

"I can drive myself."

"Not in *my* car. Let's go."

As we drove to my unknown destination I asked, "What kind of job am I interviewing for?"

She didn't answer at first, then said, "I'm not sure. A personal assistant of some sort, I think." I knew by the way my mom's jaw clenched she wasn't being honest with me. "Your hair looks really cute," she said, trying to smile. "I like the bangs."

And then it hit me like a ton of bricks. "I'm not going on an interview, am I? You're taking me to rehab!"

Chapter 2

Panic seized me and I unbuckled my seatbelt, frantically grabbing the door handle. Just as I opened the door and the highway air began rushing in she grabbed my coat sleeve with one hand and yanked me toward her, screaming, "I'm not taking you to rehab!"

I pulled the door shut and stared at her with my hand still gripping the door handle, not believing a word she said. "You're lying," I snarled.

Her face glistened with sweat as she white-knuckled the steering wheel, her chest heaving from the disaster that nearly happened.

"Are you so willing to jump out of a moving car?" she shrieked. "Maybe what you really need is a mental hospital!"

My face burned with the anger boiling in my veins. "Prude is lucky to be dead. At least she doesn't have to deal with *you* anymore."

The car swerved into the next lane as my mom kept her left hand on the wheel and clawed at me with her right. She righted the car when horns blared to get her attention, then she wiped the sweat from her forehead.

"You take that back!" she hissed. "Take it back right now!"

"Like hell I will."

"What an ungrateful little witch you are."

"I don't know Mom," I said with a laugh. "You're the one who seems pretty ungrateful to still have one daughter left. But that's okay. I know I'm not the *right* daughter."

My mom stared straight ahead and said nothing more. Her silence spoke volumes, revealing the truth of everything I'd known since my twin died four years earlier when we were eighteen. Everyone's lives would have been much better off if it had been me who died, and I couldn't agree more.

My mom parked in the lot of a small office complex, pulling out a book to read while I went inside. I was surprised to learn it really was a job interview after all, clutching my coat close to my neck as I walked inside. I hung up my coat and was immediately ushered into an office, where I was greeted by a small woman with silver hair and half-moon glasses perched on the bridge of her nose.

"I'm Audrey Campbell. My husband works with your father at the bank."

"Jude," I replied, shaking her tiny, bony hand. "Jude Hastings."

We both sat down and she shuffled through a stack of papers on her desk. I tried to be patient, but I shifted uncomfortably in my seat waiting to hear anything about the job I was interviewing for. What could possibly be taking her so long?

I'd finally had enough and my agitation was brutally apparent when I spoke. "So what job am I interviewing for?"

"Oh, this isn't a job interview, Ms. Hastings. I'm interviewing you to see what jobs you might be suitable for. I work with select clients, who contact me when they're in need." She studied the look on my face and continued, "Oh don't look so glum. I'm sure we can find something for you."

"So... what kind of jobs? Office jobs? Cleaning up dog shit?"

She immediately froze and looked into my eyes, removing her glasses. "Ms. Hastings, I would like to remind you that you're in a professional business office and I expect you to be courteous at all times. I cannot, with a good conscience, send you out on job interviews if you're going to talk like that."

I quickly apologized and promised it wouldn't happen again. I then spent an agonizingly long time listening to her rattle off myriad job skills that I had to admit I did not have experience in.

Frustrated, she exhaled loudly and said, "Why don't you tell me what jobs you *do* have experience in?"

I didn't like the way she was looking at me, almost as if one of my parents filled her in on their disdain for me and she was seeing me with their eyes. The way I used to look. The way I was; the person I *was*.

I sniffed loudly and rolled my eyes before answering, "Babysitter, grocery store bagger, bartender."

Cage dancer.

She hesitated briefly before forcing a smile. "No office work? Typing? Filing? Answering phones?"

"Everybody answers the phone," I snorted, trying not to laugh.

Audrey pulled all the pieces of paper on her desk together and stacked them neatly in a pile. She then grimaced and said, "I'm sure I can find something you're qualified for. I'll be in touch."

I took that to mean we were finished, so I thanked her and walked out of the office. As I threw my coat on I grumbled, "And fuck *you*, Audrey." I smiled at the secretary and gave her my sweetest goodbye.

I should've jumped out of the moving car.

*

I was sound asleep when my mom entered my bedroom without knocking. "You turned down a job interview Audrey set up for you?" she screamed, standing over me like a lunatic.

I was still a bit drunk from the night before, rolling over slowly to look up at her. "What?"

Her face was blood red as she stared down at me. "You're going to call Audrey and tell her you made a mistake."

I started to laugh. The more I laughed the angrier she got, so I laughed even harder. "I'm not calling her back."

"What is *wrong* with you?"

I wiped my face and grumbled, "Nothing wrong with me. Just living my life."

"*Destroying* your life is more like it."

"What do you care?" I hissed, pulling the blanket back over my head. "You don't give a shit about me. You'd be happier if I disappeared forever."

"I'd be happy if you lived a clean, decent life. I'd be happy if you stopped drinking and doing drugs and…."

Here it comes.

"I think you're a sex addict!" She gasped as she said, "People are talking about you, Jude. There are whispers all over town."

I flipped the blanket off my face and glared at her. "I'm not interviewing for that job."

"It's the only one she's been able to come up with. You have no skills!"

"I'll get another bartending job."

"No Jude, not while you're living in this house."

"Then I'll move out. I hate it here anyway."

"Where would you go?"

"I have friends. I don't need you."

"You don't even have a car!"

"I can walk. Or bum a ride."

"Then start looking. You have two weeks. If you're not out by then, you're going to rehab."

She stormed out of my room and slammed the door behind her, causing the frame sitting on my nightstand to fall on the floor. I heard the glass shatter and with it went my heart. I scrambled out of bed and sat on the floor holding the broken picture frame in my hands, staring down at the photo of me and Prude taken the day she died, New Year's Eve 1985. We were only eighteen years old. Jude and Prudence, nicknamed the Beatle Twins even though our names had nothing to do with them. The blonde and the brunette, the blue-eyed princess and her brown-eyed jester, the deaf daughter who was struck down by a brain aneurysm and the twin who had to learn how to survive without her.

I clutched the picture frame to my chest and rocked back and forth wishing I could bring my sister back. Wishing the aneurysm had struck me down instead of her. She was smart, funny and beautiful. Even before we were taught universal sign language we had our own secret sign language that no one else understood, and we used it quite often. She was my best friend in the whole world, and together we were unstoppable, even if she couldn't hear. I was her ears, and she was my everything else. When she died, my soul died with her. All that remained was the empty shell that I covered in disguises who drowned her pain in any way she saw fit. Alcohol, drugs, and yes, sex.

I never got out of my pajamas, dragging myself downstairs once I stopped obsessing over my dead sister. As I opened the refrigerator to grab a soda, the phone rang and I ignored it. My mom, who had been cleaning the bathroom, came running out to answer it, giving me the look of death on the way. After some pleasantries she held the phone out to me. I stared at her as I took my time opening the can of soda and chugging half of it before snatching the phone out of her hand.

I belched loudly before saying, "Hello."

"Hello Ms. Hastings, it's Audrey Campbell. I've just hung up with a new client, and I think you'd be the perfect fit for this job."

I rolled my eyes. "What is it?"

"He's looking for a live-in nanny for his four-year-old son."

I laughed so loudly I probably burst her eardrum. "No, no way. Not a chance."

"But this is something you're actually *qualified* for."

"Why? Because I used to babysit?"

"Well… that's part of the reason, yes."

"No. Bye Audrey."

I hung up the phone and turned around, nearly knocking my mom over. I hadn't realized she was still standing there listening to the whole thing. The phone rang and I immediately picked it up, never moving from my spot on the floor, staring directly into my mom's angry eyes.

"Ms. Hastings, please hear me out."

"I don't even like kids!" I shouted. "I'm not taking care of some snot-nosed little brat. Find some other sucker."

"Ms. Hastings, I—"

"Stop calling me that," I grumbled.

"Jude, believe me, if I had a more qualified prospect for this client, I would *gladly* present them with the opportunity," she snapped.

"How am I more qualified than any of your other *prospects*," I hissed.

"He needs someone who knows sign language."

I fidgeted as I sat in Audrey's waiting room, dressed in the same black skirt and black blouse with large white polkadots. It was the only thing I had that was considered interview presentable. I didn't want to be there, I didn't want to be anyone's nanny, and I just wanted to escape. Maybe somewhere warm where I didn't have to deal with the bitter cold anymore. Somewhere I could lie on a beach and leave everything behind me. One of the bartenders I used to work with hit the road for Florida; I'd have no qualms about giving him a call to see if I could crash with him until I found something of my own. I liked bartending; why wasn't that good enough for my parents? I made excellent tips, and the more cleavage I exposed, the better. I didn't have enormous breasts like some of the other girls, but that's what pushup bras were for.

I sat up straight when the front door opened and a strikingly beautiful woman walked in, shaking the fresh snowflakes from her long, curly blonde hair. "Fucking snow," she grumbled, thinking nobody could hear her.

With her arm outstretched she walked toward me, shaking my hand. "You must be Jude."

"Yes."

"I'm Celeste, Mr. Sullivan's personal assistant, and I'm here to interview you."

I followed Celeste into an empty office where she turned on the light and got comfortable behind the desk. She pulled a manila folder from her briefcase and flipped through a few papers, then looked up and smiled at me.

"I've contacted your references, and they all speak very highly of you."

References?

She must have seen the confused look on my face, picking up a piece of paper and saying, "It says here John and Maggie Fordham thoroughly enjoyed having you on their two week trip to Mexico with their ten-year-old daughter Cassie two years ago."

Of course they enjoyed having me on that trip. As soon as we got there they disappeared until it was time to go home, and I was stuck with their spoiled rotten brat on my own the entire time. I had to share a room with Cassie, and they made sure their room was on a completely different floor! My heart raced as I thought about how much I hated that kid and the torture she put me through for two solid weeks. I was so stressed my hair started falling out before the trip was over. Once I turned twenty-one and it was legal to be in bars, I quit babysitting for good and never looked back.

    I had every intention of sabotaging this interview in any way possible. I slouched in my chair, I rolled my eyes when I got bored, and I barely listened to anything… what was her name again… anything she had to say. I just didn't care. I was already formulating a plan to get out of my parents' house and move south.

    I was just about to doze off when Celeste asked, "So Jude, do you have any questions for me?"

    "Nah, not really."

    "Really? Nothing at all?"

    I had exactly one question. "Who is Mr. Sullivan?"

    "I'm not allowed to divulge any personal information, but Zigmond—"

    I tried so hard not to laugh, but the giggle dribbled out of my mouth so quickly I couldn't stop it.

    Celeste gawked at me. "Is there something funny about his name?"

    I continued to giggle and raised my eyebrows. "Um, yeah there is."

    I could picture him so vividly, as I'd seen his type at the Cheetah Club all the time. A rich, white-haired, old man who got his jollies with younger women and was now stuck with a four-year-old child he wanted nothing to do with. So let's hire a nanny to take care of the germ-infested runt instead. I grinned, wondering if Celeste was more than just a personal assistant to Mr. Sullivan.

    "Ms. Hastings, I really don't—"

    "For fuck's sake," I snapped. "Stop calling me that."

    "All right, *Jude*. It's obvious you're not interested in this job, so I will report back to Mr. Sullivan that we'll need to continue looking for the right candidate. Thanks *so* much for wasting my time today."

With that, Celeste shoved the papers back in her briefcase and stormed out of the office. I giggled as the bell chimed on the door signaling her exit.

Florida, here I come.

∽

I went out with my girlfriend Linda that night and as was our usual custom, we drove into the city, got drunk, danced, flirted with guys we never intended to go home with, got high, then drove back to her house. She still lived at home with her parents as well, but they weren't assholes like mine were, so we crashed in her bedroom and she drove me back home the next afternoon.

As she pulled up to the house there was a police car sitting in the driveway and I begged her to keep going. We went back to her house and I called my mom to ask what was going on.

"I'm reporting the damage to our front yard. The one you destroyed when you smashed through it with your car. While you were drunk and high and whatever else you were that night."

"You can't be serious!"

"You turned down *another* job offer from Audrey. It's the last straw, Jude."

"You gave me two weeks!"

"Your two weeks ends *tomorrow*. You don't even know what day it is," she grumbled, sounding like she had reached her breaking point. "But I do agree with you on one point. You have no business working as a nanny, taking care of a young child. You can't even take care of yourself."

She hung up the phone and left me hanging. She wasn't even yelling. She sounded as if she finally resigned herself to the fact that I was a completely lost cause and all hope that remained, however minuscule, had disappeared. And now she was reporting my front yard accident to the police, and it certainly didn't help that Walter, the Chief of Police, was my dad's best friend.

Linda drove me home and somehow I was able to sneak into the house without being seen, tip-toeing up the stairs and locking myself in my bedroom. It was time to face the music. I pulled out my suitcase and packed as lightly as possible, then stuck the shattered picture frame in between some clothes so it wouldn't further be destroyed in my travels. I counted the cash in my dresser and even though it wouldn't last me very long, it was enough to get me on a plane to Florida and spend the next few days looking for a job. I'd figure out the rest later. My plan was set; as soon as I knew my parents were asleep I would grab a taxi for the airport and they'd never have to see me again. I'd just have to stay quiet as a mouse until then.

Until I had to use the bathroom.

A quick change of plans. I could still leave under the cover of darkness, I'd just have to deal with my parents until then. I decided to go downstairs and share my last meal with them, and they didn't seem the least bit surprised to see me. They probably knew I was home all along. As I passed through the kitchen the phone rang, and for some reason I didn't want to irritate my mom, so I answered it.

"Hi Jude, it's Celeste, Mr. Sullivan's personal assistant. Do you have a minute?"

As my parents sat down in the dining room to start dinner, I sat in the corner of the kitchen on the high stool Prude and I used to fight over. I usually let her win.

"Go ahead," I said quietly.

"I don't like you," she began, causing me to grin. "You're rude, you're brash, you're arrogant and you don't give a shit about anyone but yourself. And you're just like Mr. Sullivan."

"Can't find anyone for the job?" I asked, laughing.

"Oh I found someone, but she quit after the first day, agreeing to stay until I found someone else."

"So you *need* me."

"No, *I* don't need you, but Mr. Sullivan does, and until he gets what he wants my life will be a living hell."

"No." I hung up the phone and waited. I watched the second hand on the clock — ten seconds and the phone rang again. "Hello, Celeste," I answered in the most condescending voice imaginable.

"Jude, please hear me out." She sounded desperate and I loved it.

"Oh Celeste," I cooed, "but you *do* need me. Because without me, your life is a living hell. You said it yourself."

"Jude—"

"Why would I want to help you? Or this Zigmond guy? I don't give a damn about either of you, and I certainly don't give a shit about some little devil child he has no interest in raising on his own. Leave me alone!"

I slammed down the phone; that felt good. I sat staring at the floor giggling like a child until I saw my mom's feet taking up space there. I looked up as she fanned a pamphlet in my face.

"Tomorrow," she said. "Pack a suitcase."

I snatched the pamphlet out of her hand to see it was the rehabilitation facility she was so eager to lock me up in.

"My suitcase is already packed," I snarled. "I'm out of this shit hole."

"Where are you going?"

"Florida. You won't have to see me again after tonight."

"I can't let that happen."

"Try and stop me."

"You need help, Jude. I'm begging you, please. Prudence would hate seeing you like this."

"You leave her out of this!"

She always knew how to get to me, how to make me feel guilty and worthless. Whenever she was at a loss she dragged my sister into it, and I hated her even more for doing that.

"You're going to rehab tomorrow. Whatever it takes, I can't let you continue living like this."

"I don't need rehab!" I shrieked, stuck in the corner like a small child. "You just want to lock me away so you don't have to deal with the fact that *I'm* the one who lived!"

My mom reached out and slapped me hard across the face, causing me to see stars. I knew I hit a nerve because it was rare for either of my parents to resort to physical attacks.

As her chest heaved in anger, she spoke very softly. "I will be taking you to rehab tomorrow, and if you try to leave this house before then, I will call the police and tell them you're threatening to harm yourself. Walter already knows the situation and has been put on alert."

Walter was well aware of the struggles in my family since Prude's death. I'm sure he had heard an earful about me in the last four years, and would believe anything my mom said.

The phone rang and my mom picked it up, then handed it to me with a frightening look in her eyes. I answered numbly, no longer interested in playing games with Celeste.

"Jude, can I ask you to just meet Shea before you make a final decision?"

"Shea? That's the kid's name?"

"Yes. He just turned four years old on New Year's Eve. He's a very bright little boy but he's a handful, and aside from the fact you know sign—"

"His birthday is New Year's Eve?"

"Yes."

"And he's four years old?"

"Yes."

"Can I meet him tonight?"

"I'll send a car for you in thirty minutes."

෴

As I rode in the back seat of the black sedan, I wondered if this was some ploy my parents cooked up to get me to rehab. I wasn't aware of my surroundings in the darkness, sitting quietly and wide-eyed as twenty-minutes later I saw mansions on properties that seemed to stretch on for miles.

"So what do you know about Mr. Sullivan?" I asked the driver as he pulled into the driveway with a gated entrance.

As he punched in the security code to open the gate he replied, "I'm not at liberty to say, ma'am."

"Have you ever met him?"

"As part of his car service, yes, I have."

"I hear he's an asshole."

The driver chuckled then quickly recovered, pulling up in front of a house that must have been a hundred times larger than mine.

"I'll be here when you're ready to leave," he said.

I got out of the car and walked to the front door, ringing the bell. The door soon opened to reveal Celeste, who looked like she had been through a war. Her mascara was streaked down her cheeks, her hair was a ratted mess and her breathing was heavy.

"Oh thank God," she whispered, ushering me quickly into the house.

I stood in the front foyer with my mouth open, admiring the giant mermaid fountain in the middle of the floor, which ended up being a koi pond as well. I didn't have time to admire much else as I had to run after Celeste to keep up.

As we walked up the grand staircase and down a long maze of hallways, she explained, "Shea doesn't like new people, so don't be surprised if he acts out at first. Difficulty communicating is part of the problem."

"I thought he knew sign language?"

"He knows what he's been taught, but they can't keep anyone long enough. Oh, and he's a bit mischievous, but he's cute as a button...."

I stopped listening because I knew what that meant. He was a holy terror and nobody could control him. We stopped in front of a large, double doorway and Celeste turned to look at me as her hand rested on the doorknob.

"This is Shea's playroom," she whispered. "Amanda is with him right now. She's the one who said she'd stay until we found someone new."

I nodded, wondering what the hell I thought I was doing there. *Trying to stay out of rehab.*

Celeste opened the door and we walked into the massive room filled with every toy a child could ever dream of. As we entered I looked across the room to see a woman I assumed was Amanda reaching for a small child who was climbing a floor-to-ceiling bookcase. As soon as he was secure in her hands and she pulled him off of the shelf above her head he began struggling against her, his arms and legs flailing, fighting her at every step. The sounds that came from him were alarming; grunting and groaning like… a gremlin.

Wide-eyed in fear I took a step back and fell into a wingback chair that was patterned in all colors of the rainbow. I watched in horror as the child fought so hard she dropped him to the ground where he landed in a heap and didn't move. I gasped, my hand flying to my mouth, and that's when she noticed me and seemed to wilt before my eyes.

"Don't take this job," Amanda warned me, wild-eyed. "It's like working for Satan himself."

I was speechless as she stormed out of the room in tears. I watched as the little boy rolled over and got to his feet, then glared at me. I'd seen all those demonic child horror movies and here was one in the flesh, headed right toward me.

Shea stood in front of me, staring up innocently enough with his big hazel eyes, button nose, chubby cheeks and a mouth fit for an angel. I held my breath as he got closer, then climbed onto my lap. He curled up in my arms and lay silently watching me, wiping his bangs out of his eyes. A tiny smile crossed his lips as a single tear fell from his eye and disappeared down his cheek and out of sight. And then he closed his eyes and fell fast asleep. I stared down at the little boy curled up in my arms, then glanced up at Celeste, who was gawking with her mouth open.

"Jude, I don't know what to say. This… this is not typical behavior for Shea."

I opened my mouth to speak, but I could find no words. Tears burned my eyes as I looked up at Celeste, and I knew in that instant this child needed me as much as I needed him. And for the first time in my life I understood what love at first sight actually was. I stared down at the sleeping boy in my arms, his breathing soft and seemingly content, and questioned how I would ever be qualified to take care of something... some*one*... so small. I was a mess, but something drew me to this child; something that grabbed hold of my heart and simply wouldn't let go. I was stunned to see teardrops fall against his precious face and realized they were coming from me. I gently swiped them away and tried to wipe my face with my sleeve without Celeste noticing.

"Does that mean you're interested in the job?" she asked, smiling at me.

"I... I don't know what's happening to me," I admitted. "But yeah, I'm interested."

"I need to get something from the office. Don't move."

Celeste left me there alone with Shea, looking like a doll in my arms, and all I could do was stare at him. I was in no place to be the sole caretaker to this innocent boy. Whatever was going on in his life, who was I to teach him anything? I couldn't even take care of myself let alone be entrusted with a four-year-old child.

I looked up as Celeste returned with Amanda, each pulling up a chair to sit in front of me. Amanda was no longer crying but her hands were visibly shaking. I couldn't fathom what a small child could ever do to cause that much fear and anxiety in an adult. Maybe it was lack of sleep; I didn't know.

"Before I go through the list of Mr. Sullivan's requirements, Amanda has something she'd like to say," Celeste said.

Amanda's voice cracked as she rambled, "He hates everything. He won't eat anything but peanut butter and jelly. He won't go outside. He cries all the time. He kicks me, pinches me... sometimes he bites." She paused to catch her breath, her face as pale as a ghost. "He doesn't sleep and he climbs on *everything*. This is the worst job I've ever had. Do yourself a favor and never come back." She stared at me, her vacant eyes wide with terror. I wondered if she was talking about Shea, or Mr. Sullivan. Maybe both.

"Okay Amanda, you can go," Celeste replied gently. She waited until Amanda was gone then whispered, "She wasn't a very good fit.

But as you can see, we're having trouble finding the right person for Shea."

"So what are Mr. Sullivan's requirements?" I couldn't wait to hear them. I'd probably fail in the first five words. She began to read and my eyes glazed over.

> *No smoking*
> *No makeup*
> *Fingernails must be kept short at all times*
> *No jewelry of any kind*
> *Hair must always be worn up*
> *Must wear assigned uniform (shirt tucked in at all times)*
> *No belts*
> *Sneakers only, no sandals or other open-toed shoes*
> *No visitors to the house (including boyfriends or family members)*
> *Always speak aloud while signing with Shea*
> *You will live in the house, in your own apartment*
> *Dinner will be taken in your own apartment*
> *Weekends are your own to do as you wish*
> *Never disrupt Mr. Sullivan if he is working in his home office*

The list continued on and on and I finally zoned out and stopped listening, focusing all of my attention on Shea. His breathing was calm as he softly purred against my breast and I watched as his tiny eyelids flickered, causing me to wonder what dreams were playing behind them.

"Jude, do you think you can abide by Mr. Sullivan's requirements?"

"Is he looking for a robot?" I joked. "What's with all the personal stuff?"

"Let's just say incidents with other nannies have caused the lengthy list of requirements. To protect you as well as Shea. And to avoid lawsuits."

This caused my heart to race. "Lawsuits?"

"Look, I told you Shea wasn't an easy child to deal with, and you saw what happened when we walked into the room. But for some insane reason, he bonded with you immediately, and to me that's as close to a miracle as I've ever experienced."

"And *Zigmond*?" I said with a laugh. "What do I need to know about old Ziggy?"

"Don't *ever* call him that," Celeste replied with a slight grin. "He's very rigid and set in his ways. He struggles with Shea because he works so much, but having a deaf child has its own challenges, as you can imagine."

I thought about Prude and while my parents never seemed to be challenged with her inability to hear, I'm sure it came as a shock. I was also certain having to learn sign language in order to teach their deaf child how to communicate was a challenge they never expected. I imagined it wasn't easy for them, especially with two children to teach.

"Now am I allowed to ask what Mr. Sullivan does?" I asked.

"He's part of the Sullivan publishing empire. Books, magazines, you name it. I don't know if that was his life goal, but it's the family business so…."

"Ah, I get it. You said I was just like him. Does that mean we're going to butt heads all the time?"

"Do you want the job?"

"Answer my question."

Celeste sighed heavily. "Look. Honestly, I—"

"Are you sleeping with him?" I don't know what I was thinking, but the words just flew out of my mouth. Something I always had a problem with.

Her face blanched as her hand grasped her throat. "Excuse me?"

I chuckled, trying to make it sound like a joke. "I'm sorry. He's rich, you're young and pretty so I just assumed—"

"Well *don't*. Not that it's any of your business, but I have a boyfriend and Mr. Sullivan is *not* my type."

Shriveled up old rich man.

An awkward silence filled the air as Shea shifted his position in my arms but remained sound asleep. "So what are we going to do about him?" I asked.

"Follow me."

I stood up carefully, trying not to disturb the sleeping child in my arms, and followed Celeste out of the room. From my experience, children always weighed more when they were sleeping, but Shea seemed so light in my arms. The more I watched him he seemed a lot smaller than any four-year-old I'd ever known.

I followed Celeste into Shea's bedroom, and when she turned on the light I thought I stepped into the room of a prince. Elegant furnishings with what appeared to be velvet bedding and draperies in dark purple, with elaborate artwork of famous children's book covers hanging on the walls. A large window boasted a comfy looking window seat with fluffy cushions and a bookshelf filled with books underneath. There were hundreds more toys in this room, causing me to wonder why on earth he needed a separate playroom, but maybe there were just too many. What really caught my attention was the child-sized train that sat on its own set of tracks which snaked around the enormous room.

Celeste instructed me to put Shea to bed as she pulled the drapes closed. "Don't bother with pajamas; be thankful he's asleep."

I pulled back the covers and set the sleeping boy in his bed, covering him up so he wouldn't get cold. He looked like an angel in that moment and my skin pricked as I really thought about what I was getting myself involved in. Amanda's warnings echoed through my brain and her fear was certainly not imagined or made up. She was an absolute mess. Worse than me, if that was even possible.

Celeste turned on a nightlight, turned off the regular light, and led me out of the room, back down the expansive hallway and to the front door where she handed me my coat.

"Think about it," she told me. "I'll call you in a couple of days."

"What about Amanda?"

"She promised to stay until we hired someone. If she can't manage it, I'll take over until we do. I've had to do it before."

I stood there contemplating my future and whether or not I was capable of taking this job. "Why would my weekends be free?" I asked, curious who took care of the boy during that time.

"Mr. Sullivan spends his weekends with Shea at the family cabin in Wisconsin, so you'll be free to come and go as you like."

"Well I don't have a car," I admitted. "So I wouldn't be going very far."

"As long as you're under Mr. Sullivan's employ, you'll be provided with a car to use when you're on your own time. During the day when Shea is in your care, you'll use one of the drivers if you need to take him anywhere. Emergencies, appointments, whatever the case may be. You're never to take Shea in your assigned car under any circumstance."

I was shocked anyone would trust me with a car, then remembered they probably didn't know about my fight with the tree. "Oh. Okay then."

"Thanks for coming, Jude. I'll call you."

I walked out the front door then turned around to face her. "I don't need to think about it. I'll take it."

"Are you sure?"

I couldn't shake the feeling that Shea was meant to come into my life, and that I was desperately needed in his. And I didn't want to go to rehab in the morning.

"Yeah, I'm sure."

Celeste smiled. I wasn't sure if it was a smile knowing they found another sucker, or if she knew I'd be able to handle the job. "I'll send a car for you Sunday night and I'll be here to get you settled."

Chapter 3

Celeste greeted me with a smile, and as I walked through the front door with my suitcase, I knew my life would never be the same. I had no idea what to expect and my nerves were working overtime, but I was bound and determined to prove my parents wrong. They spent the days leading up to my departure telling me I was crazy for taking the job and that I was in no way qualified, or in the right state of mind, to take care of a four-year-old child. All true statements, but they never gave me credit for anything I did right, so I had something to prove. Not to them, but to myself. And if I couldn't handle the job, I'd leave just like all the nannies before me and not look back.

I followed Celeste up the grand staircase then down a hallway that seemed to go on forever. When we finally reached the end she handed me a key ring and said, "Car keys — the white Volvo in the garage and," as she pointed to the door, "your apartment. Very private and no one will disturb you here."

"You mean Ziggy won't be paying me any visits?" I joked.

She grinned and replied, "No. If he needs you he'll call. And Shea is not allowed anywhere near your apartment."

"Got it."

I unlocked the door and walked into what was going to be my home that moment forward. I was wide-eyed and speechless as I looked around the living room area, complete with luxurious furnishings, an enormous case full of books, and a fireplace. I set my suitcase down to catch my breath, then followed Celeste as she showed me the rest of my apartment. There was a small kitchen and eating area, a bedroom with a king-sized four poster bed complete with curtains fit for a queen, and a bathroom so luxurious I could barely keep from smiling like a fool. The shower and bathtub were separate, with a beautiful claw-foot tub nestled below the most ornate and colorful stained-glass window I'd ever seen. Everything was white, crisp and sparklingly clean with accents of gold, the look completed with fluffy dark blue towels with gold trim.

"You've got a balcony off of the kitchen with a beautiful view, but you can check that out in the daylight," Celeste commented. "Now, your handbook."

Handbook?

I followed her back into the living room where we sat down on the couch and she lifted a three ring notebook from the coffee table. Holding it up as if it were something that would save my life, she explained, "This is off the record, by the way. Mr. Sullivan knows nothing about this; that's why it's in your room."

The size of the notebook made me a bit uneasy. "What is it?"

"Notes from every nanny Shea has ever had. What works, what doesn't, their experiences, their injuries, their—"

"Stop... injuries?"

"Nothing serious, but that's why Mr. Sullivan put in such strict requirements when it comes to your clothes and personal effects. The no earrings rule came into play when one of the nannies was trying to give Shea a bath and in the struggle he accidentally ripped out one of her hoops. Tore the hole clear through her ear."

What the hell am I doing here?

She must have sensed my sudden panic, placing a hand on my knee and smiling sweetly. "Don't worry, I think you'll be fine. I've never seen Shea so comfortable with anyone after first meeting them, and he crawled into your lap and went to sleep. You felt the connection, right?"

"Yeah, but what if that was just a fluke?" I replied, wide-eyed. "What if he hates me, too?"

Celeste stood to leave. "Those are just helpful notes. You'll figure out what works for you as you go along. But make sure you write everything down, you know... just in case."

"Are they home yet? Is Shea here?"

"Not yet. They probably won't get home until late." I walked her to the door and she turned to face me. "One last thing. There's an alarm on Shea's bedroom door. Be sure to set it after you put him down for a nap. He has a habit of getting up and wandering around the house, which Mr. Sullivan does *not* want him to do, understandably." I nodded.

"The alarm only sounds in here," she continued. "You're the only one who will hear it, and it's your job to take care of things when it happens." Before she walked into the hallway she smiled and said, "You'll be fine. You've got this."

"But what if the alarm goes off at night?"

"The boss cannot be disturbed."

I watched as she disappeared down the long hallway then turned to head downstairs. I felt my heart race as I slowly closed the door and locked it. I turned to face the room, leaning against the door for support. I swallowed hard, having second thoughts about whether or not I made the right decision. I based everything on pure emotion and now I was kicking myself for not thinking things through. But that was one of my biggest problems — acting on impulse and emotion without thinking anything through. And now I would be taking care of a four-year-old boy who obviously had issues and being deaf was probably the least of them.

I sat on the couch and picked up the notebook, opening it to flip through the tabbed sections. Bath Time, Food/Drink, Injuries, Morning, Parties, Toys, and the categories went on, all in alphabetical order. I rubbed my temples with my fingers, pressing harder and harder as I thought about what I'd just gotten myself into. I had no idea what I would be greeted with in the morning, so I decided to unpack my suitcase and make it an early night.

I brought my suitcase into the bedroom and threw it on the bed. I knew once I started getting a paycheck I would have to go clothes shopping, as most of what I owned really wasn't suitable for a home such as the Sullivan empire. Still, I opened the closet to hang my clothes up and spotted my daily "uniform" staring back at me — five pairs of black pants and five, long-sleeved, button-down tan shirts. I was surprised I was allowed anything with buttons based on the requirements of old Mr. Ziggy. I set the broken picture frame with the photo of me and Prude on the bedside table and took a deep breath.

"I know, I know," I whispered to the air. "I've really done it this time. I'll probably get fired before I have a chance to quit."

Even though it was late, I took a long, leisurely soak in the fancy bathtub to relax my tense muscles. I didn't realize I had fallen asleep until the sound of a nuclear alarm blared through my apartment and I immediately panicked. I hurried out of the tub and wrapped myself in a towel, running out of my apartment, then stopped short because I wasn't sure where I was going. I couldn't call for Shea because he would never hear me, and I had no idea where he might be. I seemed to run in circles, up and down hallways, around corners, looking for the little boy, clutching frantically to the towel wrapped around me. My hair, loosely piled on top of my head, was falling down in sections and I was still soaking wet. Celeste never gave me a tour of the enormous mansion so I had no idea where anything was. After nearly tripping down the main staircase I landed on the tile floor in the foyer and my wet feet slid like ice skates until my shins slammed against the base of the mermaid fountain and I flipped over, falling into the koi pond. I was surrounded by darkness as I struggled in the water, and that's when I realized my towel was gone. I splashed around until I was able to find my footing and that's when the lights came on. I spotted my towel on the floor and quickly crouched back down in the water trying to hide my nakedness.

"That was a test," I heard. "You failed."

I never saw his face, but the light was quickly extinguished and I was alone again, soaked from head to toe, naked in the koi pond. It sounded like his voice had come from above me, and if that were true, he would have seen every inch of me standing there naked. Ashamed, I climbed out of the pond and searched for my towel in the dark, in the direction where I thought I last saw it. I used it to wipe the water off the floor, then wrapped myself in its wetness and fumbled my way in the dark back to my apartment.

I dried myself off and put on my pajamas, then sat on the couch to read the Morning section of the handbook. I needed an idea what time Shea woke up in the morning in order to plan my first day on the job. I flipped through all the handwritten scrawl and found nothing about what time he woke up in the morning. *Kicking, punching, biting, throwing toys, climbing the draperies, pulling my hair...* the nightmare went on and on. I saw a section that read "Miss Blanche" and decided to see what that was all about. Note after note about the kindness of Miss Blanche, who was apparently the family housekeeper. She worked inside the home Monday through Friday, but she didn't live there. She took care of everything related to the home, including cleaning, laundry and cooking dinner, and there was a schedule posted on the inside of the notebook's cover. It looked as if the only thing I really *was* expected to do was handle Shea. It appeared that I had the most difficult job in the house, and I began to wonder if Mr. Sullivan was going to be the worst part of it.

❧

I set my alarm for four in the morning, dressed in my drab uniform, put on my sneakers, and pulled my hair up into a bun on top of my head. I then snuck out of my apartment and tip-toed down the long hallway until I came to the room I believed to be Shea's. I sat in front of his door to wait for sounds of the child waking, but instead I fell asleep. A tiny cough shook me awake and since I wasn't allowed to wear a watch, I had no idea what time it was. I pulled myself up from the floor, turned off the door alarm and slowly walked inside. Shea was still in bed, but beginning to move. I looked at the train clock on the wall — eight-thirty.

I made my way slowly to the side of his bed, not wanting to frighten him upon waking and I took a moment to admire his precious, sleeping face. He looked like an angel lying there on his back, his face turned in my direction. His tiny, puckered lips opened and closed silently, and I couldn't help but smile at the sight of his hands, signing to whoever he was dreaming about. He rolled over onto his side with a grunt and opened one eye slightly, then the other, looking up at me sleepily. I smiled down at him and he sat straight up, gasping. I wasn't sure if I scared him, because I had no idea if he even remembered who I was.

I remembered Mr. Sullivan's strict rule about always speaking as I signed to Shea, and only responding to him if he signed. Under no circumstances was I allowed to respond to Shea if he pointed and grunted.

"Good morning, Shea," I greeted as I signed. "Do you remember me?"

He nodded. I'd give him that one.

"My name is Jude." I signed my name and he watched intently. He struggled trying to spell my name so I wrapped my hand over his to stop him. I signed the letter J and said, "Just call me J, okay?"

He smiled and nodded and I gave him that one, too.

Shea threw his covers off and stood on the bed, then began jumping furiously as if on a trampoline. I wasn't sure if he was happy or angry, and then he caught me completely by surprise when he bounced off the bed and flew toward me. I was quick enough to catch him, but lost my balance and crashed to the floor with him on top of me. I was stunned at first having the wind knocked out of me, but he sat patiently on my stomach smiling down at me like he woke up the happiest kid in the world.

I couldn't remember from Mr. Sullivan's expansive list of rules whether or not Shea was to be dressed before eating breakfast, so I decided to improvise.

Still flat on my back with the child sitting on top of me, I signed as I said, "Are you hungry?"

He nodded and I realized I needed to nip this in the bud, having only myself to blame. "Are you hungry?" I asked again.

::*Yes*:: he signed as he nodded with a smile on his face.

He scrambled off of me and got to his feet, and as soon as I was steadily on mine, he took my hand and led the way out of his room, down the long hallway where we turned to take the grand staircase to the main level. My shins were still stinging from slamming into the base of the mermaid fountain so I decided to make peace with it.

"Hi mermaid! Hi fish!" I said as I signed.

Shea watched me with wild eyes, then hid behind me and clutched my pant leg before dragging me away through the massive house to the kitchen where a woman had the top half of her body inside the oven.

"Good morning?" I said quietly, not wanting to scare her.

She retreated from the oven and smiled at us. "You must be Ms. Hastings."

"You must be Miss Blanche. Nice to meet you."

"Please, call me Blanche. Only the Sullivans call me *Miss* Blanche."

I nodded understanding and replied, "I'm Jude. Will we be in your way if I give him breakfast?"

"Not at all. But I'm sure you've been told he only eats peanut butter and jelly."

"For *every* meal?"

"Yes, ma'am." The short and stocky middle-aged woman with salt and pepper hair smiled at Shea and signed as she said, "Good morning, Mr. Shea."

::Good morning, Miss B::

"He has trouble with Blanche," she explained. "So I told him Miss B was just fine."

"You're very kind."

"Mr. Sullivan left a note for you on the table."

Shit.

Blanche went back to cleaning the oven and I decided to save Mr. Sullivan's note until Shea was eating. I sat him down at the kitchen table and said, "What would you like for breakfast?" He furrowed his brow as if I should already know his every want and need. "I'm new," I explained. "Tell me what you want to eat." I heard Blanche chuckling inside the oven and grinned.

Shea rolled his eyes and smacked his hand to his forehead. Such a rough morning for a four-year-old.

::PBJ::

"What's PBJ?" I knew I was being unnecessarily dramatic, but I needed to know the extent of his signing abilities. He was only four, but I had no idea what he'd already been taught, and if the people teaching him cared enough to teach him correctly.

Shea slid off the chair and walked to the cupboard where he pulled out a jar of peanut butter, and a loaf of bread. He then struggled to pull the refrigerator door open, but managed with a grunt, then stood on his tip-toes to pull down a jar of grape jelly. He set them all on the counter and looked up at me.

::Peanut butter::

::Grape jelly::

::Bread::

I smiled and tousled his hair then told him to sit back down. "What do you want to drink?"

He pulled a thinking face.

::Orange juice::

"Shea is only allowed plastic plates and cups," Blanche's voice echoed from inside the oven. "In case you didn't get to that part in the handbook. Oh, and spoons only. No forks or knives."

"Thank you." I was relieved to have someone on my side.

I presented Shea's sandwich on a plastic plate and his orange juice in a plastic cup. He stared at the sandwich and pouted, then looked at me and rolled his eyes, as if he couldn't believe he had to teach yet *another* nanny how to do things correctly. He waggled his fingers for me to come closer and I watched as he tore the crusts off and set them in my hand. I immediately gobbled them up as I was starving, and he stared at me like I was insane, his eyes wide with horror.

"The best part!" I said, rubbing my belly. "Yum!"

He giggled at my display of crust love then began eating his sandwich.

"I go grocery shopping on Fridays," Blanche said, getting up from the floor to pour herself a cup of coffee. "Anything you want or need, write it on the list and I'll pick it up for you."

"Thank you, Blanche." As she took her first sip of the hot black coffee, I asked, "How long was Amanda here?"

"Amanda... oh, she was the last one, right? A week? It's hard to keep up."

Crap.

I pulled a blueberry yogurt out of the refrigerator and tore off the lid. "Can you tell me who was here the longest?"

Blanche had to think hard in order to answer my question, then replied, "I think it was Robin… she was here two months."

I'm dead.

I poured myself a cup of coffee, doused it with sugar and real cream, then brought my breakfast to the table to sit with Shea. I noticed he wasn't eating his sandwich like someone normally would; he was picking at it with his little fingers and popping the chunks in his mouth. He bobbed his head back and forth with his eyes closed like he was listening to music and I was entertained just watching him.

When Shea realized I had joined him at the table he sat very still and watched as I put a spoonful of yogurt in my mouth. He wrinkled his nose.

"What? You don't like yogurt?"

He shook his head.

"Have you ever tried it?

He shook his head again.

"Do you like blueberries?"

He shrugged.

"Do you like milk?"

He nodded.

I stirred the yogurt so the fruit on the bottom was well mixed then asked, "Would you like to try it?"

I could see Blanche watching me carefully out of the corner of my eye, and it was apparent this type of behavior wasn't normal for any of the former nannies. It wasn't rocket science, for God's sake.

Shea stared at me as if I'd just grown another head, so I asked again, "Would you like to try it?"

He slowly nodded his head as he set his sandwich down.

::Yes::

"Yes what?"

::Yes please::

I put a small amount of yogurt on the spoon and held it in front of his mouth. He watched it for a bit before opening his mouth and swiping it off the spoon with his lips. At first he made a face like he might die but then he sat up straight and smacked his lips and rubbed his belly like I'd done earlier.

"You like that?"

He nodded.

"Would you like to share mine?"

He nodded again.

I put half of the yogurt in a plastic bowl and gave him the spoon he'd already eaten off of and he smiled brightly, his eyes twinkling with joy.

"Blanche, does he never try anything new?"

"No ma'am," she answered. "He usually fights tooth and nail and causes such a stir the girls simply don't even try. Any other girl would've had a yogurt facial right about now."

"What can you tell me about his mom?" I dared ask.

Blanche hesitated then replied, "That's not my story to tell. I've got work to do." She smiled and went back to cleaning the inside of the oven.

Shea was happily eating his sandwich and slurping up the yogurt so I decided to open the note from Mr. Sullivan. It was short and to the point.

Ms. Hastings,

I better not find you asleep in the hallway again.
Two of my koi were dead this morning. I'm taking it out of your pay.

Z.S.

My skin pricked at the thought of him seeing me asleep in front of Shea's door, probably snoring as well. And just because I fell into the pond didn't mean I was the cause of the koi deaths! Strike number two and three and I hadn't even met the man yet. Would I still have a job when he came home that evening?

After breakfast we went back upstairs so I could change Shea's clothes, and the morning was spent watching him ride around on his train and playing with blocks and puzzles. At lunchtime we went back to the kitchen where he ate another peanut butter and jelly sandwich, and more yogurt which he indicated he wanted by smiling and rubbing his belly vigorously. He tried to be adorable and funny by lifting up his shirt to reveal his stomach, patting it with his hand, but I refused to give him yogurt until he told me that's what he wanted. It took a few minutes but once he realized I was serious he conceded, learning how to sign yogurt and smiling proudly when I congratulated him.

After lunch we went back upstairs to his playroom where I decided to find out just how much sign language he was familiar with. I tried to make it a game, otherwise I feared he would outright refuse and I wouldn't get anywhere. I remembered how my mom used to play a singing game with me and Prude, and it was all for my benefit because I was the hearing child. It certainly made it more enjoyable to learn that way. I quickly learned that Shea knew his alphabet, which made things easier for me, but that didn't mean he knew how things were spelled, or myriad other obstacles that occurred with a deaf child learning sign language. Listening to Blanche speak of the "other girls" made me realize at some point they simply gave up on Shea, letting him do whatever he wanted in order to make their lives easier. I couldn't fail him the same way.

My heart swelled as I watched Shea show me his alphabet, his little fingers working so hard to do what I asked and his puckered lips moving as if trying to speak like I was. He was absolutely precious, but in the back of my mind I wondered when I would see the other side of Shea. The side that was violent and combative and the reason for so many rules put in place.

Shea and I sat on the floor facing each other with our legs crossed and I touched his chin so he would look at me.

"Why are you afraid of the fish?" I asked.

His bottom lip began to quiver and I immediately wished I'd kept my mouth shut. I knew he was afraid; why did I need to bring it up?

"It's okay," I said, trying to comfort him. "I won't let them hurt you."

He began to cry and I felt terrible for causing him whatever anguish he was going through because of the koi. I pulled him onto my lap and held him against me, rubbing his back for comfort. His little arms were wrapped around my neck so tightly it was a bit scary for such a small child. When he finally calmed down I set him back on the floor in front of me and wiped the tears from his face with my sleeve and smiled.

::*Going to eat me*::

"Who's going to eat you? The fish?"

He nodded.

"They're not going to eat you!"

He started chomping his teeth. It was cute and I tried not to laugh, because I knew he was scared.

"Those fish are *not* going to eat you. They're small... you're big!"

He looked skeptical, but I was winning him over.

"They only eat fish food," I explained. "Not little boys."

He set his elbow on his leg and rested his chin in his hand, looking up at me, thinking about what I just told him. I melted inside as his big hazel eyes looked at me, then he smiled and nodded, agreeing that he trusted what I said. I'd never felt such relief!

"Would you like to make a blanket fort?"

He sat up straight and wrinkled his nose. I gasped, my face extra animated for effect. This caused him to laugh.

"You've never made a blanket fort?"

He shook his head.

"Well let's go then."

I got to my feet and pulled him up with me, holding his hand as I led him back downstairs to find a room with enough furniture to make it the best first blanket fort he'd ever experienced. I chose a room that looked like it was probably used for entertaining and parties, with lots of chairs, tables, an elegant fireplace and a full bar in the corner. Blanche told me where I could find extra blankets and I carried an armful into the room with Shea close on my heels. He stared at me in wide-eyed wonder as I began moving chairs and tables around to make a suitable fort that would be fun, but easy, to navigate through. It was the largest fort I'd ever created, and when I had all the pieces in place I began throwing blankets over the top to cover our super secret hideout. I kept sneaking peeks at Shea to gauge his reaction and his mouth remained in a perfect "o" while his hands pressed against his cheeks in amazement.

When I was finished I asked, "Ready?"

He jumped up and down and clapped his hands and I told him to follow me. I got on my hands and knees and he followed suit, sticking close behind me as I crawled in through the entrance. With a hearing child you could sing songs or make up stories and scenarios, but it wasn't as easy with a deaf child. Since this was Shea's first blanket fort, he was mesmerized by the idea without having to do much else.

When the grandfather clock in the room signaled it was two, I told Shea it was time for his nap, which meant we had to leave the blanket fort and go up to his bedroom. Per Mr. Sullivan's notes, Shea was only to sleep in his bed so the alarm outside his door could be set and I would hear him if he tried to leave. Shea was having so much fun he immediately began to cry at this news.

"Okay," I said. "We'll try something else." I snagged two throw pillows off of the couch we were sitting next to and set them on the floor. "We're bears, and we have to hibernate for the winter."

He held his hands in the air, palms up, signaling he didn't understand what I was saying. "Bears sleep *all* winter," I explained. "Let's pretend we're bears and we need to sleep. But just pretend, don't really go to sleep."

He seemed to like this idea, so we both stretched out in our blanket fort and set our heads on the pillows, facing each other. He held a finger to his mouth, signaling quiet and I nodded. It wasn't long before his eyelids got heavy and he started to doze off and as he did, he scooted closer to me until his forehead was pressed against my neck. I lightly stroked his scalp and he soon fell into a deep sleep; I followed shortly after.

I woke with a start and realized Shea was no longer beside me. Panicked, I exited the blanket fort and saw a man dragging him out of the room, squirming and kicking trying to be released from being carried like a football. I ran after them, catching up when they reached the kitchen.

I grabbed a butcher knife from the counter and screamed, "Let him go!"

The man turned around to look at me, setting Shea on the floor. Shea ran to my side and wrapped his arms around my leg as I stared down the intruder.

"Are you going to stab me?" he laughed.

"Who are you? Why were you taking him?"

"Oh dear," I heard Blanche say behind me. "Mr. Sullivan, you're home early today."

Mr. Sullivan?

Chapter 4

"Are you going to stab me, Ms. Hastings?" he asked, glaring at me.

I stood gaping at him, the butcher knife still held high in the air, but something didn't add up. This wasn't an old man, in fact, he was quite young. Maybe thirty at the most. And I was frozen in shock, unable to respond to him in any way.

"Here dear," Blanche said, slowly taking the butcher knife from my hands and putting it back where it belonged.

I was still breathing heavily from thinking some deranged man was kidnapping Shea right from under my nose, and apparently that was his plan all along. To come home early so he could find me failing at something else, and that's exactly what happened. I was confident this would be the last night I spent in the Sullivan home.

"Miss Blanche," Mr. Sullivan said calmly. "Would you please bring Shea up to his playroom? I'll be there in a minute."

Blanche tried to peel Shea off of my leg, but he wouldn't budge. It was almost as if he knew what was coming; that if he let go of me I would disappear and he'd never see me again. He struggled against Blanche as she pulled him free, but I placed my hand on his head to get his attention.

"It's okay," I said. "Be a good boy."

::*Okay*::

He sniffled and softly cried as Blanche took him out of the kitchen and disappeared. I finally found the nerve to bring my hand down and stood waiting for him to fire me.

"I have rules in place for a reason," he began, walking over to the counter and shuffling through the day's stack of mail. "But you seem to be so good at failing them. Do you see how easily something tragic could have happened while you were asleep?"

I couldn't find any words and simply nodded.

He folded his arms and began laughing. "Are you afraid of me?"

I don't know what came over me, but he'd gotten on my last nerve. "I don't give a shit *who* you are, you don't scare me. You're nothing but a rich, pompous asshole who can't handle his own kid, so you keep hiring nanny after nanny only to have them quit. Shea's not the problem; I'm pretty sure it's *you*."

"You certainly aren't talking like someone who wants to keep a job."

"Fuck you," I snapped. "I quit."

I stomped out of the kitchen then returned, pointing an angry finger at him. "Did you know Shea is afraid of the koi?" I hissed.

"Yes. He's terrified of them."

"Do you know *why*?" My heart was racing in my chest as every nerve in my body pricked with electric pulses of anxiety.

Mr. Sullivan wrinkled his forehead and glared at me. "Not really," he huffed. "He's afraid of a lot of things."

"*Someone* told him the fish would eat him."

He pulled a shocked face then said, "Certainly you're not accusing me?"

"No, you asshole. It was probably one of the other nannies, but maybe you should do a better job trying to figure out *why* he's the way he is. You can't blame everything on his deafness!"

He shot daggers at me with his eyes, but never said another word.

"I'll be out tonight," I told him, walking quickly away.

"I'll have my driver waiting to take you home. Make sure you clean up that room before you leave," he barked behind me.

Ignoring him, I went straight up to my apartment, grabbed my suitcase and threw it on the bed. I paced the floor with my hands balled into fists, trying not to think about how he was the most beautiful man I'd ever laid eyes on. I yanked my clothes off the hangers in the closet and threw them into the suitcase, not even taking the time to neatly fold them. My skin pricked as I thought about the most infuriating man I'd ever met, with his arrogant demeanor and holier than thou attitude, and his hazel eyes glaring at me… and the way his golden brown hair fell in a soft mullet to the bottom of his neck, not in a Michael Bolton way, but a sexy Patrick Swayze in *Roadhouse* way. He had a light peppering of facial hair that added to his physical charm, and when I thought about how perfectly tailored his shimmery blue business suit was, I could feel the steam pouring out of my ears.

I didn't realize I left my apartment door open until Shea made his way inside and started taking the clothes out of my suitcase and throwing them back in the closet. I would pick them up and bring them back to the suitcase. It was a battle of wills that he was not going to win, no matter how red his face got because he was beginning to cry. His soft whimpers and grunts shattered my heart, but there was no way I could continue working for a man who was continually setting me up for failure, especially after only one day.

"He is *not* allowed in your apartment," Mr. Sullivan growled behind me.

"Then get him out!" I shouted.

As Shea was lifted off the floor he fought and squirmed against his father, his arms and legs flailing as he sobbed. One of Shea's feet connected with Mr. Sullivan's groin and sent him crumbling to his knees. Shea ran toward me and latched onto my leg, his muffled sobs getting lost against my pants.

As Mr. Sullivan grimaced up at me from his place on the floor I hissed, "How embarrassing it must be for you to look up at a peasant like me." I grabbed the broken picture frame from the bedside table, tossed it in my suitcase and slammed it shut. I knelt on the floor and forced Shea to look at me.

"I have to go," I told him.

He refused to sign anything as the tears streamed down his face and he squeezed his eyes closed. I poked his belly and he pushed my hand away. I placed my hands on his shoulders and gently shook him until he opened his eyes. I silently cursed his father for putting me in a situation where I had to turn my back on the child I had immediately bonded with; the child I fell head over heels in love with as I held him in my arms that very first time.

Shea sniffled and touched his heart with the tip of his finger, then touched me in the same place. I brought his hand to my lips and kissed the tip of his finger, then pressed it against his mouth. I stood up and grabbed my suitcase and as I passed Mr. Sullivan said, "I'll never forgive you for this."

I raced to the front foyer as quickly as possible, grabbing my coat from the closet and struggling to put it on as Shea appeared before me, sobbing.

::I'll be good.::
::I'm sorry::
::Be good. Promise.::

He was absolutely breaking my heart and I *hated* his father for forcing my hand. "I'm sorry," I said. I held his face in my hands to kiss his forehead, then walked out the door, sobbing as I ran to the waiting car.

༺༻

I walked into my parents' house as they were just sitting down for dinner. My dad said nothing, which was his usual reaction to everything, and my mom rolled her eyes and shook her head in disgust.

"Didn't work out, I see." It wasn't a question.

As soon as I opened my mouth to speak the phone rang and since I was standing right there I picked it up.

"What have you done?" *Celeste.*

"I can't work for him. He's an asshole!"

"I told you he was an asshole!"

"He set me up to fail the minute I walked into that house," I tried to explain. "He's the worst human being I've ever met!"

Celeste heaved a sigh so heavy I could almost feel the moisture against my ear through the phone. "I felt the same way about you when we first met."

"What's your point?" I grumbled.

"All the other girls left because they couldn't handle Shea. You left because of *him*."

"Yeah, so?"

"I'll be in touch." I felt a headache coming on as the phone went dead. Now, did I sit down and eat dinner with my parents, or retreat to my bed and pull the covers over my head? I dragged my suitcase upstairs and face-planted on my bed, hoping the whole world would go away and my mom would leave me alone. I had no idea what I would do moving forward, and I knew she would start screaming at me about rehab as soon as she could.

I thought about Shea's precious face as he begged me not to go, thinking it was his fault I was leaving. I didn't want to leave him, but his father gave me no choice. I cried myself to sleep and I had no idea what time it was when my mom knocked on the door and entered.

"There's someone here to see you," my mom whispered.

"Who is it?" I groaned as I tried to wake up.

"I don't know but he looks like a chauffeur."

"A chauff...." That arrogant man sent his driver to talk to me? Or better yet, sent him to fetch me like some runaway dog?

I sat up and rubbed my eyes, trying to wake myself up before heading downstairs to tell Sullivan's driver he could kiss my ass and go back to where he came from. When I hit the bottom of the stairs, the driver smiled at me.

"I'm not going back," I said. "Sending you here to get me isn't going to change anything."

"What's your name, dear?" my mom asked him.

"Andy, ma'am."

"Hey Andy," I hissed. "You can go now. Tell Ziggy I'm not going back."

Andy chuckled and replied, "You can tell him yourself. He's in the car. He said he's not leaving until you talk to him."

As my mom offered Andy a cup of coffee, I threw on my coat and stormed out to the driveway where the luxurious black sedan sat idling, causing the neighbors to peek out their windows to see what was going on.

I flung open the back door and growled, "What's the air like up there in the high society you live in?"

Sullivan rolled his eyes and asked me to get in.

"I will not. I'm through with you." I looked around the spacious back seat then asked, "Where's Shea?"

"Ah, so you do care."

"I care about *him*, I don't give a rat's ass about *you*."

"Ms. Hastings, will you please get in so I can talk to you in private? Your neighbors appear to be far too interested in the scene you're creating."

Against my better judgment I got in the back seat with him and slammed the door shut. "Why are you here?"

He didn't seem to be able to look me in the eyes, answering, "Well, you didn't clean up the room like I asked and—"

"You came here to tell me I didn't pick up the blankets?" My face was burning fire.

"And you didn't put the furniture back where it belonged."

"I quit, remember? Do it yourself, or have Blanche do it in the morning. I'm not your servant."

He blinked several times and I watched as his hands clasped together and separated several times before finally saying, "I like things a certain way and Shea knows he's not allowed in that room. That room is strictly for entertaining when I have guests over, and I asked you nicely to clean it up before you left."

"Were you ever a kid?" I asked. "Or were you born an adult jerk?"

"Ms. Hastings, I—"

"Didn't you ever make a blanket fort?"

He hesitated before grumbling, "I wasn't allowed near the furniture."

I was beginning to get some insight into why he was such an abominable asshole.

"Why are you really here?" I asked, lowering my voice.

"Shea needs you."

"He needs me, or *you* need me?"

"Celeste told me how he bonded with you immediately, and trust me Ms. Hastings, that's an unbelievable feat. I've seen every side of that boy as you can well imagine, but I've never seen him like this."

My heart dropped. "Like what?"

"He's absolutely distraught and he doesn't understand that you left because of me."

"Who's with him right now?"

"Celeste. And she's furious with me."

A slight grin crept across my face. "Good. You deserve it."

"Ms. Hastings," he spoke softly, finally turning to look at me. "You know what a special child Shea is, and you know I've had difficulty finding a nanny that is a good fit."

"If you know all that why did you keep setting me up to fail?"

"I needed to know if you could be trusted."

The blood in my veins burned fire as my hands balled into fists in my lap. "If you didn't trust me why did you hire me?"

"Celeste told me she didn't like you, but the way Shea took to you right away, she knew you were right for the job."

"You're ridiculous," I spat. "I don't even like kids. The only reason I took the job is so my parents wouldn't—"

"We don't have to like each other," he interrupted. I was almost relieved he didn't let me finish. "But I need you because Shea needs you. And I can tell by the look on your face right now that you need him, too."

I didn't like the way he was dissecting me and it made me extremely uncomfortable. I quickly snapped out of my emotional state thinking about Shea and said, "I don't need anybody. I certainly don't need *you* or your stupid job."

My immaturity had just given Mr. Sullivan the upper hand and I knew I was blowing it. He grinned, seemingly more at ease and said, "You're young and you're apparently a hot head with a short fuse. You have no filter and you're rather immature."

"You're a pompous asshole," I grumbled.

"That may be true, but I don't care if you like me or not. And frankly, I don't particularly like you either, but Shea does. I've hired you to take care of him, and I'd like you to come back."

I stared at him, having no idea how to respond without digging myself an even deeper hole. "Why would you even want me back?" I muttered, not entirely sure I wanted to be employed by this guy.

"Ms. Hastings, you threatened to stab me with a butcher knife when you thought I was an intruder kidnapping Shea. I think you passed the ultimate test."

I stared at my hands as I picked some purple nail polish from my thumbnail. "I'll come back on one condition."

"And that is?"

"I want to go over your list of bullshit rules."

"Those rules are in place for Shea's protection, as well as your own."

"Okay, bye."

As I tried to get out of the car, he said, "Okay fine, you win. I will agree to at least go over them."

Just then the carphone rang. I'd heard of people having phones in their cars but I'd never actually seen one before. I assumed it was something only the rich could afford.

"Is he okay?" Sullivan asked. "I should be home in half an hour or so."

As he hung up the phone I asked, "Is everything all right?"

"He's gotten himself so worked up he's vomiting. If you knew Celeste, you'd understand why she's a bit uneasy at the moment."

All I could think about was Shea being so upset with me that he cried himself into such a state that he started throwing up, with no outlet or understanding of how to deal with his emotions.

"I take it she doesn't do well with vomiting," I said.

"Vomiting, kids, animals... vomiting kids and animals... and she knows very little sign language. So Shea is probably more than she can handle at the moment."

"I'll be right back."

I got out of the car and noticed the neighbors still peeking out of their windows as I ran back into the house. I raced upstairs to get my unpacked suitcase and came back down, finding Andy in the dining room having cookies and coffee with my parents.

"Andy!" I shouted. "Time to go!"

He thanked my parents and excused himself as he followed me out the door. I didn't even say goodbye.

As soon as we walked into the house, Celeste met us in the foyer and said, "He's in the blanket fort. I can't get him to come out."

I set my suitcase on the floor and handed Mr. Sullivan my coat, making my way to the blanket fort and crawling inside to look for Shea. I found him in the middle of our furniture maze, curled up in a ball with his body trembling in time with his sobs. The guilt ate me alive because I knew I was the cause. Not wanting to scare him, I pounded my fist on the floor so he would feel the vibration. Slowly he lifted his head and turned to face me. He stared at me for a moment, and I wondered if he was angry with me.

He whined and cried as he crawled toward me, throwing himself into my arms once he reached me, burying his snotty face against my shirt. I hugged him tightly and whispered, "I'll never leave you again, I promise," against his sweaty head.

Chapter 5

The next morning I was blown out of bed by Shea's door alarm, jumping up and racing out of my room in complete darkness. I saw him running toward me in the hallway, his arms extended as he jumped into my embrace. I wondered if he feared I wouldn't be there as promised, or if he was just excited to get the day started. Either way, it was far too early in the morning for him to be out of bed so I brought him back to his room and locked the door behind me. A lock that was so high on the door frame I could barely reach it myself.

"Back to bed," I told him.

::Play::

I made him get back in his bed and said, "It's not time to play, it's time to sleep."

By the dimness of the nightlight I was able to see that it was four o'clock. This kid was going to be the death of me.

Shea sat in his bed and pouted, but I convinced him to lay down and go back to sleep by crawling into bed beside him. We faced each other and he curled up into a ball with his forehead against my throat. I wondered if he did this so he could feel my pulse; to "hear" me in his own special way.

I woke up four hours later and Shea was no longer in bed with me. I sat up and frantically looked for him, seeing him sitting on the window seat smiling and signing. I watched him for a bit but couldn't understand who he was talking to. I remained still, however, because I didn't want to disturb the pure happiness radiating on his face.

Shea turned his head and caught me watching him, so he scrambled down from the window seat and jumped on the bed. He jumped and jumped like he was on a trampoline and I finally grabbed his hand and made him sit down.

"Who were you talking to?" I asked.

::JoJo::

Realizing Shea had an imaginary friend, I smiled. JoJo probably understood a lot more than anyone else ever could, and probably gave him comfort when he felt alone and afraid.

::Snowing::

I got out of bed and walked to the window where large, fluffy snowflakes fell outside. Shea climbed up onto the window seat to watch with me for a few minutes before I turned him to face me.

"Do you want to go outside and build a snowman?" I asked excitedly, thinking he would love the idea.

Shea stood up and shook his head furiously, then jumped off the seat onto my bare foot with all his strength and dove under the bed to hide. I collapsed in a heap as the pain shot from my foot and up my leg, and in that moment I understood the rule about wearing sneakers and no open-toed shoes. He peered out at me and I said, "Okay, no snowman. Come on."

I hobbled around his room to get some clothes, then pulled off his pajamas once he trusted me enough to come out from under the bed. I had to change into my uniform, and the only way to do that was to bring Shea with me, so I would have to go against Sullivan's rule there, at least for the time being.

I locked the door to my apartment and made Shea promise he'd sit on the couch quietly until I came back out, rushing into the bathroom to clean up, brush my teeth and change my clothes. When I came back out to the living room he was sitting quietly, just as I'd asked him to do. I praised him for being such a good boy as I put on my sneakers, barely able to tie the shoelaces on the foot he stomped on.

Shea held my hand as we walked downstairs and I hesitated in the foyer, waiting to see how he would react to the koi. I slowly made my way toward the pond and he reluctantly followed.

"Good morning, mermaid! Good morning, fish!" I said with a smile. I leaned over the edge of the pond so I could see the fish, showing Shea I wasn't afraid and that he shouldn't be, either.

He inched closer until his legs were touching the side of the pond, then he gasped. I told him the fish were friendly and he slowly peered over the side to look at them. His eyes were huge as he watched the koi swim around, oblivious to his presence, and certainly not looking to chomp him to bits.

"See?" I said. "Nice fish."

::Nice::
::Won't eat me::
"They won't eat you, I promise. Breakfast?"

He nodded happily and I limped a bit as I led him to the kitchen. I couldn't decide if stomping on my foot was intentional, or accidental because of his anger at me suggesting we build a snowman. What was wrong with snowmen?

While Shea ate his peanut butter and jelly sandwich for breakfast I said, "The snow is so pretty."

He nodded.

"Have you ever made a snow angel?"

He wrinkled his nose and shook his head.

"Don't you like to play in the snow?"

He shook his head quickly and stopped chewing.

"But it's fun!"

Shea flung his sandwich at me then picked up his glass of milk and threw it on the floor.

"I'll get that," Blanche's voice called from behind me.

"No, you won't," I replied. I got up and grabbed a roll of paper towels, then pulled Shea out of his chair. "Clean up the mess you made."

He folded his arms defiantly in front of him and pouted, shaking his head.

"You will clean this up," I insisted. "We're not leaving this room until you do."

Shea watched as I threw his sandwich in the garbage, then poured myself a cup of coffee.

::Blanket fort::
"Nothing until you clean up your mess."
::Train::
"No."
::Blocks::
"No."

He threw himself on the floor kicking and grunting, his clothes soaking up most of the milk he splattered all over the place. I stood over him and waited until he opened his eyes to look at me.

"No play until you clean up your mess."

He made an angry face and punched the air.

::Hate you::

"You hate me?" I asked, surprised. "I don't hate you. I love you."

He punched the air again.

"If you hate me, I should go home."

I watched as he thought about what I said, and his facial expression changed from anger to sorrow. It wasn't my intention to threaten him, but if he hated me, why should I stay? It was a simple question that he needed to think about.

Slowly Shea picked himself off of the floor and tried cleaning up the milk, but he was four and his hands didn't exactly know how to manage it easily, so I helped him. When we were finished I brought him upstairs to change him out of his wet clothes.

"That wasn't very nice," I told him, now understanding why he was only allowed to use plastic dishes and cups. I wondered if he'd ever stabbed someone with a fork or a knife, remembering he's only allowed to use spoons. Sullivan's rules were making more sense the longer I spent with Shea.

Slipping a sweatshirt over his head I asked, "Why don't you like playing in the snow?"

::Scared::

"Of what?"

::Burn me::

"Burn you? Snow is cold!"

He shook his head violently.

::Burn like fire::

"Fire? Who...." I began to realize that the other nannies used threats and lies to control and manipulate Shea, and I couldn't fathom what other nonsense the poor child had to endure because of their laziness. I started to question if they even knew sign language.

"Snow is cold," I explained. "Like ice. Brrrrrr."

I lifted him into my arms and went back down to the kitchen where I set him on the floor, then grabbed a large stock pot from the cabinet. I told him to wait, but to watch me through the sliding glass doors. I rushed outside so he could see that the snow was not going to hurt me, his little face pressed up against the glass. I filled the stock pot with snow and rushed back into the house, his eyes wild with curiosity and fear. I sat him at the table and brought the stock pot full of snow and a plastic plate over. I grabbed a handful of snow and showed it to him. He was shocked, holding his hands against his cheeks.

"Cold," I said.

He carefully reached out one finger to touch the snow, pretending to shiver and relieved that it didn't burn him.

::Cold::

"See? Cold."

He smiled, jumping up and down at his new excitement for snow.

"Want to build a snowman?"

He lifted his hands, palms up, showing confusion.

I took a handful of snow and shaped it into a ball, setting it on the plastic plate. I helped Shea shape the middle section of the snowman and we set that on top of the first ball. Then he created the head and we stuck that on top. I found some raisins that we used for the eyes, nose and mouth, then I cut a hat out of a magazine sitting on the counter and placed that on top of his head.

Shea smiled and clapped at our mini-snowman creation, and to be sure his father saw what we made, I placed it in the freezer so it wouldn't melt.

※

After Mr. Sullivan came home from work, I fixed myself a dinner plate and brought it up to my apartment to eat. Once he returned home in the evening, my time with Shea was over and I finally had a bit of the day to myself. I grabbed a can of soda from the fridge and as I sat down to dig into the pot roast, mashed potatoes and green beans, the phone rang. I knew it could only mean one thing, because nobody had my phone number. I didn't even know my own phone number. It had to be Mr. Sullivan calling to complain about something — probably the snowman in the freezer — so I chose to ignore it and enjoy my meal in peace. The phone stopped ringing then started up again and I continued to ignore it.

It wasn't long before I heard a light tapping on my apartment door and while I was really hoping for some much needed alone time, I got up and opened it. There stood little Shea staring up and smiling at me, and his father, looking a bit annoyed.

"I must admit I'm breaking one of my own rules right now," he said. "Shea has something he'd like to ask you."

I smiled down at Shea, waiting to hear what he wanted to say.

::Eat with us::

"I'm sorry, Shea," I began. "When daddy comes home, that's your time to spend with him. He misses you when he's gone."

::Want you::

"You're killing me, kid," I whispered.

"Ms. Hastings, it would be okay with me if you wanted to join us for dinner. I mean, it's up to you after all, and I understand you need your free time. Shea has never made this request before, and I'm not quite sure how I feel about it, to be honest."

"I'll make it easier for you," I said. I looked at Shea and smiled. "Dinnertime is for you and your dad. I'll see you in the morning."

Shea crumpled to the floor and began to cry. "Ms. Hastings, maybe we could talk about my list of rules over dinner… if you think it's appropriate."

"Yeah, okay. Good idea."

I picked Shea up from the floor and told him I'd meet them in the kitchen. He smiled and followed his father back downstairs. Even though I was really looking forward to a peaceful meal alone, I grabbed my plate and can of soda and made my way down to the kitchen.

"Would you like a glass with ice?" Mr. Sullivan asked.

"Yeah, sure," I replied, seating myself across from Shea.

"Ms. Hastings, why is there a miniature snowman in the freezer?"

"Shea made that today." I told Shea to turn around to see what his father was looking at.

"He went outside and played in the snow?"

"Well, no... not exactly."

He brought me a glass of ice and took his seat at the head of the table. He glanced at me, waiting to hear my explanation. It was the first time he looked at me without contempt or exasperation and it suited him. I noticed he shaved the stubble from his face and he was certainly delicious to look at.

"Shea was afraid the snow would burn him, so I brought some into the house to show him that wasn't true."

"And he built that snowman."

"With some help." I looked at Shea and said, "He loves your snowman."

Shea smiled and clapped then happily continued eating his peanut butter and jelly sandwich.

"I think your other nannies were scaring Shea to control and manipulate him for some reason. Maybe they didn't know how else to deal with him, or maybe they were just lazy. Afraid the koi were going to eat him, and the snow was going to burn him... someone put those ideas into his head."

"You could be right. What do you suggest?"

"I'm not sure... I guess I'll deal with things as they come up."

"Please keep me informed," he said, never looking at me. "He seems to be receptive to you in ways no one else was able to manage. It takes a load off my mind."

I took a bite of mashed potatoes and noticed Shea eyeing me suspiciously.

::*What's that?*::

"Potatoes," I replied. "Want to try some?"

He nodded and I stared at him, not responding in any other way.

::*Yes please*::

I got up and fetched him a spoon, then scooped up a bit of my potatoes, holding it to his mouth. He pulled them in with his lips and thought hard about what he was eating before smiling and rubbing his belly excitedly.

"Would you like some potatoes?"

::Yes please::

I put some potatoes on his plate and sat back down, seeing Mr. Sullivan staring at me with his mouth open. I did not look at him.

"So Ms. Hastings, about my list of rules—"

"Please call me Jude."

"Okay Jude, we can do this your way. What did you want to discuss?"

Thinking about the snot-covered shirt and my foot that was still aching, I said, "I really only have one complaint. Can we do something about Shea's door alarm? There has to be another way."

"But it works," he replied.

"But it's awful," I argued. "It's like a fire engine driving through my room and it scares the shit out of me."

"Sorry, but I can't budge on that one. Shea's safety is more important than whether or not the shit is scared out of you."

"Have you heard that alarm?"

"Of course I have," he said with a grin. "I'm the one who had it installed. And when I need to, I can turn it on in my room."

"So what happens when you're at the cabin on the weekend?"

"He sleeps in the same room with me, and I lock the door."

"Are you gone every weekend?"

"Pretty much, unless there's a party. Which reminds me, there's a Mardi Gras party coming up next month, so you'll get paid extra to mind Shea that evening. And you'll need to have your blanket fort cleaned up, and all the furniture put back where it belongs. Sooner rather than later."

I thought he was finally softening a bit, but then it was right back to his weird obsession over the blanket fort. He'd probably die of heart failure if I ever taught Shea how to play The Floor Is Lava.

There was an awkward silence that made me uncomfortable, so I decided to make things even more unbearable.

"What happened to Shea's mother?" I asked.

"That," he said, stabbing at a piece of pot roast, "is none of your business Ms. Hastings, and I suggest you not ask me personal questions of that nature again."

I knew I'd stepped over a line, but I didn't think there was anything wrong with asking. It might explain a lot of Shea's fears and idiosyncrasies if I knew what happened to his mother. I was obviously not going to get the answer I was looking for, and Mr. Sullivan was now in a foul mood.

I quickly finished my dinner and told Shea I was going to bed, and that I'd see him in the morning. This seemed to satisfy him and I said goodnight to his father and quickly made my escape. Once in the safety of my own apartment I locked the door, started a fire and grabbed a beer. I sat on the couch and pulled the Shea handbook into my lap and settled in for a long night of reading.

The more I read the more incensed I became. The former nannies wrote in code names and never dated anything, so it was seemingly impossible to identify them. I read it from beginning to end and back again, then read it all a second time in case I missed something. A lot of the rules put in place began to make sense as I read the reasons:

> Shea ripped a girl's antique locket from her neck
> He cut off a chunk of one girl's long hair with scissors
> He caught a girl having sex with a guy in the hot tub in the middle of the night (which meant he got out of his room and wandered downstairs and then outside)
> He stabbed one of the nannies in the behind with a fork
> He threw a glass on the floor that shattered, causing him and the nanny to go to the Emergency Room for stitches

And the list went on. I understood that he was a handful, but what infuriated me the most were the ways they used fear tactics to make their lives easier. And the "handbook" was written like a secret diary amongst the nannies, as if they were all getting a kick out of how they all found ways to manipulate this young child and deserved pats on the back and awards for their brilliance. Shea liked to play in the water where the koi lived, so he was told they would eat him. One nanny hated the cold so badly she told him the snow would burn him to keep him from wanting to play outside. And yet another nanny accidentally tried to put him in a bath with scalding water, so she got out of bathing him as Mr. Sullivan had to take over that duty. Shea wouldn't allow anyone else to bathe him because he thought they were trying to boil him.

The nannies also took pleasure in the fact that Shea couldn't read lips, so they said horrible things to him that they knew he didn't understand just by watching them. "I hate you" and "you're a little shit" were some of their favorites. They also talked about how he would go out of his way to sign incorrectly to confuse them. How on earth did a four-year-old sign incorrectly in order to confuse people? My anger extended to Celeste and Blanche, who were both aware the handbook existed, and I began to wonder if they thought it was funny as well. There was nothing funny about what had happened to Shea in the hands of his former nannies and Mr. Sullivan needed to know about that book.

I held the handbook tightly underneath my arm as I walked out of my apartment and went downstairs, but I didn't find Mr. Sullivan or Shea anywhere. I went back upstairs and walked down the hallway toward the bathroom and stopped just outside the door when I heard him talking.

"No, Miss J is not your new mommy."

I could hear the water splashing as he bathed his son and I continued to listen. I only wished I could see what Shea was signing.

"You have a mommy and you know she's in heaven."

"I know you like Miss J, but—"

"Okay, you *love* Miss J, but she's not your mommy."

"I know you don't like those other ladies. You don't have to see them ever again."

I turned around and went back to my apartment, closing the door and locking it behind me. I couldn't begin to fathom what that poor child had been through with the other nannies. It bordered on abuse and my guess was Mr. Sullivan had no idea the extent those nannies went to. I vowed then and there if I taught Shea anything, it would be how to read lips so that he wasn't in the dark when people tried to trick him just because he was deaf.

Chapter 6

The next evening I brought my dinner back up to the apartment and no sooner had I begun to eat there was a tiny knock on my door. I opened it to find Shea standing there smiling up at me with a note in his hand. He handed it to me and waited patiently for me to read it.

Ms. Hastings,

Shea requests your presence for dinner this evening.

Z.S.

"Don't you want to eat with your dad?" I asked.
::Want you::
"Why?"
He pouted as he thought about it, and I don't really think he knew how to answer that.
::Miss you::
"You saw me five minutes ago."
He clasped his little hands into a praying position and closed his eyes tightly. I tousled his hair and nodded, and he waited patiently in the hallway for me to get my plate. I followed Shea back downstairs to the kitchen where his father waited patiently for him to return.
"Oh good, I can eat now," he said with a hint of sarcasm.
"Bad day at the office, dear?" I teased as I sat down.
"I beg your pardon?"
"Oh loosen up," I teased. "You take everything so seriously."
I was hoping this might be a good time to bring up the handbook, but he was obviously in some kind of mood that I didn't dare. He ate his lasagna quietly, his suit jacket hanging on the back of the chair, his white shirtsleeves rolled up to his elbows. While Shea wouldn't have known the difference, the awkward silence was killing me so I tried to think of something to talk about.

"So what's your job like?" I asked. "How did you get into publishing?"

Sullivan rolled his eyes and answered, "I'm okay with the silence, Ms. Hastings. No need for petty conversation."

"I'm sorry, I just—"

"Please stop," he grumbled. "I invited you to eat with us because Shea insisted. I'm hoping it doesn't become habit, because I rather like eating dinner in peace."

I didn't say another word, eating my dinner silently and wishing I could just go back upstairs. I rather enjoyed being in my apartment away from him. He made me so uneasy and uncomfortable I didn't like being around him much.

I watched Shea as he happily ate his crustless peanut butter and jelly sandwich, oblivious to anything else going on around him. Then out of the blue he let out an adult-sized fart that ripped the awkward silence in half. Sullivan acted as if nothing happened, but I covered my mouth to keep from laughing.

"Is passing gas funny to you, Ms. Hastings?"

"No, but there are manners for farts, just like everything else. Just because he can't hear it doesn't mean he shouldn't apologize."

He leaned back in his chair and folded his arms in front of his chest. "Be my guest."

I tapped the table in front of Shea's plate to get his attention and when he looked at me I asked, "What was that?"

He did his usual hands in the air, palms up, to show he didn't understand.

I stood up and pointed at my behind, then pointed at him. He began to giggle, knowing exactly what I was talking about.

Between his giggles he managed to say *::Bubbles::*

"Bubbles?"

Shea looked at his father, who was watching the whole thing with amusement, then he glanced back at me.

::Butt bubbles::

"And what do you say after you have butt bubbles?" I asked.

He shrugged, clueless. He'd obviously never been reprimanded for farting in front of others before.

"You say *excuse me*."

He nodded understanding.

"Say excuse me," I insisted.

::*Excuse me*::

"That's better."

Sullivan looked at Shea and said, "Thank you, Miss J, for being the bubble police."

Shea began laughing so hard he had spittle coming out the sides of his mouth. I had never seen him laugh that hard before, and even though I wasn't amused at what Sullivan said, I was glad to see Shea so happy.

༺༻

Shea insisted I eat dinner with them every evening that week, and I knew he was never going to change his mind which probably wasn't sitting well with Sullivan. On Friday, however, as soon as Sullivan returned home from work, they were packing their weekend bags to head to the cabin in Wisconsin.

As they headed toward the front door I asked, "Are you driving up there?"

"I don't drive," Sullivan answered.

"How are you getting there then?"

"My driver is taking us to the airport, and from there I'll fly to Wisconsin. Then my driver in Wisconsin will take us to the cabin."

He said it so matter-of-factly. "You won't drive, but you'll fly a plane?"

"It's a Cessna four seater," he explained, like I had any idea what that was. "Trust me, the roads are far more dangerous than the skies, Ms. Hastings."

I shuddered to think of being crammed into one of those small airplanes.

Sullivan put on Shea's coat and said, "Say goodbye to Miss J."

Panic covered Shea's precious face as he immediately looked at me with large eyes. It was apparent he thought I would be joining them, and that was the *last* thing I wanted to do.

::Coming?::

"No," I answered. "This is your time to spend with Dad."

Shea threw himself on the floor and began to cry, punching the air angrily with his fists. I leaned over him so he could see my face.

"Stop," I said. "Be a good boy and spend time with your Dad."

::You come::

"I can't. I have work to do at home. I promise to be here when you get back."

Shea's angry face softened a bit as he lay on his back staring up at me.

::Come come come::

"I can't. This is your time with your dad. Now be a good boy. He's waiting for you."

Shea picked himself off the floor and wrapped his arms around my neck, puckering up for a kiss goodbye. After kissing me he went into the coat closet and pulled out a rubber mask that he yanked over his head. I did everything I could not to laugh out loud.

"Godzilla?" I asked.

"He's afraid to go outside. He's afraid of the car... and the plane. He thinks Godzilla protects him, so that's what he wears until we get to the cabin. It's the only way."

"I pictured him as more of a King Kong kinda guy," I teased with a smile.

"He would sit in front of the television all day watching Godzilla movies if I let him. I don't let him."

"Got it."

"We'll be back Sunday night," he said, ushering Shea toward the door. "The number is on the fridge. So is Celeste's if you need anything. Emergencies *only*."

"Go, go Godzilla," I called, waving goodbye.

And now I had forty-eight hours alone in front of me and I couldn't wait to get my weekend started. I ran up to my room and took a long, hot shower; the first one I was able to enjoy the entire week. Having to guess what time Shea might set off the siren every morning made getting ready for the day a task. I had to start taking my showers before I went to bed at night and I hated doing that. I had to come up with an idea Shea would willingly accept for our morning wakeup routine, otherwise I was never going to get a good night's sleep.

My plan was to get dressed up and hit the town to see if I could catch up with some of my old party friends. With my hair wrapped in a towel and wearing the most plush and cozy robe I'd ever touched, I sat on my bed and held the cracked picture frame in my hands, looking at Prude's smiling face. If only I'd known that she would be struck down just a few hours after that photo was taken, I would have told her I loved her. She always knew I loved her because we had that unbreakable twin bond, but I rarely said it. I was always the black sheep of the family, and I suppose in an odd sort of way I relished it. It allowed me to be the uncooperative rebel, the exact opposite of Prude's perfect angel. And since my parents treated us so differently anyway, it was far too easy to fall into the trap of always being the child who was wrong.

I stretched out on the bed and wondered what Prude would think of my new job, my new life. She was probably laughing at what a horrible job I was doing, especially with Mr. Sullivan, but I hoped I could make her proud one day. And it would've been a miracle to hear one of my parents tell me they were proud of me. I wouldn't hold my breath.

I woke up at ten-thirty Saturday morning on top of my bed still dressed in the fluffy robe with my head in a towel. I must have been more exhausted than I thought; I'd never pass up a night of partying for sleep. I got up and rewashed my hair, dried it, then dressed for the day. I was a nervous wreck taking Sullivan's Volvo out for a spin, but I decided to go shopping. I went to my favorite thrift store to purchase some clothes more sensible to residing in the Sullivan home, including a swimsuit for the hot tub (which I planned to enjoy while I was home alone) and a snowsuit for Shea (if I could coax him to play outside). I then went to the toy store to find things I could do with Shea. I picked up a few puzzles, some learning games, and a couple of books.

I picked up a pastrami sandwich and fries from my favorite deli for lunch, then headed back to the house to eat in peace. I sat in the kitchen and closed my eyes before taking a bite of my sandwich, enjoying the time alone. I was surprised at the sense of loneliness I felt, the overwhelming sorrow that something was missing. I was shocked to realize that I was desperately missing Shea. In less than a week he had become the center of my world, the best part of my life. Prude and Shea were used to a world of complete silence; I wasn't. I found myself wondering what Shea was doing at that moment and whether or not he missed me. Before I realized what was happening I burst into tears. Ugly, guttural sobbing that I could not control. I couldn't remember the last time I cried so fiercely and from the very depths of my soul. It must have been a year after Prude's death, when the boy I dated all through high school broke up with me because I was taking too long to grieve. He didn't just break my heart, he shattered it, and I vowed then and there I would never cry over a man again. Colin was my first and last boyfriend; I thought we would be together forever as he proclaimed we would. I knew then men could never be trusted and that's when my partying and long list of bed partners began. They weren't all one night stands; some of them I saw more than once and some were friends with benefits. And where was I now? Bawling over a four-year-old boy I missed almost as much as my dead sister.

After forcing myself to snap out of it, I finished my lunch and spent the afternoon perusing the bookshelves in Sullivan's library. Most of them were books his company published, but not all of them. He owned a lot of classic novels that I'd heard of, but never thought about reading. I liked to read, but because there was so much reading in school, and none of it for pleasure, I stopped thinking about books as something to enjoy. I pulled out a book by an author named Willow Kelly, simply because her name intrigued me and I really liked the cover. It was said to be the best romantic mystery of 1989, according to reviews printed on the back, so I decided to give it a shot. I didn't care much about the romantic part, but I was in the mood for a good mystery.

I spent the afternoon curled up on the couch under a blanket reading and didn't realize how long I'd been there until my stomach started grumbling for dinner. The book was so good I didn't stop reading until I was finished, and I was anxious to read more by this author. The mystery kept me on the edge of my seat throughout the whole book, and the slow burn romance was hot, especially when the two main characters finally had sex.

I went into the kitchen to fix leftovers for dinner and stood staring at the phone numbers listed on the refrigerator. I saw Andy the driver's number and wondered what he did in his free time when he wasn't at the beck and call of Sullivan? Remembering that he lived in a guest house on the property, I picked up the phone and dialed, with the intention of finding out whether or not he liked to party.

"Hello, Ms. Hastings," he answered.

I panicked, forgetting he would probably know it was me who was calling.

"Ms. Hastings?"

"Oh, Sorry," I fumbled. "Never mind."

As I went to hang up the phone I heard him say, "Did you need something? Is everything okay?"

"I was thinking about going in the hot tub later," I said, cringing at how stupid I sounded. "Do you know how to turn it on?"

He chuckled and said, "What time do you want me to come over?"

"Eight o'clock?"

"I'll see you then."

"Bring a towel," I rushed before he hung up. "If you want to stay."

"It's lonely in that big house without the little rugrat, isn't it?"

I breathed a sigh of relief and replied, "It really is."

"I'll see you at eight."

I hung up and wondered what was actually happening at eight. I cursed myself for being so weak yet so forward. It couldn't have been more obvious that I was looking for company and if Sullivan ever found out we'd probably both be fired on the spot.

At eight o'clock Andy stood on the back deck, knocking on the door. I was wearing my new swim suit and wrapped in a towel as I let him into the house.

"You're all set, Ms. Hastings. Do you need anything else?"

Andy looked much different than when he'd been in the car, or taking the coffee offered by my mom in their house. And was much younger than I thought he was; older than me but younger than Sullivan. He was about six foot tall, but dressed in a sweatshirt and pair of jeans instead of a chauffeur's uniform, he looked quite different. And without the hat, his long, blond hair flowed down past his shoulders to the middle of his chest. He was gorgeous and I was nearly speechless.

"Show me how to turn it off?" I said, my face burning a thousand shades of embarrassment.

I made a big production of taking my towel off to reveal my body to him, then stepped gently into the hot, rolling water. He showed me how to maneuver all the buttons and I thanked him.

He smiled at me and it was then I noticed his piercing blue eyes. "Look, if Sullivan wasn't my boss I'd join you in a second, but I'm sure you understand why I have to say no. He's an asshole, but I have a sweet ride here and I'm not willing to risk it."

"I understand." I grinned, embarrassed. "Why do you hide that beautiful hair?"

"Because he doesn't know I have it." With that he said goodnight and walked away.

I settled into the hot water letting it relax and boil me like a hot dog. I hadn't been that relaxed in a long time, and then my mind wandered to the nanny who was caught having sex with her boyfriend. Then I wondered how many other people had sex in that hot tub. As meticulous as Sullivan was, I assumed it was thoroughly cleaned on a regular basis, and for once I was thankful for what appeared to be his prominent OCD.

About an hour later I saw lights bouncing and soon a black sedan pulled up and parked. The driver got out and opened the back door where I saw Sullivan emerge carrying a limp Shea in his arms. As he headed toward the deck where I was sitting in the hot tub, the driver opened the trunk to pull out their travel bags.

"Ms. Hastings," Sullivan grumbled as he passed, entering the house quickly.

The driver sped past me to bring the bags into the house, then as he retreated back to the car tipped his hat and said, "Ms. Hastings."

I turned off the hot tub and jumped out, wrapping myself in the towel and running inside. My heart thundered violently in my chest as I asked if everything was okay. Drying myself as quickly as possible, I followed Sullivan into the living room where he gently placed a sleeping Shea on the couch, all bundled up in his winter coat and Godzilla mask.

"Why are you home so early?" I asked, worried something was wrong. "Is he okay?"

Sullivan shrugged off his coat and tossed it on the couch next to Shea. He signed while answering me, driving home the fact he was imitating his son.

"Miss J, Miss J, Miss J. I want Miss J. I want to go home. I want Miss J."

I couldn't help but smile, even though I tried to hide my mouth with the towel I held tightly around me.

"The crying and the begging... I couldn't take it anymore," he continued, running a hand through his hair. "He finally fell asleep in the car."

My heart swelled at this news, and I no longer felt it necessary to hide my smile. "I missed him, too," I admitted.

"You're dripping water on my carpet."

Before I turned to run upstairs and change my clothes, Shea sat straight up on the couch. He ripped off the mask and blinked his wide eyes several times, trying to figure out where he was. He looked directly at me and rubbed his eyes, then hopped off the couch and catapulted into my arms, causing me to drop the towel in order to catch him. While I was comfortable in my own skin, and bought the red bikini because I loved it, I felt Sullivan's eyes on me and it was a bit unnerving.

Shea practically strangled me as he kept trying to climb higher up my body to kiss my cheek. Nobody had ever been that happy to see me in my life, and it was almost overwhelming.

"I guess Godzilla can't protect you from everything," I mused. I set Shea on the floor and told him I had to go upstairs and change my clothes, then picked up the towel and covered my body once again.

"Don't worry Ms. Hastings," Sullivan said with a grin. "Nothing I haven't already seen."

I glared at him, remembering the incident where I fell into the koi pond. I knew he'd probably seen me naked, but I tried not to dwell on it until then. Seeing me naked was something that would *never* happen again, so I ripped off the towel and walked away from him so he could take a good look at what he'd never get a piece of. When I reached the safety of my apartment, I thanked my lucky stars that Andy turned me down.

♈

I continued to wake up to the siren in my room every morning, Sullivan seemed to withdraw further into himself, and dinners with the two of them were almost excruciating, but since it's what Shea wanted, I was allowed to eat dinner with them. I would have preferred the privacy of my own apartment, but if it meant he would eat and try new foods, I was more than happy to be part of it. There was little to no conversation with his father, and I realized it was more a blessing than a curse because he wasn't my favorite person in the world. But for Shea, I'd deal with it. I didn't know if it was me he disliked so much, or if he was bogged down at the office, but either way he wasn't pleasant to be around.

I was finally able to convince Shea that when he went to the cabin with his father on the weekends, I would be there when they came home. I didn't relish the thought of spending a weekend with them in a cabin, and I knew Sullivan had no interest in me invading that time with his son. If there were any problems after that first weekend, he never mentioned it. He may have just put his foot down and didn't cave to

Shea's begging and crying; I had no idea. I was just glad I didn't have to go with them and even more happy to be home without Sullivan. I loved my time with Shea, even though he was a handful, but with Sullivan I felt like I was constantly walking barefoot on glass shards.

The best day was when I talked Shea into making snow angels, and I used my newly purchased camera to take photos so I could show Sullivan how much he was progressing and growing, and becoming less fearful of things he should never have been afraid of to begin with. Once I explained what a snow angel was he watched intently as I demonstrated on the floor. We practiced all morning after breakfast and when he was satisfied with my approval of his technique, I bundled him up in his snowsuit, hat, mittens and scarf and he apprehensively followed me outside. I had purchased a used 35mm camera and gave Blanche a brief lesson on how to take some photos, so we would have a visual memory of this monumental event. She clicked away as we went into the yard outside the kitchen. Since we were both wearing mittens, making it difficult to sign, I explained to Shea beforehand to follow me, and when he wanted to go back inside he should just go.

He watched intently as I found a perfect patch of snow, then spread my legs, outstretched my arms and fell backward. I swept my arms and legs up and down to make the angel pattern and he stared at me with wonderment. Shea was reluctant to fall into the snow on his own, so I got up and held his hands, lowering him gently onto his back. I motioned for him to sweep his arms up and down and he mimicked my movements, giggling as he did so. I plopped down on the other side of him into some pristine snow and made a new angel as we both swept our arms and legs up and down as if we were flying.

When I was done I pulled Shea up by his hands so his angel wouldn't be disturbed, and he turned around excitedly to look at it. His hands flew to his face and he jumped up and down with pure delight as he admired his creation. I thanked Blanche for taking photos and let her go back inside, but Shea stood there staring at his snow angel. I tapped him on the head to get his attention and when he looked up at me I smiled and nodded.

Shea jumped up and down and pointed toward the snow and I extended my arm, giving him the invitation to play as he wished. He ran off into the yard and jumped head first into a pile of snow, then rolled onto his back giggling hysterically. I only wished he could hear the sound of his own laughter, because the sound made me feel as if butterflies had taken flight deep within my heart.

He was enjoying his time in the snow so much, we made a snowman then ventured into a snowball fight. He was laughing so hard he almost couldn't catch his breath, stumbling in the snow to regain his footing, but falling all over the place. He had me in stitches, looking like a drunk stumbling home from a bar. Not that I knew anything about that....

The parts of Shea's face I could see were turning pink from the cold winter air, and just as I was about to suggest going back inside to warm up I saw Sullivan standing at the sliding glass doors watching us. It was unusual that he'd be home so early in the day and I hoped there wasn't anything wrong. I got to my feet and grabbed Shea by the hands, pulling him up beside me. I pointed to the door so he could see his father and he immediately ran toward him to pound on the glass. Sullivan opened it and let us in, smiling at the fact that Shea was playing outside.

"Nicely done, Ms. Hastings," he said.

"I've got some hot cocoa ready for you kids," Blanche announced. "Just the right temperature. Mr. Sullivan, would you like some?"

"No thank you, Blanche. I'll be working in my office the rest of the day."

"It's homemade," she teased.

"Yes please, Blanche. I'll take it with me."

As Blanche poured us each a glass of cocoa, Shea jumped up and down in front of his father, pointing outside.

"I saw you," Sullivan replied. "Did you have fun?"

As I began removing all of Shea's snow gear he nodded excitedly, his fingers signing in rapid succession even though they were still hidden inside the mittens.

::Snow angel! Snowman! Snowballs!::
"Do you want some hot cocoa?" I asked him.
He nodded.
"Do you want some hot cocoa?" I asked again.
::Yes please Mommy::

I pretended I didn't catch all of what he said, bringing our wet snow gear into the laundry room to dry. I walked back into the kitchen and sat at the table with Shea as Blanche brought over our mugs of cocoa. Sullivan grabbed his mug and headed out of the room, then turned back. I was checking the temperature of Shea's drink when I caught him staring at me.

He looked as though he were struggling for words, then said, "Thank you."

I knew how hard that must have been for him, so I just smiled and nodded, turning my attention back to Shea.

Chapter 7

The Mardi Gras masquerade ball was the first big party I'd been present for, and it looked as though it was going to be huge. While I was not invited to the party, Shea and I watched from the sidelines as people came and went all day long decorating the party room for the evening's festivities. Celeste was the one coordinating all the bodies roaming around, knowing exactly what went where and who was responsible for each task.

Shea tugged on my sleeve.

::You party?::

"No, I'll be with you."

He threw his arms up in victory.

I watched in awe as an intricately carved set of doors opened from the party room where our blanket fort once stood, into a grand ballroom, where the dancing would obviously be taking place. It was difficult to fathom how much the Sullivan empire was worth, and every day I was surprised by a new discovery the massive estate I lived in revealed to me.

Since Sullivan would be eating during the party with his many guests that evening, Shea and I were on our own for dinner, so I cooked up a small batch of buttered bowtie pasta and garlic bread. I made Shea's usual peanut butter and jelly sandwich, taking his crust for myself. Shea watched carefully as I sprinkled a bit of parmesan cheese on top of the pasta, then poured us both a glass of milk. I sat down to eat and noticed how fascinated he was with my little bowties.

"Want some?" I asked.

He nodded.

::Yes please::

I placed a few bowties on his plate and watched as he picked one up with his fingers and smelled it, then slowly put it in his mouth. His face had no expression as he chewed it a bit, then he grinned at me.

"Like it?"

He rubbed his belly and nodded, smiling, and I put more bowties on his plate.

::Thank you Mommy::

I touched his arm so he would look at me. "Shea, I'm not your mommy." I smiled so he wouldn't think he was in trouble.

::Sorry Miss J::

"It's okay. You're a good boy."

::Thank you::

"Do you miss your mommy?"

::JoJo::

I had to find out more about this JoJo. "Where is JoJo?"

::With Mommy::

When given the right opportunity, I needed to ask Sullivan about Shea's imaginary friend, even though he very much hated when I asked questions. He expected me to do what I was told and never question anything and it drove me crazy. And I really wanted to know what happened to Shea's mother; something just wasn't adding up.

After dinner and cleaning up our mess in the kitchen, I took Shea up to his bedroom where he liked to play his favorite game, Damsel in Distress. I would lay across the train tracks and he'd ride his train and stop just before he hit me, jumping out to save me from being tied down by a dastardly bad guy. He had a vivid imagination for a four-year-old and I wondered if the nannies let him sit in front of the television all day to keep him occupied, knowing he was only allowed to watch television at approved times and lengths.

As Shea was pretending to untie me from the railroad tracks, Sullivan entered the room and cleared his throat to get my attention.

"Are you a nanny, Ms. Hastings, or a playmate?" he grumbled.

"Why can't I be both?"

I sat up and took him in, dressed in fancy black suit pants, a dark purple vest, white button-down shirt and bowtie, a luxurious cape with a dark purple inlay and a black walking stick. He looked very much like the Phantom of the Opera.

"How do I look?" he asked, standing regally with his nose pointed in the air.

I found words difficult because my insides were swooning over the majestic human being standing above me. His hair was perfect, his face was perfect, and I caught him glaring at me and immediately feared he could read the dirty thoughts running through my head.

"You're incomplete," I said instead. "Where's your mask?"

"Downstairs," he answered, wrinkling his forehead.

Shea took the walking stick from his father's hand.

::*Magic?*::

Sullivan explained it was a walking stick and demonstrated how it worked, but Shea wasn't impressed. He wanted to see some magic and was disappointed, but he perked up when his father told him he could have the stick in the morning.

"Ms. Hastings," he said. "I don't think I have to tell you that I do not want Shea downstairs *at all* this evening."

"Is it one of those freaky orgy parties?" I asked, giggling.

What the hell did I just say?

"What on earth... no!" he snapped. "It's an actual masquerade ball for Mardi Gras, but I suppose a person of your... *upbringing*... wouldn't understand how the other half lives."

In that instant I went from wanting to ravage him to wanting to torture him. Slowly.

"I guess people from my side of the tracks don't go to very many masquerade balls," I grumbled. "Who's on the guest list? Oh never mind, I wouldn't know any of *your* people."

"Ms. Hastings, I will need you to give Shea his bath tonight, as I'll be otherwise engaged. Do you think you can manage?"

"Of course."

"I'll see you in the morning." He said goodnight to Shea and walked out.

"Asshole," I whispered, hoping he'd trip on his cape and fall down the stairs.

~

I had a great evening with Shea, building fortresses with blocks for Godzilla to knock over, reading books, and making a game out of teaching him how to read lips. He giggled through most of it but seemed to catch on fairly quickly, and when his eyes began to glaze over I decided it was time for his bath. I didn't realize it was already nine o'clock, which was an hour later than I was supposed to bathe him, but since Sullivan's party was in full swing there was no way he'd find out. When he was freshly bathed I would read him a bedtime story, put him to bed, and our night would be done.

I brought Shea into the bathroom and ran a few inches of bathwater, and he watched wide-eyed as I checked the temperature with my fingers. I turned toward him and outstretched my arms, waggling my fingers to let him know it was time to take his clothes off. He looked terrified and shook his head violently, inching away slowly.

"I won't hurt you," I told him.

::Soup! Boil!::

"The water isn't hot. Touch it."

He turned and made a run for it, but I caught him quickly and carried him to my apartment, where I locked the door. He promised to sit on the couch quietly until I came back from my bedroom, dressed in my red bikini and wrapped in a towel. I took him by the hand and led him back to the bathroom, where he pouted as I removed his clothes.

"I'll get in with you," I said. "Trust me?"

He pushed out his bottom lip and nodded, but I could tell he wasn't buying it. I set my towel on the counter and as I stepped one foot into the bathtub, Shea sprinted away from me. I chased him into his bedroom where he began climbing the drapes. Yelling for him to come down would do no good and he had already gotten too high for me to reach him. Once he reached the top of the window he froze, not sure what to do next. I stood underneath waiting to catch him if he fell, but I couldn't help but chuckle at his bare bottom just dangling there. I noticed the drapery rod begin to bend under his weight and watched in amusement as it crumpled, sending Shea and the draperies crashing down on me. Once I managed to untangle myself from the material I was horrified to see Shea take off running out of his room, naked as the day he was born. Not even thinking about what *I* was wearing, I took off after him but he had already disappeared. I panicked, hoping he had gone to his playroom, but he wasn't there. I ran down the hallway drenched in nervous perspiration then gasped as I saw his bare bottom reach the bottom of the grand staircase. I ran as fast as I could to catch him before anyone saw him, but as the sound of my bare feet slapped against the foyer tiles, he had already burst into the party.

Partygoers may not have noticed a naked cherub running through the party, but they were definitely intrigued when I flung myself into the room, dressed only in a red bikini that was probably the same shade as my face in that moment. My skin pricked with humiliation as masked faces turned their attention to me, their cacophonous eruption of laughter echoing off the walls and reverberating back into my head. I was dead and I knew it.

I caught Shea crawling under a table that held a giant mermaid ice sculpture, hidden underneath by the long, flowing tablecloth. I tried to slip out of sight behind the table, knowing full well everyone was still watching me. On my hands and knees, I poked the top half of my body underneath and saw Shea sitting there, cross-legged and nibbling nervously on his fingers. I didn't want to startle him, fearful the ice sculpture would end up shattering all over the floor, and then I'd *really* be dead.

I realized my ass was still on the outside of the table when I heard someone say, "Do you believe in love at first sight?" followed by a roar of laughter. I knew I had to act fast because my time spent as Shea's nanny was getting shorter by the minute and I still had hope that I could catch him and disappear before Sullivan knew what was happening.

Shea spotted me and tried to make a run for it, but I lunged toward him to grab his arm and as I did so, hit my head on the table, sending it and the ice sculpture catapulting forward. Shea managed to escape the melee but I lay there on my stomach surrounded by the remains of the disaster. When I finally found the nerve to look up, I saw the decapitated head of the mermaid in front of me, which was soon replaced by a set of shiny black shoes. I saw Sullivan glaring down at me, holding a naked Shea on his hip. Feeling more naked than if I'd actually been naked, I got to my feet and brushed the ice shards from my limbs before Sullivan pushed Shea into my arms. I held the naked child close to me and lowered my face as I left the ballroom and carried him back upstairs, never before feeling the shame that burned my soul.

I tried so hard not to be angry with Shea, but I couldn't help it. I held his hand tightly so he couldn't run away as I stepped into the bathtub, then pulled him in with me. He kicked and punched until he realized the water wasn't hot; it wasn't even what could be considered warm. We sat there staring at each other and I was at such a loss, I had no idea what to say to him.

::I'm sorry::

I pouted at him. "It's okay. But your daddy is mad at me."

I soaped up a washcloth and started to bathe him just as Sullivan charged through the door. His mask was gone but his eyes shot laser death beams at my face when I glanced up at him.

"Would you like to explain—"

"I'm sorry," I said. "He was afraid and got away from me. You'll want to get his drapery rod replaced in his bedroom."

"Why?"

I sighed heavily and continued. "Before he crashed your party he climbed the drapes."

Sullivan sucked in an angry breath and turned away from us, his hands on his hips. After releasing the breath he turned back to face us. "And bathing *with* him is your solution?"

"Hey," I snapped. "It's working, isn't it?"

Shea looked up at his father with big doe eyes and a pouty lower lip.

::Sorry::

"I'm taking your train away," Sullivan signed. Then to me, "Ms. Hastings, I have just been humiliated in front of my clients, employees and friends. You have made a complete mockery of me and you've left me no choice. Your days in my household are numbered and as soon as I can find a replacement, your services will no longer be needed here."

My heart dropped, but I recovered quickly as I replied, "Good. Then you're telling Shea."

"Fine," he hissed, turning to leave.

"Have fun with that, *Ziggy*," I grumbled.

After Shea was bathed, dried and put into a pair of clean pajamas, we took a detour to my apartment so I could put on some proper clothes, then we got comfortable on his bed with a book.

::*Me read*::

I smiled and nodded. I held the book as he pointed to each page and rambled his own version of the story, which to me was much more enjoyable than me reading the real thing. I was angry with Sullivan for firing me like that, but part of me knew he would have difficulty finding someone to replace me, as evidenced by everything I knew of the nannies before me. He was probably speaking out of pure anger but I still had to come up with a way to get through to him — nobody was better for Shea than I was. *Nobody.*

I tucked Shea into bed and we gave each other a hug goodnight, but before I turned out his light he asked me to stay.

"Just until you fall asleep."

::*Okay*::

I lay on top of the covers as he curled up into a ball in front of me, resting his forehead against my throat. This seemed to be a sense of comfort for him, and oddly enough, it was comforting for me as well.

It was the middle of the night when Sullivan came in to check on Shea, and I was startled when I realized I never made it back to my own bed. I waited until he turned to leave before saying, "Wait."

"Not *now*, Ms. Hastings."

I slowly slipped off of Shea's bed and followed him into the hallway. "Yes, *now*," I growled. I did the unthinkable, even for me, grabbing his hand and dragging him all the way to my apartment. And I wasn't thinking at all about how soft his skin was, and that he probably never did a hard day of physical labor in his life. He was probably one of those rich guys who had manicures. I went inside but he stood in the hallway like a statue.

"Oh for fuck's sake," I said, grabbing his hand and yanking him inside. "Sit down!"

"Such language, Ms. Hastings," he spoke softly, sitting on the couch.

I paced as I desperately wrung my hands. "Was this another setup? Are you still trying to prove what a failure I am?"

"Ms. Hastings, I—"

"I'm not finished! You knew damn well you were the only one who could give Shea a bath without a fight. Why would you do that to me?" He didn't answer, waiting to make sure he was allowed to speak. "I'm finished."

"Ms. Hastings, I—"

"Please don't fire me," I blurted. "As much as I don't like *you*, I love Shea. I can't explain it, but he's everything to me. I *need* him."

"May I speak now?"

"Yes, I'm sorry."

He took a deep breath then replied, "I can promise you this was not a setup. You've been making such great progress with Shea, I thought he would be no trouble at bath time. Obviously I was wrong."

Did he just tell me he was wrong?

I pulled the handbook off the coffee table and dropped it in his lap.

"What's this?" he asked.

"Well, according to what I've read, it's the nanny handbook on how to handle Shea."

"I don't understand."

"Open it."

I watched as Sullivan opened the binder, then ran his finger along the tabbed sections as he read their titles. He flinched as I sat down next to him.

"These other nannies didn't care about Shea," I tried to explain calmly. "This is a handbook of all their notes on how to get by the easy way. They used fear and manipulation because they couldn't properly care for him. Maybe they were lazy or didn't know sign language very well, I don't know, but that's why he's afraid the snow will burn him, or that the koi will eat him."

Sullivan slowly flipped through the pages without really reading any of them, then looked at me with wet eyes.

"Are you saying they were abusing Shea?"

"In a way… yes. But unless you can identify them by their handwriting, it's hard to know who wrote what because they all used code names."

Sullivan got to his feet. "Would you mind if I took this with me?"

"Sure, go ahead."

He tried to wipe his eyes without me noticing, then walked out the door. I wasn't trying to get anyone in trouble, but I wouldn't be able to bear it if he fired me. Shea was a lifeline I could never explain to anyone, including myself.

꽃

I woke up at eight o'clock the next morning on my own… no siren. This was highly unusual and I immediately panicked, throwing off my covers and running down the hall until I reached Shea's room, where the door was closed and the alarm was still set. I turned the alarm off and opened the door a crack, the room filled with bright, morning sunlight as the drapes were no longer covering the window. Sullivan was lying on his back in his costume pants and shirt with Shea curled up in his left arm, both of them sound asleep. They both looked so peaceful I hated to disturb them, so I closed the door and went back to my apartment.

This was the first weekend I'd spent at the house with Sullivan and Shea home, so I had no idea what was expected of me. I assumed my nanny responsibilities wouldn't continue until Monday morning, so I brushed my teeth, took a quick shower and dressed in a pair of comfortable jeans and a sweatshirt. I was about to make myself a pot of coffee when I heard a tiny knock. I opened the door to see Sullivan and Shea standing in the hallway — Sullivan still in his costume pants and shirt with Shea wearing his father's cape, golden Mardi Gras mask and holding his walking stick.

"Shea requests that you join us for breakfast, Ms. Hastings."

"But where is Shea?" I shrugged with my hands in the air, palms up, like Shea always did when he didn't understand. "Who is this man in the cape?" Shea pulled off the mask, giggling, revealing himself to me. "Oh thank goodness!" I cheered.

::Breakfast?::

"Yes, okay."

As we walked down the hall, then the grand staircase, I said, "I think Shea should be the one to feed the koi. We say hello to them every morning, but he needs a better connection than that."

"I like your thinking," Sullivan replied. "Let's start right now."

"Does that mean I get to stay?"

"Yes, Ms. Hastings."

As we hit the bottom of the stairs, something caught Shea's eye and he continued walking into the party room, returning to the scene of the crime. We followed him and found a naked man lying face down on the floor. Shea stood next to him poking his bare butt cheek with the walking stick. I covered my mouth so Shea wouldn't see that I was holding back laughter, but I heard Sullivan grumble something under his breath.

I touched Shea's shoulder and he looked up at me.

::Dead?::

"Sleeping," his father replied. "Take him to the kitchen, please."

I turned Shea away from the naked man, who was obviously a drunken leftover from the party, and brought him into the kitchen. I was surprised that Sullivan would even consider going to bed before knowing everyone was out of his home, considering how weird he was about everything.

I sat Shea at the kitchen table, but not before he removed his mask and cape and set it on another chair with his walking stick. I couldn't stop giggling over the image of him poking the naked man in the butt and eventually burst into uncontrollable laughter. This caused Shea to laugh as well, even though he had no idea what I was laughing at. Sullivan entered the kitchen and as hard as I tried to stop, the tears streamed down my face as I covered my mouth with my hand.

"Is he gone?" I managed to squeak out.

"Yes, he's gone."

"Who was that charming man?"

"No one worth mentioning," he grumbled. Then he slapped his hands together and smiled at Shea. "What should we make for breakfast?"

Shea put a finger to his cheek to think about it.

::Eggs::

"Eggs?" Sullivan said, shocked.

"He loves eggs now. Only scrambled though," I explained.

::Toast::

"So eggs and toast? Anything else?"

"He likes his toast with a little bit of butter and jelly," I told him.

"Well all right Ms. Hastings, how about I make some bacon and eggs... you like bacon don't you... and you make the toast?"

"Love bacon," I answered.

And so our Sunday morning began.

Chapter 8

At the end of March I was instructed to take Shea to the doctor's office for his annual shots, and I was not happy about it. Sullivan usually took care of things of this nature, but he had a very important meeting he couldn't miss and trusted me to handle it. As we headed to the front door, Shea slipped on his Godzilla mask and grabbed my hand as Blanche shoved a plastic bag toward me that held what looked like a rubber pretzel with teeth marks in it.

"It's a dog toy," she explained. "But unless you want him chomping onto *you*, this is the best option."

I rolled my eyes and shoved it into my purse, leading Shea outside to the waiting sedan. I secured him into his carseat as Andy said, "Doctor's visit?"

"Yes, thank you."

"It's not far," Andy said. "But just as a warning, there's a donut shop on the corner with a huge chocolate donut on their sign. As soon as he sees it, he'll know where he's going."

"Thanks." I held my breath, waiting for the meltdown.

We drove in silence and as we approached the dreaded donut, Andy said, "There it is."

I knew the very moment Shea saw the donut because he began to kick his legs and punch the air, and I could hear his grunts underneath the mask.

"Did any of the other nannies take him to the doctor?" I asked.

"Not while I was on duty."

Andy pulled into the parking lot and found a spot for the car, then I unbuckled Shea from his carseat and forced him to look at me.

::Stab me!::

"You have to get your shots so you can grow up strong like Godzilla," I tried to explain. "Don't you want to be strong like Godzilla?"

He was silent for a moment before nodding, still wearing his mask.

"I promise I'll take care of you. Would you like a donut after we're done?"

He shrugged, probably never having a donut in his life. I pointed to the giant chocolate donut sign and he shook his head.

Even though I had never watched a Godzilla movie with Shea, I knew where the stash was kept. "Would you like to watch a Godzilla movie when we get home?"

Shea sat straight up in his seat and nodded vigorously.

::*Yes!*::

"We have to do this first, okay? Then we'll stop and get some donuts, and go home and watch a movie."

He stared at me for a moment then nodded.

"You'll be a brave boy?" I asked.

He nodded, and with his mask securely in place, I pulled him out of the car and walked him into the doctor's office. The waiting room was packed, and because Shea was wearing his mask, all eyes were immediately on us. I didn't give them the satisfaction of appearing embarrassed, especially as one child sat picking his nose and eating whatever he dug out of there. After checking in we sat in the corner with Shea on my lap, as he stared at people who had the nerve to look at him. At one point Shea ripped off the mask, his hair sticking up electrically in all directions, and glared at the room of mothers with their children. I was happy to see that he wasn't going to be intimidated by them, but my nerves jumped when the nurse called his name.

He held my hand as we followed the nurse into the examination room, then she instructed me to remove all of his clothing, except his underwear. I explained to Shea what needed to be done, and he let me take off his jacket, shoes, pants and sweater, but I left his socks on.

"I need to explain to him what you're doing," I told the nurse. "He's completely deaf so he can't hear you."

"Oh sure," she replied sweetly. "Tell him I'm going to weigh him and then see how tall he is."

"Thank you." I explained what the nurse was going to do and he nodded.

"Dr. Browning will be right with you," she said, exiting the room.

::Cold::

I pulled Shea onto my lap and wrapped him in my arms to warm him until the doctor joined us. I held him close to me, and bent my head so he was able to press his forehead against my throat, and I mindlessly hummed a tune I knew he couldn't hear. He pulled his head back and touched my throat with his fingers.

::What's that?::

I wasn't sure what he meant until I started humming again and a huge grin crept across his face.

"Singing."

::Me sing::

He held his fingers to his own throat but was disappointed when he didn't feel the same vibration.

I made him look at me and said, "I'll teach you later."

He smiled and nodded and the door opened, causing him to latch onto me so tightly his little fingers were digging holes into my arms, even through my thick coat.

"Hello, I'm Dr. Browning," she said. "You must be…."

"Jude. Hastings. I'm Shea's nanny. Have you seen him before?"

"I'm new to the practice, so this will be my first time with Shea."

This made me nervous. "Did you go over his files? Did you know he's deaf? He has a lot of fears we deal with on a daily basis and —"

"Can you put him up on the table please?"

I got to my feet and placed Shea on the table, saying, "I need you to tell me what you're going to do so I can explain it to him."

"I really don't think that's necessary."

"You don't understand his anxiety. Trust me on this."

"Okay… I'm going to check his ears, nose and throat."

"Will it hurt?"

"It shouldn't."

I explained what the doctor was going to do then said, "It might tickle. Sit still."

He watched Dr. Browning with huge eyes as she checked his ears, nose and throat. "Has everything been normal for Shea?"

"Normal?"

"Bathroom habits, eating, sleeping? Nothing out of the ordinary?"

I'd only been with him for two months, how was I supposed to know? Everything *seemed* normal. "Yeah, I think so."

As the doctor's hands touched Shea's shoulders he stiffened like a board and gaped at me with his mouth wide open.

"It's okay," I said. "Be brave."

"I thought you said he was deaf," the doctor mused at hearing my words.

My face burned as my hands balled into fists at my side. "He's completely deaf, but we speak when we sign. *And* I'm teaching him how to read lips. How dare you question me! Why would I lie about something like that?"

"Ms. Hastings, please calm down."

"Don't you dare tell me to calm down! I'm responsible for this boy and I don't appreciate you condescending to me like I'm some idiot who just fell off the turnip truck!"

Shea was watching me closely and started to look scared, so I smiled at him and said, "Everything's okay. Almost done."

"Ms. Hastings, maybe you should leave the room while I give Shea his shots."

"That's not going to happen. He's not leaving my sight. *Ever*."

"Sometimes the child does better when the parent or guardian isn't in the room. It'll only be for a minute; I'll just get one of my nurses —"

I smiled at Shea and through my teeth growled, "I am *not* leaving this room. So get on with your business or I'm taking him home *without* shots and you'll have to deal with his father later. Trust me, you don't want to deal with him."

She glared at me as if I had no business talking to her the way I did, then nodded. "Fine."

"Are you done with his head?"

"*What?*"

"Are you done messing around with his head?"

"Yes."

I took the pretzel dog toy out of my purse and handed it to Shea. "Bite on this *really* hard, okay?" He nodded and I put it in his mouth, which he thought was funny. "Keep your eyes on me. Only me."

I kept my eyes locked with his as the nurse returned with a silver tray, then saw the doctor getting the needle ready out of the corner of my eye. The nurse smiled and tried to distract him and he tried to look away, but I snapped him back to attention. "Eyes only on me! Don't look at her."

Too late. He saw the needle then lunged off the table at me, crawling up my body to get away from her. As he did this, the rubber pretzel shot out of his mouth and as I tried to keep him from squirming, she administered the first shot into his thigh. I didn't realize what happened at first until Shea sunk his teeth into my shoulder, through my coat, causing me to cry out. I had never felt such searing physical pain before.

"Hurry the fuck up!" I screamed at the doctor, knowing Shea couldn't hear what I said anyway.

As she quickly finished the round of shots I could hear him wailing as his body shuddered against me. It was the most heartbreaking sound I'd ever heard because it was the first time I'd heard him vocalize anything.

"Okay, all done," the doctor said in a sing-song voice that churned my stomach. "Get him dressed and his paperwork will be at the front desk."

Dr. Browning and the nurse walked out and I hugged Shea desperately to my chest, trying to comfort him. I sat him on the table and wiped the tears from his face, holding his cheeks in my hands until he opened his eyes to look at me.

"You were very brave," I told him, trying to keep myself from crying along with him. "Very brave."

I got him dressed, put on his coat, and let him pull the Godzilla mask over his head. I then carried him out of the room and out of the office without stopping for any paperwork. If it was that important they could mail it to the house. I wasn't about to spend another minute in that office after being treated the way we were.

Shea was still sniveling when we reached the car and as I secured him into his carseat I burst into tears. I didn't want Shea to see that I was crying, so I didn't get in behind him, pacing the parking lot instead.

"Ms. Hastings," Andy called. "Are you okay?"

"Just give me a minute."

"Is Shea okay?"

Not even answering his question, I started to ramble as I paced maniacally. "Stupid bitch talk to me that way... just because I'm not a rich, pompous asshole... I can still be all the asshole you need lady... and because of you he bit me!"

"Ms. Hastings?"

"I'm sorry." I wiped my face with my coat sleeves and took in a deep breath. "Can you swing by the donut shop on the way home?"

"Sure thing."

I got in the back seat and made sure Shea was buckled in tight, then asked, "Are you okay?"

He nodded.

"Okay Andy, to the donut shop."

By the time we got back to the house Shea was sound asleep. Andy got out of the car and opened my door, leaning in to check on us.

"Need help carrying him inside?" he asked with a sexy smile.

I turned to face him and took advantage of half his body being inside the back seat with me, removing his hat and letting his gorgeous hair spill forward.

"You're going to get me in trouble."

"Once they're gone on Friday night can we go somewhere? Anywhere? I'm lonely and I'm horny and I don't care if you take me back to wherever you park this car at night. Just *somewhere*." He didn't need to know Friday was my birthday.

He leaned close to my face and whispered, "I'll swing by and pick you up when I get back from taking them to the airport… wear the red bikini."

A gasp caught in my throat as I smiled, relieved he didn't turn me down. As I got out of the car he quickly shoved his hair back up into the hat and rushed to open Shea's door. I pulled the sleeping boy out of his carseat and followed behind Andy, who carried the box of donuts and opened the back door for me. He set the donuts on the kitchen counter then winked before walking back outside.

〜

Shea was sound asleep cuddled under a blanket next to me as I sat on a couch in the family room. I was reading another book by Willow Kelly and he fell asleep before the Godzilla movie even began. It was difficult for me to see Shea so listless and still; I wanted him to be running around and playing like normal.

It was well past Shea's bedtime when Sullivan finally came home, dark outside as well as through the house. The only reason I didn't put Shea to bed myself was so I could explain what happened at the doctor's office, and he was so peaceful I didn't want to disturb him. Sullivan shrugged off his suit coat and loosened his tie as he sat in the chair across from me.

"Willow Kelly," he remarked. "She's our most popular author."

"I really love her books."

"She was the reason I couldn't take Shea to the doctor today."

"Is everything okay?"

He leaned back in the chair and brought his right foot up to rest on his left knee. He rubbed his mouth and said, "She's an enigma. Our most popular author and yet I've never met her. Apparently she's a recluse and *nobody* has ever met her. All of our dealings are with her agent, but today she agreed to come into the office for a meeting. If it were anyone but Ms. Kelly, I would have taken Shea to the doctor myself."

I was astonished that he was revealing so much to me. "So how did it go?"

"She was supposed to meet us at the office at four o'clock and she never showed." He ran his fingers anxiously through his hair and let his head fall back against the chair. "All that waiting and she didn't even have the decency to call."

"That was pretty rude."

"And what can I do? She's one of our biggest money makers… it's not like I can drop her from our roster. That would be professional suicide."

As we sat in silence I couldn't help notice what a delicious looking neck he had, completely exposed with his head thrown back. If I weren't in his employ, in his family room with his four-year-old son asleep beside me, in any other situation, I would have placed myself in his lap and started to nibble. I was trying so hard not to be that girl anymore… trying desperately to be someone Shea could grow up to respect and admire. But I was lonely for physical touch and male companionship and my thoughts drifted to Andy and how he agreed to meet me Friday night. I was exhilarated by the thought of getting down and dirty with him, especially if it meant his long, luxurious hair was falling on my naked body.

"I got a call from Shea's doctor before I left the office," Sullivan's voice disrupted my thoughts.

I was ready for battle. "Don't talk to me like you're my father getting ready to ground me."

He sat up straight and glared at me. "Why is everything a fight with you?"

"You weren't there… you didn't see how—"

"Ms. Hastings, I just wanted to thank you. If I couldn't be there with him, I'm glad it was you. Thank you for being his advocate."

Sullivan got up from the chair and walked toward me, leaning over to lift Shea into his arms. "Goodnight, and thanks for the donuts," he whispered.

My cheeks flushed as I watched him walk away into the darkness, the sight of him carrying his sleeping son taking my breath away.

❧

I woke up on Friday, surprised to see the sun shining and the clock telling me it was eight o'clock.

No siren.

I jumped out of bed and sprinted to Shea's room. The door was closed and the alarm was still set. I turned off the alarm and opened the door a crack to see him sitting on top of his bed, smiling, giggling, and signing. I stood there watching him, so innocent and precious, and oblivious to the fact that he lived his life in complete silence. He'd never hear his father say he loved him, he'd never hear the sounds of music or laughter, and he'd never hear me tell him how grateful I was that he came into my life.

In order to break myself from the emotions I was beginning to exhibit, I walked into the room and as soon as Shea saw me he jumped back into bed, hiding under the covers completely. I walked over to the bed and pulled the covers off of him, finding it hard not to laugh at his curled up body giggling out of control. I poked his belly and he rolled over, then got to his feet and started jumping up and down on the bed. I managed to grab hold of his hands to stop him from jumping and he grinned at me like he was the keeper of the greatest secret in the entire world.

"What are you smiling at?" I asked.

::You::

"Me? Why?"

He held his little fingers to his lips and scrunched up his face in giggles.

::Happy birthday::

Every part of me was warm with a feeling I couldn't begin to describe. How could he possibly know it was my birthday?

"Who told you that?"

::JoJo::

"JoJo?" I was a bit lightheaded trying to figure out where all of this was coming from, and where it was going.

::And P::

My hands trembled as I sat down on the bed, then fell onto my back. Shea crawled onto my stomach and wanted to play patty cake, but my brain was numb as my hands mindlessly followed through with the motions. I stopped his hands and looked up at his cherub-like face.

"Who's P?"

::Sister::

"Whose sister?"

He pointed directly at me.

"How do you know her?"

::JoJo::

"Is that who you were talking to when I came in here?"

He nodded, smiling happily and nibbling on his fingers.

"Did you talk to P?"

He nodded.

"What did she tell you?"

::Happy birthday::

::Miss you::

::Eat brownies::

This was hitting me hard in itself, but what really pushed me over the edge was he didn't sign to me in our regular language. He signed to me in the secret language that Prude and I used since we were old enough to communicate with our hands. A memory of the handbook flashed in my head of the nannies complaining they didn't always understand what Shea was signing, implying that he didn't always know what he was doing. How was it possible that he knew our secret sign language? And how did he know brownies were our favorite birthday treat?

I was numb, trying to understand what was happening. Who the hell was JoJo and how did Shea know about Prude? It was surreal and I felt like I was living in a dream, that it couldn't be real. I could tell by the way his face changed expression that I was beginning to make him sad. I thanked him with a smile and brought him to my room so I could change my clothes.

I floated through the day in a state of flux, knowing I had to get some answers from Sullivan whether he liked it or not. The rendezvous I had planned with Andy later that evening was a bit of a distraction, and I wondered exactly how I was supposed to wear my red bikini for him. Did the guest house have a hot tub? Should I wear it under a big coat with nothing else underneath? Under a dress? I assumed by his request we wouldn't be going out on the town, and I was certainly okay with that, thinking only of the intimacy my body was craving.

As soon as Sullivan got home from work I hugged and kissed Shea goodbye, told him I'd see him Sunday night, and ran up to my apartment to shower and figure out how I was going to present myself to Andy. I tried to push the morning incident to the back of my head and concentrate on the evening ahead of me, but I couldn't get the image of Shea talking to Prude out of my mind. And until I could sit down peacefully with Sullivan and have a real conversation, it was going to haunt me.

I was in the bathroom brushing my teeth when I heard a knock on my door. I tightened my robe around me, adjusted the towel on my head and opened it. Of course it was Sullivan and Shea, who smiled up at me, positively beaming.

I think I surprised them by opening the door in my robe, obviously just having showered. This seemed to throw Sullivan off a bit, as he cleared his throat to regain his thoughts.

"Ms. Hastings, Shea tells me today is your birthday."

"You told him?" I asked Shea.

He grinned and nodded happily, as if he were the best little boy in the world.

"Yes, it's my birthday."

"He would like to invite you to spend the weekend at the cabin with us. You know... to celebrate."

This threw me off my game. "Oh," I stammered without signing. "Well I... I don't want to impose on your time with Shea."

"It looks as if you already have plans. I apologize for disturbing you."

I looked at Shea, who's happy smile quickly turned to a quivering bottom lip. "Wait, no," I said. "Do I have to wear my uniform?"

Sullivan laughed and said, "No, casual is just fine."

"Give me half an hour?"

"Perfect." He pulled Shea into his arms and walked away.

Shea bounced in his father's arms and waved happily at me as they disappeared around the corner and down the staircase. I had just given up an evening, possibly a weekend, with a hot chauffeur for a four-year-old boy. I needed to have my head checked.

※

I met Sullivan and Shea down by the front door, and as Shea slipped on his Godzilla mask, Andy came in to grab our bags.

"I see you'll be joining the men this weekend, Ms. Hastings?" he asked.

"Yes," I answered quietly. "They've invited me for my birthday." As Sullivan carried Shea outside to settle him into his carseat I whispered, "I'm sorry... I wasn't expecting—"

He winked and replied, "Maybe another time. Happy birthday."

I grinned with regret. "Thanks."

I got comfortable in the back of the sedan as Andy threw our bags in the trunk and then we were off for the airport. I didn't have the heart to tell Sullivan I was terrified of flying, and the thought of being in what I assumed was a small plane set me on edge. If I had proper time to prepare for this trip I would've gotten some tranquilizers or something to take before getting on the plane. As it was, my stomach clenched into a giant knot as we reached the airport.

Shea stretched his arms my way, so I unbuckled him from the carseat and carried him out of the car as Sullivan headed toward what I assumed was his Cessna. As Andy put our bags inside the small airplane, I momentarily stopped breathing. I was frozen in place as

Sullivan took Shea from my arms and climbed into the aircraft, securing him in his seat.

"Have a nice weekend," Andy said to me.

I stared at him wide-eyed and he chuckled, then helped me into the airplane. I sat down on the leather seat next to Shea and buckled the seatbelt, feeling the color drain completely from my face. I searched frantically for a vomit bag and began to sweat when I couldn't see one. I covered my mouth with my hand and tried to collect myself, not wanting to scare Shea in any way. He was always so concerned about my well-being, and he was wearing a Godzilla mask to help him with his fears already.

Shea reached over and tapped my arm. I turned to look at him and he began signing in his secret language.

::Close your eyes::

I nodded and smiled, but as soon as the plane began to move my stomach was in my throat and I was searching desperately for air. I gripped the armrests so tightly my knuckles were turning white. Shea tapped my arm again and I turned to look at him. He pulled the mask off his head and handed it to me. His sweet face with his chubby cheeks and his hair sticking out in all directions melted my racing heart.

::You wear it::

::Safe::

"Thank you," I said, sliding the mask over my head.

Inside the mask was hot and smelled like sweaty rubber, and the mouth area was moist. Something wet was touching me but I couldn't let my head go there. Was it spit? Food? My stomach lurched as I thought about green, gooey boogers. I needed to calm down and suck it up for the short plane ride to Wisconsin. I almost burst into tears thinking of Shea, terrified of flying, but giving his security mask to me because he was worried about my fear, not his own. I reached my hand out to him, letting him wrap his little hand around my finger as he closed his eyes and took a deep breath, like a brave little boy.

Chapter 9

We stopped for some fast food on the way to the cabin and once Ryan, Sullivan's Wisconsin driver, brought our bags inside, he went home to his cabin further down on the property. It was pitch black outside and I felt like we were in the middle of nowhere as there were no other houses nearby and the night was still and quiet. It was a bit unsettling.

Sullivan turned on the lights and I was standing in an open-spaced, rustic cabin made completely of wood, from the floors to the beams overhead. Sullivan put the food bags on the table and I waited for Shea to remove the Godzilla mask before taking off his coat. Sullivan hung all of our coats on a rack near the door and picked up our bags; I followed. He stopped before two doors that I assumed led to the bedrooms, and hesitated.

"Ms. Hastings, would you prefer the room with two twin beds, or the king sized bed? The bathroom is down the hall, so everyone has to share that."

He was giving me a choice? Maybe he was being nice because it was my birthday. "Where do you usually sleep?" I asked.

"Shea and I usually sleep in the king sized bed together."

"Then I'll take the twin room. Thank you."

Shea stood watching us with wide eyes. I knew he had just woken up from the car ride, but he looked concerned. I watched as Sullivan brought their two bags into the king room and Shea quickly followed, grabbing his little bag and bringing it back out. I chuckled and brought my bag into the twin room as Shea entered behind me, setting his bag on the bed farthest from the door.

"Are we having a slumber party?" I asked.

He thought about what I said, then nodded and smiled happily. Until Sullivan came in and grabbed his bag, bringing it back to the other room. Shea tore after him and I followed.

"I don't mind," I told him.

"We're not going to get into that habit," he argued.

"But it's one weekend. And it's my birthday."

Sullivan sighed heavily as he rolled his eyes, then handed Shea his bag. Shea left immediately to put his bag in my room and Sullivan raised his eyebrows as he looked me in the eyes.

"You don't like rules much, do you Ms. Hastings?"

"Not much. But there's nothing wrong with bending them a little bit once in a while."

"Let's go eat."

While we ate burgers and fries, Shea ate his usual peanut butter and jelly sandwich, saving me the crusts. He wanted nothing to do with what we were eating, even though he eyed my fries with a bit of longing. I put one on his plate to see if he'd try it, but he waited until he was finished with his sandwich before picking it up and smelling it. Sullivan watched him with a curious eye, as smelling new foods before trying them had become a recent behavior. I had no idea where it came from, to be honest.

"What's with the smelling?" he asked.

"It's new."

Sullivan tapped on the table in front of Shea's plate to get his attention. "To bed after dinner. It's late."

Shea pouted and rested his forehead on the table. His back soon began to tremble as he cried. It broke my heart when he cried, but I was exhausted and ready to go to bed as well.

Shea lifted his head, his face wet with tears, his bottom lip quivering.

::Story::

"Yes," Sullivan agreed. "I'll read you a bedtime story."

::No J::

I held a napkin against my mouth to hide my grin.

"Fine. If Miss J wants to read you a story, she can."

"Yes, of course," I replied.

Shea immediately stopped crying and hopped off his chair, then started to take off his clothes. I brought him into the bedroom and pulled his pajamas out of his bag and helped him change. We went back into the living area where Sullivan added a log to the fire and I waited for him to choose a book from the shelf. I sat on the floor and pulled a blanket off the couch to get comfortable. Shea sat in front of me and handed me the book.

::Me read::

"Daddy, I think you should hold the book so Shea can read to us," I said, feeling a little more relaxed around Sullivan than I did at the house.

::Hold please::

Sullivan held up a finger for him to be patient, then asked me if I would like a glass of wine.

I hesitated before saying, "Not around Shea. Thanks though."

"I don't have a problem—"

"It's okay." The *last* thing I wanted was to be drinking in front of Shea, but even worse, his father.

Sullivan shrugged then got comfortable on the floor with us and took the book from his son's hand, opening to the first page. We both watched enthralled as Shea made up a story based on the drawings on the pages, his vivid imagination astounding both of us.

When Shea was done reading us the story, we clapped excitedly as he got to his feet and took a proud bow, over and over again. It was the sweetest thing I'd ever seen. He was such a character he could have been his own cartoon.

"Bedtime," Sullivan told him when he finally stopped bowing.

Shea crawled onto my lap and curled up with his face against my chest. "He slept on the plane and in the car," I stated the obvious. "He's probably not very tired."

::Cuddle::

Sullivan sighed and wrapped the blanket around his son, and myself by extension, then pointed a finger at him and said, "Close your eyes." He got up to stoke the fire and said, "You're spoiling him."

"Every kid deserves to be spoiled once in a while. Weren't you ever spoiled as a kid?"

"No, never. My parents were very strict. It was all business all the time."

That explains a lot.

"This kid is going to face enough challenges as he gets older and experiences the real world. There's nothing wrong with spoiling him a bit now while he's still little. You're going to blink and he'll be all grown up."

"But spoiling a child only brings headaches later on."

"There's a difference between spoiling a child with affection and spoiling one with gifts and material items they don't need."

"You're pretty smart for having such a foul mouth."

I had to laugh at this, then said, "I was salutatorian at my high school."

Sullivan couldn't hide the visible shock that covered his face. "Really… and did you beat up the valedictorian for besting you?"

"Very funny. It was my sister."

"Sister? I guess I don't really know much about you, do I? Tell me about this smarter sister of yours."

"I'd rather not."

He seemed a bit flustered, not having the proper social skills to deal with being shut off from a conversation he thought he was leading. Then he smiled. "He's already asleep."

"See? I know things."

He chuckled and said, "He's never connected with anyone the way he has with you. I have to admit, it's a great relief."

"I haven't connected with anyone this way since…." I couldn't finish my sentence.

"Since?"

"Um… I just… hey, can I get that wine now?"

"You bet."

Sullivan got up and went into the kitchen and I closed my eyes as I listened to Shea breathing sleepily on top of me. I touched my nose to the top of his warm head and inhaled his little boy scent, a mixture of sweat, rubber and peanut butter. Sullivan returned and set a glass of red wine on the floor next to me as he fluffed up a group of large pillows and got comfortable a few feet away from me.

I felt the heat from the fire on my cheeks and took a sip of wine as he watched me. Seeing him so relaxed, lounging on the floor against a bunch of pillows with a glass of wine was a little too much for my libido to handle. Then just as if I needed protection from my own devious thoughts, Shea farted in his sleep and we both started laughing like little kids.

"Bubble police," I said, trying to hold back my laughter so my convulsing body didn't wake Shea.

"That was *hilarious*," he said.

"How could you not tell your own son that people knew when he farted? That's not cool, dude."

"I guess it wasn't something that was really on my radar. I was always worried about more important things. Like why can't he hear? Why is he different? The worst was how I was going to handle it. I didn't think I could."

"But you did. Because you had no choice."

"Exactly. We all have our crosses to bear, and I'm guessing you've had a few."

I emptied my glass of wine and held it out to him. "Please."

Sullivan left and returned with both our glasses refilled, then got comfortable on the floor again. He just watched me, waiting for me to finish my thought from earlier. This seemed a really good opportunity to ask about Shea's mother and JoJo, so I decided to see how things looked after I gave him a bit of information on my personal life.

"Prude was my twin sister."

"Prude?"

"Her name was Prudence but I called her Prude."

"Prude and Jude. Beatles connection?"

"Please don't go there."

"Sorry."

"A brain aneurysm killed her when we were eighteen."

"Holy shit, I'm sorry."

It was surreal to see Sullivan behaving like a normal human being with feelings, and swear words.

"She was my best friend, and I fell apart when she died."

"Understandable."

"Prude was deaf, and that's why I know sign language."

"Well that can explain Shea's connection to you. Celeste told me how he bonded with you the minute you met. She's the one who scolded me and made me drive to your house to beg you to come back."

He was grinning and I said, "You deserved it."

He shrugged. "So tell me, Salutatorian Hastings… what were your plans after high school? Did you go to college?"

"When I was little I dreamed of being a ballerina," I said, the memory bringing a smile to my face. "But because Prude was deaf I wasn't allowed to listen to music."

His brow furrowed. "A bit over the top, don't you think?"

"When my parents took that away from me I started acting out. It was wrong, but it seemed the only time I could get attention from them was when I misbehaved. Prude was treated differently because she was deaf and she hated it, but what could she do?"

"I'm sorry you had to grow up that way."

I rested my cheek on Shea's soft hair and said, "As long as I had Prude, it didn't matter. But when I lost her, I lost everything."

I was telling him a lot more than I had planned. I wondered if I was revealing too much, letting him inside my head like that.

"I was going to be a zoologist and Prude wanted to be a teacher. Going to college was the first time in our lives we were ever separated and it was really hard for me."

"Was she much different from you, other than her hearing?"

I accidentally grunted. "She was the beautiful blonde, blue-eyed princess and I was her antithesis. My parents never held me in the same regard."

Sullivan held up his glass and said, "A toast to using the word antithesis."

I laughed and held up my glass. "Cheers."

"A zoologist. That's mighty impressive."

"Yeah, well…." How much did I want to tell him? Since he was being a decent person at the moment I continued. "We came home for Christmas break that first year and Prude died on New Year's Eve from a brain aneurysm. I never went back to school and I spent the next four years self-destructing."

"Well... you should never compare yourself to your sister or anyone else. You're not treating yourself fairly."

An awkward silence fell upon us and he said, "Oh look at that, we're out of wine." He jumped up and retrieved the bottle from the kitchen, emptying its remaining liquid into our glasses. As he got comfortable once again on his bed of pillows he said, "I apologize. I'm not very good at being comforting."

I looked at him sideways and gently replied, "You're better than you think you are." I snuggled Shea closer to me, allowing myself to get lost in his mere presence in my arms, feeling more connected to him than ever. "You haven't mentioned the handbook," I spoke quietly, hoping it wouldn't evoke an ugly response.

He took a sip of his wine and nodded, looking as though he were searching for just the right words. "I've read it. Over and over again. The first time broke my heart, thinking of the way those girls psychologically messed with Shea's head. Then I got angry. Angry with them, angry with myself for not realizing what was actually happening. How could I have been so blind?"

"You couldn't possibly know what they were doing. You trusted them to take care of your son and—"

"I still should've sensed something was wrong. I failed him and I'll never forgive myself for that."

I was stunned at his admission. Maybe I needed to ply him with alcohol more often in the evenings so he wasn't so tense, robotic, and asshole-ish.

His face contorted in anguish as he continued, "And those girls had the *audacity* to write about how Shea didn't know proper sign language! Maybe they were the ones who didn't know what they were doing. How could I have been so careless?"

I wasn't sure how to respond to his outburst, so instead I emptied my glass. Again. Three glasses of wine and I could feel it swirling around in my head.

"You've made so much progress with Shea in such a short time," he said reflectively, not looking at me. "Obviously you were meant to come into his life. He's never bonded with anyone the way he has with you. Looks like your sister prepared you well for this job, if nothing else."

"I think it goes much deeper than that," I said, almost in a whisper. "What time was Shea born?"

He pulled a face, looking at me strangely, then answered, "Around ten forty-five, the evening of New Year's Eve, 1985."

"Prude died at ten-thirty, the evening of New Year's Eve, 1985."

He stared at me, then drank the last of his wine. "I don't understand."

I looked directly into his eyes as tears burned my own and asked, "Who is JoJo?"

Sullivan nervously ran a hand through his hair then rubbed his lips. "Ah shit," he grumbled. He sat up straight and said, "Joella is Shea's twin sister. He calls her JoJo."

My heart stopped. Shea had a twin... where was she?

I slowly relayed that morning's experience of watching Shea signing in a secret language I actually understood, and that it was the same one Prude and I shared.

"I haven't celebrated my birthday since Prude died," I explained, my voice cracking. "I never told Shea today was my birthday."

He looked at me strangely. "Well how did he know then?"

"He said that JoJo and Prude told him. JoJo... his sister... and Prude... *my sister.*"

Sullivan shot to his feet and paced the floor in front of me. I'd never seen him look more vulnerable or unsure of himself. It was a bit unsettling, even though it made him more likable. Then he shocked me by falling on the floor next to me, so close he almost knocked Shea in the head.

"He talks to JoJo?" he asked, his eyes wide.

"All the time."

He closed his eyes and pinched the bridge of his nose with his thumb and forefinger, then blew out a long, anguished breath. He brushed a strand of hair off of Shea's face and watched him closely as he began to tell me what I could sense was very painful for him.

"My wife, Shea's mother, was killed in a car accident a year and a half ago." My breath caught in my throat as he watched Shea sleep, reaching out to touch his hair. "She was killed instantly... thrown from the car on impact. The car was so badly damaged they had to cut the kids out of the back seat...." His voice cracked and I could tell he was holding back a flood of emotion, not wanting me to see how vulnerable he really was. "Shea and JoJo were holding hands when they finally reached them... they worked on JoJo at the scene but she was pronounced dead at the hospital."

My hand flew to my mouth as I gasped louder than I ever intended.

He wiped a tear from his cheek as he whispered, "Her blood alcohol level was twice the legal limit. Shea somehow survived with nothing more than a few cuts and bruises and a concussion. But he was never the same. JoJo's death destroyed him; it was like his already closed off world became that much smaller, and everyone he came in contact with was the enemy. Including me."

As hard as I tried to control my emotions, it was hopeless. I was blinded by tears as I said, "I'm so sorry."

"As much as I despise what those other nannies did to my son, I can admit he's been a terror."

"No," I cried. "What they did is on *them*. Don't you dare put this on him."

"I'm not blaming him, but as his father I can admit that he wasn't the easiest child to handle after losing his mother and JoJo. Being deaf just made everything more difficult."

I pressed my lips softly against Shea's head and cried. I cried for the loss of his mother and his beloved sister, and I cried for the loss of my own twin, barely able to catch my breath.

Getting to his knees, Sullivan said, "I should put him in bed." As he reached for Shea his face was so close to mine I could smell the wine on his breath. The wine was certainly doing a number on me and there were so many emotions electrifying the air. I didn't want to let go of Shea; I was clinging to him with every ounce of sanity I had left.

"Please don't take him," I whispered, wiping the wetness from my face. I looked up to see him watching me, seemingly unsure what he should be doing.

"This might be the wine talking but," he whispered. "do you think Prude and JoJo brought you to Shea?"

A lump formed in my throat as I looked into his eyes, both of us fighting to hold back tears we didn't want to cry in front of each other.

"I think so," I answered in a whisper, swallowing hard. "Why are we whispering?"

I saw him swallow before he whispered, "Because saying it any louder makes this all real and I don't know how to deal with that."

"I don't either," I admitted, my eyes darting down at Shea and back to Sullivan.

His face was so close to mine, and I was certain our baffled expressions mirrored each other, experiencing something neither of us understood or dared talk about out loud. I don't know what came over me but I leaned forward and kissed his mouth. He said nothing, pulling Shea into his arms and carrying him to the bedroom.

You idiot!

I hugged my knees to my chest as I watched the burning embers in the fireplace through a curtain of tears that I could no longer control. Everything was so overwhelming and I had probably just kissed my way out of a job. It wouldn't have been the first time, but losing this job would destroy me.

I rested my forehead on my knees as I tried to relax my breathing and stop the tears from falling, and then I felt his presence come back into the room.

"Why are you crying?" he asked.

Without lifting my face I mumbled something I realized he couldn't understand due to my muffled cries against my legs. He sat on the floor next to me and briefly touched my arm to get my attention. I lifted my head so I could see him, even though I was mortified by what I'd done.

"Why are you crying?" he asked again.

"I don't know… I just… please don't fire me. I couldn't handle it."

"I'm sorry for wrangling you here tonight like a bully. It was obvious you had something else planned. Nobody should be crying on their birthday."

"I was only going to do something stupid anyway," I grumbled. "Stupid is what I do best."

He placed a hand on my knee as he scooted closer. "No, what you do best is take care of my son. He was a lost soul and you singlehandedly brought him back to me." His eyes became wet and his voice shook as he cried, "I lost my wife and daughter and live with the guilt every single day. Guilt I could never really explain to my surviving deaf child because he can't hear the sound of my grieving voice, or because he completely shut down and became something I had no idea how to deal with."

His emotional admission was almost too much to take in. I covered my mouth with my hand as the tears nearly choked me.

"You give Shea *all* of yourself," he continued. "Everything you do, you do for him, and he's not even your child. You are the most important person in his life, even more important than me, and he needs you. I'm not going to fire you Jude, because if Shea needs you, *I* need you."

"You called me Jude," I squeaked.

He grinned and said, "Don't get used to it."

I chuckled as I wiped my face with the sleeve of my sweatshirt. I thought about getting up and going to bed, but he didn't move from his spot next to me. He looked so different dressed casually in a relaxing atmosphere away from home; and he looked damn sexy. I wasn't sure if he was expecting me to say anything further, but I was frozen in place, mesmerized by the way he was looking at me with his soft hazel eyes. He leaned closer and grinned before pressing his lips against mine, holding them there as my heart banged like a drum in my chest.

And just like that he pulled away and said, "Now we're even. Goodnight, Ms. Hastings."

My heart choked me as I watched him get up and walk into his bedroom, closing the door behind him.

Chapter 10

I woke the next morning with Shea cuddled beside me, grinning, just waiting for me to open my eyes. Sullivan's kiss was still imprinted on my mind, even though I realized after going to bed that he did it so I would stop feeling mortified over what I'd done. Unfortunately that didn't calm my swelling heart when I thought about his lips on mine.

I pulled Shea into my arms and nuzzled him as he giggled, his face pressed against mine. I batted my eyelashes against his cheek and he wriggled free, sitting up and rubbing his face where I tickled him.

::Tickle::

"Butterfly kiss," I explained.

::Butterfly?::

"Butterfly... kiss."

I pointed to my eyelashes then touched his cheek.

::Me::

I nodded and leaned toward him, giving my cheek up for his version of a butterfly kiss. I clapped with my mouth in a big smile and he joined in clapping, too. He was always thrilled to learn something new; I was happy he was so receptive.

I got out of bed and Shea hopped onto my back for a piggyback ride, and as we walked into the living area of the cabin I saw some deer nosing around in the snow through the sliding glass doors that led to the back deck. I set Shea on the floor so he could see outside, pointing to the deer. He gasped and froze.

::Eat me::

"No, they won't eat you. Deer are nice animals."

::Nice?::

"Nice."

He frowned and I sat down on the floor, setting him in my lap to watch. We sat there quietly for some time before he reached out his hand to bang on the glass, but I managed to grab him before following through.

"No," I gently scolded. "You'll scare them."

Shea was sneaky, however, as I gently held his arms down, kicking out his foot to make contact with the glass, sending the deer running off immediately. He hopped up and down in my lap clapping, proud of his accomplishment. I stood up and looked down at him with a stern look on my face.

"That wasn't nice. That was *mean*. You scared them away."

He thought about what I said for a moment, then stuck his tongue out at me. Before I could react Sullivan was behind us asking what we wanted for breakfast.

༄

Later that morning I took Shea outside to play in the snow and his unbelievable energy wore me out. We made snow angels, made a snowman family, and went sledding down a tiny hill not far from the house. It was really private seeing the area in the daylight, and I wondered how much of the property belonged to Sullivan. I could see another cabin in the distance, assuming it was where Ryan, his Wisconsin driver, lived. Initially I believed Sullivan had drivers because he was rich and pompous, but after spilling his heart out to me I realized the accident that killed his wife and daughter was probably the reason. I definitely saw him in a different light and even though he acted as though our lips never met, I couldn't stop thinking about it.

Sullivan himself bundled up and joined us for a little while, and watching the two of them playing and laughing together melted my heart. Everything came to a halt, however, when Shea needed to use the bathroom, so we all filed back inside. Shea ran to the bathroom to do his business, Sullivan announced he was going to make peanut butter and jelly sandwiches for lunch, and I hung all of our wet snow gear up to dry.

When Shea returned from the bathroom in his adorable little long-johns, he bounced up and down on the balls of his feet and exaggeratedly rubbed his arms to show me he was cold. I pulled him into my arms and sat in the recliner, wrapping both of us in a warm blanket to wait for lunch to be served. When Sullivan walked over to tell me our sandwiches were ready he chuckled.

"He's already asleep," he said.

"Oh good," I replied dreamily, pushing the chair all the way back and snuggling Shea close to me. "I'm tired, too."

"Good thing I'm hungry," he teased.

I closed my eyes but stretched out my arm. "I'm starving."

He walked away and returned, placing a sandwich in my hand, which I devoured quickly with my eyes closed. I got snuggled back under the blanket with Shea on top of me, and fell asleep instantly.

I don't know how long I'd been asleep, but I could hear voices and didn't know if they were in my dream, or if Sullivan was actually speaking to someone in the cabin. Once I realized the voices were real, I kept my eyes closed to listen.

"You didn't tell me you had a girlfriend," an unknown male voice spoke quietly.

"She's the *nanny*," Sullivan corrected him.

"The nanny! You've never brought a nanny here before!"

"This one's different. It was her birthday yesterday and Shea really wanted her to come with us."

"Are you getting soft, old man?"

"I need you to go into town and get a birthday cake."

"Birthday cake? You *are* getting soft!"

"A birthday cake and maybe some ice cream, and just pick up some pizzas for dinner. A large sausage and a large cheese."

"Whatever you say."

I heard the front door open and close and just listened… complete silence. Shea began to squirm on top of me so I stretched my limbs and put the chair in its upright position. I pretended I heard nothing and didn't ask who he was talking to. Instead I brought Shea into the bathroom to do his business, then into the bedroom to put on some clothes. When we came back into the living area Shea hopped onto Sullivan's lap on the couch and I sat on the floor next to the stereo.

"Mind if I flip through your records?" I asked.

"Be my guest."

I could hear Sullivan chatting behind me to Shea as I flipped through the records in his collection. A lot of Beatles, a lot of oldies, a lot of classical. I guess I wasn't too surprised. As much as it pained me, I pulled the Beatles' *Hey Jude* from the record cabinet and placed it on the turntable. I played some songs, just a few seconds each, to see what might work for what I had planned, then chose "Paperback Writer."

I twisted my body around to look at Shea, then waved him over to where I was sitting. He immediately hopped off his father's lap and joined me, and I positioned him in front of the tall speaker with his hands palm down on the top of it. I gently placed the needle on "Paperback Writer" and waited to see his reaction. He stared down at the speaker as if waiting for it to move, or jump, or become animated in some way, but nothing else.

"Cover your ears, dad," I warned.

I turned the song up loud and watched as Shea's mouth turned into a perfect circle as he slowly turned his head to look at me.

"Music," I said.

His eyes grew large as he placed his cheek down on the speaker and gasped at feeling the vibrations against his face. He nibbled on his fingertips and jogged in place at this new experience and I was relieved it worked. As he alternated feeling the vibrations with his hands and his cheek, I searched for another record. When the song was over I placed the record back in its cover and put on another. I started to play "Yummy Yummy Yummy" by Ohio Express, only this time I sang the words.

"Yummy yummy yummy I got love in my tummy," I sang, signing as I went along.

Shea gave me a strange look and I knelt on the floor next to him, placing one of his hands on the speaker and the other against my neck. As I sang the words he could feel the vibrations in my throat and his face was a mixture of emotions.

"Singing," I told him. "Music and singing."

He removed his hand from my throat and placed it on his own, but was disappointed there was no singing there. He frowned.

::*No sing*::

"We still have to find your voice," I explained.

He nodded and placed both hands back on the speaker. I tried to play songs with heavy bass lines or lots of drums, and Shea was having the time of his life feeling the vibrations and dancing along to the music. He really liked the words to "Yummy Yummy Yummy" so we played that one over and over again so I could sing it to him.

At one point Shea became distracted and ran away, jumping into the arms of a man who had just entered the cabin. I turned off the stereo and put the record away as I heard him say, "Hey buddy!"

"Ms. Hastings, this is my brother Jasper," Sullivan said. "And his friend...."

"Darla," a girl answered.

I wiped my palms on my jeans then turned around and extended my hand, coming face to face with the guy I hooked up with in the back of my car on New Year's Eve.

My stomach roiled as he smiled at me and shook my hand, his kaleidoscope eyes trying to figure out if he'd met me before.

"Nice to meet you...."

"Jude."

"Like Judith?"

"No."

"Like Judas?" he teased.

"Like hey," I finally said.

He wrinkled his forehead then grinned, beginning to sing, "Hey Jude—"

"Please don't."

As Shea bounced excitedly in his arms he replied, "Oh, sorry."

I waved him off, thankful he didn't recognize me, but still paranoid enough that I kept pushing my bangs over my eyes like some kind of hair curtain to hide my true identity.

Shea reached his arms toward me and I pulled him to me as Jasper said, "Jude, this is my friend Darla."

"Hi Darla, nice to meet you."

She was the most beautiful woman I'd ever laid eyes on, with long curly black hair and eyes so green they sparkled like emeralds. She stood taller than Sullivan and his brother, and could certainly have been a supermodel.

"Nice to meet you," she replied, her megawatt smile illuminating the room.

"It's apparent the two of you are already intimately aware of each other," Sullivan chimed in, causing sweat to bead on my forehead.

"What?" I gasped, sounding guilty of every crime ever committed.

"The naked man face down on the floor," he replied. "My charming brother."

I pointed at Jasper and started laughing until he said, "And that was *your* ass in the red bikini!"

The two of us laughed together, causing Shea to laugh and clap, having no idea what was so funny. If Sullivan had any idea how intimate I'd actually been with his charming brother, my situation in his home would be in great peril, I was sure of it.

"One of my finest moments," I grumbled with a grin.

"Are we eating these pizzas or what? I'm starving," Darla interrupted.

Jasper rolled his eyes, then turned to face her with a smile and said, "Yeah, let's eat."

As we all munched on pizza I noticed Jasper staring at Shea in disbelief and he finally asked, "When did he start eating pizza?"

"Ms. Hastings has been a wonder in getting Shea to try different foods," Sullivan explained. "He even eats scrambled eggs and yogurt."

"Wow!" Jasper exclaimed. "Impressive." Then after some hesitation, "He seems so… content."

"He's a different child," Sullivan replied. "Ms. Hastings has been nothing short of a blessing."

I saw Jasper give Sullivan a sideways look and I wondered what was going through his mind. My heart swelled when I looked at Sullivan and thought about his lips touching mine, but my ovaries banged together like a set of castanets when I looked at Jasper and thought about what we'd done together. Only I could end up in a situation so bizarre, but as long as Jasper didn't recognize me I was safe.

Darla disrupted my thoughts when I heard her ask, "How old are you, Shea?"

Shea was too busy eating his slice of cheese pizza and bobbing his head back and forth in pure bliss to know she was talking to him.

"He can't hear you," Jasper explained. "Little guy is deaf."

I got Shea's attention and told him, "Miss D has a question for you. Watch her mouth." He nodded as everyone looked on, wondering what I was doing. "Ask him again," I told Darla. "But slowly."

"How old are you?" she asked again, his eyes fixed on her lips.

This was a question we'd done over and over again so there was no reason he wouldn't be able to answer, unless he was nervous with everyone watching him. He thought about what she said then raised his hand and extended four fingers.

Sullivan and Jasper looked astounded as Darla smiled and nodded her head at Shea. I gave him a hug and tousled his hair, letting him know how proud I was of him.

"Lip reading, Ms. Hastings?" Sullivan stammered. "I don't even know what to say."

Is he looking at my mouth?

"You're welcome," was the only thing that came to mind.

"So will he have to learn braille?" Darla asked.

The look on Jasper's face was priceless as we all grasped Darla's question. "He's deaf, not blind," I quipped.

Darla looked at me like I was a new found enemy, her green eyes stabbing me with an icy glare. I suddenly felt quite small and insignificant.

"So… Jasper," I decided to change the subject. "Do you work in publishing too?"

Sullivan laughed loudly. "He likes to think he does."

"Kiss my ass old man," Jasper retorted. "I do, Jude, but I like to venture into other opportunities, not just publishing."

I was genuinely interested in getting to know more about my New Year's Eve conquest. "Like what?"

"Nothing but failures," Sullivan smirked.

"And you've never had a shit real estate deal?" Jasper countered.

I couldn't decide if they were engaging in normal brotherly banter, or if the two genuinely disliked each other. Either way it was entertaining to watch.

"So tell us of your latest brilliant idea," Sullivan urged.

Jasper's face lit up as he looked at me and said, "Wine. My new company is called Sign of the Times Wine, and every bottle will have a sign language diagram on it, starting off with each letter of the alphabet, then actual words and phrases. Half of the proceeds will go to charities that directly benefit the deaf."

This brought a warm smile to my face. "I think that sounds wonderful."

"The point is, Ms. Hastings, my brother spends so much time on other projects that our publishing companies have taken a back seat."

"You wanted Willow Kelly and I gave her to you on a silver platter, Ziggy," Jasper argued.

He called him Ziggy!

"And yet every time I schedule a meeting with her, she's a no show," Sullivan replied.

"How is that my fault?"

The air in the cabin became thick with animosity and while Shea was oblivious to anything that was said, I was extremely uncomfortable.

"I love Willow Kelly," I announced, thinking it would ease the tension. "I've read a lot of her books since living at the house."

"Frankly, Ms. Hastings, her plot lines are so intricate and twisted, I'm surprised you understand them at all."

My face fell and my skin pricked with the heat of anger as Sullivan's insult rattled around inside my head like a pinball. It became eerily quiet from all the ugliness being flung around the room and no one said another word until Darla decided the silence in itself was too much to take.

"I can't imagine what it must be like to have a disabled child," she said, thinking this would help the situation somehow.

"He's deaf you idiot," I growled. "He is *not* disabled!"

I got up from my chair and went to my room, slamming the door behind me. I angrily paced the floor trying to understand why Sullivan turned on me, insulting my very intelligence with his comment. He knew I wasn't stupid; he knew I was only second in line to being the smartest in my graduating class because of my sister.

I didn't have a chance to think about it long before Sullivan stormed into the room and closed the door behind him.

"You can't talk to people like that in my home," he raged. "I won't allow it!"

"And what about the way you talk to *me*? You're such an asshole!"

"Ms. Hastings, I—"

"Stop calling me that!"

He ran a hand through his hair, then rubbed his eyes in frustration.

"I'm sorry," he said softly. "I'm always on edge in the presence of my brother."

"That's no excuse! You've been a complete asshole since the day I met you!"

"Please, can you just calm down so they don't hear you screaming at me?"

"Oh, it's all about you and your image, isn't it, *Mr.* Sullivan? Maybe you need to take a look in the mirror and see how *you* affect the people around you? It's like walking on eggshells all the time — no, worse than eggshells — it's like walking on broken glass, afraid of saying or doing the wrong thing, worried I'm going to get fired for something stupid when we both know I'm the best thing that ever happened to you!"

We stared at each other speechless until his mouth turned into a slight grin.

"Shea, I meant Shea!" I corrected myself. "The best thing that's happened to Shea since… you know…."

Sullivan stepped closer to me and whispered, "That genius my brother brought along… you know I don't do well with strangers. I barely tolerate you."

This made me chuckle. "Why have you never mentioned your brother?" I asked. "It might've been something helpful to know."

He sat on one of the beds. "I don't know, I guess I didn't think it would matter… until it mattered."

"And now it matters." It mattered to me more than he'd ever know.

"I was ten years old when Jasper was born," he explained, staring into his lap. "Such a big age gap, we never got along very well."

"Let me guess… you were the studious, disciplined child, never stepping one toe out of line and he was the wild child who broke all the rules and got away with murder."

He looked up at me and nodded. "Pretty much."

"And you resent him for it."

"He never takes anything seriously. I've worked my ass off for my father since I was fourteen, and *he* comes and goes as he pleases, living life in the fast lane and getting involved in opportunities outside of the family business. He doesn't give a shit about Sullivan Publishing; he's always looking for the next big adventure or investment."

"I think his wine idea sounds pretty cool."

"Are you taking his side?" He briefly looked like a child needing to know that somebody liked him best, even though he was the uptight, condescending, holier than thou sibling.

My head had been spinning since setting eyes on Jasper, but I finally had a moment of clarity. "I lost my sister. Shea lost his sister. Both in unimaginable ways. Like him or not, he's your brother and you're lucky to have him in your life. You still have a chance to develop a relationship with him, but you're so stubborn you don't even want to try."

"*I'm* stubborn? You just met him and you're already—"

"Stop it! This argument is about how *you* spoke to *me*, so don't think you can get out of it by changing the subject!"

Before he could respond there was a tiny knock on the door, which was followed by three loud fist pounds.

"What!" Sullivan shouted.

Jasper's voice spoke from the other side of the door. "Shea wants to know why his new mommy is mad, and *I* want to know why my brother is fighting with his nanny like she's his girlfriend."

Sullivan's face twisted. "I'm sorry for insulting you," he grumbled. "I will apologize in front of Jasper and Darla, but you owe them an apology as well."

"Fine," I hissed, opening the door to see Shea standing there. I walked back to the table and sat down as Sullivan pulled Shea into his arms and followed suit, setting his son on his lap.

"Ms. Hastings," he began, "I apologize for insulting your intelligence in regards to your reading comprehension. I hope you will forgive me."

Why couldn't he talk like a normal person?

"Apology accepted," I replied. I looked at Darla, who was still shooting me daggers, and said, "Jasper... Darla, I'm sorry for calling you an idiot. I'm very protective of Shea and I went overboard. I meant no disrespect."

She spent a long time admiring her long, red fingernails before saying, "Yeah, okay."

When everyone was finished eating, I brought Shea over to the fireplace where we stretched out on our stomachs to color in his coloring books. Being the nanny, I didn't feel it was my place to sit around talking with the adults while they enjoyed their after dinner coffee or drinks, and I certainly didn't need to be looking at Jasper more than necessary.

"Watch how he does the dishes," I heard Jasper whisper to Darla. "Washes one dish, dries it, puts it away. Talk about OCD."

"I can hear you," Sullivan grumbled. "And I don't see *you* offering to help."

"That's because I could never do it as perfectly as you," Jasper teased. And then to Darla, "Trust me, there's no pleasing this guy."

Even though it was probably true, I thought Jasper was being a bit harsh, especially for someone who apparently just barged in on Sullivan's family time without warning or invitation, and with an unknown female companion. I was trying desperately to figure out what their relationship was, which was stupid because what did I really care, but where were they going to sleep?

"Can I smoke?" Darla asked.

"Outside," Sullivan insisted.

I heard her chair slide across the wood floor, then the sounds of her pulling on her coat and exiting the front door. Without moving from my place on the floor, or even turning my head, my eyes followed Jasper as he walked closer to us and sat on the couch. It was here I got a better look at his worn out jeans, especially the threadbare area of his crotch that fully accentuated what was hidden there. His flannel shirt was unbuttoned to the middle of his chest, his legs spread wide as he silently watched us. Why did guys always sit that way? With Jasper it made me think about the time I spent on his lap in the back of my car and it was almost unbearable. I remembered how he claimed he could turn me on without ever touching me and he was *right*. There he was, his long dark hair spilling onto his shoulders, his adorable face watching us, and I had to pretend I didn't even know him.

Darla soon returned and took her place beside Jasper on the couch as he put a protective arm around her and asked if she was okay.

"Yep, I'm fine," she replied.

"Are you sure?"

She patted his thigh and said, "Yep." She kissed him quickly on the mouth and I put all of my attention back on the page I was coloring, confused at why I felt so deflated. It wasn't long before I noticed Shea fidgeting in front of me and when I locked eyes with him he was grinning, then he covered his giggling mouth with his little hands. Shea jumped to his feet and rushed toward me, covering my eyes with his hands and I had no idea what was going on, though I should have guessed based on the conversation I heard between Sullivan and Jasper while pretending I was still napping.

I kept my eyes closed as I got to my feet and let Shea lead me to the table. When I opened my eyes there was a birthday cake with a sprinkling of lit candles and I could feel a smile so wide cover my face I thought it might swallow me whole. Shea bounced up and down nibbling on his fingers, giggling like he had kept the most precious secret in all the world.

"Did you do this?" I asked him.

He nodded.

::Happy birthday::

"Thank you."

"Happy birthday, Ms. Hastings," Sullivan said. "You can blow out the candles now if you like."

"Help me?" I asked Shea.

He nodded excitedly and I lifted him into my arms so we could blow out the candles together. When the last candle was extinguished, he raised his arms in victory then wrapped his arms around my neck as he nuzzled his face against my hair. I could see Jasper giving me the side eye and thought about his comments through the door about me being Shea's new mommy, and how Sullivan was fighting with me like I was his girlfriend. Did he think I was sleeping with my boss?

After eating the delectable half cheesecake, half brownie birthday cake, it was time for Shea to go to bed, and of course because he was having such a wonderful time celebrating me, he threw himself on the floor and punched the air as he cried.

"I'm going to bed, too," I told him, peeling him off the floor. "Now, where is everyone sleeping?"

"Oh… uh….," Sullivan stammered. "Well, I guess I'll sleep in the twin with Shea, and they can have the other room."

"We don't want to put you out of your bed," Jasper replied.

"Well I'm not sleeping with *him*," I quickly responded. "No offense."

"None taken Ms. Hastings, goodnight."

"Give me five minutes to change, then bring him in. Goodnight… it was nice meeting you both."

I made a quick exit to my room and closed the door, thankful I didn't have to be in the presence of Jasper Sullivan any longer. I prayed they were early risers and would be gone when I got up in the morning. I ripped off my clothes and slipped into my flannel pajamas, then crawled into bed waiting for Sullivan's knock.

He entered cautiously, as if there would be something improper to be seen, but closed the door quietly as he sat on the other bed with Shea. He sighed heavily as he began to remove his son's clothes to get him ready for bed.

"I'm sorry, Ms. Hastings," he grumbled. "He never drops by unannounced. I don't know why he chose today to… as you can see, I'm a bit flustered."

"I see that," I chuckled. "So how old is he, anyway? You two are worlds apart, obviously."

"Twenty-two, and yes, we're galaxies apart."

"At least he has a loving relationship with Shea. And Shea obviously adores his uncle."

Sullivan carried Shea over to give me a hug and kiss goodnight, but he squirmed away from him and crawled under the covers next to me.

"Your own bed," Sullivan told him.

::Sleep party::

Sullivan was visibly exasperated. "Ms. Hastings, I can't even argue with him anymore, do you—"

"Yes, it's fine if he sleeps here with me."

"Behave," he told Shea. As he turned to leave he stopped and said, "I'm very grateful Jasper loves my son as his own. It's his one redeeming quality."

"Oh come on, just one?" I could think of a few others.

"Goodnight, Ms. Hastings."

He turned out the light and walked out, closing the door.

Chapter 11

I fell asleep to the sound of adult chatter from the other side of the bedroom door, and sometime during the night I was startled awake by the most spine-tingling snoring I'd ever heard in my life. I sat up in bed trying to remember where I was, then tried to wrap my head around who would be snoring that loudly in my room. Then I remembered that Sullivan was forced to sleep in the twin bed opposite me and laughed. But only briefly, as his snoring made me understand why some women lost their minds and murdered their husbands while they slept. It felt like a serial killer was loose in the room threatening to slaughter us all with his rusty old chainsaw.

As Shea slept peacefully against the wall, I quietly slipped out of bed and tip-toed to where Sullivan was sleeping on his back. I lightly tapped his shoulder, but he didn't budge. I tried to coax him to roll over with a sexy voice whispering in his ear, but still nothing. I'd never be able to go back to sleep with his log splitting concert going on in the room, so I pinched his nose closed. Nothing. I saved my mother's remedy as the last resort, sticking my finger in his open mouth and swirling it around to mimic an invading insect. I managed to pull my arm away before he swatted it with his hand, then he rolled over and closed his mouth.

Since I was up I slipped out and went to the bathroom, then headed to the kitchen for a glass of water. As I swallowed the last drop in the dimness of the nightlight, I heard a stifled commotion from the bedroom where Jasper and Darla were staying. I couldn't help but glance in that direction only to see Jasper standing there naked as the door was slammed in his face. I giggled a little too loudly and he immediately covered himself with his hands and turned to face me.

"This is *your* fault!" he whisper shouted, heading my way.

How on earth could anything that happened in his room be my fault? "You standing out here holding your dangly bits is my fault?" It was so ludicrous I had to laugh in his face.

"I accidentally called her Marla," he explained. "She kicked me out and locked the door!"

"Marla? So what?"

"I know who you are," he accused. "You might look different now, but I know it's you."

"I don't know what you're talking about." Meanwhile, my heart was thumping violently in my ears.

"I waited for you to come back and you blew me off."

"I don't know what you're talking about," I repeated.

"Oh come off it *Marla*, or whatever your real name is. What kind of scam are you pulling on my brother?"

"Stop it," I hissed. "You're wrong; you have me mixed up with someone else."

"Do I?" His eyes were wild as he touched the "P" hanging from my neck. I went against Sullivan's rules about no jewelry, always hiding the necklace I refused to remove underneath my shirt.

I slapped my palm against his bare chest and pushed him away as he was a little too close for comfort.

"What was that for?" he screeched.

I was going to turn this around and put it back on him, where it belonged. "How dare you suggest my relationship with Shea is some sort of scam!"

"I'm not… that's not what I… I've been looking for you for two months!"

Every stressfully tightened muscle in my body relaxed at the same moment as I took a deep breath. I could physically feel my facial expression change.

"You have?" I whispered breathily.

"Ha! It *is* you!" he flung back at me.

"Please don't ruin this for me," I begged. "I'll tell him whatever you want me to, but please don't—"

"Why didn't you just tell me the truth?"

"Are you going to keep standing there holding your junk?"

He raised his arms in the air and shrugged. "There." As I covered my eyes he said, "Nothing you haven't seen before."

"Well… I really didn't see anything before."

"I saw everything," he teased. "We have history together, you know."

"We have no history, we had a one time fuck."

"You were going to meet me back inside."

"And you left a used condom in my back seat!" He opened his mouth to speak but blew air out instead. "Can you please cover yourself?"

I watched his ass as he stomped over to the couch and grabbed the granny square quilt, wrapping it around his waist. "You're sleeping with him."

"*What?*" I walked to where he was standing and shoved him onto the couch. "You take that back!"

"He sleeps with *all* the nannies," he grumbled.

For some reason I felt every ounce of life drain from my body and fell onto the couch beside him. This changed my whole perspective of Sullivan, who I believed was a lonely man that worked far too many hours in a day to compensate. How many nannies had there been in just one year? Was that the real reason they all ended up leaving? But it couldn't be... I saw the handbook. Were they seducing the lonely boss to keep their inexcusable behavior even further from coming to light?

"I'm not sleeping with him," I whispered dully. "He's my *boss*. I would never jeopardize my position with Shea." My voice was barely audible as I added, "He's everything to me."

Jasper poked his finger in and out of the holes of the crocheted quilt, avoiding eye contact with me. Staring at what his finger was doing he said, "I'm sorry, I shouldn't have said that."

"I'm not pulling a scam, I swear. I'm a loner and I didn't want to get involved. I didn't even want to know your name. I went home and drove my car over the front yard and into a tree. My parents were furious, and then my mom saw not only my panties in the back seat, but the used condom *and* your vial of coke. I was forced to make a life change or they were going to throw me in rehab."

"Holy shit, that's crazy! It was a wild night, that's for sure. I gave up the coke after that because I thought maybe that's why you blew me off, and I really liked you."

"Please don't tell me that."

"I kept going back to the club but everyone told me I was wasting my time, that you didn't work there anymore. I thought they were lying to me, but I see it was true. You were working for my brother the whole time."

"Please don't take it the wrong way. You wouldn't want to get involved with me. I'm not a good person."

Still refusing to look at me he asked, "Did you ever think about me?"

I couldn't decide if he wanted the truth or fantasy, so I told him the truth. "Not until I saw you today."

"Ouch."

"I'm sorry, but I told you... I'm not a good person."

"It's okay, my feelings have changed."

Relief rushed over me and I finally felt relaxed enough to smile.

"Yeah, you know, when I walked in and saw you asleep with Shea cuddled in the chair you looked like a horrible person."

This was not going as I thought it would.

"Then I came back and you had him feeling music, and dancing to it... nobody has ever bonded with him like that. Not me, not even Ziggy. You must be the most despicable person in the world."

I said the only thing that made sense. "Shea has made me a better person."

"And you've given him his childhood back."

I was quite uncomfortable with his praise. "That's not true."

"I haven't seen Shea since his birthday party three months ago. He was like a zombie, you know? Blank look in his eyes, didn't interact at all. He sat there most of the time staring into space like there was no one else around. When it came time to blow out the candles on his cake he crawled under the table and wouldn't come out."

"He just needed some time."

"No, it's because of *you* and I can even see the change in Ziggy. He'll always be uptight and never any fun, but he seems much more relaxed. He's never brought a nanny to the cabin before!"

I humphed. "He only brought me here because Shea begged him. He thought I was going to be alone for my birthday."

"See what I mean? He's only four, and he's already been through so much. To see him smiling and giggling and enjoying life… *you* did that. It's all you, and I love you for it."

I scooted away from him as far as I could go, the arm of the couch pressing against my back. "I should get back to bed before Shea wakes up and starts looking for me."

"Do you believe in love at first sight?"

"No, I don't. I told you that the first time you asked me."

"I never did either. It was always a line that seemed to work with girls. Until today." He finally lifted his head and looked me in the eyes. "I accidentally called Darla Marla because I haven't stopped thinking about you today."

"Marla was the unlovable crazed blonde slut you banged three months ago. She doesn't exist anymore."

"I liked her… I had fun with her… but I didn't love her. I'm in love with you, Jude. From the minute I saw you sleeping in that chair with Shea. You're the miracle my family needed to heal."

"You're getting everything confused. You're grateful, you're not in love."

He slid as close to me as he could get and whispered, "I know the difference."

"How can you say something like that with your girlfriend in the next room?"

"I just met her a couple weeks ago; she seemed fun at the time. She's like a sexy toothache… beautiful on the outside but painful every time she opens her mouth."

"Where did you meet her?"

"The Cheetah Club." He grinned then said, "I kept hoping I'd find you there."

"Instead you found Darla."

"I kept asking for Marla and they finally sent Darla," he said with a laugh.

"You need to start hanging out someplace new," I teased.

I flinched when he lifted his hand to brush the bangs out of my eyes. "What would you do if I kissed you right now?"

He placed his hands on my cheeks and I immediately batted them away. "Gross! You were holding your junk and now you're touching my face!"

He exaggeratedly flung his head back in frustration then said, "Ziggy was right about one thing… you *do* make everything difficult."

"Are you going to tell him about me?"

He hesitated before answering. "No, I have no reason to." When I stood to leave he said, "Guess I'm sleeping on the couch alone," then got comfortable with a pillow and pulled the quilt over his naked body.

"Did you think I was going to stay with you?"

He pouted, his bottom lip protruding like a child. "I just wanted a kiss."

"Goodnight, Jasper."

I tip-toed back to my room and quietly closed the door, my ovaries clanging a protest beat against me the whole way there. My body knew it wanted Jasper, my heart knew I wanted to kiss him, but my head won out, knowing it was the worst thing I could have possibly done. I crawled back into bed beside Shea, whose face looked like an angel as he purred quietly into the pillow. He was the only boy I was willing to lose my heart over.

༄

Between Jasper's declaration of love and Sullivan's snoring, I didn't get much sleep that night. I was torn between the girl I was striving to become and the girl I used to be, stuck in the middle not knowing who I was at all. I could easily do without the alcohol and the drugs, but the sex… my body was craving physical interaction so badly it ached. I was afraid if I gave in to Jasper, even for just a kiss, I would end up right back where I started before being thrust unwillingly into Sullivan's life. I couldn't risk losing Shea, not even for a kiss. Not even for something that could possibly be a lasting relationship. Nothing would be worth losing him.

I took a quick shower and when I joined the rest of the group, Darla was fixing breakfast, Sullivan was reading the Sunday paper, and Jasper was on the floor with Shea in front of the fireplace having an animated conversation with their hands. In anyone else's life it would have looked like a happy family moment, but in my life it was nothing but weirdness, secrets and overactive hormones.

Jasper pulled a shocked face when he spotted me, causing Shea to turn his head. As soon as he set eyes on me, he giggled and covered his face as if he were embarrassed, then flopped onto Jasper's lap to bury his face against his leg. I grinned and Jasper winked at me, causing my heart to flutter. I didn't want him to cause my heart to flutter.

"Breakfast is ready!" Darla announced cheerfully, as if she hadn't kicked a naked Jasper out of their room the night before.

Sullivan was already at the table enjoying his coffee with the newspaper, but Jasper picked Shea up off the floor and as he passed me whispered, "I'm not the only one in love with you. You're this kid's whole world."

While his comment made me happy, it also made me nervous. I wasn't sure it was healthy for Shea to think so highly of me. I wanted to be the best person I could be for his sake, someone he could look up to and admire, someone to be proud of. But I wasn't his mother, and I certainly wasn't going to be his nanny forever.

Darla put everything on the table, then sat next to Jasper with their backs to the window. Sullivan was already seated at the head of the table, which meant I would have to sit with Shea facing the window, which was always a struggle because he got distracted so easily.

"Would you mind if me and Shea switched places with you?" I asked them. "He gets too distracted if he can see out the window."

Jasper jumped to his feet and immediately gave up his chair, but Darla gave me the evil eye, acting like moving was going to ruin the breakfast she prepared for all of us. I noticed Jasper give her bug eyes without saying anything and she finally got up and switched places.

"Thank you," I said, taking my place next to Shea at the table.

As Darla began to dish the food up onto our plates, I noticed hardly anything she cooked looked edible. The toast was burnt, the bacon looked soft and wiggly, and as soon as a fried egg hit the plate the yoke spilled out like golden bloodshed. It wasn't the least bit appetizing looking and I watched Shea's face as she placed a plate in front of him. I knew this was not going to end well.

Shea wrinkled his nose but sat like a stone. Sullivan never complained, putting bits of undercooked egg in his mouth and washing it down with coffee. Jasper picked up a limp piece of bacon and wiggled it in front of his face.

Shea angrily pushed his plate away.

::PBJ::

As Sullivan set down his napkin I said, "It's okay, I'll get it."

Before I could even stand, Shea picked up the runny eggs with his fingers and flung them at Darla, hitting her in the face. As her mouth opened in shock, Jasper busted out laughing, and before anyone else could react, a piece of blackened toast and fatty bacon followed. Sullivan got up from his chair so fast it skidded across the floor as he lunged at Shea, pulling him into the air and dropping him onto the couch.

"Why did you do that?" he asked, furiously wiping the food off Shea's hands with a napkin.

I could barely see Shea's hands, but I thought he said *::Don't like that lady::*

"You're naughty!" he scolded. "You sit here until you can behave!" Sullivan made his way back to the table and said, "Darla, I'm sorry, he's just—"

"He's a spoiled little shit, that's what he is!" she shouted, getting up from the table and storming into the bathroom.

Jasper continued laughing like a dumb high school boy and I glared at him, disapproving of his immaturity.

"What?" he hissed. "Are you going to eat that shit? Have fun with botulism."

"Do you even know what botulism is?" Sullivan quizzed, making me chuckle.

"Yes I do, asshole."

Shea wasn't used to being excluded from everyone else and began to cry. Loud, guttural sobbing that was unusual for him. It broke my heart that the only time I heard his voice was when he was distraught.

I caught Sullivan's eye and carefully asked, "Can I...?"

He nodded, staring at all the uneaten food still sitting on the table. I went to the couch and held my fingers to Shea's throat but he pushed my hand away, punching the air in anger. I then took his hand in mine and held it to his throat as he continued to cry. It wasn't long before he began to calm down and opened his teary eyes to look up at me. His grimace turned into a smile, but he was soon disappointed when he no longer felt a vibration against his throat. He started crying again and threw himself backward on the couch, punching and kicking the air above him.

As he wailed I placed his hand on his throat and as soon as he felt the vibration he was quiet, looking up at me with a smile.

"Your voice," I told him.

Shea jumped off the couch and ran toward his father, jumping into his lap and signing furiously about finding his voice. Sullivan smiled and hugged his son, then thanked me. Our tender moment was interrupted when Darla flew back into the room and grabbed a handful of eggs and smeared them all over Jasper's face and hair.

"You think it's funny, you son of a bitch?" she shrieked.

Shea jumped, clinging to his father's neck at the madness he saw before him, and I stood frozen in place even though Jasper deserved everything he got. Jasper stood up and grabbed a fistful of limp bacon and grabbed her by the back of the neck, shoving it down the front of her blouse as she howled in protest. Shea thought this bizarre behavior was hilarious, laughing and slapping his legs in delight. No one was prepared for him to pick up a piece of toast and throw it into the melee.

"What's wrong with you people?" Darla screamed, pulling greasy bacon out of her blouse. "Jasper, take me home *now*."

As Sullivan tried to get up from his chair he slipped on a piece of bacon and fell backward, nearly sliding underneath the table. I clasped my hand over my mouth, trying so hard not to laugh. Shea scrambled away from his father and crawled on top of the table to start flinging breakfast foods at Darla and Jasper, who were still embroiled in a messy food fight despite her loud protests.

By the time Sullivan was able to collect himself and get to his feet, Jasper, Darla and Shea were covered in runny eggs, bacon grease and burnt toast crumbs. If Sullivan didn't look like he was about to blow a gasket I would have burst into hysterics.

"Get out!" his voice thundered.

"You're really going to talk to me like that?" Darla hissed.

"Get out of my house," he spoke through clenched teeth. "Grab your shit and get out. Now."

"Come on man, at least let us clean up first," Jasper had the nerve to argue.

Sullivan folded his arms across his chest and Jasper grabbed Darla's hand, leading her back to the bedroom where their bags were. It wasn't long before they returned wearing clean clothes, throwing on their coats and heading toward the front door.

"Nice meeting you, Jude," Jasper called, pushing Darla outside. "See you around."

After they were gone and we were left in complete silence, Sullivan quietly said, "I'll clean up in here if you wouldn't mind giving him a bath."

꘎

After the kitchen and Shea were cleaned up, Sullivan jumped in for a quick shower as I packed up our bags for the trip home. He was in such a foul mood that he didn't want to stay at the cabin any longer. He wanted to get home and forget everything that happened that weekend — most likely Jasper and Darla's antics, but perhaps the tender moment we shared before they showed up and disrupted everything.

He hadn't spoken a word in so long, I was startled when he addressed me in the car on the way to the airport.

"Why do you think he did that? Why would Shea throw the eggs at Darla like that?"

I had to think very carefully about how I answered. "Well, Shea is a lot like you. He doesn't like new people and Darla was intruding on what he probably considered family time. Then she had the nerve to present him with those nasty eggs without consulting his food choices. I think it was just too much for him."

"I suppose you're right. Was I too harsh in kicking them out like that?"

He was asking *my* opinion?

"I don't really think it's my place to—"

"I'd really like your opinion." He looked at me with his soft hazel eyes and pouted like a child, causing me to laugh.

"They were out of control," I answered honestly. "I didn't like how it was affecting Shea."

He nodded in deep thought, but had no response. As he stared out the window I noticed he'd done something different with his hair, and by something different, he did nothing at all. He was in such a hurry to leave the cabin he took a shower and left his hair to dry naturally. I didn't know what his normal morning routine was like, but it was obvious he took the time to style and spray his hair every day.

"I like your hair," I said, instantly regretting that I allowed my thought to escape through my mouth.

"Oh… thanks?"

It was obvious he was unprepared for me to make such a statement and I swore his cheeks flushed after hearing my words. His discomfort became clear when he immediately changed the subject as opposed to sticking with the silence he was so good at.

"My brother is brilliant," he admitted. "He's the smartest guy I know. But he takes nothing seriously and he's immature. He's always bouncing around from one idea to the next, one money maker after another, and all I've ever wanted was for him to be one hundred percent committed to our publishing company. I guess I'm expecting far too much for someone so young."

The fact that he would rather continue talking about Jasper instead of addressing a compliment I gave him spoke volumes.

"What would you change if you could?"

"I would like him to show up to the office every day. I would like him to work side by side with me to learn all the intricacies of the family business. I would like him to…." He stopped speaking for a moment then finished with, "I want him to be my partner, I want the two of us to be able to share in each other's lives, but the only thing we're ever on the same page about is Shea."

"At least you have that."

He shifted in his seat. "I suppose. I guess I shouldn't expect his dreams to be the same as mine. I have a list of lifelong resentments where Jasper is concerned. We can only stand each other in small doses, and I know we're equally to blame."

"Well if the business isn't suffering, and what you're doing works, why fix what isn't broken?"

"But it's *all* broken," he argued.

"Why? Because things aren't the way you think they should be?"

"Ms. Hastings, do you know anything about running a business?"

I knew this conversation had taken a turn that was going to end up in some sort of argument, especially since Sullivan was so prickly after the food fight that morning. I decided to end it before he became angry with me.

"No, I don't. I'm sorry."

And that was it. Nothing more was said the rest of the way home.

As Sullivan carried a sleeping Shea into the house and I headed toward the grand staircase to go to my apartment, he asked me to join him in the family room. As he placed Shea on the couch and began removing his coat, he said, "I'm sorry you had to deal with my family drama on what was supposed to be a nice birthday weekend."

"It was still a nice weekend."

"Even with my crazy brother and his genius girlfriend?"

"I kinda like your brother," I admitted. "The genius I can do without."

We chuckled and then his face became serious again. "Thank you for loving Shea the way you do… and this weekend showing him music, and dancing, and then his own voice. As hard as it is for me to admit, I'm happy you stumbled into our lives, even though you never wanted to be here. And you're right when you say you're the best thing that ever happened to Shea… to *me*."

Before that moment I'd never faltered in finding something to say in response to anyone, whether sincere, obnoxious or combative, but my mouth dried up leaving me speechless. I watched Shea's face as he began to smack his lips and started signing in his sleep.

Since I hadn't come up with a response to Sullivan's high praise, he then said, "You're dismissed, Ms. Hastings. Goodnight."

"Goodnight."

I threw my overnight bag over my shoulder and went upstairs to my apartment, falling back against the door once I closed and locked it. My heart swelled in my chest as I played Sullivan's words back in my head over and over again. He repeated my own words back to me, agreeing that I was the best thing that ever happened to Shea… to *him*. What exactly did he mean by that?

As I got ready to slip into bed my phone rang, and my heart raced wondering if Sullivan had more kind words to tell me. I wasn't prepared to hear Jasper's voice on the other end.

"Hey Jude," his voice sang.

"Hey Jasper."

"I can't stop thinking about you."

"Well you have to," I insisted.

"I was just calling to thank you."

"For what?"

"For the progress you've made with Shea, the way you love him. But mostly for how you've affected my brother."

"How do you mean?"

"He's still a rigid, uptight pain in the ass, don't get me wrong, but even I can see he's loosened up some. Maybe because of your relationship with Shea, I don't know, but he's *different*. It's hard to explain."

"Well I'll take it if it means he's a better person. We don't always see eye to eye, and we certainly don't get along very well most of the time."

"I don't believe that. You two were like an old married couple, very in sync when it came to Shea, even arguing in private behind closed doors. And then he came out and apologized… he *never* apologizes for anything! You've got something that speaks to him, whatever language that is."

Jasper's revelation made me uneasy, even though the idea that I had some sort of hold on Sullivan made my heart soar. I just didn't want to hear it from Jasper's mouth.

"Do you have any advice on how I can smooth things over with Ziggy? Get in his good graces?"

"How should I know?"

"Come on, help me out here. I promise I won't repeat anything you tell me."

I thought about the things Sullivan revealed to me in the car ride earlier that day, but I wasn't sure it was something that should be shared. If it could help repair their relationship, however, maybe I could divulge just a little bit of what I knew.

"I don't know," I grumbled. "Maybe spend more time at the office, or act like you're interested in learning the business. You know how important it is to him, but maybe you're too young and immature to take it seriously."

"But it's so *boring*," he groaned.

"Well it's not to him! His whole life is that business and you act like you don't even care. You're part of a family legacy and he's doing all the work."

Jasper was seemingly at a loss for words, saying nothing in return.

"I'm sorry." I felt guilty for being so harsh. "It's not my place."

"No, it's okay."

"He thinks you're brilliant," I tried to soothe the sting. "But please don't tell him I told you that."

"Huh. Well that's something I guess. Thanks, Jude, I'll talk to you later."

And with that he hung up the phone.

Chapter 12

The nasty egg incident caused Shea to revert to his fear of food, so it was back to peanut butter and jelly sandwiches at every meal. I had made so much progress and along came Darla to traumatize him back into his old ways with just one bad meal. Honestly, it was enough to turn me off eggs and bacon for a while.

A week after my visit to the cabin I was playing with Shea inside a newly constructed blanket fort, the most elaborate I'd ever created, and I was surprised to hear Sullivan calling my name. I must have really lost track of time, not realizing he was already returning home for the day. I poked my head out from inside the fort and looked up at Sullivan, who was grinning at me.

"You have a visitor," he said. "Someone who followed me home like a lost puppy."

Shea and I followed Sullivan into the kitchen where I saw Jasper greeting Blanche with a hug and a kiss, exchanging pleasantries like they were long lost friends. Shea ran at him full force, jumping excitedly into his arms.

"Goodnight everyone, I'll see you tomorrow. Enjoy your dinner." With that Blanche went home for the evening and I wasn't quite sure what to make of Jasper's visit, but I was taken aback by his appearance, wearing a business suit and a radiant smile.

"Jasper has decided to spend more time at the office," Sullivan explained. "Would you have anything to do with this, Ms. Hastings?"

"Not me, no," I answered far too quickly, shaking my head. I knew Sullivan wasn't buying it, so I quickly changed the subject. "You guys sit down and eat; I'll make Shea's sandwich." As I slathered the bread with peanut butter and jelly, I asked Jasper, "So… how's Darla?"

"Oh she dumped me in the car on the way home," he replied. "Longest ride of my life." He chuckled, which made me smile in response.

As the three sat down to eat their dinner, Sullivan said, "Thank you Ms. Hastings, we'll see you tomorrow."

This was extremely odd behavior, especially since I had eaten dinner with them since Shea requested it that first time. He was sending an obvious message, and the message was he didn't want me present as he ate dinner with his family. I placed some fried chicken, cauliflower and cornbread on my plate and excused myself with a smile.

"Wait, where are you going?" Jasper asked.

"My day is done," I answered with a smile, knowing it was also a bit of a lie. "It was nice seeing you again."

With that I went upstairs to my apartment and ate dinner alone. For someone who was such a loner I'd never felt more lonely in my life. The more I got to know Sullivan and his idiosyncrasies, likes and dislikes, and odd personality, the more I liked being around him. He was more relaxed than when we first met, and seemingly more at ease in my presence. He apparently listened when I said I liked his hair because he was wearing it naturally without fuss, and he looked more handsome than before. He smiled a lot more and sometimes when our eyes met.... No! What was I doing? Kissing the boss was one thing, but falling for him was something I couldn't allow.

I took a long, hot shower before bed, trying to rid my mind of Sullivan and Jasper both, knowing getting involved with either of them in an intimate way would ruin everything. I liked them both, in very different ways, but I needed to stay focused on Shea. Shea was the only one who truly mattered, and the other two would have to figure their relationship out on their own. I couldn't get caught in the middle.

I threw on my fluffy robe and dried my hair, and as I headed to my bedroom to settle in with some television, I heard a knock on my door. I knew Jasper was going to be relentless and I was a little annoyed, so when I opened the door expecting to see him, my facial expression took Sullivan by surprise.

"Is everything okay?" I asked, recovering quickly. "Is Shea okay?"

"Everything's fine, Ms. Hastings."

"Did I do something wrong?" Why else would he be knocking on my door without Shea in tow?

"I wanted to apologize for sending you away at dinner," he explained. "I realize we've been… going against my own rules for some time and I didn't want my brother to think I was getting soft."

I did everything I could to hold back a giggle. "I understand."

"You want to laugh, don't you?"

I covered my mouth with my hand and nodded as I watched his lips curl into a grin.

"Shea was quite unhappy that I sent you away, but Jasper was quick to fill the void."

"He loves Jasper."

"Everybody loves Jasper," he admitted with a sigh. "Look, Ms. Hastings, I don't want you to think I don't enjoy our time together, because I do. I just have rules in place for a reason, and I—"

"You don't have to explain. I understand."

"My brother is apparently quite smitten with you, but I'm sure you can see how problematic that is."

"Is that one of the rules I missed?" I teased.

"No, but perhaps I need to make it a rule since he has a fondness for fondling my nannies."

My stomach lurched hearing his words.

"Don't look so disturbed, Ms. Hastings. He's young, he's a party boy and he's quite charming. I'm well aware of his shenanigans."

"Where is he now?"

"He's reading Shea a bedtime story."

I cleared my throat. "Would you like to come in for a drink?"

He opened his mouth to speak, then paused, as if he were actually considering coming into my apartment. "Maybe another time, Ms. Hastings. Goodnight."

As he turned to leave I blurted, "I want a do over."

"I'm sorry?"

"The cabin. I want a do over, without Jasper and Darla and nasty eggs and gross bacon. I want the three of us to enjoy a weekend together without any disruptions."

Sullivan looked as though he wasn't sure how to respond to my request.

"We were having a nice time before they showed up and ruined everything," I added.

Sullivan smiled with what appeared to be a new twinkle in his eyes and replied, "As you wish. Name the date."

"This weekend," I answered quickly.

"Goodnight, Ms. Hastings."

He walked away and I closed my door, wondering what the hell I was doing.

༺༻

Jasper continued to follow Sullivan home every night for dinner that week, much to Shea's delight, but then I was forced to eat in my apartment alone and I resented him for it. On Thursday as I was leaving the kitchen with my plate Shea got up from his chair and yanked the back of my shirt. I looked down at him as he reached for my plate then let him take it to see what he was planning to do. The plate tipped in his hands as he wobbled back to the table and set it down at the seat next to his. Jasper and Sullivan stopped eating to watch the scene playing out before them.

::Sit::

"What?" I asked.

::Sit please::

"I have to go upstairs. I'll see you in the morning."

Shea threw himself on the floor and began punching and kicking the air in anger, as was his custom.

"Behave yourself," I scolded. "Get up and eat your dinner."

::No::

"Goodnight, Shea."

As I reached for my plate he kicked the chair and sent it crashing against my shin, causing me to howl in agony. Sullivan was quickly on his feet but instead of going to Shea like I thought he would, he placed his hands on my shoulders and gave me a look of concern.

"Are you okay?"

"I'm fine," I answered, glaring at Jasper as if it were his fault. His eyes grew large as he watched us, but he remained silent.

Sullivan then grabbed Shea off the floor and put him back in his seat.

"Enough!" he shouted. "You will *not* behave like that!"

::I want J::

"You will see her tomorrow. Now apologize!"

Shea's bottom lip began to quiver as he lifted his little hands.

::I'm sorry::

::I love you::

"I love you, too, Shea. Be a good boy and eat your dinner. I'll see you tomorrow."

I picked up my plate and went upstairs, limping from the bruise I could feel developing on my leg. I poured myself a glass of milk and sat at the kitchen table, staring at the lasagna and garlic bread on my plate. I hated it when Shea acted out like that, but what I hated even more was Jasper impeding on our family time. Then I realized how ridiculous I was being because I wasn't family at all, and Jasper *was*. Jasper was the one who had every right to be at that dinner table, not *me*. Once again I was learning a lesson in selfishness and I was the sole perpetrator of my own misery.

༄

I half expected Jasper to come home with Sullivan after work on Friday, but was relieved when he didn't. I wasn't sure if he knew whether or not I was going to the cabin that weekend, imagining he might call or stop by thinking I was at the house alone.

We were delayed heading to the airport, as Sullivan had a late office meeting, and then stormy weather kept us from taking off as planned. As we waited in the car, we all ate peanut butter and jelly sandwiches that I packed for the trip, then shared a thermos of milk to wash it all down. By the time we finally reached the cabin, it was long past Shea's bedtime and we decided to turn in for the night. Shea was sound asleep as Sullivan placed him on the couch to remove his coat, then I saw him push his sweaty hair away from his face and press his lips against his forehead.

"He's burning up," he said. "Could you please get me a cool cloth?"

I went into the kitchen and wet a washcloth with cold water, then brought it to the king bedroom where he was removing Shea's clothes. Placing him in the bed wearing only his underwear, he blotted the sleeping child's skin with the cold cloth and I was in awe of what a wonderful father he was. He had been through so much since his wife and daughter were killed, and he lived his entire life for the son who survived. I found myself wondering if he ever did anything for himself, anything out of the ordinary, anything *fun*. Upon first meeting him I thought he was a rich, arrogant, pompous ass, but in reality he was the exact opposite. I felt I was one of the few people fortunate enough to see the real man behind the façade, and it made me sad.

"Goodnight, Ms. Hastings. I'll see you in the morning."

"Do you need me to do anything?"

"Thanks, but no. Nothing out of the ordinary, really."

I went to bed and fell asleep as soon as my head hit the pillow, and in the morning as I went to use the bathroom I saw that Sullivan was lying on the couch with Shea stretched out on top of him, both sound asleep. I tip-toed into the kitchen to make a pot of coffee, then took a quick shower. When I came back out dressed and refreshed I could see it was still pouring rain. It was the first weekend in April and while the weather wasn't as bitterly cold, the rain didn't want to let up.

I was standing in front of the sliding glass doors enjoying the view and a cup of coffee when I spotted the lake that I somehow missed when the area was covered in snow just a week prior. I wondered if they had ever fished off the dock, or swam in the water, or caught fireflies on warm summer evenings. I didn't know how long Sullivan had owned the cabin, if it was a recent purchase, or something that had been part of his family for years. I tried to imagine Sullivan and Jasper playing there as boys growing up, but knowing the difference in their ages, it was probably just a fantasy playing in my head. Sullivan was already ten years old when his brother was born, and while Jasper probably looked up to him, Sullivan most likely wasn't interested in having him as a shadow.

I was stirred from my daydream when I heard movement behind me, turning to see Sullivan sitting up with a groggy Shea in his arms. Shea began to whimper, though his eyes were still closed, as Sullivan carried him to the bathroom. I couldn't help but notice he was wearing only his pajama bottoms, and his shirtless upper body looked good enough to eat for breakfast. I slapped my forehead, reminding myself why I needed to stop thinking about my boss in that way, and the reason I hadn't shaved my legs for the weekend.

When Sullivan returned with Shea whining and clinging to him, he sat at the table and threw his head back in frustration, closing his eyes.

"Did you get any sleep?" I asked.

"Not much. Between his tossing and turning, kicking, and vomiting, it was a pretty rough night."

Shea looked like a limp dishrag in his father's arms, trying to open and focus his eyes but losing the battle quickly. I set a cup of coffee on the table in front of him and asked if he was hungry.

"Coffee is fine, thank you." I caught him looking at the hot liquid before bringing the mug to his lips.

"Two spoonfuls of sugar and enough cream to make it blonde." He wrinkled his nose and I teased, "I pay attention."

"I guess you do. Thank you, Ms. Hastings."

"Can you please knock it off with the formality? Do you have to be in stuffy suit guy mode all the time?"

"Those are the only relationships I'm any good at."

"You need to loosen up. It's just *me*. You obviously took it to heart when I said I liked your hair when it's natural. Hair is a very personal thing you know."

He nodded and pursed his lips. "Yes… I listened. Leaving it natural saves me time. And I no longer smell like hairspray. It's quite freeing, actually."

"And has anyone noticed?"

"I don't think anyone has the nerve to mention such a thing to me, but Celeste certainly did."

"And?"

Sullivan took a sip of coffee and pressed his cheek against the top of Shea's head, causing my heart to swell. He replied, "She wanted to know why I hadn't told her I was seeing someone, then proceeded to badger me for her name."

I felt my cheeks flush and turned to pour myself a cup of coffee so he couldn't see my face. "And what did you tell her?"

"Of course I told her I wasn't seeing anyone, then she went off into fantasyland going on and on about how I've grieved long enough and it's time I put myself out there. She even offered to set me up on a blind date! Can you believe that? Who has time for dating or getting to know someone well enough to trust them with my son? Celeste needs to realize what it's like to live in the real world."

"Celeste does live in the real world. You're the one who lives in a bubble." He opened his mouth to protest but I was quick to cut him off. "I'm not saying that's a bad thing. Nobody understands what you've gone through, or the way you have to live your life with a deaf child. But *I* do, and if you're interested in someone to spend time with...." His eyes grew large as he sat up straight and took another sip of coffee. "I'd be happy to stay with Shea if you want to go out and have fun, or go on a double date with Celeste. All you have to do is ask."

He pulled a face that told me he had no idea how to process all of that, then Shea sat up and started to whimper, weakly raising his arms to speak.

::I want JoJo::

Sullivan got to his feet and shifted Shea onto his hip as he grabbed his coffee mug. "I'm going to give this one a bath. He stinks."

෨෯

The rest of the day was spent quietly inside, not only because it was still raining, but because Shea wasn't interested in doing anything but lie next to his father on the couch and watch his beloved Godzilla movies, even though he struggled to keep his eyes open most of the time. If Sullivan got up for any reason Shea would slide off the couch and chase after him, grabbing for him and whining, trying to pull him back to the couch. One thing was certain — when Shea was sick he wanted nothing to do with me. It was as if I didn't even exist.

"I'm sorry this weekend didn't turn out to be very exciting," Sullivan said, pulling a blanket over Shea once he settled back down.

I tucked my legs underneath me on the recliner as I replied, "Except for Shea being sick, it's all the excitement I need. The change of scenery is nice, and...."

He turned to look at me with a grin on his face. "And?"

"And it's nice to get to know you better. You know, without the stick up your ass."

"Have you been talking to my brother?"

"Nope. I make my own observations." He chuckled, taking it as the joke I meant it to be and then I asked, "Do you think Jasper will show up?"

"I certainly hope not. Having him at the office all week was unbearable enough."

"But I thought that's what you wanted!"

"So it was you!"

I squirmed in my seat. "Maybe."

"It *is* what I want, but not all at once like a blender ready to shred my face off. He can be overwhelming and I need him in small doses, if that makes sense."

"That's how you need *everyone*."

He pursed his lips and slowly nodded his head. "Perhaps." Changing the subject he added, "It's a little bit early for dinner, but I'm hungry. How about BLT's?"

"Sounds great."

As Sullivan tried to get up from the couch Shea immediately began to cry, even though he was sound asleep.

"I've got it," I told him.

"But the bacon...."

"I know how to cook bacon."

Shea's fever finally broke after we finished eating, but he was still cranky and clingy. He allowed me back into existence when I asked if he would like some apple juice, nodding and giving me a weak smile. He sat up on the couch as I handed him his special plastic Godzilla cup with an attached straw. He took a long sip of the cool liquid, then handed the cup to his father for safe keeping.

::*Thank you*::

"You're welcome."

::*3! 3! 3!*::

"Three? Three what?"

Shea hopped off the couch and opened the cabinet underneath the television where all the VHS tapes were housed. He pulled out a tape of *The Three Stooges* and handed it to me.

"He must be feeling better," Sullivan mused.

I put the video into the VCR and sat on the floor, leaning against the couch. Shea plopped himself onto my lap, reaching toward Sullivan for his cup of apple juice. He sat there quietly giggling at the antics of Moe, Curly and Larry and I was relieved to see he was feeling better.

"So do you really have a problem with Jasper wanting to see me?" I decided to ask. When he didn't answer I turned my head to see that he was sound asleep behind me, his head resting on the arm of the couch. I knew he was probably exhausted from being up all night with Shea and I took over from there.

I was able to put Shea to bed without argument around eight o'clock and as I returned from the king bedroom, Sullivan was sitting up and stretching his arms high over his head.

"I'm sorry for falling asleep, Ms. Hastings, I—"

I held a closed fist in front of his face, pretending I was ready to punch his lights out. "*Stop* calling me that."

He raised his hands in surrender and said, "I'm sorry, I guess I'm just used to being formal."

"Can you at least try to be a normal person while we're here?" I asked.

"Normal," he groaned, getting up to stoke the fire. "I don't even know what normal is."

"I can help if you let me. And maybe you should listen to Jasper once in a while."

"Listen to Jasper!" he choked out, walking into the kitchen. "Would you like some wine?"

"Sure."

I could hear him clinking glasses, opening and shutting drawers as he said, "You and Jasper have no idea what it's like to be my age, working all the time and taking care of a young child. A very needy deaf child, I might add. You're too young to know what real life is all about with your grand ideas about life and love."

He came back in and handed me a glass of wine, setting his down on the table, then disappeared back into the kitchen. I glared at him as he returned with a wooden tray topped with an assortment of meats, cheeses and crackers. He sat on the floor next to me and looked startled when he finally noticed I was glaring at him.

"You think I don't know what it's like to take care of a needy deaf child all day?" I hissed. "He may not be *my* child but *I'm* the one who takes care of him every day until you get home."

"Ms. Hastings, I—"

"Ziggy, if you call me that one more time—"

"Ziggy? Is that what you think you can call me?"

"What do you want me to call you? And don't tell me Mr. Sullivan. We've moved beyond that, don't you think?"

"Ziggy is fine, Ms… *Jude.*"

I grinned and took a sip of wine. "Thank you." I popped a piece of cheese in my mouth and said, "I love cheese."

"I know. I pay attention, too."

This took me by surprise, because I couldn't imagine for one moment why he'd be paying attention to anything I liked.

After an awkward silence, he said, "You're the only one who knows what my life is like. You're there for all of it… good, bad, insane."

"I know how hard that must have been for you to admit. Thank you."

"It might not seem like it, but I'm trying. We may be like oil and water most of the time, but I do listen."

"I feel like the stick is halfway out of your ass," I teased.

"So you and Jasper…."

"There is no me and Jasper. And I don't like that you're sending me away at dinner just because he's there. Do you know how that makes me feel?"

"Please don't take it personally."

"Do you really have such a problem with Jasper liking me? I mean, why can't we be friends? Isn't it better for Shea if we all get along?"

"Yes, but I know how Jasper operates and I think it'll end up in disaster if he gets what he wants from you."

He had no idea that ship had already sailed.

"Well I'm not interested in Jasper, but what does that say about me? It sounds like you don't trust me."

"I don't trust *him*."

"I'm done talking about Jasper. Let's talk about *you*."

He threw his head back, revealing his delicious neck as his hair bounced against his shoulders. "What do you want to talk about?"

He rested his elbow on the couch, then held his head in his hand, watching me with eyes that told me he was willing to let his guard down, even if it were only a little bit. My heart skipped a beat when I realized he had no intention of breaking eye contact with me.

"Your hair," I stammered. "You look younger."

"We've already talked about my hair."

"Okay, well… do you ever get lonely? Would you like to have a special woman in your life?"

"Why do I get the feeling you're trying to marry me off?"

We both laughed and it was nice to see he was more relaxed in my presence, comfortable enough to make jokes.

"Not marriage, but do you ever wish you had someone to do things with, just for fun?"

"I guess I don't really think about it much."

"What do you like to do? For fun?" I couldn't wait to hear his answer.

"Fun? Fun...."

Was it really that difficult to come up with something he enjoyed? "Wow, okay... it shouldn't be that hard."

"I'm really pretty boring."

"Oh stop it. You can't be crusty and boring *all* the time." I popped a piece of prosciutto in my mouth and enjoyed the way my tastebuds tingled at its mere presence. It was heavenly.

"I love the art museum," he began. "All museums really. Golf, baseball, the theater, the symphony, boating, travel, classic cars... I have a weird obsession with the Titanic...."

My skin pricked at the word Titanic. "I'm totally obsessed with the Titanic!" I nearly shouted.

"Well look at that," he teased. "Something we have in common."

"Real golf is pretty boring," I replied. "But I like putt-putt golf."

"Putt-putt... you mean miniature golf?"

"Yeah, same thing. Hey, I bet Shea would love to do that!"

He grinned and nodded. "He might, actually."

I wanted to change the subject back to *him* so I said, "You should take Celeste up on her offer. She probably knows some nice ladies you might be interested in."

He rolled his eyes then went to the kitchen to grab the bottle of wine, refilling our glasses before sitting down again. "You and your young, starry-eyed view of the world."

"I'm not starry-eyed at all. I'm the most cynical person I know."

"What about you then? Don't you get lonely? Don't you want to date? You haven't really left the house since moving in."

I didn't like that he kept turning everything back to me but decided to play along. In a nutshell, I told him all about my one and only boyfriend Colin, how we were together all four years of high school and until a year after Prude's death. I told him how he dumped me when I was taking too long to grieve, and that I'd never had a serious boyfriend since.

"I'm not very trusting when it comes to guys," I added.

"Can't say I blame you. After my wife…."

I waited for him to finish, but he took that time to eat some meat and cheese instead.

"I understand survivor's guilt better than anyone," I told him.

He nodded, his face holding an expression I couldn't place. After draining his second glass of wine, he filled it up again and wrinkled his forehead before taking a sip.

"I'm so out of the loop. I haven't been with a woman… I mean, I haven't dated in a very long time. I wouldn't even know what to do anymore. Everything's changed."

"Stop acting like an old grandpa. You're still young, you're good looking, and you have a lot to offer."

"You think I'm good looking?"

"You're okay."

We both tried desperately not to laugh, but burst into uncontrollable giggles. Once we gained our composure he cleared his throat and said, "Let's say I agree to Celeste's blind date idea… it's not likely I will, but just for discussion purposes."

"Okay first of all, you need to stop talking like you're your own grandpa."

"What's with the grandpa references?"

"You talk like an old man. So proper all the time. You don't have to be so stiff. You don't *always* have to be the smartest man in the room."

"Now you don't like the way I talk?"

"Stop." In my excitement to get him to understand my point, I scooted closer and he flinched, taking a sip of wine to recover. "You just need to loosen up. It would be one of those times when being more like Jasper has an advantage."

He looked like I just stabbed him. "I think this conversation is headed in the wrong direction."

"Okay okay, you said you wouldn't know what to do on a date. Did you mean where to go, what to talk about?"

"I suppose, but I'm always so stuck in a business mindset, how would I know if a woman even liked me? How would I know if she found me interesting or if I bored her to tears?"

"Well you might not always be able to tell, but pay attention to her body language. If she's into you, she'll probably smile a lot, but most likely she'll want to touch you."

He looked mortified. "Touch me?"

"Yeah, touch you." I moved the meat and cheese tray out of the way and sat as close to him as I could. "Depending on how close you are, she might touch your arm." I softly ran my fingers down his arm, then held his hand. "She might try to hold your hand. Hey, you have really soft hands. Anyway… um… she might rest her hand on your leg." I set my hand on his thigh and felt him tense up like a rubber band ready to snap. "Some women have a thing for hair, so she might curl a chunk around her finger like this." I got to my knees and gently wrapped a strand of his hair around my index finger. "Most importantly, pay attention to her eyes," I said breathily as I leaned closer to his face. "Smiles can be fake, but the eyes never lie. If she only has eyes for you, that's a good thing. If her eyes are darting around while you're talking, she's interested in everything but you. If you ask a personal question and she looks at the ceiling, she's probably getting ready to lie."

"How do you know so much?"

"I'm a woman."

"Your own playbook?"

"Maybe."

He swallowed hard and looked directly into my eyes as he whispered, "And what if I really like her?"

I touched the tip of his nose with my own and whispered, "You kiss her goodnight."

Chapter 13

A million thoughts went through my mind in the split second it took to decide whether or not I should let him make the first move. I touched my lips to his cautiously at first, fearing he would flinch or push me away, but to my surprise he leaned in for more as his hands gently grasped the back of my head. For a man his age he seemed unsure of himself, peppering my mouth with sweet, innocent kisses and sending my heart crashing into my ribcage like violent waves against an unsuspecting shore.

As he slowly introduced his tongue to mine I slid onto his lap and melted into him, surrendering completely as the sensations in my body drowned out the screaming protests inside my head. He tasted like wine and fancy cheese and it was a combination I liked very much. As his hands slid down and grabbed my ass I could feel his excitement growing underneath me, and as my body began to ache I wondered how long it had been since he was intimate with anyone.

He kissed a trail from my lips to my neck, and I threw my head back to give him better access. My skin was blanketed with his warm breath as his lips and tongue devoured me like a favorite snack he'd been deprived of for an eternity.

He kissed his way down my neck and toward my chest, where he stopped and whispered breathily, "Tell me when to stop."

"Keep going," I begged.

As he released each button on my shirt, he softly kissed the skin revealed underneath, sending chills rippling across my skin. I tossed my shirt on the floor then helped him out of his as he pulled me against him and kissed me hungrily, my fingers mangling his soft hair. As he successfully unhooked the back of my bra, a tiny cough was heard in the distance and I crab crawled away from him so quickly there could've been flames sparking between my palms and the throw rug.

He scrambled to his feet and pointed at me saying, "Don't move," then went to check on Shea.

Sullivan may have thought I was trying to ease his mind about hitting the dating scene again, but there was so much more to it than that. I knew he was too old for me, I knew his description of us being like oil and water was true, and I knew I didn't want to be involved in a relationship with him, or anyone for that matter. He was the furthest thing from my type so why was I falling so hard for him and why did I feel so guilty?

I lay back against the stack of pillows on the floor near the fireplace and covered my chest with my arms, waiting for him to return. I watched him exit the bedroom and fasten the hook lock at the top of the door before walking back to me.

"Is he okay?"

"Sound asleep."

"His fever hasn't come back?"

"Cool as a cucumber."

Relief rushed through me but it was soon replaced with an awkward feeling in my bones as he smiled at me.

"I can't do this," I said.

He ran a hand through his hair and said, "Okay. Why exactly?"

I glanced around the room, embarrassed to tell him the real reason. "I didn't shave my legs," I answered quietly, chewing on my knuckle.

He towered above me with a look on his face that told me he didn't know whether I was telling the truth, or pulling an unfair prank.

"So it has nothing to do with me being your employer… or being Shea's father… or that I don't own a condom?"

"All valid points but… seriously, my legs."

He fell to his knees on the floor beside me and grabbed my left foot, pushing up my pant leg to see the evidence for himself.

"You don't know what it's like to be a dark-haired girl," I tried to explain. "I have to shave every other day or I look like—"

"Do women really worry about things like that?"

I nodded.

"And in the heat of the moment do you really think guys care about that?"

I shrugged.

"We *don't*," he insisted. "*I* don't."

I smiled and sat up, pulling off my bra and tossing it on the floor. I stood in front of him and unfastened the button on my jeans, then slid down the zipper. He curled his fingers over each side of my waistband and slipped my jeans and panties off in one swift motion. There I stood before him, vulnerable and naked and wondering if he was going to follow through or decide sleeping with his nanny wasn't a very good idea.

I sat on his lap, wrapping my arms around his neck and my legs around his waist, whispering against his mouth, "I want you, Ziggy."

He grabbed my bare ass with both hands, lifted me into his arms and placed me onto the pillows before deftly removing his own pants and lowering himself on top of me cautiously. I kissed him hard, letting him know all I wanted at that moment was him, and he wasted no time breaking every employer moral code ever written.

To say Ziggy knew his way around a woman's body would be an understatement and as he expertly tantalized every one of my nerve endings, I briefly wondered how many nannies had been in the same position with him. The thought quickly left my mind because I was consumed with how it felt to finally be pleasured by a real man for a change.

I don't know what time it was when I woke up under a blanket on the floor next to the dying fire, but I couldn't help but smile at Ziggy's handsome, sleeping face next to me. I gathered up my clothes and pulled the blanket off of him, hoping to wake him. I admired his body and bit my lip as he began to stir, and looked up at me with half-closed eyes.

"Where are you going?"

"To bed. You need to get back in bed with Shea before he wakes up and gets scared because you're not there."

He looked so much like a disheveled teenager as he sat up and rubbed his face, then got to his feet and stumbled around trying to put his pants on.

"Goodnight, Jude," he mumbled, heading sleepily toward the king room.

"Goodnight, Ziggy."

I didn't sleep much that night, not that I expected to after the steamy connection I'd just had with Sullivan. I had no idea what the morning would bring, but I was prepared to accept it for what it was — one night of passion between two lonely adults who were in desperate need of each other. It's how I'd lived my life the last four years and I had no regrets.

As I opened my eyes the next morning, however, my heart swelled at the thought of seeing him, and all I could think about was greeting him with a good morning kiss. I was in serious trouble.

I hopped out of bed and swung open the door, but when I entered the living area I stopped dead in my tracks when I saw Sullivan sitting at the table with Shea and Jasper. What the hell was he doing there?

"We have a visitor," Sullivan explained the obvious.

"I brought donuts," Jasper said, his face covered in an infectious smile with a dimple in each cheek I'd never noticed before.

"He brought donuts." Sullivan took a sip of coffee as I tried to gauge the expression on his face, but I was clueless.

Shea finally realized they were talking to me and jumped off his chair to grab my hand and pull me to the table to join them. Being a little gentleman he pulled out a chair for me to sit in.

::Sit::

I smiled at him and sat down, then had to chuckle when he tried to push in my chair with my added weight. He struggled a bit before I helped him along, letting him think he'd suddenly developed the strength of a superhero.

I made a strongman muscle with my arm and said, "Strong!"

He grinned and I was so happy to see he was finally feeling like his old self.

::Drink?::

"Yes, please."

Shea patted his father on the leg.

"Would you like some coffee, Ms. Hastings?" he asked me, looking quite aggravated.

Ms. Hastings?

"Yes, please."

As he went to the kitchen area to make me a cup of coffee, he asked, "So Jasper, to what do we owe this unexpected visit?"

"Dad wants to know what we're doing for Mom's 50th birthday."

"You drove four hours for that?"

Sullivan placed a steaming mug of coffee in front of me as Shea climbed onto the chair next to me, pushing the box of delectable donuts my way. Shea watched me with a smile on his face, waiting excitedly to see which donut I would choose.

"Her birthday isn't for another two months," Sullivan groaned.

"Yeah, well, you know how impatient Dad is."

"And it couldn't wait until we got home this evening?"

Jasper glanced my way then shrugged, looking a bit embarrassed. "I guess it could've."

"Drink?" I asked Shea.

He smiled and pulled his glass of milk closer to him.

"Donut?"

He nodded and we peered into the box together. He pointed to a chocolate covered donut then pointed at me, knowing those were my favorite. I smiled at him and pulled that one out of the box as he continued to consider his options.

I pointed to a juicy looking jelly-filled donut and told him, "Jelly."

His mouth turned into a perfect circle as he reached in to pick up the jelly donut. As he set it on a plate I gave him a napkin and noticed the two adult men at the table weren't eating anything. I shrugged and took a bite out of my breakfast treat, the thickness in the air threatening to choke us all.

"They just opened a miniature golf place near here," Jasper mused. "Maybe we could check it out today since it finally stopped raining."

"Sure, whatever you want," Sullivan replied curtly. "I'm going to take a shower."

As he got up and disappeared I realized he hadn't made eye contact with me since I entered the room. I waited until I heard the water running in the bathroom before glaring at Jasper and whisper shouting, "What are you doing here?"

"I told you why I was here."

"I don't believe you."

He grinned devilishly and said, "Well, it was partly true. Why didn't you tell me you were coming here?"

"Because it's none of your business. I don't have to give you an itinerary of my life."

"But I love you."

"Stop saying that. You don't love me."

Shea had sucked all the jelly out of his donut and left its sugary remains on the plate, smiling at me with the sticky residue coating the corners of his mouth. He suddenly pulled a shocked face and pointed to the stereo system.

::Music::

::Please::

I cleaned off his sticky face and hands and we made our way to the stereo where I pulled out Ohio Express album to play "Yummy Yummy Yummy," his favorite song. He placed both hands on the speaker and bobbed his body up and down to the beat as I danced in place and signed the words of the song to him.

Jasper soon joined us and leaned close to my ear whispering, "See? *This*! This is why I love you! Nobody has ever connected with Shea the way you have!"

"Stop it. You love that I've made a connection with him, but you don't love *me*. It's two different things."

"You're wrong. What do I have to do to prove it?"

My eyes grew large as I replied, "I don't want you proving anything."

"I'll tell Ziggy, that's what I'll do. That'll prove it to you."

"That wouldn't prove anything and you better not!"

I heard the door to the bathroom open and grabbed one of Shea's hands to take my attention off of Jasper and focus solely on him. I swung his arm as he continued to bob up and down to the beat under his palm and Jasper boogied in place trying to fit in.

"Ms. Hastings," I heard Sullivan call. "Has Jasper told you that he's the reason my nannies are not allowed to have boyfriends at the house, or in their apartment?"

Jasper blanched and rolled his eyes, lowering his head.

"I'm sure he'd love to tell you the story," Sullivan goaded.

I looked toward Sullivan's voice and saw him standing there with a towel wrapped around his waist, revealing the rest of the body I devoured just the night before. He shook his head to get the wet hair out of his eyes and crossed his arms in front of his chest as he waited for Jasper to respond.

"Nothing, little brother?"

Jasper put his hands on his hips and exhaled loudly. "I'm the one who was in the hot tub with the nanny when Shea got out in the middle of the night."

From what I remembered he wasn't just *in* the hot tub with that nanny, but having sex with her, and because she couldn't hear Shea's door alarm he was able to escape. I couldn't believe that Jasper would put his own nephew in danger that way!

My shock at Jasper's admission subsided as it found another place to fester. Why would Sullivan tell me something so awful about his brother? Was he trying to turn me against him, or cause me to see him in a bad light so I'd stay away from him? I began to wonder if he was jealous of his younger brother, worried that I might actually succumb to his flirtation and persistence.

I left Jasper to care for Shea as I took my turn in the shower, trying to wrap my head around what just happened. It was painfully obvious the two could barely tolerate each other and I didn't appreciate being caught in the middle.

When I emerged from my room dressed and fresh as a daisy, Sullivan announced, "Let's get this over with," as he grabbed a jacket for Shea.

"Look, it was just a suggestion. We don't have to go," Jasper grumbled. "I thought it would be nice to do something as a family."

"I guess Ms. Hastings will be staying behind then?"

"I don't... I thought... why would she stay behind?" Jasper stammered.

"You want to do something as a family, and she's not part of this family."

Sullivan pulled Shea into his arms and walked toward the front door, leaving me speechless and Jasper struggling for what to do next. Sullivan opened the door and turned to glare at Jasper.

"Sorry Jude," Jasper said, following his brother to the door, leaving me stranded.

"Have fun!" I called behind them, almost relieved they were leaving me behind.

I knew the moment Shea realized I wasn't going with them, watching me from over his father's shoulder with wide eyes and a quivering lower lip.

::Come::

"Have fun," I said with a smile. "I'll be here when you get back."

Shea went into meltdown mode, throwing his head back and stretching his arms and legs out as far as he could muster. Tiny groans could be heard in his throat as he began to cry and frustrated, Sullivan set him on the floor to cool off. Shea ran to my side and grabbed my hand, trying to drag me to the door. I knelt in front of him and kissed his forehead.

"I can't go with you all the time," I tried to explain. "This day is for you, and Daddy, and Jasper. I'll be here when you get back."

::NO::

"We were having a perfectly good time until you showed up," Sullivan hissed.

Jasper laughed loudly. "You were having a good time? I doubt that very much."

"Go on," I urged Shea. "Ryan is waiting outside with the car."

Shea threw himself on the floor, kicking and pounding his fists as he bawled quietly beside me.

"Maybe it's time to go home," Sullivan suggested.

"Why can't she just come with?" Jasper hollered. "Is the nanny so beneath your highness that you can't stand to have her along?"

I could see Sullivan's nostrils flaring from where I knelt on the floor and the tension in the room was so thick I could almost chew it.

"Ms. Hastings," he began, slowly and quietly. "If you'd like to join us, it's entirely up to you."

He could barely look me in the eyes. I began to wonder if he regretted everything that happened between us the night before, and just wanted me to go away so he'd never have to face me again. I started to realize that maybe his antagonistic behavior that morning had nothing to do with Jasper at all, but everything to do with me.

I gently poked Shea's belly with my finger and forced him to look at me. "You can't do this every time you don't get your way."

::Mean::

"I'm not mean, you're being naughty."

::NO::

"Yes, you are. Now get up, be a good boy, and go have fun."

::Hate you::

"You don't hate me."

::Yes::

"You don't mean that. I love you, even when you're naughty."

Shea crossed his arms angrily and glared up at me, refusing to get up from the floor. Sullivan walked over and stood above Shea, giving him a death stare that caused him to squirm a bit as he nibbled on his fingers.

"Get up," Sullivan told him. "Or we're going home."

Shea scrambled to his feet then launched himself at me, wrapping his arms around my neck so tightly I almost couldn't breathe.

"That's settled then. Are you coming with us, Ms. Hastings?"

"Apparently," I whispered, getting to my feet while holding onto Shea, who was permanently attached to my neck.

As we exited the front door I set Shea on the ground and handed him his Godzilla mask, which he promptly pulled over his head. As the four of us walked down the sidewalk toward the waiting sedan Shea stopped dead in his tracks, his arms flying out to the side, frozen in place. The warmer temperatures brought the rain and now that the rain had finally stopped, worms were scattered all over the sidewalk.

Shea ripped off his mask and flung it in the air, slapping Jasper in the back of the head and causing him to stumble forward, knocking Sullivan onto his backside in the wet, muddy grass. Shea lunged at me, his fingers like claws as he tried to climb up my torso to get away from the wriggly creatures. Sullivan was shouting expletives at Jasper, who was laughing so hard he slipped on the wet grass, slammed against the side of the car and landed with a thud, the lower half of his body ending up underneath the car.

::Snakes::

::Eat me::

As I looked at the chaos in front of me I could do nothing but laugh. And laugh, and continue laughing. It served all of them right for being so unbelievably presumptuous, crabby and naughty that morning. I set Shea down on the front stoop as Sullivan and Jasper peeled themselves off the wet ground.

"They aren't snakes, they're worms," I explained. "They can't eat you, you're too big!" Shea looked up at me with his large, scared eyes and nodded. "The worms won't hurt you. They're sad because they need to get back into the ground. We have to help them."

Shea gasped and shook his head violently, backing as far away from me as possible until he was pressed against the front door. I didn't relish the idea of using my hands to pick up all the worms from the sidewalk, but I needed to prove a point to Shea.

As Shea watched terrified from the front stoop and Sullivan and Jasper stood wet and muddied from their tumble on the ground, I carefully picked each worm up with my fingers and placed them back in the grass. I didn't realize how many there actually were until it was obvious I was the only one who was going to help them.

Shea made his way cautiously toward me, taking a step back when he was too close for comfort. I pretended I didn't know he was there, and he inched his way closer wanting to see what I was doing. He slowly reached out his arm and I held a worm in my palm for him to examine at close range. He touched my hand with his fingertip and grinned at me. I nodded and smiled, letting him know it was okay. I plucked a few more worms off the sidewalk as he supervised my every move. I could feel the men, including driver Ryan, watching us intently but never offering a hand to help. Why was I not surprised?

Shea nervously reached a hand toward me, palm facing the sky, and I searched for the tiniest worm I could find to introduce. I placed the worm against his skin and he stood there like a statue, unsure what to do. His eyes were huge and his mouth was a perfect circle as he stared at the creature wriggling in his hand. He brought his hand up to his face to examine it more closely and when he'd had enough he placed it atop the grass and clapped excitedly.

::Helping::

"You are helping! I'm so proud of you!" I cheered.

"Are you seeing this?" I heard Jasper ask.

"I have eyes, don't I?" Sullivan sneered.

Shea and I were able to remove every last worm from the sidewalk and return them to safety, and when we were finished he jumped up and down for joy clapping his hands and smiling brightly. He ran over to his father and tugged on his pant leg, looking up at him.

::Helping::

Sullivan tousled his hair and smiled. "You're the best helper in the world."

We never ended up going to play miniature golf, opting instead to head home after cleaning up for the second time that day. After the tumultuous morning I was relieved, looking forward to going home and leaving Jasper behind.

As we returned to the house, Shea made sure to keep an eye out for any stray worms that might have found their way to the driveway or sidewalk, and quickly helped them back to the safety of the grass. As we entered the kitchen Sullivan pulled him up to the sink to wash his hands.

"I appreciate your patience with him," he said, never looking my way.

"You have the patience of a saint," I replied, trying to establish a line of communication so he wouldn't shut me out. "With Shea being sick all weekend and clinging to you like a vine, you never complained once."

"You don't get days off from being a parent."

"No, I guess not."

"Besides, complaining is for the weak." He dried Shea's hands with a towel and said, "You can go now, Ms. Hastings."

And just like that I was dismissed. I turned and went up to my apartment, falling on the couch when I got there, trying to understand his bizarre behavior. He didn't seem the type to take advantage of his nannies by sleeping with all of them; I didn't believe it for one minute. Yet he so easily shut me off as if nothing had happened between us. Was he that ashamed or embarrassed in the harsh light of day? The worst part was he hadn't looked me in the eyes once that day, and I'd never felt so insignificant. I wasn't expecting a romance to develop, but an acknowledgment of our time together would have been nice. A smile, or a knowing look would have been perfect. But there was nothing, and I had no idea if it was because he regretted what happened, or because Jasper showed up unannounced and set him off, leaving me out in the cold in the process.

Around Shea's bedtime I heard a knock on my door and took my time answering it, not wanting to look too anxious. Sullivan stood there with Shea in his arms, still avoiding eye contact.

"Shea wanted to say goodnight."

::*Goodnight*::

"Goodnight, Shea."

Shea held out his arms so he could give me a hug and a kiss goodnight, and I obliged with a smile. As he pulled away I realized I was lost for words for probably the first time in my life. I had never hesitated to spew whatever thought came into my head, and this time as they stood before me, I was silent. Had I finally been tamed?

"Goodnight, Ms. Hastings."

As he turned to walk away my wounded soul choked me as I mumbled, "Goodnight."

He turned back to face me and finally had the nerve to look in my eyes. I wasn't sure what I saw there but it resembled the same thing that clouded Colin's eyes when he broke my heart — pity.

"Last night was a mistake," his voice shook. "And if you want to stay in my employ we need to forget it ever happened."

I could feel the color drain from my face as my whole world seemed to float above my head, threatening to crash on top of me like a lead balloon.

"Yes," I managed to respond. "I understand."

"And stay away from Jasper."

He turned and walked down the hall as Shea blew goodnight kisses at me until they disappeared around the corner. I closed and locked the door, falling against it and sliding slowly to the floor where I ended up in a miserable, crying heap. I knew exactly what I wanted when I requested a do over at the cabin with Sullivan, and I had every intention of seducing him and I succeeded. So why did it feel like my heart was breaking all over again?

Chapter 14

The rest of that week was awkward, to say the least. The Sullivan I first met had returned and I was once again walking on eggshells in his presence. All the original rules that had relaxed a bit were firmly back in place, and even though Jasper was nowhere to be found, I ate dinner in my apartment alone. Monday was rough as Shea chased after me when I didn't join them in the kitchen to eat, and I was forced to turn my back on him. He kicked and pounded on my door until Sullivan brought him back downstairs and it broke my heart. On Tuesday it was the same thing, only Sullivan grabbed him before he could follow me. Wednesday he threw his sandwich at me and as I bent to pick it up from the floor he dumped his milk over my head. Thursday he ignored me and on Friday I was not invited to go to the cabin, unsurprisingly.

When Shea realized I was not accompanying them to the cabin he threw himself on the floor and added a new action to his temper repertoire — spitting. But the spit had to come down after leaving his mouth, spraying his face every time he did it. Sullivan's face looked like it was ready to pop as he snatched Shea off the floor and forced him back on his feet.

"You stop that nonsense right now!" he scolded. "Miss J is your nanny, not your mother!"

Shea burst into tears and my eyes burned, threatening to do the same. I hated seeing him so upset, especially about things he couldn't control, let alone understand. He was far too young to grasp why he was suddenly without a mother and his twin sister, and while he wasn't consciously trying to use me as a replacement, I was the closest thing he'd come to since that unimaginable loss.

"You're being too hard on him," I mumbled, kneeling to give Shea a goodbye hug. He glared at me with such icy eyes I could feel goosebumps erupt across my skin. "Maybe if you let yourself *feel* once in a while, you wouldn't be so angry."

"Maybe you should listen to your own advice," he spat.

Here we were, using secrets we revealed in a vulnerable moment at the cabin against each other in anger, like a bitter divorced couple.

I smiled at Shea and said, "Have fun with Daddy. He'll need help saving all those worms."

Shea cocked his head and shrugged, then nodded in agreement even though he still wasn't happy that I had to stay home. I didn't even wait for them to leave, getting up and heading back upstairs to my apartment. The truth was, without Shea I was lonely. He had become my whole world and I began to realize how dangerous it was for me to let that happen.

Having no appetite for dinner, I lit some candles in the bathroom and sank low into the lavender scented bath water. I had to figure out a way to have a life away from Shea. I wasn't his mother and I would never be his mother; I was simply the nanny hired to take care of him during the day and when his father was home, I was no longer needed.

Soaking in the silence of my own misery, it hit me like a ton of bricks. I was fearful that I was falling for Sullivan, that my heart had finally found a new man to send it aflutter, but that wasn't it at all. In the years after my heart-shattering breakup with Colin, I chose who I wanted to sleep with, and whether or not I wanted to see them more than once. Everything was on *my* terms, and I played by *my* rules. With Sullivan all of that was out the window as I couldn't just walk away after sleeping with him and never see him again. I had to face him every single day because he was my boss. I cursed myself for getting into that situation and knew I was the only one to blame.

I knew I had to start going out again, meeting up with friends, having fun like I used to. From here on out my weekends were mine to use as I wished and I needed to get back out into the land of the living. I decided I would give Linda, my party partner in crime, a call to see what she was up to.

My phone rang, startling me from my thoughts, and I rushed to get out of the tub without slipping, wrapping a towel around myself on the way. My skin pricked thinking something might be wrong with Shea, or worse, Sullivan wanted to apologize and profess his undying love for me.

"What are you wearing?"

"What the hell, Jasper! I was in the tub!"

"So you're naked?"

"What do you want?"

"I wanted to see if you went to the cabin this weekend. Looks like you didn't."

"Jasper, I really don't—"

"Aw come on, I'm just trying to be friendly."

"I know exactly what you're trying to get, and it's not going to happen."

Jasper sighed heavily into the phone. "I just thought you might want to hang out with someone fun for a change. Someone who isn't a four-year-old and someone who isn't my brother."

"I'd rather hang out with the four-year-old," I teased.

"You're breaking my heart."

"You haven't been over for dinner this week."

He was silent for a moment before he chuckled and said, "I don't think I'm really welcome."

"I don't understand why you two—"

"It's complicated. Besides, Ziggy made it clear he wants me to stay away from you."

This information didn't sit well with me. It was one thing to tell me to stay away from his brother, but to make the same demand of Jasper?

"I have to go," I said, hanging up without giving him a chance to respond. To keep from getting an immediate call back, I dialed Linda's number.

"Hey!" I said excitedly when she finally answered.

"Who is this?"

I was taken aback by her weirdness; she had always recognized my voice before. "Duh, it's Jude," I replied.

"Oh. What can I do for you, Miss High and Mighty?"

Her words struck me down like a sword. "What? Why would you say that?"

"You've been working for that rich asshole three months, and you're just *now* giving me a call?"

"It's been kind of crazy," I tried to explain. "My time hasn't really been my own most days."

"You got a taste of the high life and forgot about all us peasants," she grumbled.

"That's not true!" I argued. "You don't know what it's like here!" Before I could say another word she hung up on me.

I stared at the phone in my hand and really wanted to leave it off the hook if Jasper tried to call back, but knew I couldn't do that in case Sullivan tried to reach me for some reason. I dried myself off, put on my pajamas and went to bed early, wanting to pretend that day never happened.

At around nine o'clock the following morning, I was shocked awake by Shea's door alarm, and thinking they must have come home in the middle of the night I ran to find him. When I reached his bedroom, however, I found Jasper riding on Shea's child-size train wearing his conductor's hat, his knees up to his chin. He was clearly enjoying himself, his smile taking up his entire face. While I was relieved nothing was wrong, I was trying to wrap my head around what was going on.

"How'd you get in the house?" I asked, my hand over my racing heart.

"I have a key."

"Why are you here?"

"I need someone to play with today."

I sat on Shea's bed, thankful nothing was wrong, but disappointed they hadn't come home. Jasper stopped the train and plopped onto the bed next to me.

"Are you okay? You look like you just saw a ghost."

"I'm okay, I just… never mind. You wouldn't understand."

"You miss him when he's not here."

My face flushed at his accusation. "What?"

"Shea's a handful, but I know how much you care about him. And things aren't really the same when he's not around."

Regaining my composure I said, "That's true. He's my whole world and I don't really know what to do with myself when he's not here."

"You need to get out of this house."

"I tried calling my best friend last night and she hung up on me." Why did I feel the need to confess all this to him? "She called me high and mighty and was pissed I haven't called since I started working here. Maybe she's right."

"I know what being in this house does to people. It's gloomy, it's depressing and it messes with your head. I think what you need right now is a friend."

I did need a friend, but I didn't think Jasper was the person to fill that void.

"I know a great dive with the best breakfast. Hungry?" he asked.

"I don't think that's a good idea."

His face grew serious as he said, "I promise I'll keep my hands to myself."

"I just can't handle you hitting on me right now."

He grinned like a kid with a secret and lifted his hands in surrender. "I promise. Just friends."

I got up to leave Shea's bedroom, knowing any time I spent alone with Jasper would only end up in disaster. "No, I can't, but thanks."

"Why do you think Ziggy wants us to stay away from each other?"

I stopped in my tracks and turned to face him. "Conflict of interest I guess."

"You work for him, but he doesn't *own* you. Are you okay with him interfering in your personal life? Telling you who you can and can't see?"

No, I wasn't okay with that. Sullivan had no business telling me what to do during my free time, and I certainly didn't appreciate him dictating who I could and couldn't spend time with.

"I don't want to lose my job," I said, knowing losing Shea would destroy me. "I love working with Shea."

Jasper laughed out loud. "That's the first time I've ever heard a nanny say that."

I cocked my head and watched him for a moment before asking, "Just how many nannies have you slept with?"

Jasper looked at the ceiling as if he had to calculate the number in his head before answering me honestly. Whatever number he came up with I had no room to judge because my laundry list of faceless encounters would certainly put me in the slut category.

"Out of twenty nannies—"

"Twenty!"

"I'm not counting you, because, you know...."

"Twenty?"

"Out of twenty nannies there were four."

Four wasn't so bad, but my question was *why?*

"Did you do it to spite your brother? Did you like them? Why go for the nannies?"

He patted Shea's bed, encouraging me to sit back down. I got comfortable and waited for him to explain, a feeling of dread roiling in my stomach that Sullivan and Shea could return home at any moment and find us there.

"There's something you need to understand about Shea," he began, his kaleidoscope eyes very blue as he looked at me. "Shea was treated differently by his mother. Because he was deaf, not perfect in her eyes, she didn't treat him the same way she did JoJo. He almost didn't exist most of the time, and never really knew a mother's love."

"Don't tell me that!" I shrieked, covering my mouth with my hand to hide the shock and despair his revelation caused to flow through me.

"Ziggy was so desperate to keep a nanny that I thought a little seduction might help. It was a temporary fix though, because while those girls liked me okay and stayed longer than they would have, it wasn't enough to keep them from leaving."

"He never slept with any of the nannies, did he?"

"No. For all his faults and weirdness and unlikeable qualities, Ziggy has been an amazing father. And you're the first woman who has ever connected with Shea the way he deserves… with the love of a mother."

I continued to cover my mouth as tears burned my eyes, standing and walking to the door. I turned back, then headed to the door again, speechless. The last thing I wanted was for Jasper to see me crying, to be so emotional and vulnerable in front of him.

"I have to take a shower," I squeaked.

"Breakfast then?" I nodded and he said, "I'll meet you downstairs."

As the weeks went by I secretly saw Jasper on the weekends and he was a man of his word, refraining from hitting on me, touching me, or professing his love for me. It was nice to get out of the house and he left no experience ignored. We went to the zoo, to play miniature golf, horseback riding, to amusement parks, to the movies, to see local bands play in venues around the city, and to breakfast, lunch or dinner. He was behaving like the friend he promised to be, and the friend I so desperately needed at that time. It was a wonderful relief as my calls to Linda continued to be ignored.

Sullivan remained aloof in my presence and I continued to eat dinner alone in my apartment. He made it very clear I was not welcome to join them, and it was easier on both of us if we spent as little time as possible with each other. I did notice a change in Shea, however, and knew it was something I needed to bring to his attention. Shea and I had mostly good days with a difficult day thrown into the mix once in a while, but I noticed his demeanor would completely change once his father came home. He was always excited to see him, jumping into his arms for his daily kiss and hug, and he was eager to tell him about what we did during the day, or about something new that he learned. As soon as I would get my dinner, however, I could see him wilt in his chair and the twinkle in his eyes would completely disappear. Jasper's revelation about Shea's mother only caused the despair in me to grow and I couldn't let on to Sullivan that I knew anything personal about her.

One Friday at the end of May, Sullivan informed me that they wouldn't be traveling to the cabin that weekend, then asked if I would be willing to stay with Shea Saturday evening.

"Of course," I said with a smile. "Got a hot date?"

As he sat at the kitchen table and loosened his tie he replied, "Actually yes, Celeste set me up with an acquaintance of hers."

My heart fell into my stomach and thrashed violently as I put on a smile and pretended to be happy for him.

"That's great! Where are you going to take her?"

"I'm not sure. Celeste has everything planned; I just have to meet them where she tells me to go."

"So a double date?"

"Celeste knows me pretty well," he joked. "It's probably better to meet her in a group."

I swallowed hard and asked, "Do you know anything about her?"

"Her name is Antoinette. That's all I know."

"Well I'm sure you'll have a great time." I gathered up some leftovers for dinner, said goodbye to Shea, and went upstairs to my apartment where I promptly called Jasper to tell him we wouldn't be able to see each other that weekend.

The next evening Shea and I were in the kitchen eating peanut butter and jelly sandwiches with milk and a side of yogurt when Sullivan joined us and asked how he looked.

"Like you're going to work," I answered, eyeing his ensemble up and down. "You need to take it down a notch."

"How do I do that?"

He was a wreck and I felt a little bit sorry for him. It was like watching a teenage boy getting ready for his first date.

"Do you trust me?" I asked.

"Of course."

I stood in front of him and reached for his tie, causing him to flinch. "That doesn't look like trust to me."

"Sorry."

I loosened his tie and slid it out from his collar, setting it on the table. As I released the top two buttons of his shirt I heard his breath catch. "I think dressy casual is what you're aiming for. Keep the suit jacket, but the tie is too much. You're trying too hard."

He nodded, seeming to listen to what I had to say.

"Now your hair."

"What's wrong with my hair?"

"If you get too close to fire your head is going up in flames. What's with all the hairspray again?"

"I don't know, I just…."

"Go get your brush."

Sullivan rolled his eyes as if he were a child being scolded by his mother, but he didn't question me and left to retrieve his hair brush. I took Shea by the hand as we all went into the small bathroom off the main hallway. I set Shea on the sink and made Sullivan sit on the toilet and bend over as I brushed the hairspray out of his hair. His body jerked and he grunted as I hit some snags, but eventually I was able to brush his hair free of the sticky substance.

"Now blow it around with your hair dryer to bounce it back into shape, and no more hairspray."

Standing, he asked, "You enjoyed that, didn't you?"

I grinned. "Maybe." I looked up at him and pulled a face. "Dude, unless you want her to braid those nose hairs, you better do some trimming."

"*What?*" Mortified, he examined his nostrils in the mirror.

As he ran out of the bathroom I shouted, "No tiny hairs on the shirt!"

I noticed Shea was smiling at me.

::*Daddy funny*::

"You have no idea."

Sullivan returned home around midnight, finding me in the family room reading a book on the couch with Shea sound asleep on top of me. He shrugged off his jacket and sat in the chair across from me.

"Were you painting? You know I don't like paint," was the first thing he said.

"Water colors," I groaned. "Can't you just be happy he wanted to paint a picture for you?"

"Why is there tape on the floor in the front foyer?"

I rolled my eyes so hard I could see inside my skull. "I used the squares to teach him how to play hopscotch. Were you ever a child?" As he leaned back in the chair I asked, "So... how did it go?"

He rolled up his sleeves and ran a hand through his product-free hair. "She seems very nice, divorced, no children. She's a plastic surgeon, very independent, very active and quite beautiful."

I asked the only question that mattered. "Does she know about Shea?"

"She does."

"Will you see her again?"

He got up and walked over to the couch, bending down to slip the blanket off of a sleeping Shea. His face was so close to mine and all I could think about was whether or not he kissed his date goodnight, or more.

"I haven't decided yet," he whispered, lifting Shea into his arms. "Goodnight Ms. Hastings, and thank you."

Chapter 15

It was always clear to me that Sullivan's top priorities were Shea and the family business, so it wasn't a surprise that he didn't spend a lot of time obsessing over Antoinette and whether or not their relationship was going to develop into something more intimate than drinks or dinner here and there. The times they did go out together, which was always a weeknight, I was more than happy to stay with Shea, enjoying our extra time together and secretly hoping his father wasn't falling in love with this beautiful mystery woman.

Weekends continued to be family time at the cabin with Shea, however, which was a relief to me. I knew once Antoinette invaded that part of Sullivan's life, there would be no turning back. He rarely let anyone in as it was, and if he began taking her to the cabin on the weekends it meant he let her all the way in and I would quickly and easily be squeezed out. I couldn't stand the idea that any other woman could connect with Shea the way I did; to be as fiercely protective as I was. I couldn't bear the thought.

On a Saturday morning in early June, after being out late clubbing with Jasper the night before, I received a phone call from Celeste informing me we were going shopping together that afternoon.

"You need to find a dress for the party," she explained.

"Party? What party?"

"Mother Sullivan's 50th birthday party."

"I'm not invited to that."

"Oh, but you are. Zigmond told me to make sure you have a proper dress for the occasion."

"Why didn't he ever mention it?"

"I don't know, but today we're going shopping. I'll pick you up at one o'clock."

Celeste picked me up promptly at one o'clock and whisked me into the city to a dress shop I couldn't afford to pay attention in. When I asked the price of a sparkly red dress I saw hanging on a mannequin, Celeste pulled me to the side and gave me a stern look.

"No red dresses," she whispered. "And this is *not* the kind of shop where you ask what the prices are."

"What does that mean?"

"If you have to ask, you can't afford it."

"I *can't* afford it," I argued. "Why did you bring me here, and what's wrong with red?"

She was already visibly frustrated with me and we'd only just arrived. I couldn't imagine how the afternoon would progress from there.

"It's a black tie affair and you need to find something elegant, something black. After your red bikini fiasco, trust me when I say you don't want to stand out at this party. And Zigmond is paying for everything, so let's just find something you like."

The old me would have an argument ready to go as soon as she finished speaking, but the person I was in that moment chose to remain silent and let her do the job Sullivan assigned her to do. And apparently that job was to make me look presentable to his family and friends, and whoever else would be attending his mother's 50th birthday party. What I didn't understand was why he never mentioned it to me if he was so insistent I be there.

I settled on a sleeveless, knee-length, black satin A-line cocktail dress reminiscent of what Audrey Hepburn wore in the movie *Sabrina*, with tiny bows on the shoulders. Celeste promised it was the perfect dress for me and for the first time in my life I actually felt comfortable in my own skin, beautiful and elegant at the same time if that were possible.

"All you need is a set of pearls," she cooed, smiling at me through my reflection in the mirror as the shop owner finished marking up the alterations on the dress.

I smiled and replied, "I've got that covered."

When Celeste dropped me off at the house, I hopped into the Volvo designated for my use and took a drive to visit my parents. My mom looked surprised to see me when she opened the door.

"Jude... did you get fired?"

"Hi Mom, it's nice to see you, too."

She shook her head as if coming back to her senses and said, "Come in, come in. Would you like some coffee?"

"Yes, please."

I sat at the kitchen table as she poured me a cup of coffee, then smiled at her as she set it down in front of me. I added my regular amount of sugar and milk and said, "You haven't returned any of my calls."

"Well you know… we've been busy."

"I've been gone for five months."

Evading the question she smiled weakly and asked, "So what brings you by today?"

"I have a very important party in a couple of weeks and I was hoping I could borrow your pearls."

"Those were your grandmother's."

"I know, but they'll go perfect with my dress and I'm hoping they'll bring me good luck."

"Luck? Luck for what?"

So I don't make a fool of myself.

It was difficult to explain. "I don't know… it's a very fancy party and I just want to fit in."

"By the looks of that car you're driving you can afford to buy your own pearls."

"That's not my car," I protested quietly. "It came with the job."

"I'm sorry Jude, I just can't allow it. Your grandmother is the only one who ever wore those pearls, and the thought of something happening to them—"

"Never mind, Mom. It's okay. I don't need them that badly."

I took a sip of coffee and she looked at me strangely, as if she didn't recognize the person sitting in her kitchen.

"You've changed, Jude."

"What do you mean?"

"What have they done to you in that house?" she quizzed. "You're weak. You have no fight left in you."

When her comments didn't cause rage to boil inside me, I smiled and said, "That's because I finally found a place where I no longer have to fight to be seen. I love my job and they love having me there, and my opinion actually matters."

I got up and walked out of the kitchen and toward the front door, my mother chattering behind me, "Where are you going?"

"Home. Thanks for the coffee."

I walked to the car and I could see our neighbor nosily peeking out at me through her living room curtains. I got in and sat down, glaring at her through the windshield. Five months ago I would have flipped her the bird, then bent far over as I pulled my pants down and mooned her. I thought about the person I wanted Shea to look up to and admire, started the car and left without incident.

Thirty minutes later I walked into Sullivan's house, oddly enough the only place that felt like home at the moment, and found Jasper waiting for me in the kitchen. I had no explanation for what came over me, but seeing him caused me to burst into tears and he was there to catch me when I collapsed in his arms.

Jasper did nothing but hug me tightly and let me cry, which was exactly what I needed at the moment. It had been so long since I'd felt the strong arms of another person around me, wanting to be there, wanting to comfort me. We made no plans to meet at the house after my shopping day with Celeste, but I was so thankful he was there.

When I was finally calm enough to speak, I sat down at the kitchen table and he sat next to me, holding both of my hands in his. But as soon as I began to speak, to try and explain my out of character emotional outburst, my words came out in one jumbled whine.

"Only dogs can hear you right now," Jasper teased, his smile making me laugh. He got me a glass of water, then sat back down to listen to whatever it was I decided to reveal to him.

I had never intended to reveal anything personal to Jasper but ended up telling him my entire life story. I told him about Prude and my parents, her death, my boyfriend Colin, my path to self-destruction, how I ended up working for his brother, and that day's visit with my mom. For the first time since knowing Jasper, he wasn't quite sure what to say.

"And I'm not crying for myself," I insisted through my tears. "It breaks my heart that Shea was shunned by his mother because he was deaf. It's bad enough he lives in complete silence, but to be nonexistent to your own mother... it's not right! He deserves better than that!"

Jasper grasped my hands and gave them a gentle squeeze. "It's no wonder you and Shea made such a connection."

"But it's more than that," I sniveled with wide eyes.

I was beginning to realize that Jasper wasn't the person to share this information with. I wasn't sure he could handle it the way Sullivan had, and then he might only think I was out of my mind.

"I made an instant connection with Shea," I recovered quickly. "The night I met him he was like an uncontrollable animal grunting and climbing the shelves in his playroom, but as soon as he saw me he crawled right up onto my lap and fell asleep. And he doesn't know my parents rejected me for being the hearing child."

Jasper smiled. "Well however you ended up here, it's the best thing to happen to Shea. He's a completely different kid."

I wiped the tears from my face and nodded, knowing I was a completely different adult than I was before meeting Shea.

"You hungry?" he asked. "Want to go get some dinner?"

"I really don't feel like going out."

"Okay, that's cool." He hopped up and went to the refrigerator to inspect its contents. "Is that Blanche's lasagna?"

"Yep."

"Excellent."

"Do you mind if we go upstairs? Just in case your brother decides to come home early?"

"Sure, no problem," he answered with a wink.

Jasper pulled the pan of leftover lasagna out of the refrigerator, grabbed a bottle of wine and followed me upstairs to my apartment. I panicked when I thought about Sullivan coming home early and seeing his car in the driveway, but he assured me he had the perfect hiding place and it would never be seen.

As we ate a quiet dinner in my kitchen Jasper said, "At least now I understand the meaning behind your necklace."

I lightly touched the "P" hanging from my neck and nodded. "Did you know Shea talks to JoJo?"

"I've had my suspicions, but didn't really know for sure. Things were just never the same after he lost JoJo. I thought it was his way of coping."

We were both quiet for some time before Jasper asked, "Does Ziggy ever talk about this woman he's been seeing?"

"Antoinette? We don't really talk about personal things like that."

"He's so secretive about the whole thing. He won't even talk to Celeste about her, and she's the one who set them up."

"Maybe he doesn't want to jinx things."

"This might come as a surprise, but I just want him to be happy."

"I believe you. I also believe you love each other very much, but you're both just too stubborn to let your walls down and let the love in."

He chuckled and immediately changed the subject. "Do you think he'll bring Antoinette to my mom's birthday party?"

It hadn't even dawned on me, but now the thought of Sullivan bringing a date to the party made my insides churn. I quickly turned the tables on him. "I'm still trying to figure out why I've been invited."

He quickly swallowed the bite of food in his mouth and said, "Oh come on! You're part of the family!"

"I'm not part of the family. He's made that *very* clear."

"Maybe he thinks Shea will be more comfortable if you're there. He hasn't been in a crowd since the accident."

"Then why doesn't he just stay home with me then?"

"Oh no," Jasper said with a grimaced face. "My mom's only living grandchild will be at her party; it's not an option."

"But what if he gets scared? What if he can't handle it?" Having a meltdown in the middle of their swanky party was a very real threat.

"I'm sure Ziggy has thought about all the possible scenarios."

"But Shea shouldn't be put on display for all those people to gawk at or feel sorry for. You know he hates being the center of attention, and he's still afraid of so many things. Things I haven't even discovered yet, I'm sure."

"We just have to trust Ziggy's judgment. Or maybe you need to tell him what you're thinking."

"Maybe."

"Promise me one thing?" he asked, that familiar twinkle in his eyes. "Save at least one dance for me?"

"Only if your brother gives you permission," I teased.

⁂

Two weeks later was the day of the big celebration. Sullivan left early to meet Jasper at the Palmer House, where the birthday shindig was being held for their mother. They needed to make sure everything was in place and in perfect order before guests began to arrive for cocktail hour. I was honestly surprised he hadn't tasked Celeste with that job, but apparently there were things his OCD just couldn't let go of.

This put the burden of getting Shea dressed in his little tuxedo on me, so I locked him in my apartment to dress myself first and when I was all set I joined him back in my living room where he was quietly playing with a puzzle. He looked up at me from the floor with a smile that covered his whole face.

"What?"

::Pretty::

"Thank you. Now it's your turn."

We went to his bedroom where I dressed him according to Sullivan's instructions, but I'd never put anyone into a tuxedo before so I prayed I was doing it correctly.

As I put the finishing touches on his little bow tie I asked, "Are you excited to see Grandma and Grandpa?"

He wrinkled his nose and shrugged, his palms face up to the sky. I wondered how often he actually saw his grandparents, considering they lived in New York and the only place Sullivan ever traveled with Shea was to the cabin on the weekends. I learned from Jasper that the main hub for Sullivan Publishing was in New York City, and while their father controlled everything there, the brothers were in complete control of their Chicago office. Since Jasper was the unattached free spirit of the two, he was the one who traveled back and forth between offices when the need arose, leaving Sullivan to stay behind with his son.

::Handsome?::

"You are the most handsome boy in the whole world," I replied, smiling brightly at him. "Your dad will be so proud of you."

I knew that Andy was outside waiting to take us to the party and walked Shea to the front door where I knelt on the floor and presented him with a box.

"I have something for you," I explained. "Today is a special day for your family, and you need to be a very good boy. Open it."

I watched Shea's little fingers as he opened the box and pulled out a pair of child-sized aviator sunglasses. He shrugged at me, not understanding the sentiment.

"When you wear these, you will be safe and very brave."

Shea went into the coat closet to pull out his Godzilla mask, holding it out to me. The strong stench from the mask reached my nose quickly and I had to try every trick I knew to keep him from wearing it that day. It wasn't something Sullivan asked me to do, but I had to try.

I pulled a pair of matching sunglasses out of my bag and put them on. "I have some because I need to be brave, too. We can be brave together."

I helped Shea put the sunglasses on and his head was on a swivel, looking from one part of the foyer to another, up and down and sideways and he even walked over to the koi pond to check them out. He raced into the bathroom to see himself in the mirror then finally walked back and held his hand out for me to take, nodding.

"Are we ready to go?"

::Ready::

I took Shea's hand then grabbed my black bag, which I managed to fashion into an elegant cooler to hide away food he would actually eat, having no idea what the menu was going to consist of.

As I walked him out to the waiting sedan, Andy smiled and said, "You're a genius, Ms. Hastings."

I smiled and thanked him, hoping the rest of the evening went as smoothly.

Shea sat quietly looking out the window as we drove into the city, my stomach in complete turmoil thinking about the evening ahead of us. I had no idea what my responsibilities were supposed to be — was I there to enjoy myself as an invited guest, or was I doing my job and taking care of Shea? Sullivan never said a word about it and Jasper had no idea either.

Andy disrupted my tortured thoughts when he pulled up to the curb in front of the Palmer House and announced our arrival. He helped me out of the car then plucked Shea out of his carseat and deposited him on the sidewalk next to me, telling me to call whenever we were ready to head home. As he pulled away I swallowed hard, took Shea by the hand and walked with my head held high through the front door of the hotel.

It was never my intention to make a grand entrance, but with Shea strutting alongside me looking like my own personal miniature secret service agent, all eyes were on us as the entire cocktail crowd seemed to glimpse us at the same time. I took off my sunglasses and slipped them inside my bag, but Shea was allowed to keep his on as long as he needed them.

Sullivan was the first to reach us, lifting Shea into his arms and smiling at me.

"You're incredible," he whispered, looking astonished. "I thought for sure I'd be seeing Godzilla tonight."

"It took some coaxing, but—"

"It's time to be seated for dinner. The place settings are on that table over there." He pointed to a table filled with little gold cards, then walked away, carrying Shea with him.

I searched the table for a card with my name on it and heard Jasper's voice behind me. "Whoa. Is that really you?"

I plucked my place card from the table and turned to face him, smiling. "Like what you see?"

"Yeah, so let's get the hell out of here and go somewhere a little more private."

I laughed and tried to figure out which table I would be sitting at. "I can't make heads or tails out of this numbering system," I groaned.

"Jude!" Celeste greeted. "You're sitting with us."

"Why isn't she sitting with us?" Jasper asked, making a face.

I knew exactly why. I wasn't part of the family, as Sullivan made sure to tell me on numerous occasions.

"It's okay Jasper," Celeste cooed. "You can talk to her after dinner." And with that, she placed her hand under my elbow and led me to the table where she was the only soul I knew. She introduced me to her boyfriend and the rest of the people sitting in a circle, but never mentioned my relation to the family.

I craned my neck to look for the family table, spotting Shea standing on his chair and searching the room. I could only assume he was looking for me, but I had no way of being certain.

"Relax," Celeste told me. "You're off duty tonight."

I thought about the food in my bag and wondered how long it would be before the ice packs started to leak condensation all over the floor. I sat quietly as the salad was placed in front of everyone, knowing Shea wouldn't touch anything on the plate. I watched as Sullivan tried to get him to sit in his chair and he folded his arms in protest, standing his ground and refusing to budge. I tried to get a glimpse of the woman sitting next to Sullivan, assuming it was Antoinette, but he was blocking my view of her. All I could see was a mass of curly blonde hair fit for a runway model.

"Your dress looks fabulous," Celeste said. "Nice entrance, by the way."

The rest of the table agreed with her statement but I insisted it wasn't planned, that I was only trying a different approach to get Shea to the party without wearing his Godzilla mask.

As soon as I put a bite of salad in my mouth I saw Shea jump off his chair and march with purpose to where I was sitting. He was still wearing his sunglasses and pouted as he stared me down.

::Come::

"I have to sit here for dinner. Go back and eat with Daddy."

::No::

::Come with me::

"Shea, go sit down like a good boy, and I'll see you after dinner."

I knew exactly what was going to happen next, and I hated that he was going to throw himself on the floor in front of the hundreds of guests who were all watching us at that very moment. Before I could beg him to behave, Jasper appeared out of nowhere and placed a strong hand on Shea's shoulder, keeping him from throwing a tantrum.

"You're at the wrong table," he told me.

"No Jasper, really, it's okay."

"Take Shea, I'll grab your chair."

I was mortified as Shea grabbed my hand to lead me and my food bag to his table, Jasper following close behind us with my salad in one hand and my chair in the other. My face flushed with an intense fire as Sullivan and everyone to the right of him moved their chairs over to fit me in, nestled snugly between Jasper and Shea.

"Jude Hastings," Jasper announced as he pointed to each member of the family party, "this is my Aunt Sadie, my father Zigmond senior, my mother Yvonne, and Ziggy's date, Antoinette. Everyone, this is Jude."

"Nice to meet all of you," I spoke softly, embarrassment burning through my core. "Happy birthday, Mrs. Sullivan."

"Hello dear," Yvonne addressed me with a smile. "Please call me Yvonne. Jasper, you didn't tell us you had a girlfriend."

"No, no," I quickly corrected her. "I'm Shea's nanny."

"That's too bad," Zigmond grumbled. "He could use some settling down."

I could see the look on Sullivan's face out of the corner of my eye and he wasn't pleased. If his jaw clenched any tighter he would destroy half of his teeth.

"We've heard a lot about you, Jude," Yvonne said. "Except for the little tantrum Shea just had with his father a moment ago, I can see a remarkable difference."

"He's a remarkable little boy," I replied.

Shea shoved his salad plate away from him, knocking over a glass of water that I jumped up to grab before it ended up in someone's lap. I pulled a handful of grapes out of my bag and placed them in front of Shea, who smiled, removed his sunglasses and bobbed his head back and forth as he happily ate them. I could feel everyone staring at me and just wanted to run away. I quickly slipped his sunglasses back into my bag for safe keeping.

"Since when does he like grapes?" Sullivan whispered out the side of his mouth at me.

"Since last month. Keep up," I whispered back.

"I see you've come prepared," Aunt Sadie commented. "Smart girl."

Jasper patted my knee underneath the table, letting me know I was doing okay and that I should relax. As the family made small talk and I attended to Shea, I got a good look at Antoinette, who seemed to hang on Sullivan's every word, smiling and laughing and touching his arm whenever she had the chance. She was absolutely gorgeous, almost too perfect, like a doll. I wondered if plastic surgeons did favors for each other as they obviously couldn't perform surgery on themselves. As much as I didn't want to like her, I hoped her personality was as flawless as the rest of her.

When the servers set the main course in front of us — filet mignon with seafood newburg sauce — I thought Shea was going to jump out of his skin. He hopped off his chair and hid underneath it, Sullivan giving me an exasperated look.

"May I?" I whispered.

He rolled his eyes and nodded.

I asked the server to take Shea's plate away, since he wouldn't be eating it anyway, then pulled out a sandwich bag and showed it to him. He soon crawled out from under the chair and sat back down as I placed the sandwich in front of him, again with everyone at our table gawking at me. I pulled a small carton of milk out next and opened it for Shea, setting it on the table.

Jasper was happily digging into his steak and chuckling as he said, "I told you she was good."

Antoinette watched in amused horror as Shea enjoyed his crustless peanut butter and jelly sandwich while the rest of us ate like royalty. As the family talked animatedly around me, except for Sullivan who never broke from his normally quiet demeanor, I tried to get a read on everyone at the table. At fifty, Yvonne was a striking beauty with short dark hair and hazel eyes, her makeup impossibly perfect with diamonds decorating her neck and earlobes. Aunt Sadie must have been her sister, because they looked almost like twins. The business world had either aged Zigmond beyond his years, or he was quite a bit older than Yvonne, his hair as white as cotton and his facial features ragged with deep lines and a permanent scowl. Based on the few moments I experienced their personalities, Jasper was an exact replica of their mother, while Sullivan seemed to favor their father. The family dynamic was all beginning to make so much sense.

"When do we get to start dancing?" Yvonne asked. "I better get a birthday dance from *both* of my sons this evening."

"As long as I get the first dance," Zigmond said, cracking a smile as he kissed the top of his wife's hand.

"All of my first dances belong to you, sweetheart," she cooed, quickly kissing him on the lips.

Jasper cheered loudly and began clanking his glass with his fork as people usually do at weddings, and the whole room followed suit. Yvonne feigned embarrassment, but it was obvious she was enjoying the attention, and leaned in for a smooch from her husband. It was evident how much they loved and adored each other and I wondered if either of their sons were capable of the same kind of devoted affection.

Shea had no idea what was going on, but smiled and started clapping, mimicking what everyone else at the table was doing. He was so precious and within the depths of my soul I hated that he had to live in silence, even though he didn't know the difference. He deserved to hear the sound of his father's voice, the sound of laughter, the sound of music, and every sound his little four-year-old self created, including his butt bubbles.

Shea finished eating before the rest of us did and I pulled out two little cars for him to play with. He rested his head on his father's thigh and played quietly as the family stared with mouths agape. I couldn't stand feeling like I was under a microscope any longer and excused myself. I went to the restroom to pull myself together and when I exited Jasper was there waiting for me.

"Are you okay?" he asked.

"I just needed to use the bathroom," I said with a laugh that didn't even fool me.

"They're not staring at *you*," he said. "Believe me, they think you're amazing. They just can't believe the change in Shea. Six months ago he would've been hiding underneath the table, refusing to come out. He was always so miserable, crying and misbehaving, and now he's a loving, fun little boy. My parents were worried about having him at the party."

My heart swelled and tears burned my eyes as I touched the "P" hanging from my neck. "Thank you," I said, dabbing the tears with my finger before they ruined my makeup. "I just wish your brother had such nice things to say about me."

Jasper chuckled and replied, "You'll hear it from Shea's mouth before you ever hear it from Ziggy's. It's just not part of his character."

"I better get back. Thanks, Jasper."

He smiled and his eyes lit up as he did so. "My pleasure."

As Jasper headed over to talk to the DJ I went back to the table and sat down as the servers were clearing away all the dirty dishes. Shea sat up and held his arms out to me, so I pulled him onto my lap where he quietly snuggled against me.

"Everything okay?" Sullivan asked.

"Yes, everything is fine," I answered with a smile.

He smiled and nodded, then turned his full attention to Antoinette. I didn't have too much time to feel brushed off as Jasper was on the microphone addressing the room full of partygoers.

"Thank you to everyone who could make it to my mom's 50th birthday soirée. Everyone here means the world to my family in one way or another and we're glad you could all be here to celebrate with us. Mom, can you join me please?"

"Oh here we go," Sullivan grumbled as everyone in the room turned in their chairs to watch.

Yvonne got up from her chair and glamorously walked to where Jasper was holding court, her long dress sparkling with gemstones and beads flowing behind her. He handed her a microphone where she thanked everyone for being there and then they looked at each other and smiled.

"I promise we did not rehearse this at *all*," Yvonne joked, laughing and winking.

The sounds of the Beatles "Birthday" ripped through the crowded room and we were soon entertained by Jasper and Yvonne singing the song word for word to each other, then to the rest of us. As Yvonne held Jasper's microphone close to him, he sang and signed the song for Shea's benefit. One by one people got to their feet pumping their fists in the air, jumping up and down in their formal attire and singing along as a group. I had never seen so many happy, smiling faces in one place in my life. It was obvious that this family was well-loved and with the exception of Sullivan, a whole lot of fun.

As much as I wanted to remain in the background at this party, I hopped to my feet with Shea on my hip and pointed to Jasper so he would know what was going on. I danced in place as Shea bounced up and down clapping and smiling. It was then I noticed a photographer roaming through the crowd and hoped I didn't end up an overexposed party favor because of my connection with Shea.

::Dancing::

"Yes, dancing!" I replied, nodding.

Shea wiggled to be set free, and as soon as I put him on the floor he ran toward Jasper and Yvonne. Sullivan moved quickly past me to run after him, but I grabbed his hand and pulled him back. He gave me a stern look but stayed put, letting the scene play out without interfering.

Shea ran up to one of the speakers and placed his hand against it, then glanced over at Jasper and Yvonne and smiled, bouncing up and down to dance along with everyone else. She audibly gasped and stopped singing, then handed her microphone to Jasper as Shea reached out his free hand for her to take. Together they bounced as Jasper continued singing and the rest of the crowd spilled onto the dance floor, unable to help themselves.

I soon felt a hand on my shoulder and turned to see Zigmond standing beside me. "Looks like I lost the first dance," he said with a smile. "You're a good egg, Ms. Hastings."

I grinned because I couldn't think of anything intelligent to say.

Chapter 16

After Yvonne blew out the candles on her decadent chocolate cake with chocolate icing and cashew topping, Jasper pulled her out onto the dance floor for "their" song, "Dancing Queen" by ABBA.

"Remember how your mother used to dance to this song with Jasper when he was little?" Zigmond asked Sullivan.

The server put a piece of cake in front of all the place settings at our table.

"I remember," Sullivan replied, taking a sip of his coffee.

Shea wrinkled his nose at the cake and I pulled a container of blueberry yogurt from my bag and handed him a spoon. He ate it quietly and made no further fuss over the cake.

"Ms. Hastings, Jasper tells me you're a big fan of Willow Kelly," Zigmond commented.

I assumed Antoinette was feeling a bit left out when she blurted, "I love her books! She's an amazing writer. I've read all her books and I'm eagerly awaiting her next novel."

"Well you girls are in for a treat," Zigmond said, looking like a child with a big secret. "In December we will be publishing Ms. Kelly's very first illustrated children's book."

"That's awesome!" I exclaimed as Sullivan absentmindedly picked cashews off his cake and dropped them onto my plate.

"What about a new novel?" Antoinette asked, looking deflated.

"Probably not until next year," Sullivan answered.

"A children's book is sweet," she said.

Jasper, Yvonne and Aunt Sadie returned to the table to eat cake and Jasper pointed at Shea.

"You're in my seat, buddy."

Shea giggled, yogurt spurting out the sides of his mouth.

::Mine::

"Fine, I'll sit over here," he said, plopping himself between me and Sullivan. "Hey Ziggy, am I allowed to dance with your nanny?"

My face flushed at his brashness, but it really burned when Sullivan turned to glare at Jasper, saying, "I'm not her father. She can dance with whomever she chooses."

Jasper exaggerated a playful slap to Sullivan's back as he smiled and said, "Thanks, bro!"

Sullivan sucked in a breath and turned slowly to face Antoinette. "Would you like to dance?" he asked, taking her hand and helping her up from the chair. We all watched as they walked to the dance floor, embracing each other for a slow dance that made me cringe. Shea watched them intently, never taking his eyes off them. I continued to watch Shea as Jasper chatted with his parents about birthday memories of the past. Shea finally turned around in his chair and looked at me, pouting. I couldn't figure out what he was thinking, and he didn't seem to know how to express what he was feeling.

"The next song is for you and Shea," Jasper whispered.

"What did you do?" I didn't want anymore attention given to me.

"You'll see."

The next song the DJ played was "Yummy Yummy Yummy," by Ohio Express and I smiled at Jasper, plucking Shea out of his chair and pulling off his shoes then carrying him to the dance floor. I set him on the floor and danced while signing the words to the song he knew well and loved more than any other song in the world. He was frozen at first, not understanding why I took off his shoes, but as soon as he realized he could feel the beat of the music with his feet, he began to dance and sign along with me. I didn't plan for us to be the center of attention, but that's exactly what happened as the crowd on the dance floor parted to give us the spotlight in our publicly private moment. When the song was over and I stopped dancing, Shea noticed all the people watching him and ran into my arms, burying his face against my shoulder as I lifted him off the floor.

I returned to our table and sat down with Shea straddling my lap, his face pressed hard against my chest, trying to block out all the people he thought were still watching him. I slipped off his tuxedo jacket and removed his tie, hoping to get him more comfortable but he still clung to me like plastic wrap.

I was suddenly alone at the table with Zigmond, as everyone else disappeared to get drinks or head back onto the dance floor. He watched me carefully, then drank down the wine left in his glass.

"You know, I raised two sons, but you'd never guess it by their hair."

I giggled and said, "I like long hair."

"That must be why they keep it that way. *Girls*." After a pause he said, "My boys… different as the moon and sun, like trying to mix oil and water. But you seem to have a hold on both of them in some way. How is that?"

I wasn't sure what he was getting at, but it made me extremely uncomfortable. "I don't know what you mean."

"I see the way they both look at you. Both of them protective but trying not to let it show."

My jaw dropped at his revelation, but I wondered if he was just seeing something he wanted to see.

"Ziggy was taking the cashews off his cake and giving them to you. Why was that?"

"He knows they're my favorite." As soon as I said it, I wished I hadn't.

"I see," he said with a grin.

I tried to recover, and quickly. "Honestly, Ziggy is my boss and Jasper has become a good friend. What you're seeing is their appreciation for my relationship with Shea. Nothing more." Was I trying to convince Zigmond, or myself?

"Maybe my emotions over seeing Shea so transformed are clouding my judgment. I used to be good at this sort of thing."

I winked at him and replied, "That must be it."

"Are you enjoying yourself tonight?"

"I am, very much."

"Are you a guest, or are you working?"

"To be honest, I'm not really sure."

"That boy clings to you like a life preserver. He didn't do that with his own mother. *Witch*."

I wasn't comfortable with the way the conversation had turned, changing the subject. "Great music selection tonight."

"My wife and Jasper... their connection has always been music."

"And Ziggy?"

"Books. Ziggy was always the serious, studious child. Jasper is a free spirited goofball like their mother, and Ziggy is a curmudgeon like me I suppose. He can be like sand in your crack most of the time, but deep down there's a heart and soul in there. He just likes to keep it a secret."

"Well he brought a date to the party. That must mean something."

Zigmond waved his hand dismissively and rolled his eyes. "For our benefit, I'm sure."

"But he's been seeing her for several weeks now. I think they might be serious."

"She doesn't even know sign language."

"Is that a problem?"

"It is if she's going to have any kind of relationship with my grandson. Have you noticed she's made no effort to engage the child at all since he got here?"

"I'm sorry, I was too busy worrying about Shea."

"Exactly. What else do you have in that bag of tricks? It's like watching a clown car escape out of a Prada purse."

I started laughing, covering my mouth with my hand for fear of drawing attention to myself. "All that's left is a very wet ice pack."

"What's so funny?" Jasper asked, dropping down in the chair next to me.

Before I had a chance to answer, Sullivan was standing next to me with his hand extended. "Ms. Hastings, would you like to dance?"

"Back off old man," Jasper growled under his breath, taking my hand and pulling me off the chair with Shea still clinging to me. I passed

Shea to Sullivan and let Jasper lead me to the dance floor, where Huey Lewis & the News began to sing "Do You Believe In Love?"

"Did you plan this?" I asked.

"Of course." Jasper smiled as he wrapped his arms around my waist. "He'll do anything to keep us apart."

"First of all, there's no *us*. We're just friends, remember?"

"I really want to kiss you right now."

"Well that's not going to happen, and if you try I'll never speak to you again."

"Harsh."

"Your parents are wonderful," I said, wrapping my arms loosely around his neck.

"Yeah, we lucked out. My dad seems to be taken with you."

"Oh I don't think so. It's all because of Shea."

"Isn't Shea the key to everything?"

I smiled. "He certainly is, and he's the only boy for me."

"You're breaking my heart," he teased.

"Seems to me your heart needs a little breaking, Mr. Playboy."

He clutched his heart and pulled a face. "Mission accomplished."

I glanced over at the family table where Sullivan was struggling with Shea, who was crying and trying to get away from him.

"Something's wrong with Shea," I said.

Jasper turned to see what was going on then said, "Let his father take care of him. He's probably just tired."

As soon as the song was over I made a beeline to the table to see what the problem was.

"Well Ms. Hastings," Sullivan began, handing Shea to me like a football. "Shea thought it might be fun to rub chocolate frosting on Antoinette's dress. I'm going to see if I can get some seltzer from the bar."

"I'm so sorry," I apologized for the child. "Not that it's an excuse, but he's not used to being around so many people."

"Maybe that little animal needs to stay hidden at home where he belongs," she hissed.

"He's not an animal," I growled. I sat Shea on the table and said, "That was naughty! You say you're sorry to Miss A right now."

::No::

"Shea, you say you're sorry *right now*."

Shea pouted as he stared at Antoinette, who refused to look at him.

::I'm sorry::

"You need to be looking at him for this to work," I scolded. "Give the kid a break."

She turned her perfect head and glared at him, waiting for the apology he had already given her.

"Shea, she didn't see you. Tell her again."

::I'm sorry::

"How do I know he's apologizing?"

"Do you think I'm lying? He's four years old!"

"Are you his nanny or his *mother*?"

"Is that hair natural or does it come from a bottle?"

Sullivan returned with a clean towel and a bottle of seltzer water. "This should work," he told Antoinette. "Again, I'm so sorry. Shea doesn't usually—"

"So I've been told," she scoffed.

::Potty Mommy::

"I'll take him," Sullivan said, unhappy at Shea's choice of words.

"No that's okay, I'll take him. Stay with your date."

I passed Yvonne and Aunt Sadie on the way into the restroom. "Everything okay?" Yvonne asked.

"Yep, just a potty break," I answered, smiling.

"Here, let me," she offered.

As she reached for Shea he grunted and pouted, grabbing onto my dress so tightly I thought it might rip.

"Okay then, never mind. Looks like you have it handled." She smiled and they walked away.

Shea had to poop, which could explain his behavior toward Antoinette, but I wondered if it was more than that. Did he think

Sullivan was trying to replace me? While the idea brought a smile to my face I couldn't condone his behavior.

"Why did you rub cake on Miss A?" I asked as he sat on the toilet staring up at me.

He shrugged and raised his palms to the air.

"She's a nice lady. Daddy likes her."

::No::

"Well you don't have a choice. You need to be a nice boy."

::Sorry Mommy::

"Who?"

::Sorry Miss J::

"Are you ready to go home? I think you're tired."

::No!::

::Dancing::

"You want to dance?"

He nodded and smiled and I wanted to kiss his whole face.

"Here's what you're going to do."

I explained that he was going to dance with Antoinette, and when we found her, he would ask her properly and behave like a perfect gentleman. He seemed eager to comply.

When Shea was finished doing his business we washed our hands and headed back to the party. He walked up to Antoinette, who was sipping her wine at the family table. Everyone watched anxiously to see what he was going to do.

::Dance?::

He took one of Antoinette's hands in his and bowed, then stood upright and waited for her to respond.

"He's asking you to dance," Sullivan told her.

Antoinette smiled and nodded, getting up from her chair and following Shea to the dance floor. Sullivan breathed a sigh of relief as he leaned back in his chair and looked up at me.

"Did you do that?"

"Yes."

"Thank you. I owe you a dance. Or something," he joked.

By the time the birthday bash began to wind down, Shea was passed out cold in his father's arms and it was certainly a scene that pulled at the heartstrings. Sullivan and Antoinette were involved in a deep discussion where they spoke in hushed tones and I sat listening to Aunt Sadie complaining about how the party ruined her diet and that she'd have to get back on track on Monday. Jasper was dancing with Celeste but I was too busy watching Yvonne and Zigmond, dancing cheek to cheek with their arms around each other and their eyes closed, absorbed only in each other and that special moment. It seemed as though the affection they had for each other was handed down disproportionately to their sons — Jasper had too much and Ziggy didn't have nearly enough. It was odd to think about, but I wondered if true love really existed for my generation. Priorities were so different, and it seemed as though people were no longer willing to fight for what they loved, opting instead to just walk away when things got tough.

Sullivan and Antoinette got to their feet and he turned to me asking, "Would you mind taking Shea for just a moment?"

"Of course."

He gently placed Shea in my arms and walked away with Antoinette, his hand on the small of her back as they left the room completely. Jasper soon took Sullivan's place, sitting in the chair next to me.

"He'll sleep good tonight," he said with a smile.

"Let's hope!" The thought of hearing Shea's door alarm early in the morning set me on edge.

"The family is all getting together for breakfast in the morning. Will you be joining us?"

"I don't know anything about that, so my guess is probably not."

"Aw come on, you're part of the family."

"You may think so, but at the end of the day I'm just your brother's employee. And that's how things need to stay."

"We still get to sneak around behind Ziggy's back right?" he asked with a wicked grin.

"As friends, yes."

Jasper took in a breath then said, "You might not believe this, but I like having you as a friend. You're one of the few people I actually trust."

"Oh yeah? Why is that?"

"Because you never want anything from me."

My cheeks flushed as a huge smile crossed my face, only to be disrupted by Sullivan, rubbing his hands together and telling me Andy would be there shortly to take us home. He then slapped Jasper on the back and said, "Great party, well done."

Jasper looked stunned to be receiving praise from his brother, and frankly I was taken aback by it as well.

"Thanks, man," he replied. "We make a good team."

Sullivan didn't quite know how to respond to that, nodding and managing to say, "It's nice when we're all able to be together."

"It is," Jasper agreed.

"Where are his shoes?" Sullivan asked, turning his attention to Shea.

"Everything's in my bag."

Sullivan pulled Shea into his arms and he remained peacefully asleep as we said our goodbyes to everyone who was still there, reaching his parents and Aunt Sadie last. They were all hugs and kisses, even when saying goodbye to me, and I couldn't help but wonder why Antoinette wasn't there.

Yvonne was the last to say goodbye to me, placing her hands on my cheeks and looking directly into my eyes. "You are the miracle we needed in our lives," she whispered, causing tears to form in my eyes. "You've given my grandson life, and it's everything we've prayed for."

She kissed me on the cheek and hugged me tightly, causing my insides to quiver because I wasn't used to a mother — *anyone's* mother — loving on me so hard. It was almost overwhelming and just as I was about to burst into tears Jasper saved the day.

"Okay mom, my turn, my turn. Go kiss Ziggy." Jasper pulled me in for a friendly hug and whispered, "My mom made you cry, didn't she?"

I dabbed at the tears with my finger to keep them from falling down my face, her words more special to me than anything I'd ever heard in my life.

"Your family is so loving," I sniveled. "I'm not used to that."

"You make it easy."

"Don't say that," I gently scolded. "I can't handle it right now."

"Sorry. I'll see you soon," he whispered.

I followed Sullivan out to the car where he secured Shea in his carseat, then helped me into the sedan. With one hand on the roof of the car he leaned in and peered at me, but made no move to get in.

"I'll see you in the morning," he said.

"You're not coming with us?"

He looked hesitant to answer, then replied, "I've booked a room for the night."

I knew what that meant, and now it made sense why Antoinette disappeared before everybody said their goodbyes. She had probably gone up to the room to wait for him while she became a distant memory to his family.

"Oh," I said quietly. "Okay. Goodnight."

"Thank you. For everything. Tonight would have been an absolute disaster without you."

"It was nothing. Just doing my job." My throat began to constrict because I was close to losing control of my emotions completely.

"See you tomorrow."

Sullivan closed the door and slapped the top of the car to let Andy know he could drive away, and as soon as we began to move I burst into tears.

"You all right, Ms. Hastings?"

"Yes," I cried, embarrassed to be such a blubbering mess. "I'm just so proud of Shea." It was true, but that wasn't why I was such a wreck, and I scolded myself for being so stupid. Hadn't I learned my lesson the hard way years ago?

As Andy pulled up to the back door he asked if I needed help carrying Shea into the house, but I assured him I was fine, pulling him out of his carseat and bringing him inside. I thanked Andy for opening the door for me and he was off into the night.

I brought Shea upstairs to his room and placed him gently on the bed. By the glow of the nightlight I undressed him, careful not to wake him up. As I did so I wiped the tears from my face, angry with myself for letting my guard down and messing up my sensibilities. Once I slipped on Shea's pajamas, I put him into bed and pulled the covers over him. He began to whimper and even though he was still sound asleep I kicked off my shoes and stretched out next to him to let him know I was there. He curled up next to me and quieted down, and I felt some comfort being with him as well. It was such an exhausting day it didn't take long for my eyelids to feel heavy and I soon fell asleep.

I don't know what time it was when I was awakened by the light in the hallway, opening my eyes to see Sullivan stepping through the door. I sat up quickly trying to get my bearings and wondering why he was home.

I immediately began apologizing, thinking I was going to be reprimanded for falling asleep in Shea's bedroom. "I'm so sorry," I stammered, trying to fully wake up. "He was crying in his sleep and I —"

"You're not in trouble, Ms. Hastings."

"Oh God, please stop calling me that. That's what your father calls me now."

"I'll do my best," he chuckled.

"Why are you home?" I asked, getting to my feet.

"I didn't think it was fair that you took care of Shea nearly all day, and now I was leaving him with you for the night as well."

"I don't mind."

"You've gone above and beyond today, and I am more than happy to compensate you."

"Not everything is about money," I said, walking toward the door.

"Perhaps not, but there is another matter." I turned back to face him and he said, "I still owe you a dance."

"You don't owe me anything," I replied, thankful he couldn't see my burning cheeks in the dim light.

He held out his hand as I admired his uncharacteristically haphazard look, with no jacket and his bowtie hanging down his shirt that was unbuttoned low enough to reveal his toned chest. I hesitated, frozen in place, until he grinned at me and waggled his fingers urging me to join him. I didn't understand what was happening. Why did he leave the hotel to come home? Where was Antoinette? Why was he insisting on dancing with me in the dim light of Shea's bedroom? Had he gotten drunk between the time I left the hotel and he arrived home?

I let him take my hand as he pulled me close to him, my cheek pressed against the smoothness of his chest, soft and warm just as it had been the night I fell asleep in his arms in front of the fire at the cabin. My heart raced like a train as I tried to make sense of what was happening, and I knew I couldn't let myself get sucked into whatever head game he was trying to play with me. I couldn't put my wall back up and willingly give him the key to open the door.

We danced slowly together, barely moving much at all, as he wrapped his arms around me and rested his face against my hair. There was no music playing, only the soft sounds of Shea's breathing in the background. I could feel myself falling under his spell once again all the while my own voice was screaming inside my head to walk away.

"Thank you for loving my son," he whispered, causing a lump to form in my throat.

I wanted so desperately to look at his face, to see what he was feeling, but I didn't dare. I couldn't let myself be tricked by the intensity of the moment, or worse yet, fall into my usual trap of seducing a man there was no future with.

But isn't that what you do best?

I lifted my head to look at him and as he bent his face close to mine I stepped away and said, "Goodnight," making a quick exit and racing to my apartment.

I woke up to the sun shining through my bedroom sheers, no alarm, no panic. It was nine-thirty. I dragged myself into the kitchen, remembering I was out of coffee, so I headed downstairs to snag some from Ziggy knowing he and the rest of his family were out for breakfast on that sunny summer morning.

I shuffled into the kitchen with my eyes half closed and heard Jasper shout, "Morning, sunshine!" to which I was wide awake and face to face with the entire family eating a home cooked breakfast at the dining room table.

"Shit," I grumbled under my breath. "Sorry, I thought you were going out for breakfast."

"Join us dear!" Yvonne exclaimed, pulling out a chair for me.

"No, that's okay, I was just looking for some coffee."

"Don't be silly, Ms. Hastings. You have to eat breakfast," Zigmond encouraged.

Shea hopped off of his chair and took me by the hand, leading me to where he was sitting between Sullivan and Aunt Sadie. He pushed on her leg and glared at her, frowning.

::Move::

"Shea!" Yvonne shrieked, signing at him. "Don't be rude!"

I looked like a slob in my pajamas and crazy bedhead, and my morning breath probably smelled like something had died in my mouth, but there they all were staring at me. Jasper was trying so hard not to laugh, covering his mouth with his hand as I slowly made my way to where Yvonne had pulled out the chair for me, placing me between her and Zigmond. This did not sit well with Shea, who was at the opposite end of the table. As Yvonne dished up pancakes, scrambled eggs and bacon, Shea gave me a look of pure hatred, sitting with his arms folded in front of him and refusing to eat.

Sullivan patted him on the leg and said, "Come on, eat your breakfast."

He shook his head as he continued to stare me down, every eye turning to look at me. "I should go upstairs," I said, standing.

"Sit down," Yvonne ordered, and I obeyed without hesitation. She waved her hand in the air to get Shea's attention then told him,

"You are not the master of this house. You do not tell us what to do. You are the child, we are the adults. You do not own Miss J and she can sit anywhere she chooses, whether you like it or not. Now eat your breakfast and get that scowl off your face."

I don't know how much of her speech Shea actually absorbed, but his facial expression didn't change as he glared at her. I saw him slowly lift his hand and pick up a piece of bacon from his plate. The food fight at the cabin flashed before my eyes and I jumped to my feet.

"No!" I told Shea.

He grinned as the attention was taken off of him and placed on me, then took a tiny bite of the bacon he was holding in his fist. He kept his eyes locked on mine as his arm seemed to move in slow motion, raising the bacon in the air.

"Don't you dare!" I scolded, shocking everyone but Sullivan with my unexpected outburst.

Shea threw the bacon with all his might and it was unclear who he was actually aiming for as Jasper quickly caught it before reaching its intended target. I quickly apologized and went back upstairs, embarrassed that Shea had behaved that way because of me. All I wanted that morning was some damn coffee.

It wasn't long before I heard a tiny knock on my door and I flung it open to see Shea standing there crying. Yvonne was quickly behind him, scooping him up into her arms.

"So this is where the nanny lives," she commented.

Shea kicked and punched and squirmed until Yvonne set him back on the floor.

::I'm sorry::

"You can't behave like that," I replied. "That's naughty."

::Come::

He reached for my hand but I folded my arms in front of me so he couldn't touch it.

"He's certainly got an attachment to you, Jude," she marveled. "I'm not sure if it's healthy, but at least most of the time it seems to be good for him."

"He's come a long way, but he still has temper issues. I'm sorry if I overstepped—"

"Don't be silly. Now you need to come back downstairs and eat your breakfast or I'll never hear the end of it from my husband."

Shea threw himself on the floor, punching and kicking and spitting into the air, staring me down with angry eyes.

"The spitting is new," she mused with disgust.

"Yep, it sure is. Excuse me." With that, I closed the door and waited.

I soon heard a tiny knock on the door and opened it to see Shea standing there looking remorseful.

"Can I help you?" I asked him.

::I'm sorry::

"What are you sorry for?"

::Bacon::

"And?"

He thought about it for a moment.

::Spitting::

"And?"

He wrinkled his forehead, pulling a really hard thinking face.

"What did you do to Aunt Sadie?"

I could almost see the lightbulb go off over his head as he realized what I was talking about.

::Hit::

"That's right, you hit her and that's naughty."

::I'm sorry::

"You need to tell Aunt Sadie you're sorry, not me."

His bottom lip quivered as he nodded and looked up at me with the saddest puppy dog eyes I'd ever seen. He nodded and one huge teardrop slid down his cheek as he held his hand out for me to take. I held his hand as he led me back down to the kitchen where I took my place at the table next to Zigmond. Shea patted Aunt Sadie softly on the leg to get her attention.

::I'm sorry::

::Sorry I hit::

He lifted his arms for a hug and Aunt Sadie gladly accepted his apology. Shea then crawled back up onto his chair to eat his breakfast as the rest of the table fell back into normal conversation.

"So Ziggy," his father said. "Tell us more about this plastic surgeon you've been seeing."

"Antoinette is no longer in the picture," he replied.

I felt needles all across my skin at this news, staring at my eggs to keep from looking at Sullivan's face.

"That's too bad," Yvonne said, visibly disappointed.

His father humphed and grumbled, "Well that didn't last long."

"I don't need a woman in my life to be happy," he insisted.

"So you won't be seeing her again?" Yvonne prodded.

"Not likely, no."

It was clear his mother wasn't satisfied with that answer, and was really hoping he'd found a woman he could settle down with. "But she's smart and independent and beautiful. And she's a *plastic surgeon*." As if that would make or break the deal.

I looked up as Sullivan cleared his throat and wiped the corners of his mouth with a napkin. "Apparently someone overheard Antoinette referring to my son as an animal who needed to stay hidden at home."

Everyone around the table gasped at this revelation and my eyes grew huge as Sullivan looked right at me.

"That bitch!" Aunt Sadie exclaimed, quickly covering her mouth with her hand and apologizing for her language.

"Well good riddance to her then," Zigmond growled.

Jasper quickly changed the subject, saying, "We're all going to the zoo after this. You'll come with us, won't you Jude?"

"No that's okay," I declined politely. "I wouldn't want to intrude."

"Nonsense!" Yvonne said. "No intrusion whatsoever, dear. We'd love to have you join us."

"That's okay," I declined again. "I'm spending the afternoon with my parents."

Jasper knew that was a lie and raised his eyebrows at me, causing me to look away. I was pretty sure Sullivan knew I was lying as well. When Yvonne mentioned that Shea's attachment to me might be unhealthy, I began to wonder myself. He needed to spend more time away from me, and today was the perfect opportunity to make that happen.

I stood to leave, saying, "Thank you for breakfast, I'll clean up here after I take a shower. You all go ahead and have fun at the zoo."

I had nearly reached my apartment when Sullivan caught up to me. He looked so out of character and magnificently handsome in a pair of jeans and a t-shirt as he nervously rubbed his hands together.

"You're not going to see your parents."

"No, I'm not."

"Why won't you come with us? It'll be fun."

"Because I think Shea needs time away from me. He needs to understand that he can't always be attached to my hip and that I'm a separate entity from his family. I won't be here forever to take care of him, but his family will."

This seemed to catch him off guard. "Okay," he replied shakily.

"After what he did at breakfast, don't you think I'm right?"

"I suppose."

"Have fun," I said with a smile, opening my apartment door.

"Jude, why didn't you tell me what Antoinette said about Shea?"

I knew that was coming, I just didn't know when. *And he called me Jude.*

I turned to face him and said, "I didn't want to ruin your night. And I didn't want you to think I was…." I couldn't even bring myself to say the word.

"Jealous?"

I nodded, embarrassed, but he was looking at me differently than he ever had before.

"Who told you?"

"Jasper heard the whole thing."

"And you believed him?"

"Jasper may be a lot of things, but he's not a liar." After an awkward silence he said, "Jude… were you jealous?"

How was I supposed to answer that? Did he want me to be?

"No," I answered matter-of-factly. "But you can understand why I might be afraid you'd think that."

"Of course."

I looked into his eyes and said, "I just want you to be happy." I didn't give him a chance to respond, making a quick exit into my apartment and closing the door behind me.

Chapter 17

Sullivan and I came to an agreement that would help Shea begin to understand schedules and boundaries. He needed to realize that I was not his mother, and that his father was the one who made the rules and was in charge of everything, including my role in their lives. I ate dinner with them on Monday and Wednesday evenings, and weekends at the cabin were off limits to me, and understandably so. Evenings were when Sullivan and Shea had their family time together and when it was bedtime, I would get a knock on my door so Shea could say goodnight to me.

My days with Shea hadn't changed and with the warmth of summer in full swing I managed to coax him outside to play every day and more often than not he didn't want to go back inside. There was a side yard off of the kitchen where Sullivan had a jungle gym built that included a spiral slide, monkey bars, tire swing, trapeze bar, rope ladder, attached swing set and a secret roofed fort at the top of it all. There was room for a small children's pool where I attempted to teach Shea how to swim, and plenty of grassy area left over where we could play catch, tag, and soccer. Sullivan was actually thrilled on the days he came home to a dirty and sweaty little boy, and as long as the weather permitted, he would spend his time after dinner with Shea playing outside — no fears, no hangups, no tears. Just pure joy and contentment between a father and his son.

While my relationship with Sullivan had become more relaxed but strictly professional after the birthday party, I was no longer walking on eggshells and I continued to spend my free weekends with Jasper without his knowledge.

One hot Friday night in July not long after Sullivan and Shea left for the cabin, there was a knock on my door and I smiled, knowing exactly who I would find on the other side. I opened the door to find nothing but a note on the floor. I unfolded the piece of paper to see what Jasper had in store for me that evening.

You're It. Come find me.

Being with Jasper was often like playing with Shea, the only difference was Jasper could hear. I think that was why we had so much fun together; he wasn't afraid to be silly or embarrass himself or be the center of attention. The complete opposite of his brother, whose very own father called him a curmudgeon. He was far too young to be curmudgeonly.

I had no idea how I was supposed to find him in that expansive house, but I was on board to play his little game. Instead of searching feverishly for him at first, however, I took a detour to the kitchen and enjoyed a drink, then went into the family room to browse the bookshelves to see which novel I might like to read next. After about half an hour of pretending to search I made a concerted effort to look for him, and went into the party room where Shea's elaborate blanket fort was still set up. Just as I was about to leave, he poked his head out of the fort entrance looking all of fourteen years old.

"You're it," I said with a smile.

"What took you so long?" he teased, climbing out and running a hand through his hair.

"It's a big house."

"Great make out spot, by the way."

"Fat chance." We both laughed and I asked, "So what's the plan for tonight?"

As we walked out of the room and into the front foyer he said, "Pack a bag for the weekend. It's my birthday Sunday and I have a lot planned."

"I'm not staying at your place."

"I swear I'm not trying to seduce you," he promised. "You can stay in the spare room. I like having you as a friend and I don't want to mess that up."

I felt my cheeks flush at his admission. "I like having you as a friend, too."

"Besides, there might be some drinking involved and neither one of us should be driving."

"So what's the plan?"

"Tonight I'm playing in a charity softball game, tomorrow night I'm having a wine tasting at my place, and—"

"*Your* wine?"

"Yeah!" he said with an infectious smile.

"That's so exciting!"

"So yeah, my birthday is Sunday and I want to go out to dinner, maybe some dancing, and definitely club hopping. And I want to do it with you."

"Okay, sure. It sounds like fun."

"Jude, I know I'm a goof off and most people get tired of me pretty quickly. My humor can get annoying, and I really appreciate that you haven't pushed me away. Your friendship means a lot to me."

"It means a lot to me, too."

"And you might not believe this, but I think it's helping me get closer to Ziggy."

"I just want you both to be happy." And I meant it.

He smiled at me, his eyes twinkling like stars in the night sky. "Need some help packing your bag?"

"Actually yeah, since I'm not sure what to wear."

"Lead the way."

୨୧

Jasper lived in the penthouse of a new building on Lake Shore Drive, seventy floors up with breathtaking 360 degree views of Lake Michigan on one side and the Chicago skyline on the other. I loved to escape to the city so I completely understood why Jasper preferred to live there than in the suburbs like Sullivan. It was hard to fathom someone as young as Jasper living the high life with so many business ventures and a bank account I couldn't begin to understand the math for. He and his brother were both pretty grounded when it came to being successful not only in the business world, but in finances as well. Unless I'd seen it with my own eyes, I would never have guessed they were part of any publishing empire.

Jasper gave me the grand tour and my mouth hung open in awe the entire time. Everything was in perfect order and top of the line, which surprised me somewhat based on his childlike personality. He showed me his playroom last, which was full of model cities he had built himself, including trains of all types and sizes. It was a child's dream come true.

"I see where Shea gets his love of trains," I said, afraid to get too close in case I bumped into something.

"He loves coming to visit. I break the rules a bit and we stay up all night playing in here."

I wasn't sure why this revelation surprised me so. "He comes here to stay with you?"

"Only a few times a year, but yeah. It's nice to have him to myself once in a while."

I could feel my cheeks blush as a warm smile crept across my face. "That's incredibly sexy, you know."

"Maybe I should take him out to help me meet girls."

"Maybe you should."

That night at Jasper's charity softball game I was talked into playing as they ended up being short one player. We were on opposing teams and as I tried to score the tying run at the end of the game, Jasper, who was the catcher, stood waiting for me with the ball firmly in his grasp. I couldn't tell if he was going to let me score, but as I ran full speed to home plate, I tripped over my own feet and fell face first in the dirt. As the dust settled Jasper dropped the ball then grabbed my hand and placed it on home plate, ending the game in a tie, which for a charity event made everyone happy. As I tried to get the dirt out of my mouth I was informed that everyone was going for pizza and beer to celebrate. I imagined I looked like a dirty, sweaty mess, but nobody else seemed to care. Throughout the game and our pizza and beer celebration, I noticed a cute blonde girl with shoulder length bouncy curls paying a lot of attention to Jasper and I wondered if he had ever given her a second look. Aesthetically they would have made an adorable couple.

At one point during the evening, the cute blonde found me in the restroom and asked if Jasper was my boyfriend.

"God no!" I laughed. "He's just a really good friend."

"Is he seeing anybody?"

"Not that I know of. What's your name?"

"Tabitha."

"I take it you're interested?"

"He's cute, and he's really funny."

She seemed nice, and harmless enough. "I'll put in a good word."

She bounced on her toes and thanked me before running into one of the stalls to take care of business.

൪

After returning to Jasper's condo we each took a shower and met outside on the balcony where he had beer, chips and salsa waiting. It was a beautiful summer night and the view from where we sat was breathtaking.

"Nice game," I said.

"Thanks for being a good sport," he replied as we clinked our beer bottles together.

"So… Tabitha…."

"Who?"

"The bubbly blonde with the curly hair."

"Oh. What about her?"

"Are you blind? She's really into you."

"She is?"

I looked at him like he had just grown two more heads. "Seriously? Maybe you need glasses."

He grinned. "She's cute."

"You two would be adorable together."

"Trying to set me up?"

"I told her I'd put in a good word."

"Great, so it's all set. Now all we need to do is find someone for my brother." He clinked his beer bottle against mine and laughed.

"Aw, leave him alone," I groaned.

"You have a soft spot for him, don't you?"

I took a swig of beer and stared out into the twinkling Chicago night before answering without looking at him. "I see him differently than everyone else does, you know? I see him every day and working so closely with Shea... it's a complicated relationship but deep down I think he's a lost soul trying to raise his son the best way he knows how."

"Wow." He pulled a face that looked like I was feeding him a line of crap.

"Why do you two dislike each other so much? You should be thankful you still have each other."

"You think your relationship with him is complicated?" he teased. "There isn't enough time in a day to tell you all the reasons we don't get along."

"I have time."

He threw his head back, his long dark hair dangling behind the chair. "I didn't invite you here for the weekend to talk about *him*."

I curled my legs underneath me and smiled. "Fine. Let's talk about you then."

"My favorite subject," he laughed.

We talked late into the night and I learned that Jasper didn't want anything to do with the publishing business originally. Growing up all he wanted was to be a professional baseball player but once he discovered sex, everything else went out the window. All he cared about was girls and when he graduated high school he had no interest in following his brother's college path, instead choosing to dive head first into the family business so he could start earning a paycheck and living his own life. He claimed to have no regrets, but something in his voice made me wonder if he was truly being honest.

When I got up the next morning, I went into the kitchen to find Jasper frantically spraying the air, a cloud of moist particles floating down around him.

"Hold your nose!" he warned when he saw me. "Beer farts are the *worst*."

I began laughing until the stench reached my nostrils and the air freshener he was drowning in tickled the back of my throat, then I lifted a hand to my face. The next thing I saw was Jasper slipping on the air freshener that wet the floor, crashing to the ground. As I tried to help him up, I slipped and landed next to him, both of us flat on our backs staring at the ceiling and giggling so hard we could barely move.

"What's for breakfast?" I asked.

"Leftover pizza or cereal."

"Ooooh pizza...."

"I'll get right on that."

As we continued to laugh I asked, "Did that stench come from you?"

"Beer isn't my friend."

"I can see that."

"Have you ever farted during sex? Talk about embarrassing."

"Stop it!" I yelled, unable to control my laugher.

"That's why I never drink beer on a date," he continued. "Beer farts are the worst, but during sex you might as well have just shit the bed."

"Right now I don't know what's worse... your farts or the lavender scent mixed with farts!"

"You're right," he said, coughing and laughing. "Let's go out for breakfast."

We walked to a local place to eat then made our way to a street festival where artists were selling their handmade wares. Jasper said he was looking for a painting to hang over the fireplace mantel and he wanted something in place for the wine tasting that evening. After hours of walking and searching in the August heat, he finally settled on an oil painting of two hands, intertwined. It was the hand of a man and a woman, but the details were so intricate it looked like a photograph.

After getting the large painting safely back to his condo in one piece, Jasper pulled out a ladder and hung it over the mantel himself, then stood back with me to admire his new piece of art.

"Why this painting?" I asked, thinking it was a strange choice for him.

He stared at it with his arms folded in front of him for a while before answering. "I'm trying to envision my future, and I see myself settling down with the perfect woman for me and starting a life together."

This was certainly not the response I was expecting. "That's actually really romantic."

He smiled at me and said, "I have my moments."

☙

I emerged from Jasper's spare bedroom in the black dress I wore for Yvonne's birthday bash and found him helping a young woman with a harp get set up in front of the living room windows. This wine tasting was going to be a fancy affair, it seemed. Jasper pulled on his suit jacket and hurried toward me.

"How do I look?" he asked nervously.

Famous last words. "Do you ever look in the mirror?"

His face blanched. "Why?"

"Nose hairs! What is it with you and your brother? Get some scissors."

"Scissors?" He looked mortified, then grabbed my hand and dragged me into his bathroom. "I don't have any scissors." He pulled out a set of tweezers and handed them to me. "I can't do it."

"You want me to do it?"

"Please."

"I'm not pulling your nose hairs!"

"People will be arriving soon. I can't greet them with wandering nose hairs!"

He sat on the toilet and threw his head back, his eyes squeezed shut waiting for the pain. "You should really get some little scissors—"

"Come on!" I placed my left hand on his forehead to hold him in place, then yanked out the first hair. He nearly catapulted into the wall, screaming out in agony. "Are you done?"

"Nope. Hold on."

I pulled a few more hairs out of each nostril and he stood up, pinching his nose with his fingers, his eyes watering.

"Get some scissors," I said again, trying not to laugh.

"You pulled Ziggy's, too?"

"Um, no. He took care of them himself."

"Well thanks for doing mine."

"Between your beer farts and nose hairs, I don't know how you haven't landed your perfect woman yet."

"Very funny." He looked at himself in the mirror, examining the inside of his nostrils and I left him to it, heading back out into the living area where the caterers were beginning to set up the food and wine in the kitchen.

Jasper's wine tasting party consisted of twenty people and their guests, from wine distributors to newspaper journalists to high end restauranteurs, and while I had no idea who anyone was I felt comfortable enough to schmooze and mingle with all of them. Jasper, looking dapper and confident, was not only easy on the eyes but a joy to watch as he engaged everyone like a veteran who had been doing it for many years. He was utterly charming as he explained the concept behind Sign of the Times Wine, talking about Shea and his vision for charities who specifically work with the deaf. The passion he exuded was evident and he never faltered as he introduced each bottle of wine, its name and its unique sign language diagram. All in all there were six bottles, consisting of champagne, riesling, moscato, pinot noir, cabernet sauvignon and a sparkling cider for those who preferred a non-alcoholic option.

For someone who was so young, goofy and a bit childish at times, none of those things were apparent during Jasper's wine tasting. I was sorry that Sullivan couldn't see his brother in this environment, where he had everybody entranced when he spoke, hanging on every word. I'm certain he would have been extremely proud of him and found myself disappointed he wasn't there. If he had been there, however, I wouldn't have been, and I wouldn't have changed it for the world. It was an eye opening experience to see Jasper in such a mature, businessman role and I found it suited him well.

When the party ended, every guest left with their very own case of the six Sign of the Times wines, including the catering personnel and the harpist. I couldn't help notice that every person left with a smile on their face and fond words on their lips and even though I knew nothing about how the wine business worked, I felt deep in my heart Jasper had been a success.

As the last person exited the condo and we were finally alone, Jasper pulled me into his arms and danced around the room, deliriously happy at how things went that evening.

"That. Was. Amazing!" he announced, a smile permanently fixed on his face.

"You were fantastic!" I cheered.

"Time to celebrate!"

He opened a bottle of the Sign of the Times champagne, popping the cork without a single drop spilled, and poured two glasses. We took them out to the balcony and stood admiring the beautiful summer night sky over the lake.

"Thank you for being here tonight. I couldn't have done it without you," he said.

"Oh sure you could have."

"Well I could've, but I wouldn't have wanted to."

"To friends," I said.

"To friends," he repeated, clinking his glass to mine as we then took a sip. "You must be my best friend because I'd never let anyone else yank out my nose hairs."

"What do you normally do with them?" I laughed.

"Shove 'em back up and out of sight I guess."

"I think you're my best friend, too," I said dreamily. "I don't trust many people but I trust you."

He smiled and gazed at me with his stunning kaleidoscope eyes. "You really impressed me tonight."

"I did?"

"Nothing phases you. Money, wealth, big name business executives… none of it seems to make you uneasy. You talked to people like you owned the place and didn't have a care in the world."

"Money doesn't impress me," I replied. "We all shit the same way."

"Good point."

"I judge people by their hearts, not their bank accounts."

"Don't ever change, Jude."

"You had all those people captivated with every word tonight," I said with a smile. "You were absolutely amazing. Ziggy would've been so proud of you."

"Yeah, well… I didn't invite him because I wanted you here, so…."

"I can appreciate that."

"Whattya say we slip into something more comfortable and play with my trains?"

"Let's go."

❧

Jasper was still sound asleep when I got up the next morning, so I went into the kitchen to fix him a birthday breakfast. We were up fairly late in the evening drinking and playing with his trains, but I mostly listened with great interest as he painstakingly showed me every inch of the city he built entirely by hand, what materials he used, and the significance of every piece that was incorporated.

As I flipped the smiley face blueberry pancakes and cooked the bacon, Jasper appeared out of nowhere, flying past me on a skateboard wearing only a pair of cutoff shorts.

"Birthday bacon!" he cheered, his fists pumping in the air as he whizzed by.

He made a complete pass around the entire condo before stopping to sit at the counter where I was cooking. He looked like a teenager just waking from a party binge, his hair a shaggy mess and slits for eyes.

"Coffee?"

"Yes, please."

As I poured him a cup of life elixir I asked, "Aren't you going to tear up your floors skateboarding like that?"

"Nah. I had them specially treated." I didn't realize I was looking at him any particular way until he asked, "What are you grinning at?"

"You act like a goofy teenager who doesn't care about much, but the reality is you're brilliant. You're intelligent and you're a shrewd businessman. Why don't you ever let Ziggy see that side of you?"

"I guess it's more fun to live up to his stereotype. I'd hate to disappoint him."

"You really don't give him enough credit."

"I'd argue with you, but you're the one currently making my birthday breakfast," he teased.

"Your personalities might be like oil and water, but you're more alike than you think."

"It's my birthday, right?"

"Yeah."

"So my rules, right?"

"Okay."

"No more talking about Ziggy on my birthday."

I locked my lips with my fingers and made an exaggerated motion to throw away the key.

Chapter 18

After pulling on my mini-skirt of brightly colored faux peacock feathers, I pulled on the opalescent suit vest with nothing underneath and buttoned it up. I loved how it covered everything snugly and perfectly, but allowed just enough peaking cleavage to be sexy. I slipped on my favorite sandals then placed the finishing touches on my curled hair, securing it in an updo with sparkling butterfly bobby pins. I met Jasper out on the balcony, looking dapper yet casual in a pair of black slacks and a crisp, summery, white button-down shirt.

He took my hand and twirled me around to get a better look then said, "Looks like you're ready to hit the town."

"I'm always ready."

"But first, my present!"

He held my hand and pulled me inside, then to his bedroom where he handed me a small, gold box.

"It's your birthday," I said. "Why are you giving me a present?"

"Because I like to give gifts to people I care about on my birthday. Go on, open it."

I opened the gold box to see an antique necklace with a cameo pendant hanging from it. The cameo was a mermaid on a blue background and I gasped as I held it up to admire.

"It's carved from a shell," he explained.

"It's beautiful."

"My grandmother was obsessed with mermaids. That's why it's our company logo."

Of course! That's why there was a giant mermaid fountain in the foyer of Sullivan's house! The decapitated mermaid ice sculpture at the party… how had I never figured it out?

"Jasper, it's beautiful but I don't think—"

"Give me one good reason you don't deserve a nice gift like this."

I gazed into his kaleidoscope eyes, looking mischievously green at that moment, and smiled. "Thank you."

He took the necklace from my hand and turned me toward the mirror. I watched our reflection as he unclasped the hook from behind me and secured the pendant around my neck where the cameo fell perfectly at the point where the top of my vest ended.

With his hands on my shoulders he smiled at me through the mirror and said, "And see? It doesn't interfere with your 'P' at all."

I automatically touched Prude's "P" with my finger and nodded.

"Let's hit the road... I'm starving!"

Jasper's birthday rule number one was no talking about his brother. Birthday rule number two was no drinking and driving, so we hopped into a taxi and headed to dinner. We noshed on surf and turf served over a bed of rice, then had decadent chocolate mousse for dessert. I made sure to mention it was Jasper's birthday, so he was treated to the whole song and dance routine with sparklers to celebrate. The entire restaurant sang happy birthday to him, and while he tried to act embarrassed I knew he was enjoying every minute of the attention.

As we exited the restaurant to head to our next adventure, Jasper stopped to give a homeless man a wad of cash and the leftover food containers from our dinner. The man thanked him profusely as we continued on our way and I was amazed, but not surprised, by his kindness.

"How do you know he's not going to just buy liquor or drugs or something?" I asked, skeptic that I was.

"There were no conditions attached to that money. While I hope he uses it wisely, ultimately it's his decision."

I smiled at him, and slid my arm through his as we continued walking.

"What?" he asked, grinning.

"You just amaze me every single time I'm with you."

"Well prepare to be amazed even further because now we're getting to the fun part."

We walked a few blocks to a place called The Players Club and there was a line down the block waiting to get in. Jasper held my hand and walked up to the front door where the bouncer recognized him and led us straight past the velvet rope.

"How'd you do that?" I asked, wide-eyed.

"I paid for his daughter's braces."

I assumed a place named The Players Club was going to be a high society off-track gambling sort of establishment, but I couldn't have been more wrong. The three level building was thumping with sixties and seventies music, furniture and decor from the same decades, and games as far as the eye could see. Pinball machines, pool tables, table tennis, and board games every kid in our age group grew up playing; it was a literal playground for people who loved to play games of any and all types.

We walked up to the first bar and Jasper asked me what I wanted to drink. "Martini, lots of olives," I told the bartender.

"I thought so, but I didn't want to assume," Jasper said with a grin.

"This place is so cool!"

Jasper leaned close to my face so I could hear him without yelling. "It just opened last week. What do you want to do first?"

"It's your birthday, you decide!"

"You want to play games or dance first?"

"Games!"

He laughed at my excitement and took my hand, leading me through the crowded club until we found a table where a couple just abandoned a game of Battleship. I couldn't believe how excited I was to play the old games from our childhood and sat down to set up the ships on my game board.

We eyed each other menacingly over our games, sipping our martinis, eating olives and shouting "hit" or "miss" over the crowd noise, and I was enjoying every minute. I had never been with anyone who was as fun to spend time with, and I cherished the fact he was in my life. While I missed Shea horribly when I was away from him, Jasper was the perfect substitute.

As we were getting closer to the end of our game, "Gimme Gimme Good Lovin'" by Crazy Elephant blared through the club and I began chair dancing and singing the opening lines.

"From Atlanta, Georgia… to the Gulf Stream water… up to Califor-ni-ay… I'm gonna spend my life a-both-a-night and day and say…."

To which Jasper continued with, "Gimme gimme good lovin' every night…."

"J7!"

"Dammit!"

I loved winning just as much as anyone, but when I got up to rub his face in it I noticed he let me win, as I wasn't even close to hitting the final target. I drank the rest of my martini and sucked down the last olive and we moved on to our next conquest, first stopping at the bar for another drink.

We made our way to the top of the building where the dance floor was and found a table in the corner to people watch while we enjoyed another martini. When the Beatles' "And I Love Her" played and people began to dance closely and lovingly, I groaned loudly and threw my head back.

"You don't like the Beatles?"

"I do, I'm just sick of them."

"Why?"

"Jude and Prudence… Hey Jude… all the Beatles jokes growing up. We were dubbed the Beatle Twins and it stuck, and I *hated* it."

"What about Wings? You like Wings?"

"Wings?"

"Paul McCartney and Wings."

"I *love* them! Much prefer them over the Beatles!"

"I'll be right back." Jasper disappeared and returned a few minutes later with a smile on his face. "Let's dance."

Draining our drinks he pulled me onto the dance floor to the tune of "Lay A Little Lovin' On Me" by Robin McNamara and of course neither one of us could dance without singing the words at the same time.

Jasper sang, "Ever since we kissed that night…."

"Ever since I held you tight…."

"I just don't want nobody else…."

"So put your lips on mine...."
"Leave them there 'til the morning time...."
"Lord don't leave me by myself!" I screeched.

People were laughing as we continued to entertain those around us with our fabulous vocals and smooth dance moves. When the song ended, "My Love," by Paul McCartney and Wings began to play and I smiled at Jasper who was grinning like a kid at Christmas. He pulled me close to him as we slow danced in each other's arms and I'd never felt more comfortable with him. I closed my eyes and brushed my cheek against his soft hair, feeling his breath against my neck. My thoughts left Jasper and joined Sullivan and Shea at the cabin, wondering what they were doing at that moment. They were probably both sound asleep, but I couldn't stop thinking about Shea's precious face and how much I missed him when we were apart.

When the song ended we were off to get another martini and find a new game to play, sitting at a table with another couple to play a rousing game of Operation. They were no match for me and Jasper, as they were too drunk to grab a game piece without setting the buzzer off, so that was an easy win. More drinks, more games, and what was supposed to be a club hopping evening for Jasper's birthday turned into us having a blast at one place, and we were both okay with that.

We eventually joined a group of three other couples for a sloppy game of 8-Ball at the pool table, and it was decided that it would be men versus women. This made things even more interesting because the other three women were doing everything possible to distract their partners when it was their turn, so drunk they didn't care if they flashed a boob or a butt cheek. Jasper and I found them utterly ridiculous but amusing, laughing along with them while not participating in their game of distraction. They assumed we were shy and awkward young twenty-somethings on a first date, but they had no idea what our entire history consisted of. We just laughed and let them think whatever they wanted. At one point I leaned over to take a shot with my pool cue and looked up to see Jasper grinning, realizing he could see straight into my vest.

We lost that game, but said goodbye to our new drunk friends and moved along, my head feeling a bit fuzzy as the alcohol consumption caught up to me. We stumbled to the back of the room where a separate bar was set up specifically for shots, accompanied by a row of six vintage barber chairs. I leaned hard against Jasper as we watched what was taking place and he seemed eager to give it a try. The way it worked was a person sat in the barber chair which was then reclined as far back as it would go, and the bartender accompanying that particular chair would pour the alcohol straight into the person's mouth, no shot glass in sight. On a blackboard behind the chairs was a huge list of all the flavorful shot concoctions they offered and some of them were mouthwatering to think about. The bartenders were very good at what they did, because every drop they poured made it into the customer's mouth without any spillage.

"You wanna try it?" Jasper asked, smiling.

"You first."

Jasper chose a fiery cinnamon concoction and when he got up from the chair stumbled my way, falling into my arms as I caught him.

"That was intense!" he cheered. "You next!"

I chose a chocolate covered cherry mixture, then sat in the barber chair and closed my eyes as they reclined it as far back as it would go. I opened my eyes to see Jasper grinning like a mischievous child as I opened my mouth and welcomed the alcoholic liquid. It really did taste like a chocolate covered cherry and when they whipped the chair back into the sitting position I was a bit lightheaded, stumbling toward Jasper as he had done to me. Clinging to each other to stay upright we laughed and decided what to do next.

"I need food," I said unapologetically.

"Me, too."

Jasper took me by the hand and we walked out of the club into the fresh air, which was warm and breezy, but not stifling like it had been all day. We walked hand in hand if for no other reason than to hold each other up.

"There's a great diner a couple blocks down," Jasper said. "Let's split a burger and fries and then we can get a banana split."

"I'll share your burger and fries, but I'm not sharing a banana split."

"Hell no! I don't share my ice cream. Not even with you."

"Harsh," I teased.

He put an arm around my neck and gently squeezed, further cementing our friendly bond. We had sobered up a bit by the time we walked in the door of the diner and Jasper ordered for both of us before the waitress even brought menus. We quickly chowed down the burger and fries we shared, and when the banana splits were set in front of us Jasper looked at me with sadness in his eyes.

"Why don't you love me?" he asked.

After the night we'd been having I was blindsided by his question, but it was easy for me to answer as I reached across the table and cupped my hand over his.

"I do love you, Jasper. Just not the way you want."

"I honestly don't know what I want. I mean, it would be nice to have someone to share my life with, but I enjoy the time we spend together and—"

"Don't you dare use me as an excuse not to get involved with someone."

"But it's so easy with you."

"You're the only one who's ever said that to me."

"You don't give guys much of a chance," he teased.

"Touché."

He smiled at me and the twinkle in his beautiful eyes was almost difficult to resist. "So where to next?" he changed the subject.

"How about returning to the scene of the crime?"

A mischievous grin crept across his face as he said, "I like the sound of that. Now tell me what you're talking about."

"The place where we first met. It's not far from here."

"The Cheetah Club?" he laughed loudly, slapping his hands together.

"It might be fun for some of those hateful bitches to wait on me. I say we walk in and own the place."

"Like you and Shea owned my mom's birthday party?"

"Stop. We did not."

"Oh you certainly did," he chuckled. "All eyes were on the two of you when you walked in. Getting him to wear those sunglasses instead of his mask... you're a genius. Ziggy was nervous about mini-Godzilla making an appearance and he had nothing to worry about. My parents love you, by the way."

My face warmed as I covered the smile that immediately crossed my face. "I think they're pretty great. They made me feel like part of the family."

"It doesn't matter what Ziggy thinks. You *are* part of the family."

Ziggy. I was sure he only thought of me as the slutty nanny who took care of his son.

Jasper paid the bill and we headed back out into the night, in the direction of the Cheetah Club. I wondered if Carl was still a bartender there, and if I would recognize any of the others who currently worked there. And if I did, would they recognize *me*?

Jasper, who refused to let me pay for anything that evening, paid the door charge and held my hand as we walked in. My stomach clenched being in that building because I wasn't very well liked when I worked there, and I knew why. I was always shooting my mouth off and people didn't like hearing things that made them uncomfortable, whether it be the truth or some variance of it. I didn't know any other way to live, feeling everyone in my orbit should be forced to hear my thoughts and whatever came out of my mouth. The flip side of that was whenever someone didn't have the guts to say something themselves, I was always recruited to be the one to do the talking.

"Hey bacon grease!" I heard a woman shout, looking up to see Darla dancing in a cage above our heads.

"Hey brain surgeon!" Jasper hollered back at her, causing me to burst into a fit of laughter I nearly couldn't control.

Continuing to hold his hand I dragged him into the first floor bar where we met, and much to my surprise Carl was holding court as bartender. We sat down at the bar and Jasper ordered two martinis with extra olives. Carl looked at me and cocked his head.

"Hi Carl," I said with a smile.

"Marla?"

"It's Jude, but yeah. How have you been?"

"It's certainly a lot less lively around here without you," he replied. "You seem to be doing all right for yourself. I've never seen you smile like that before."

"I'm very happy," I said.

"It looks good on you."

I knew he was being genuine. He was one of the few men in that place that actually looked out for the rest of us. "Thanks, Carl."

"Dollar shots in the VIP club tonight. Elevator code is the same."

He winked and I thanked him as we grabbed our drinks and Jasper took my hand, leading me out of the bar area to the elevator where I punched in the code that would take us up to the top floor.

"I think dollar shots might be dangerous," Jasper practically whispered.

"So Darla," I teased.

"Hopefully she stays locked in that cage all night." He exaggerated a shudder and we both laughed all the way to the third floor.

Once the elevator doors opened we went to the bar to finish our martinis, and when I popped the last olive in my mouth the opening "Jitterbug" lyric to "Wake Me Up Before You Go Go" by Wham! got the room jumping and I dragged Jasper out onto the dance floor.

"You put the boom boom into my heart," I sang to him.

I saw him pull a face and looked to see why. Darla was relieving the bartender and I explained, "Cage girls always bartend up here after their cage shift. Just one of those things."

"That girl is psychotic! She slashed my tires after the whole food fight incident and she *still* calls me at least three times a week!"

"She probably didn't like seeing you come in here with me."

"I tried to convince her I had a girlfriend, but she doesn't believe me."

I pinched his cheek and said, "Follow my lead."

I held Jasper's hand and led him back to the bar where we sat down and Darla avoided us as long as she could, before finally smiling and pretending she just saw us.

"Hey Jasper," she greeted with a big smile. "Who's your friend?"

"Jasper's girlfriend. Jude," I answered for him. "We met at the cabin, remember?"

"Oh right, the *nanny*."

My head was feeling a bit light. "Yes, the nanny who knows that braille is for the blind not the deaf, and knows how to sign in four different languages."

Jasper raised an eyebrow and I rolled my eyes at him.

"Four languages? What can I get for you, genius?" Darla did everything to hold back a yawn.

"Four tequila shots, please." She placed four shots of tequila in front of me and I waited a generous amount of time before asking for salt and limes. After she plopped them down next to the shots I turned to face Jasper and smiled, placing a lime wedge in his mouth, flesh side facing me. I licked the side of his neck, sprinkling the wetness with salt then licked that off, drank one of the shots then grabbed the lime out of his mouth with my own and sucked the juice out of it.

I could see his Adam's apple wiggle as he chuckled at my antics, but he was more than eager to take his turn as Darla watched us with jealous, steely eyes. I moved my mermaid necklace out of the way so I could nestle one of the shot glasses in my cleavage as Jasper waggled his eyebrows at me. He licked my neck like I did his, sprinkled and licked the salt, grabbed the shot glass with his lips and threw back the liquid then sucked the lime from my mouth.

I wasn't sure what condition he was in, but I was certainly feeling no pain and all I wanted to do was dance and….

I threw my arms around Jasper's neck and nuzzled my lips close to his ear as I whispered, "Think she believes you have a girlfriend now?"

"Maybe."

I pulled away from him and slurred, "Okay… next shot we do together."

The room began to get smaller and it felt like bodies of strangers were closing in on me. We did the second shot of tequila at the same time and it didn't go down as smoothly as everything else had that evening. At that moment I was thankful we ate burgers, fries and a banana split because otherwise I might have been passed out on the floor.

Jasper untwisted my mermaid necklace and pressed the pendant gently against my chest, the way it was supposed to sit around my neck. I thanked him with a drunken smile and leaned over so I was closer to his face.

"Jasper," I whispered. "Did you have a nice weekend?"

"The best."

"Did you have a nice birthday?"

"Yes. Thank you for spending it with me."

"I didn't give you your present yet."

His face lit up with a smile brighter than the sun. "You have a present for me?"

"But you might not like it."

"If it's from you, of course I'll love it."

Our eyes were locked on each other and I moved even closer, pressing my mouth against the softness of his, waiting to see what he would do next. My heart was banging like a drum as my head screamed at me to stop whatever I thought I was trying to do. I tried to rationalize my behavior by reminding myself how lonely I was but I knew in the end I would only end up hurting Jasper and that was the last thing I wanted to do. Still, every sensible thought was pushed out of my head as his lips covered mine in soft, sweet kisses and I melted into him as he placed his hands gently against the sides of my neck.

"God Jasper, get a fucking room!" Darla snarled.

The spell was broken and I pulled my face away from his, saying, "Take me home."

"Take you home?"

"Your home."

Jasper hopped off his bar stool, left a tip and grabbed my hand, pulling me toward the exit as we heard Darla shriek, "Jasper, you fucking prick!"

We rushed out of the club and onto the sidewalk where Jasper quickly hailed a taxi and gave the driver his address after we piled into the back seat. We both stared straight ahead as we fidgeted in our seats, then Jasper slowly lifted his arm and slung it around my shoulders. I didn't dare look at him as my heart thumped wildly in my chest at the same time my head was screaming at me to put a halt to everything that was happening. Everything *I* put in motion.

My head was spinning from the amount of alcohol I'd consumed and I could barely feel my face, but I closed my eyes as I became entranced by Jasper's fingertips lightly caressing my shoulder. The next thing I knew the taxi was pulling up to Jasper's building and he held my hand tightly as he led me inside. I finally had the nerve to look at his face as the elevator doors closed. He devoured me with his eyes without ever touching me and I could no longer control myself, grabbing the front of his shirt and pulling him against me as our mouths crushed against each other. He pressed his body against mine, pinning me against the wall of the elevator as we became a heated frenzy of lips and tongues and groping hands.

By the time we reached the top floor Jasper had my panties in his hand as he ravaged my neck, my heart racing so quickly I almost couldn't catch my breath. Upon entering the condo his kisses were hot and desperate as we stumbled toward his bedroom, frantically removing our clothing along the way. While I knew an ongoing romantic or sexual relationship with Jasper was out of the question, he was exactly what I needed that evening, and I would have to face those consequences in the morning. I was in no frame of mind to think rationally as my body selfishly had one mission, and Jasper was fulfilling every want and need deliciously.

When I opened my bleary eyes the next morning face down on the bed, Jasper was heading toward me on his skateboard, completely naked. I slowly lifted my head to get a better look as he hopped off before reaching the bed, and as his feet touched the floor he swiveled his hips from side to side quickly, his junk slapping back and forth against his thighs. I couldn't help but laugh but then realized I needed to get home, and as quickly as possible.

As he slipped into the bed beside me smiling cheerfully, I got out and struggled to stay upright as I followed the path of clothes, pulling them on as I found my own. Jasper jumped out of bed, pulling on a pair of shorts as he rushed to my side, stopping me with both hands on my shoulders.

"What's the matter? Where are you going?" he asked, his eyes wide.

"I have to go."

"Why?"

"Last night was a mistake."

"But I thought… wait a minute… am I just a charity case to you? Stupid Jasper, let's give him a good time on his birthday and bail the next morning?"

"No, it's not like that."

"Well tell me what it is like then!"

Looking into Jasper's eyes was pure torture. "I care about you Jasper, I really do."

"I'm beginning to think what you're really good at is fucking with people's heads."

He had every right to be angry with me and I had no intelligent response, so I went into the spare room to collect my clothes and toiletries, stuffing everything haphazardly into my overnight bag. When I turned to leave he was standing there with his arms folded in front of him.

"I told you I wasn't a good person," I said weakly.

"You're so full of shit."

"I know you're pissed, but I don't want to lose you."

"You know I'm in love with you. Why would you do this to me?"

"I love you, Jasper, I swear I do. I have the best time with you but I'm not in love with you. I've always been honest about that."

I watched his face as it slowly changed from anger to confusion until it completely drained of all color. "Oh my God," he finally said, his hands resting on top of his head. "How did I not see it?"

I didn't like the way he was looking at me. "What are you talking about?"

"You're in love with *him*!" he shouted.

"With *who*?"

"My brother!"

I knew I had to get out of there and I couldn't move fast enough. I grabbed my bag and stormed out of the room, snagging my purse off the floor as I passed it on my way to the elevator.

"You're not even going to deny it?" he asked behind me.

I turned to face him, reaching to unclasp the mermaid pendant from my neck.

"It was a gift," he said, his voice softening. "I want you to keep it."

I stepped onto the elevator and saw my panties on the floor, so I picked them up and shoved them into my purse, my face burning as I did so.

As the elevator doors closed Jasper shouted, "Jude, wait!"

But it was too late. I knew I'd never be able to face him again without tremendous guilt eating me alive, and maybe it was for the best. Once outside I hailed a taxi and headed home. I was relieved it was early enough in the day that Sullivan and Shea wouldn't have returned from the cabin so I was able to exhale and relax a bit during the drive. On the other hand, I would never forgive myself for hurting Jasper, especially since he was my only friend and now that relationship was destroyed.

Once home I walked in the back door, dragging myself through the kitchen to the front foyer. As I attempted to walk up the stairs I heard someone call my name. I turned to see Sullivan standing there, glaring at me.

"Can you come to my office, please?" he asked.

I set my bag and purse on the bottom stair and followed him. I could only imagine what I looked like dressed in my outfit from the night before and never once looking in a mirror before leaving Jasper's condo. I followed him to his office where I saw Shea sound asleep on his fancy leather couch.

"Is everything okay?" I asked. "Why are you home early?" And why were they in his office?

Sullivan leaned against his desk, half sitting, half standing as he cleared his throat and folded his arms in front of him.

"It's Monday, Ms. Hastings," he spoke calmly, but angrily. "Monday afternoon."

Shit!

I had to rethink my weekend to get it straight in my head. Friday was the charity softball game, Saturday was the wine tasting, Sunday was Jasper's birthday... panic rushed through me as I realized how much danger I had put Shea in by not being there when Sullivan left for work that morning.

"I'm so sorry," I said. "I lost track of time and... oh my God, did anything happen to Shea?"

"We knocked on your door last night when it was time for him to go to bed, as we do every night, but you didn't answer. Since that was odd I tried to rouse you this morning before I left. When there still was no answer, I went into your apartment to make sure everything was okay, but you were nowhere to be found. I had to work from home today, which isn't the best way I like to handle business."

"I'm sorry, I can explain—"

"It seems you don't take me seriously, Ms. Hastings. I asked you to stay away from Jasper, yet here you are. I can only imagine it was quite the weekend based on your current appearance."

"Jasper had nothing to do with this," I lied.

"You're wearing my grandmother's necklace!"

I touched the mermaid around my neck and swallowed hard as I looked at the floor. I was absolutely busted and there was nothing I could do about it.

"I have very valid reasons for the rules in this house. *Especially* where Jasper is concerned. Maybe you should reread the contract you signed to work here."

Contract... *contract*! After everything *he'd* done with me how could he throw the contract in my face like that? I finally lifted my head and met his glare head on.

"I'm a screw up," I said softly. "I freely admit that. But whatever this thing is between you and Jasper… you're lucky you still have a brother. I mourn my sister every day, wishing I could do *anything* to bring her back."

"You will *never* understand the situation between me and my brother!"

"Maybe not, but here's what I do know. Jasper is smart, kind and generous. He's loving and fun to be around. He's a good soul who loves his family more than anything else in the world. He would do *anything* for you and you push him away every chance you get."

"Ms. Hastings, you—"

"He's the exact opposite of you!" I screeched, my frustration with him reaching peak level. "Yes, I was with Jasper this weekend! He just wanted to spend it with someone he cares about and yesterday was his birthday… did you even bother to give him a call? Of course you didn't. Because you're all caught up in your own bullshit so you don't give him a second thought. He's a good friend to me, and he could be that friend to you if you'd just let him. But no, you have that stick shoved so far up your ass the only one you think about is yourself! You could take some cues from Jasper because you know what? He's everything you're not, and that's a *good* thing!"

I stomped out of the room, but as I reached the stairs and grabbed my bag and purse he was right behind me, asking, "Are you in love with him?"

I turned slowly toward him with a smirk on my face. "No," I answered with complete certainty. "And you'll be happy to know that I screwed up my relationship with him, too."

I unclasped the mermaid pendant and handed it to Sullivan then ran up the stairs to the safety of my apartment, locking the door behind me and heading to the bathroom for a look in the mirror. I looked like a street junkie with matted hair, black mascara caked to my eyes and streaked down my face with shades of purple eyeliner and eye shadow mixed in. I managed to dig the remaining butterfly bobby pins from my hair before stripping out of my clothes and getting in the shower, hoping to wash the day's heartache I was responsible for down the drain. But even I knew it wasn't going to be that easy to right the wrongs I caused that day.

Before going to bed that evening I noticed an envelope had been slipped under my door. I opened it to find the mermaid necklace and a note from Sullivan.

She would want you to have this.

Z.S.

Chapter 19

July rolled into August and while my relationship with Sullivan was strained to say the least, I missed Jasper terribly. I missed his smile and laughter, and the fun we had together. I had no one to blame, and I kicked myself for sabotaging anything good that ever came into my life. I had screwed things up so badly in the Sullivan family, possibly creating a further divide between the brothers, my only recourse was to continue making strides with Shea, so that's what I concentrated on. I kept my attention focused solely on my job and the small boy who was the center of everything.

As we reached the first week of September, I was enjoying a quiet breakfast with Shea when Jasper walked through the back door, surprising the hell out of me. My heart swelled when I laid eyes on him, wondering why he was there. We hadn't spoken to each other since my abrupt departure from his condo and seeing him in the flesh made me realize just how much I missed his friendship.

Shea jumped out of his chair and straight into Jasper's arms when he saw him, hugging and kissing him while he bounced happily in his embrace.

"Hey, Jude," he said, a weak smile crossing his lips.

"Hey. What're you doing here?"

"Shea's coming with me for the day. I'll bring him back tomorrow."

"Oh? I was never told that."

"You can check with Ziggy if that makes you feel better."

"I'm not going to bother him at work."

"He's not at work."

"How do you know that?"

Jasper placed Shea back in his seat and asked him to finish his breakfast. He hesitated before he looked at me and replied, "Today is Ziggy's birthday."

"It is? Why didn't you tell me?"

Jasper's face grew stern, something I wasn't used to seeing on him. "Listen to me; this isn't about his birthday. Today is the two year anniversary of JoJo and Jenny's death."

My skin pricked with sadness hearing this news. "I had no idea."

"I told you Shea stays with me a few times a year… this is one of those times."

The sadness covering Jasper's face was almost unbearable to witness, but I still felt it was my duty to clear this with Sullivan before Shea was taken away for the day.

"It's not that I don't believe you because I do, but I need to hear it for myself if that's okay."

"Sure, if it makes you more comfortable. I'll take Shea upstairs and pack his bag while you disturb my brother, who's probably in bed a complete wreck right now."

"You don't have to be an asshole about it," I grumbled, getting up and going upstairs. The closer I got to Sullivan's bedroom the more my stomach rumbled, nervous about disturbing him in such a fragile state. But as Shea's nanny I couldn't let him leave without confirming it with his father, even if it was Jasper taking him.

I tapped lightly on his door, listening carefully for his voice. When I didn't hear anything, I opened the door a crack and knocked a little louder.

"What?" his voice called from the darkness.

"Jasper is here to take Shea. I just wanted to make sure it was okay."

"Yes, it's okay."

I closed his door and went back to the kitchen to clean up the breakfast mess and Jasper wasn't far behind, with Shea bouncing along beside him, excited to be leaving with his uncle.

"Just make sure to check in on him every once in a while, okay?" Jasper said.

"Sure, I can do that."

Jasper threw Shea's little bag over his shoulder and lifted him up to say goodbye to me. Shea gave me a hug and a kiss and had a huge smile on his face.

::Bye::

::Miss you::

"I'll miss you too," I answered with a smile. "Have fun with Uncle J. I love you."

::Love you::

"Are you driving him in your car?" I asked Jasper.

"Oh no," he said with a laugh. "It's against the rules. Andy will be driving us so I'm leaving my car here."

"Got it."

Jasper cleared his throat and finally made eye contact with me. "I miss you," he said.

I wrinkled my nose to keep my eyes from tearing up. "I miss you, too."

Jasper and Shea slipped on their matching aviator sunglasses and he said, "Call me if you need anything, otherwise I'll have him home before dinner tomorrow."

With that, Jasper walked out the back door and I mirrored Shea's goodbye waves until we could no longer see each other. I had an entire day to myself and without Shea, what was I supposed to do?

"Hello Miss Jude," Blanche's voice greeted me as she entered the kitchen.

"Hi Blanche," I said with a smile.

"You look perplexed."

"I just found out today is Mr. Sullivan's birthday."

"Ah yes," she said, nodding slowly. "An unfortunate day, for sure."

"Is there anything he likes on his birthday? Cake? A special dinner?"

"You probably won't get him to eat much today. He hasn't celebrated his birthday since the accident, but I know his favorite ice cream is mint chocolate chip."

"Thanks, Blanche."

Around lunchtime I made my way to Sullivan's room and knocked, hoping he was okay. I couldn't begin to fathom the grief he was feeling on such a tragic anniversary and I didn't imagine he was too keen on me bothering him, but Jasper did ask me to check on him once in a while and I felt I needed to oblige.

"Come in," his weak voice called.

Come in? I didn't want to go into his bedroom, I just wanted to see if he was okay.

"Just wanted to see how you were doing," I said, standing firm in the hallway speaking through the door.

"Come in," he said again.

I slowly opened the door and saw him lying in bed with only the flickering light from the television illuminating the room. I walked in cautiously, not sure he really wanted me to be in the room with him. I first saw his face, eyes open and wet with tears, then I glanced at the television and saw home movies playing on the screen. I was so taken aback by seeing Shea as a baby that I found myself sitting on the bench at the end of his bed to catch my breath.

"You should watch from the beginning," I heard his soft voice say as he clicked the remote to start at the beginning.

"No it's okay, I just wanted—"

"You're the one person who should see Shea growing up," he said, as soft as a whisper. "And get to know JoJo."

"I don't—"

"Please."

I turned to face him and I was surprised by how young and fragile he looked. My own eyes burned with tears and my voice croaked as I asked, "Is there anything I can do for you?"

He sat up straight and positioned a pillow behind him as he leaned back against the headboard, then patted the bed next to him. If that's all he wanted from me, it was the least I could do on such an awful day. I kicked off my flip-flops and sat on the king-sized bed next to him, but not too close, taking his lead and leaning against the headboard. I observed he wasn't wearing a shirt, and I hoped he was wearing something underneath the covers.

He started the video over, which began right after Shea and JoJo were born, snug in the arms of their beaming mother, who looked beautiful even though she was completely worn out after giving birth. I watched the emotional video as he explained everything that was happening in great detail, as if he were living it at that moment.

"That's Jenny, my wife," he struggled to say. "Shea is in her left arm and JoJo is in her right."

It was the first time I had ever seen what JoJo looked like, as Sullivan had no photographs in the house whatsoever. I had always thought it was strange, but as I saw his grief in person for the first time, it made sense that he might not want a reminder of everything he lost staring him in the face every time he turned around.

Shea and JoJo reminded me of myself and Prude in a way — one dark haired child, one blonde… one hearing and one deaf. While Shea was the dark haired twin with hazel eyes, JoJo was blonde and blue-eyed like their mother.

Seeing Sullivan in these videos with his infant children brought about emotions in me I never expected, and I tried not to let him see my eyes getting moist as we watched the videos together. He was so happy and the smile on his face lit up the universe as he held his tiny babies, and while I'd seen him smile on occasion since knowing him, it would never be the same as when his wife and daughter were still alive.

I watched eagerly as newborn Shea was placed into Jasper's arms for the first time, and not only did he look incredibly young, but terrified. It was heartwarming to see them in their first moment together knowing how close they would become. I never stopped to think about how JoJo's death would have affected Jasper, and realized it must have been almost as devastating for him to lose his niece and sister-in-law in such a tragic way.

While watching video of Shea and JoJo's first birthday party, Sullivan said, "Jenny and I weren't getting along at the time of the accident. I had filed for divorce and she was served with the papers that morning."

I sucked in a breath at his revelation. "I'm so sorry."

"If I'd just set my feelings aside and stuck it out, my daughter would still be alive," he cried.

I turned my head to look at him as he covered his eyes with his hand and began to sob. Ugly, guttural sobbing that was so heartbreaking it brought me to tears.

"No, don't say that," I argued. "It's not your fault. You couldn't have predicted what would happen."

"I destroyed everything because I could no longer live with my wife," he howled in agony.

The last time I saw someone in that much emotional pain was when Prude died, and it was my own. I tried to remember if there was anything that might have soothed me and the only thing that came to mind was desperately needing comfort from my parents, which never happened.

I reached out and smoothed Sullivan's hair away from his forehead and he dropped face first into my lap, sobbing against my leg. It was overwhelming to see him so distraught, as he was always so put together and calm in every other situation he seemed to find himself.

"I'll never forgive myself," he sobbed. "And when Shea is old enough to understand I'll lose him forever because he'll never forgive me either."

I caressed his shoulder with my left hand as I ran my fingers through his hair with my right. "What happened was your wife's fault. She's the only one to blame."

"I miss JoJo so much," he cried. "And Shea… no one has suffered more than he has. JoJo was his whole world."

"That might be true, but I think he's doing pretty well. He talks to JoJo all the time. He's happy."

"I couldn't stand her drinking anymore," he whispered, the crying subsiding somewhat. "She needed help, but no matter what I tried she refused. It was tearing apart my family."

"You have to stop blaming yourself, or you'll never be able to heal."

"I don't deserve to heal. I'm tortured every day and it's a reminder of what I did to my children."

I was used to the tough love approach in the way I did everything, but I knew that wasn't the way to handle Sullivan in his fragile state. I had no idea what to say to ease his pain or help him find comfort, so I thought it might be best for me to say nothing at all. I continued to watch the video as his body shook under my touch every time a new batch of tears choked him. Shea grew up before my eyes as I gently caressed Sullivan's arm, knowing he was watching, too.

I watched as he taught the twins sign language, something his wife refused to do, according to Jasper. This didn't surprise me based on her inability to cope with Shea's deafness and shunning him because of it. It was painfully obvious watching the video that Jenny favored JoJo and it was everyone else showering Shea with love and affection. It was heartbreaking to witness, but when I saw how loved Shea was by his father, Jasper and their parents, it brought tears to my eyes. They were such a loving family and I was happy to be in their presence, if only in small amounts.

"This was the morning of the accident," his voice cracked.

I watched as Sullivan walked into the kitchen, sharply dressed in his suit and tie, smiling as the twins ran to greet him. As he lifted them both in his arms JoJo's little voice said, "Birthday Daddy!" as she signed to Shea. Shea smiled happily and clapped, giving his father a birthday kiss.

::Birthday::

::Daddy::

The smile on Sullivan's face was priceless as he kissed each of his children and placed them in their highchairs for breakfast, then sat at the table.

"Blanche made your favorite," Jenny's voice could be heard off-camera. "Blueberry pancakes."

"Happy birthday, Mr. Sullivan," Blanche said as she placed breakfast plates in front of Sullivan and the twins.

"Thank you, Blanche," he said with a smile. He looked into the camera and smiled, saying, "We don't need video of me eating breakfast."

I heard Jenny grumble something I couldn't decipher as the camera panned to the twins who were happily plucking at their pancakes, their little syrupy fingers feeding their hungry mouths.

"My precious JoJo," Jenny squealed, completely dismissing Shea, who was oblivious since he heard none of it.

"Hi Mommy," JoJo said, smiling brightly for her mother.

I watched closely as Shea took all his cues from JoJo, who was not only his ears but his voice as well.

"I love you, JoJo," Jenny whispered.

"Love you Mommy," she replied. She watched her mother for a moment and when she didn't hear what she wanted, she turned to Shea and in the secret sign language I knew all too well, told him, "Mommy loves you." Shea smiled and nodded as JoJo placed her sticky hands on his cheeks, pulling him close for a kiss and a hug.

I shocked myself when an audible gasp escaped my throat. As a toddler JoJo knew that her mother treated Shea differently, even if she didn't understand why.

"This was the last time I saw her," Sullivan howled. "I finished my breakfast, kissed them goodbye and went to work."

The agony in the room was devastating and when the video ended I leaned over and pressed my face against his head as I wrapped my arms around him in the hopes he would find some comfort in my touch. The devastation I felt when Prude died returned with a vengeance and I found myself crying along with him, even though I would never understand the pain of losing a child.

I don't know how long we cried together, but eventually his body relaxed and he seemed to calm down, wiping his face with his hand and sighing with exhaustion.

"Is that why you don't have any pictures in the house? Because you feel guilty when you see JoJo?" I asked quietly.

"That's part of it. Losing JoJo destroyed Shea, and I was afraid seeing her picture would make things worse."

"Maybe you're not giving him enough credit."

"You could be right."

"I was salutatorian, remember?" He chuckled, which was a great relief, easing the mood quite a bit. "When was the last time you took a picture of Shea? Or made a video?"

"Nothing since losing JoJo."

"I have to show you something."

I eased myself away from him and hopped off the bed, going to my apartment and retrieving a scrapbook. When I returned to his bedroom he was just coming out of the bathroom wearing only his boxer shorts, getting back into bed and leaning against the headboard. I'd never seen him look so disheveled and distraught; it was heartbreaking.

"It's not finished yet, but since today is your birthday it seems the perfect time to show you this," I said, handing him the scrapbook. "Shea and I have been making this for you."

I sat on the edge of the bed and watched as he slowly flipped through the pages, his eyes wet with a new onslaught of tears.

"Shea loves posing and looking at pictures of himself," I told him. "I've been trying to show his progress visually with photographs, crafts and pictures he's drawn or colored. You can see his first attempt at learning to write his name on the last page."

Sullivan looked at me with red eyes as tears rolled down his face, his hand robotically covering his mouth as he said, "I don't know what to say."

I swallowed hard and cautiously replied, "Say you'll stop blaming yourself for something that wasn't your fault. Say you'll stop torturing yourself and put the blame where it belongs."

"It won't be easy but I promise I'll work on it."

I smiled. "Good. And instead of watching that video once a year to torture yourself, you should watch it to remember your little girl. And you should watch it with Shea. Maybe in small doses at first, but he deserves to see his sister."

Sullivan rubbed his face vigorously and heaved a heavy sigh. "You're probably right."

I got up and headed for the door, saying, "I'll need that back before Shea gets home. When he gives it to you for Christmas, act surprised."

"Where are you going?"

"I'll be downstairs if you need anything."

I went to the kitchen to make something for lunch and it wasn't long before Sullivan joined me, looking a lot better than he had that morning and I was glad to see he'd thrown on a pair of gym shorts.

"You hungry?" I asked.

"Not really."

I pulled a gallon of mint chocolate chip ice cream out of the freezer and said, "How about now?"

"Now you're speaking my language."

He reached into the cabinet for two bowls but I stopped him, shoving two spoons into the ice cream and telling him to follow me. I led him into the party room where Shea's elaborate blanket fort was still intact, and crawled in until I reached the middle. I almost thought he wouldn't play along and was pleasantly surprised to see him right behind me.

"Welcome to Shea's secret world," I said, handing him a spoon.

"How can you talk to each other in here? It's a bit dark."

I surprised him by turning on a handy flashlight and held it up to my face, looking as scary as possible. He laughed loudly and it warmed my soul. Not that he ever looked old, but he looked so young sitting there eating ice cream straight from the carton wearing nothing but a pair of shorts. He was like a completely different person from any other day I'd known him; he was relaxed and didn't look like a windup toy ready to snap.

"Are you happy here, Jude?" he asked quietly, taking another bite of ice cream.

"Very happy."

"I'm glad you're here."

My cheeks flushed as I grinned and said, "Me, too."

"I've lost sight of so many things since losing JoJo, and Shea is the one who has suffered the most. I should've done a better job as his father but instead I shut down and put up barriers that have probably caused a lot of his fear and anxiety."

"Maybe. But all you can do now is move forward."

"Will you take me through Shea's day and show me his life? I think I need a reminder of what it's like to be a child."

"You bet."

"And maybe I need a reality check into your life as well. I'm guessing it's obvious why I've been keeping you at a distance."

My face burned fire and I nodded, shoving another spoonful of ice cream in my mouth, and was more than surprised he would bring up our steamy cabin encounter at all. He left the last bite of ice cream for me, gentleman that he was, and we headed into the kitchen where Blanche was pouring a cup of coffee.

"Oh!" she gasped, startled. "It's good to see you up and about, Mr. Sullivan."

I guessed she wasn't used to seeing him walking around in a pair of shorts and nothing else. It was startling for me if I had to be completely honest, but it was definitely easy on the eyes to see him relaxed and so vulnerable.

"Thank you, Blanche," he replied with a smile. "Why don't you take the rest of the day off and be with your family?"

Her face dropped. "Have I done something to make you unhappy?"

"Not at all. You do so much for me and my family... you deserve more time with your own."

"Mr. Sullivan, I don't know what to say."

"Say you'll enjoy the afternoon with your husband. Oh, and since tomorrow is Friday, take tomorrow off, too."

Blanche looked as though she were going to burst into tears.

"And tell your husband I'm giving you a raise," he added with a smile.

Blanche glanced at me and I nodded at her, mouthing, "Go!"

She swiped away tears that began to spring from her eyes, saying, "Thank you, Mr. Sullivan. Thank you."

"We'll see you on Monday."

She thanked him all the way out the door and when she was gone I turned to him and smiled.

"What?"

"What was that all about?" I asked.

"She's not getting any younger and neither is her husband. Now that their kids are all grown they deserve to have more time together."

Was Sullivan finally becoming human?

"Are you ready to take a walk in Shea's shoes, Mr. Sullivan?"

"Ready, Ms. Hastings," he replied with a grin.

We spent the rest of the afternoon going through Shea's daily routine, starting from our first foray down the stairs to greet and feed the koi. He was a good sport about everything, taking a serious interest in how I spent my time with Shea, playing games, reading books, playing with toys, teaching him new words, teaching him how to write, and everything else in between. He seemed surprised that we squeezed so much into our day, but I reminded him that not every day was the same and sometimes Shea was stubborn and refused to do things he wasn't in the mood for. I explained that I had to find ways around his moods, but that most of the time he was willing and compliant. For example, he absolutely hated brushing his teeth but because I turned it into a game, he no longer fought me to get it done.

To end Sullivan's day in Shea's life, he put on shoes and a shirt and we went outside to play on the jungle gym. He stood there watching me with a grin on his face as I climbed onto the slide, having no interest in joining me.

"Come on," I urged. "You promised to play along."

"Slides aren't really my thing."

"Bad experience?"

"You could say that."

I enjoyed my trip down the slide and said, "Swings?"

I got comfortable on one swing while he sat in the other but neither of us moved.

I didn't know if it was the right time, or if I should say anything at all, but something in me felt I needed to come clean, and I blurted, "I have a confession."

"Oh?"

Staring at my feet kicking up dirt, I said, "I hooked up with Jasper on New Year's Eve when he came into the club where I was working. I never knew who he was... I didn't even know his name. I never thought I'd see him again and then he showed up at the cabin with Darla."

"Why are you telling me this?"

"I'm not sure. I was drunk and hated my life and was a bit lonely I guess. He pretended he didn't recognize me at the cabin but he was very protective of you and Shea, thinking I was pulling some sort of scam. He realized that wasn't true when he watched me with Shea, but I want you to know my position here has never been anything but on the up and up."

"I've never doubted that. One only has to see you with Shea to know your motives are pure."

This made me feel better as I breathed a sigh of relief. It felt good to get that off my chest, even though I wasn't obligated to tell him about my first meeting with Jasper all those months ago. It seemed like a lifetime ago when I thought about it.

"I was a different person then," I continued. "But even now, I know excessive partying only gets me into trouble and ruins everything good in my life."

"Jasper?"

"Jasper," I admitted with a sigh. "What happened on his birthday was a mistake and I really hurt his feelings. He was a really good friend to me and I screwed it all up."

"Do you love him?"

I hesitated before answering. "I do love him. He's fun to be with, he makes me laugh, and we have a lot in common, but I'm not *in* love with him."

"I'm not judging you. I wanted you to stay away from him because I didn't want you to end up getting hurt."

For some reason I believed him, but I didn't want to talk about Jasper or ending up in his bed anymore.

"I have one more thing to show you," I said, changing the subject.

I took Sullivan by the hand and brought him to Shea's favorite patch of soft grass, where we would lay to watch the birds and clouds. I stretched out on my back and he followed suit, both of us staring up into the summer sky.

"When the weather is nice, we'll lie out here before Shea's nap. He likes to watch the birds, but some days we have really great clouds floating by and he loves to tell me what he thinks they look like."

"And what does he see?"

"Animals mostly. Once he insisted he saw JoJo."

"Does he still talk to her?"

"Every day."

"And Prude?"

Goosebumps covered my skin as I answered, "Once in a while he'll give me a message from her."

We were silent for a while until he cleared his throat. "Do you still believe she brought us together?"

I felt a tear escape my eye as I turned my head to look at him. "Yes, I do."

He turned his head to face me. "What makes you happy, Jude?"

"Living here, feeling like part of your family."

"You are part of the family."

"What makes you happy?"

"You do."

I felt my breath catch in my throat. "I do?"

"Yes." Sullivan slid his hand closer to mine, taking it in his and squeezing gently.

"Jasper accused me of being in love with you," I whispered, my insides quivering nervously.

"Is he right?"

I looked deeply into his eyes and replied, "Yes."

His silence was unnerving as he watched me then whispered, "I'm not good at this stuff."

Another tear slowly rolled down my face as my voice croaked, "Please tell me I'm not alone."

Sullivan reached to wipe the lone tear from my cheek as he leaned closer and kissed my mouth softly. He pushed a strand of hair out of my eyes as he smiled and said, "You're not alone."

As I opened my mouth to speak he silenced me with soft, feathery kisses and I felt like I was floating high above the clouds looking down on myself in disbelief. Things like this didn't happen to me; *love* didn't happen to me.

In between kisses he whispered, "We should probably go inside."

"Why?" I asked devilishly, continuing our innocent make out session.

"I'd hate for Andy to see us and think I was taking advantage of my nanny."

I thought about my birthday and how Sullivan unknowingly thwarted the rendezvous I had planned with Andy that evening. I was never more relieved that things didn't happen the way I planned, and agreed it was probably a good idea to take things inside.

Sullivan stood first, reaching out a hand to help me to my feet. As we walked toward the house I brushed the loose grass off the back of his shirt and he reciprocated. I had no idea what to expect once we went back inside, and I certainly wondered how the rest of our evening would play out.

As we entered the kitchen he said, "It's almost dinnertime. Are you hungry? I'm hungry."

"Sure, I could eat something."

"Got anything in mind? What do you have a taste for?"

"It's your birthday. You decide."

He opened the refrigerator and while he stood there examining what was inside, I took the opportunity to admire him from behind. He stood on one leg looking like a human flamingo, his long legs toned and the lean muscles in his arms flexing as he held the refrigerator door open. He started humming a song I didn't recognize as his head rocked back and forth, his long, golden brown hair bouncing on his shoulders as he did so.

"Ever have a cold meatloaf sandwich?" he asked, turning to look at me.

"I never have."

"You don't know what you're missing!" he cheered, pulling out a container of leftover meatloaf, a jar of mayonnaise and a loaf of bread. I sat at the counter as he made us each a sandwich, accompanied by some left over caesar salad. He excused himself for a moment and returned with a bottle of wine that I immediately recognized as one of Jasper's.

He poured us each a glass and I grinned, saying, "Jasper's wine?"

"He sent me a case. This is the first bottle I've opened."

"He really has some brilliant ideas, you know."

Sullivan gave me the side eye and said, "Sure, if you say so."

"Oh come on, you said yourself he was the smartest guy you knew."

"Are you going to remind me of everything I've ever said?" he teased.

"I wouldn't dream of it."

"Eat."

I smiled and dug into my sandwich, letting him know he made a good food choice as it really was delicious. I had never thought of eating meatloaf that way and I found I liked it better than when it was hot and on its own.

"What's even better is a layer of mashed potatoes on the sandwich, too."

"Maybe next time," I replied.

After we finished eating and he cleaned up the dinner dishes, he grabbed my hand and led me to the party room where he pointed to Shea's blanket fort and said, "Ladies first."

I had no idea what he was up to, but giggled as I got on my hands and knees and crawled in. When I reached the middle, or the Grand Ballroom as Shea and I referred to it, I stopped.

"I can be fun, too, you know," he said with a smile. "I'm just a little out of practice."

My insecurity suddenly got the best of me and my head started screaming that this was all a trick. In real life the attractive, older employer didn't fall for his son's nanny. He may have had a steamy affair with her, but a happily ever after? Not in my lifetime. Hello sabotage, my closest friend.

"Hey, what's the matter?" he asked, making me realize I wasn't very good at hiding the emotions that always showed so prominently on my face.

"You said I wasn't alone, but...."

Sullivan placed his hands gently on either side of my neck and smiled, whispering, "I love you, Jude. But to be fair you didn't exactly say the words either."

Though I knew how strong my feelings were I found the words difficult to say, as I'd only uttered them to a man once in my life and he shattered my heart. "I love you, too."

His eyes were moist as he continued, "You came crashing into my life like hell on wheels but you saved my son and you made me realize that my whole life was passing me by because I thought I was powerless to change it."

"So what happens now?" A million thoughts were running through my head at lightning speed. Did this mean we were dating? A couple? Would we tell people? What would his family think? What would *my* family think? The thought that was in the forefront of my mind, however, was how would this affect Shea?

"There's something you need to understand," he said, letting his hands fall from my neck as he stretched out on his back. "I met Jenny when we were both sixteen. She was my first girlfriend... my *only* girlfriend... and after high school we went to college together. After college we got married then had kids and she's the only one I ever really had a relationship with. You know I'm not good with this kind of stuff, and I just need you to be patient with me."

"I think taking it slow is a good idea. There's no reason to rush."

"Everything we do affects Shea, and he's my main concern."

I smiled and said, "He's mine, too."

"That's why I love you," he replied, smiling from ear to ear. He took my hand in his and pulled me onto the floor next to him. "Our situation is a bit complicated and I don't want outside influences making this more difficult. Are you content with keeping this between us until we figure things out?"

"I like the way you think," I whispered, leaning over to kiss him. "I've always wanted to make out in a blanket fort."

"Well now's your chance to make out with Chicago's former most eligible bachelor."

"Oh you *are* funny," I teased.

I knew things would be different once Shea returned home, and I had no idea what this thing with Sullivan could even be described as. I was more reserved than in the past, deciding to let him make whatever moves he chose so as not to overwhelm him. I was abysmal at relationships and if this was going to be something that lasted I was only bound to screw it up.

We watched each other for a while before I began to feel awkward and said, "I'm not good at this either. You know, relationships. But you obviously know that already." I was also famous for talking too much when I didn't know what else to do, especially when silence was perfectly acceptable.

"I want to show you something."

I followed him out of the blanket fort and into the family room, where he opened a cabinet door and pulled out an armful of photo albums. We sat on the couch and started with the first one, which were photos of Sullivan as a baby and as he grew, and then Jasper entered the picture. I was thrilled that he allowed me a peek into this part of his life, because I knew it wasn't easy for him to reveal. Based on the relationship I knew they had, I was amazed to see smiling, happy faces in the photos where Sullivan and Jasper were together. The eldest brother seemed to dote on his much younger sibling, and the adoration from both of them was obvious by the look on their faces.

"Your mom looks like Gina Lollobrigida," I said, marveling at her exquisite beauty.

"She was seventeen years old when she married my father. He was thirty-seven."

"Thirty-seven!" I gasped.

"Her parents were furious when she told them they wanted to get married. Apparently they married in secret and she continued to live at home until she turned eighteen. She got pregnant with me as soon as she moved in with him and her parents disowned her. I've never met them."

"Wow, I'm sorry to hear that."

"My mother has never faltered when it comes to what she wants. And she always gets what she wants."

"But she was so young!"

"Jasper was born ten years later. I'm pretty sure he was an accident." He chuckled, but I was still trying to wrap my head around the age difference between his parents. I knew he looked older but I never would have guessed it was twenty years.

"How did they meet?"

"She worked in a flower shop and my father ran in one day to buy roses for my grandmother's birthday. They both said it was love at first sight and the rest is history."

"It's a beautiful story," I gushed. "What did his parents think?"

"They loved my mother immediately and took her in as their own."

The parallels to my own situation didn't go unnoticed as I'm sure the expression on my face betrayed me.

"What do you say we finish that wine and watch a movie or something? I don't usually have the time to do that with Shea around."

"Sure, that sounds great."

"I'll get the wine, you pick out a movie."

He put the photo albums back in the cabinet then left to get our wine, so I pored over the movies on the shelf and pulled out *The Breakfast Club*, which was one of my favorite movies. I thought a comedy was probably the safest bet since I was still so uncertain what was really happening between us.

He returned with two glasses of wine and what looked like a cookie tin. "Blanche made my favorite — snickerdoodles!" He was so excited he looked like a kid ready to burst.

I popped the movie into the VCR and we got comfortable on the couch, and when he saw what we'd be watching he said it was one of his favorites. When the movie started we were simply sitting next to each other, sipping our wine and noshing on snickerdoodles. It was as if neither one of us really knew what we should be doing so we concentrated on watching the movie and nothing else. At one point about half way through the movie, Sullivan shifted in his seat a little bit and put his arm around my shoulders, causing me to lean into him. He smelled like cinnamon and all I could think about was kissing him, but I remained frozen in place. Is this how two people behaved after admitting their love for each other? Were we both so far out of our league — at opposite ends of the extreme — that we had no idea how to deal with it? Maybe love wasn't really an honest factor in what we were experiencing. Maybe it was just a bunch of emotions getting mixed together and we didn't really know what we were feeling. Maybe it was more the idea of being in love than actually being there, and it had everything to do with Shea.

As the movie ended and the credits began to roll Sullivan turned his head and smiled at me and the butterflies in my stomach were released, their fluttering wings causing every nerve ending in my skin to tingle. He kissed me softly at first, then more urgently as our bodies made the slow slide into a reclining position with him on top of me. His kisses were gentle but sexy and when his tongue danced with mine it was all I could do to keep my breathing at a normal rhythm. My fingers worked their way through his hair as his lips devoured my neck and his hand slid under my t-shirt. My fingers made their way down his back to the hem of his shirt, which I tugged up and over his head and threw on the floor like a magician, quickly and stealthily without missing a single kiss.

He pulled his face away from mine as I caressed his bare shoulders and smiled up at him, his hair a shaggy mess.

His breathing was labored as he whispered, "Do you want to go upstairs?"

I realized that sleeping together was the furthest thing from taking things slow, and I surprised myself by saying, "We should probably stop."

"Oh. Okay." He sat up and snatched his shirt off the floor, pulling it back over his head. "Anything wrong?"

"We agreed to take things slow. Ending up in your bed isn't taking things slow."

"You're right. I'm sorry."

Sullivan put the movie away and turned off the television, then grabbed the empty glasses and tin of cookies and left the room. I followed him into the kitchen, feeling a bit of guilt in bringing things to a halt the way I did.

"I want to," I told him. "I really do. But I—"

"You don't have to explain. I'm getting ahead of myself and to be honest, it's a little overwhelming. I had more confidence as a sixteen-year-old. Pretty sad, isn't it?"

"You're doing just fine," I assured him. "This is about me." I could have come right out and told him I was a tramp, but is that the way I wanted to start this romance? It probably wouldn't have been well-received and I would've certainly blown it from the start. I needed to show some restraint otherwise how would I know if we were just in it for the sex or if it was really love?

Sullivan put the lid on the cookie tin and said, "Well that was an interesting first day of this romance."

"Will you walk me home?" I asked with a grin.

"Of course I will." He held my hand as we slowly walked upstairs to my apartment door, where he smiled and said, "Here we are."

"Such a gentleman."

"May I kiss you goodnight?"

"You better."

His mouth kissed mine softly as he whispered, "I'll see you in the morning."

Chapter 20

I was excited to jump out of bed the following morning, showering quickly and heading downstairs to the kitchen where Sullivan was pouring a cup of coffee. He smiled at me and before he could say anything I rushed him, throwing my arms around his neck and kissing him.

"Good morning," I said.

"Morning. Coffee?"

"Yes, please."

"What would you like for breakfast?"

"No, me! Let me make breakfast for you!"

He plopped himself down at the counter and said, "You're on."

After treating him to a delicious, cheesy omelet filled with anything I could find in the refrigerator, he cleaned up the breakfast mess then took me by the hand and led me outside.

"I'm going to conquer my fear today," he said, smiling. "For Shea."

He led me to the jungle gym where we both stood staring at the slide. "What did the slide do to you?" I asked.

"Slides were extremely tall death traps when I was a kid. I climbed all the way up the ladder and once I reached the top it started wobbling and I fell off. Broke my arm in three places."

I gasped at the thought. "No wonder you hate slides!"

"But this one… this is short… and manageable. And has a lid… cover."

"You can do it, honey. I'm here for you."

He kissed me quickly and climbed up the child-sized slide and exhaled loudly. "Okay, be sure to catch me!"

I waited at the bottom of the slide for him to come down, and as soon as his feet hit the ground he stood up and pumped his fists in the air, announcing his victory. I hugged him tightly, congratulating him on his fearless effort.

"Shea will love seeing you come down that slide," I said.

"Shea and I are very lucky to have you helping us with our issues." He smiled, kissed the tip of my nose, then sat down on a swing.

It was extremely warm for an early September day, and as soon as I sat on the swing next to him, the sky opened up and we were caught in a torrential downpour. As the rain soaked us to the bone we laughed like children, swinging as high as our legs would take us. It was hard to believe the Sullivan I came to work for was laughing and swinging and enjoying playing in the rain; I only hoped that he would continue to be the playful father once Shea came back home.

The rain ended as quickly as it began, the sun peaking through the clouds as we both kicked off our drenched shoes. I stood up to wring out the excess water from my shirt and as Sullivan came to a stop I grabbed the chains of his swing and hopped onto his lap, facing him. I pushed the wet hair out of his face and he did the same to me as we watched each other, taking in and appreciating the beauty of the moment.

As raindrops dripped from the ends of his hair and the tip of his nose he whispered, "I'm in love with you, Jude. You believe that, don't you?"

Holding tightly to the chains I nodded and said, "I do." I gazed into his kind eyes and whispered, "I would've stabbed you if you were really an intruder kidnapping Shea. You believe that, don't you?"

His mouth turned into a beautiful smile as he laughed and answered, "I do."

He cupped the back of my head with his hands and pulled me closer, surprising me with a kiss so sensual it made my toes curl. I refused to pull away, continuing the deep tongue kiss as our bodies pressed closer together and we balanced on the swing like a well-trained circus act.

The sound of someone clearing their throat sent me scrambling off of Sullivan's lap, struggling to untangle myself from his limbs and the chains of the swing. I stood there gaping at Jasper and Shea, who were looking at us with two very different expressions.

"He was ready to come home," Jasper said. "He missed Jude."

Shea ran into his father's arms, wanting him to swing him and I ran after Jasper who walked away without another word.

"Jasper, wait!"

He turned to face me, his eyes burning holes through my face. "Are you in love with him?" he asked as tears welled in his eyes.

"Yes, and he feels the same. We agreed to take it slow so we can figure things out… because everything affects Shea."

"I will never forgive you if you hurt him."

"I would never intentionally—"

"I'll get over it," his voice shook. "But he *won't*."

Jasper didn't give me a chance to say anything else as he walked away quickly, getting in his car and driving away. I walked back to the yard where Shea was clinging to his father on the swing as they enjoyed a very special moment together. I stayed back to watch for a while, not wanting to interrupt the beauty I was witnessing between them. The only thing I could hear was the sound of the swing's chains chirping against the metal that they hung from as Shea pressed his face against his father's chest, smiling and content.

Sullivan looked around for me and when our eyes met, he smiled and motioned with his head to join them. When Shea realized I was there, he wriggled off of his father's lap and raced to greet me. He jumped into my arms and as I lifted him up he leaned in for a kiss.

::Swinging::

I smiled brightly and nodded, then asked Sullivan, "Do you think he understands what he saw us doing?"

"I'm not sure, but I guess we'll find out. How's Jasper handling it?"

I blew frustration out through my mouth as I answered, "He's pretty upset with me."

"He falls in love every other week, so he'll forget about this sooner than you think. He'll be fine."

"He's worried about you getting hurt."

"Well that's certainly unexpected."

I didn't want to talk about Jasper anymore. "Are you taking Shea to the cabin tonight?"

"No. I'd like the three of us to stay home and spend the weekend together."

My insides quivered. "That sounds nice."

That evening after dinner, we went up to Shea's playroom and the three of us played with whatever he was interested in. It seemed that Sullivan was prepping him for something I didn't know he was planning to do, but when he pulled a photo album off of a high shelf I knew what was coming.

Sullivan got Shea's full attention and said, "I want to show you something."

He looked at his father with wide, curious eyes and nodded as Sullivan placed the photo album on the floor in front of him, opening to the first page. Shea cocked his head as he looked at the first few newborn photos he saw, but didn't react in any other way.

Sullivan pointed to one baby and said, "That's you," then pointed to the other baby and said, "And that's JoJo."

Shea looked confused; obviously he had never seen these photos before and didn't understand how it could be JoJo when she looked nothing like he probably remembered. Sullivan flipped through the pages until Shea gasped and slapped his hand down for him to stop. He stared at a photo of JoJo who was probably a year old, her sparkling blue eyes taking center stage over her bouncy blonde curls and happy smile. Shea leaned over and kissed JoJo's face then exhaled loudly.

::JoJo::

"Yes, JoJo!" Sullivan responded with a smile.

Shea sat quietly as Sullivan continued to flip the pages, giving him time to peruse and react to each photograph. Shea excitedly patted my leg and pointed to the photo album.

::JoJo::

"Yes, I see," I replied, smiling at him.

Shea cocked his head again and ran his fingers over a photo of him with his twin sister. They were hugging each other and smiling brightly for the camera and it was then I realized that Shea had no reaction whatsoever when seeing photos of his mother.

::JoJo::

::Want JoJo::

Shea leaned over and rested his head on Sullivan's leg, his eyes still glued to the photo album. His stomach began to quiver and I watched as he rubbed his eyes. Within seconds he burst into tears so heartbreaking I could barely contain my own emotions. Sullivan pulled him into his arms and Shea buried his face against his shoulder, his quiet sobs the only sound in the room.

"I shouldn't have done that," Sullivan said. "It was a bad idea."

"He just needs time," I tried to assure him. "Baby steps."

Sullivan rocked back and forth trying to comfort Shea, tears beginning to escape his own eyes. Seeing them both in so much pain was almost too much to bear and I reached over to close the photo album, then got to my feet.

"I'll be right back," I whispered.

I went to my apartment and sat on the bed, taking the framed photo of me and Prude off the table and eyed it with great heartache. I had no idea what was best for Shea anymore and wondered if a romantic relationship with his father would cause more harm than good. Shea had already been through so much in his young life and I certainly didn't want to add to his pain.

I took the photo to Shea's playroom where he and his father were still clinging to each other for comfort and sat on the floor next to them. I gently touched Shea's hand with my finger and he opened his eyes to look at me. I smiled, then held up the photo for him to see. He lifted his head to get a better look then turned in his father's lap to face me.

::P::

"Yes, that's P."

He placed both hands against his cheeks as he took in the photograph, then reached to pull it out of my hand. He pointed to my face in the photo, then pointed at me and I smiled. He crawled out of Sullivan's lap and opened the photo album searching for something specific, then placed the framed photo of me and Prude next to a photo of him and JoJo.

::Sad::

"I'm sad, too," I said.

::P loves you::

I smiled as the tears burned my eyes, wiping them away before Shea saw them.

::JoJo happy::

::P happy::

"Who told you that?" I asked as Sullivan looked on in wide-eyed wonder.

::P::

"Tell P I love her, too."

Shea smiled and nodded and began using sign language Sullivan didn't recognize.

"What's happening here?" Sullivan whispered.

"He's talking to Prude," I whispered back.

Shea giggled and nodded as his fingers did all the talking and Sullivan sat entranced watching him.

::JoJo loves Daddy::

Sullivan's hand shot up to his mouth as he gasped in disbelief, the emotions overwhelming him as the tears streamed down his face. Shea looked at his father and shrugged, palms to the sky.

"Do you have something to say to JoJo?" I asked.

He wiped the tears from his face and signed, "I love you, JoJo. I miss you so much." He was so overcome he couldn't speak.

Shea relayed his father's message and smiled at him, giving one nod to indicate it was received.

"Thank you," his voice croaked as he stared at me in astonishment.

Sullivan and I kept our new romance low key, and agreed not to tell anyone about it. Jasper obviously knew about it, but we were pretty sure he had no desire to mention it to anyone as he was still quite bitter about the whole thing. Around Shea it was business as usual with no touching or affection of any kind, and the rare moments we did find ourselves alone together, we were so worried about being discovered that we only engaged in a brief hug or innocent kiss. I was beginning to wonder how we'd ever manage any intimacy at all if we were so afraid of Shea seeing us. I started to think that maybe it just wasn't meant to be.

Slowly, Sullivan shared more photographs of JoJo with Shea and his reaction was far less tearful as he was excited to see his twin and talk about her. Framed family photographs, especially of Shea and JoJo, began turning up around the house which made it feel more like a home. It became part of Shea's daily routine to greet each and every photograph as we passed them, just like we did with the koi. The most heartwarming moment came when Sullivan introduced the videos to Shea, and while he cried the first time he recognized JoJo, it was pure joy moving forward. It appeared Godzilla had taken a back seat to the special treat of seeing his beloved twin on the television, and this was a step in the right direction.

One chilly night in October as I settled on the couch with a book in front of the fire, I heard a soft knocking on my apartment door. I couldn't help but smile as I slowly opened the door to see Sullivan standing there holding a bottle of wine with a rose clenched between his teeth.

"May I help you?" I teased.

He flashed a seductive smile and said, "I have wine."

"By all means, come in."

I closed the door and followed him into the kitchen, where he put the rose in a vase and pulled two wine glasses out of the cabinet. As he poured the wine I hopped up onto the counter and watched him.

"Are we just dreaming here?" I asked, not sure I wanted to hear his answer. "Are we fooling ourselves?"

"What do you mean?"

"We're so afraid of people finding out about us… so worried Shea will see us… maybe this isn't going to work."

He was quickly standing in front of me with his hands on my shoulders. "No, don't say that. We said we were taking things slow... nobody in history has gone as slow as we are."

This made me laugh. "I guess so."

Sullivan gently cupped my head in his hands, lifting my face so I would look at him. "We were brought together for a reason," he said, his kind eyes smiling at me. "You still believe that, don't you?" I nodded and he continued. "I know there's an age gap. I know we're like oil and water. But you've made me a better man and I can't remember the last time I was this happy."

"I'm happy, too."

"And the love you have for Shea... he never knew a mother's love until you walked into this house. You may not have birthed him, but you're the one who gave him life."

I couldn't help but smile as the tears burned my eyes, slowly trickling down my face until he wiped them away. It was the most beautiful thing anyone had ever said to me. *Me.*

"Let's make a pact," he said. "Come Thanksgiving when my family is all here, we'll tell everybody. Including Shea."

"Only if we tell Shea first."

"It's a deal."

He leaned in for a kiss which I gladly accepted, wrapping my legs around his waist to pull him closer. As he peppered my lips with soft, sensual kisses I asked if he wanted to watch a movie but he didn't answer, continuing his romantic assault and further putting me under his spell. He surprised me by lifting me off the counter and stumbling toward my bedroom as he continued to kiss me while I held on tightly with my arms and legs. We tumbled onto the bed in a heated entanglement of lips, tongues and limbs, groping each other like two teenagers hoping not to be discovered by their parents. As soon as his shirt hit the floor, Shea's door alarm sounded and we both scrambled to our feet because there was no time to wait — he was already out of his room.

Sullivan pulled on his shirt as he ran out of my apartment toward Shea, who was crying and sleepily trying to find his way down the hall.

::JoJo::

His little hands kept saying her name over and over again. Sullivan picked Shea off the floor and looked back at me.

"Come with me," he said.

I followed him into his bedroom, where he tucked Shea under the covers in the middle of the bed. He then popped in the video of Shea and JoJo and got comfortable next to his son.

"Your turn," he said to me, smiling. "If we can't be in bed together over *there*, at least we can be *on* the bed here."

I couldn't really argue with his logic if he was inviting me onto the bed with them. I got comfortable on the other side of Shea, who rolled over to snuggle against me, not even watching the video. I leaned over to kiss the top of his head, then treated him to a butterfly kiss on his cheek with my eyelashes. He giggled and turned toward his father, tugging on his shirt so he would lean closer to his face. He gave Sullivan a butterfly kiss on the cheek and smiled when he realized he tickled him.

"What's that?" he asked his son.

Shea put a finger to his lips trying to remember what I called it.

::Butter::

::Fly::

::Kiss::

"A butterfly kiss," I reiterated, in case he wasn't quite sure what Shea was getting at.

"Do you do that often?"

I smiled. "As often as he lets me."

"I wouldn't mind getting some of those myself," he teased.

Shea turned back toward me and in minutes he was sound asleep with his little arm around my leg and I turned my head to see Sullivan smiling at me. He leaned over to kiss my forehead as he scooted closer to me and pulled both of us into his embrace.

"We were meant to be a family, Jude."

The look on my face must have given away the trepidation that shot through my body, wondering what he could possibly say next.

"This isn't the way I planned it, but the moment couldn't be more perfect."

I watched as he reached into the bedside table and pulled out a ring. I was so blinded by tears that I couldn't even make out what it looked like.

"Jude, will you marry us?"

"This isn't taking things slow," I stammered.

"It is if we don't tell anyone," he teased with a grin. He lifted my left hand and slid the ring onto my finger, but it wouldn't budge past my knuckle. "And it'll need to be resized."

My mouth remained agape, my thoughts drifting from how tiny the ring was to wondering if he really just asked me to marry him.

"It was my grandmother's favorite ring," he explained. "She was exceptionally tiny."

I brought my hand closer to my face so I could see the ring's details, marveling at the beauty of the simple and elegant princess cut amethyst with diamond accents on each side.

"I know I'm not good at this stuff," he said. "But this isn't something I'm taking lightly. I love you, and I want you to share our life."

I was so shocked I couldn't form words. I kept staring at the ring, then glancing back at him. Even if there were no ring, a marriage proposal was something I never thought I'd hear in my lifetime. I didn't realize how emotional I'd become until he reached to wipe the tears from my cheeks. I looked down at Shea, who was still sound asleep in my arms, then back at Sullivan, who didn't pressure me for an answer but smiled and waited patiently while the enormity of the moment registered in my brain.

"I love you, too," I finally whispered. "And I love Shea. So, so much."

"Is that a yes?"

I could only nod as he placed his hand behind my head and gently pulled me closer for a kiss.

"We'll make the announcement at Thanksgiving."

Chapter 21

Sullivan's parents and Aunt Sadie arrived from New York late Tuesday evening the week of Thanksgiving, taking up residence on the opposite end of the house in the visitor's quarters, which until that time had not been occupied once since I'd been there.

On Wednesday morning Shea and I went through our normal routine, but as we headed into the kitchen for breakfast, he stopped in his tracks when he spotted Yvonne and Aunt Sadie having coffee.

"My handsome boy!" Yvonne greeted Shea as he ran toward her and jumped into her waiting arms. He giggled as she kissed his whole face, then he squirmed to get away so he could get the same greeting from Aunt Sadie.

Yvonne held her arms out to me, motioning with her hands. "Jude! It's so good to see you, dear."

I said hello and melted into the loving embrace she welcomed me with, trying to remember the last time my own mother wrapped her arms around me. I was pretty sure it happened at Prude's funeral and it was purely selfish as she used me for a crutch to keep her upright in her grief.

I greeted Aunt Sadie with a hug that was just as warm as Yvonne's, then got Shea settled at the table for breakfast.

"What would you like for breakfast?" I asked him.

He tapped his lips with a finger to think carefully, causing Yvonne and Aunt Sadie to chuckle.

::*Eggs please*::

I pulled the carton of eggs out of the refrigerator and asked the ladies if they would like eggs for breakfast.

"Thank you dear, that would be lovely," Yvonne answered.

"Shea only eats scrambled; is that okay?"

"Hell yes," Yvonne replied. "I'm happy the kid is finally eating something other than peanut butter and jelly."

"He's making progress. He doesn't always like everything he tries but at least he's not afraid of food anymore."

"You're a miracle worker, Jude. Shea was a lost soul and a prisoner in his own life. You changed all that."

"I'm no miracle worker. All it took was patience and understanding. And love."

I placed plates of scrambled eggs and buttered toast in front of Yvonne, Aunt Sadie and Shea, then grabbed the orange juice and jelly from the refrigerator and sat down with my own breakfast.

"I've never seen Ziggy so relaxed and happy," Aunt Sadie remarked. "You've changed his life, Jude. Shea can finally be the little boy he was meant to be."

Their praise embarrassed me and I just smiled in response as I spread jelly on Shea's toast. Sullivan had given Blanche the week off to spend with her family and to prepare for the holiday and I wondered how the two sisters were going to spend their day.

"With the boys at the office, we're going to make the desserts for tomorrow," Yvonne said. "Later this afternoon we have mani and pedi appointments. Would you like to join us?"

"Thank you, but it's probably better if I stay here with Shea. He'll just be bored, and we're still working on patience in public."

Both ladies agreed that was probably best, then Aunt Sadie said, "I understand your parents will be joining us for dinner tomorrow."

My sphincter clenched and my throat constricted as I tried to find my voice. "Yes," I croaked. "Ziggy thought it would be a good idea for our families to spend the holiday together."

Sullivan and I went round and round about inviting my parents; I was vehemently opposed to the idea but he thought they should be there when he announced our engagement. I was worried they would ruin the day for everyone else but he won the argument, and while they were shocked by the invitation they accepted. As hard as I tried not to think about it, I stressed over whether or not my parents would go out of their way to humiliate me.

༄

I changed my clothes five times before settling on a comfortable pair of black slacks and a pink button-down blouse, accented with the mermaid cameo necklace and Prude's "P" pendant that never left my body. I ran a brush through my hair one last time, my bangs completely grown out and falling in waves along the side of my face. I heard a knock on my door and my heart raced as I hurried to answer it. Sullivan stood there smiling like the Cheshire Cat as he stepped into the apartment and closed the door behind him.

"Shea's waiting for you downstairs. He wants to dance, but he won't do it without you."

"I taught him a new song," I said, my stomach clenching. "Are they here?"

"Not yet." He lifted my left hand and slid the amethyst ring on my finger. "We can't make the announcement without the ring."

I smiled and stared at the gorgeous ring adorning my hand. "It's perfect."

He put his hands on my shoulders and kissed me softly. "Breathe. Nobody in this house is going to let them hurt you. Those days are over."

I nodded and took a deep breath, trying to clear my head. I admired his handsome face and said, "Thank you."

"I love you, Shea loves you, my family loves you, and Jasper *really* loves you," he teased. "You're surrounded by so much love, that's what you should concentrate on. Soak it in and let our love be your armor, because nobody can take that away from you."

"How did you get so smart?"

"I know things."

We both chuckled and I asked, "So when's the big announcement?"

"I haven't decided yet. Whenever it feels right."

I followed Sullivan down the stairs and into the party room where Zigmond was bouncing Shea up and down on his knee. Jasper walked toward me and pulled me into a hug, wishing me a happy Thanksgiving.

"You remember Tabitha from the softball game?" he said with a smile, extending his arm toward the cute blonde as he pulled away from me.

"Tabitha!" I cheered, greeting her with a friendly hug. "It's so good to see you!"

"Thanks for putting in a good word," she whispered in my ear.

"You're welcome."

Shea was soon tugging on my pant leg.

::Music::

::Dance::

I walked over to the giant record cabinet that was a piece of furniture in itself and pulled out Sullivan's Kiki Dee Band album, *I've Got The Music In Me*, and placed it on the turntable.

"Are you ready?" I asked him.

He nibbled his fingers and nodded, smiling.

"Okay, here we go!"

Shea placed his hand on the record cabinet where the built in speaker resided inside and waited. I set the needle on the song "I've Got the Music in Me" and turned it up so he could feel the beat. As soon as he felt the vibration on his little hand he began to bounce up and down and I signed and sang the words to him, my back to the rest of the room.

"Ain't got no trouble in my life…."

Everyone was on their feet dancing and clapping along with us and the smile on Shea's face lit up the entire room.

"I got the music in me… I got the music in me… I got the music in me… yeah, I got the music in me."

Sometimes Shea would remove his hand from the speaker in order to sign along with me because he was so excited about learning a new song and wanted to share it with everyone else. He was adorable dressed just like his father in a pair of blue slacks, white button-down shirt and blue sports coat, topping the whole ensemble off with a pair of shiny black shoes.

I noticed that Shea was distracted by something happening behind me and I turned to see Sullivan standing with my parents as they watched, their blank expressions telling me nothing but causing great turmoil inside of me. Feeling like I was silently being reprimanded because I wasn't allowed to listen to music, I turned off the record player.

"Mom, Dad," I said with a smile. I gave each of them a hug that felt wooden and forced and pulled away quickly to introduce them to everyone there. After going through the entire family and Tabitha, I turned to Shea who was looking at them expectantly.

"Shea, this is my mom and my dad. Mom, Dad, this is Shea."

Shea clung to my pant leg as he watched them, unsure what he was supposed to do. They each waved weakly at him and when he didn't respond, Sullivan took matters into his own hands.

"Shea," he said. "Say hello to Miss J's parents. Don't be rude."

Shea wiggled his fingers at them as Yvonne announced, "Let's eat!"

I lifted Shea into my arms as everyone filed toward the dining room and I gasped as I tried to calm my breathing.

"Don't tell them," I begged. "Not today. Please not today."

"I promise I won't do anything unless you give me permission."

"Thank you."

"Breathe, Jude. It's going to be okay."

I nodded, trying to believe it as we followed the group to the dining room, where Yvonne, Aunt Sadie and Jasper were setting delectable side dishes on the table. Sullivan brought the turkey platter in next, setting it at the head of the table in front of his father and taking his seat at the opposite end. Shea sat between his father and myself, as my parents were seated directly across from me.

"Let's join hands for our prayer of Thanksgiving," Yvonne announced.

For some reason this sent a jolt of terror through me and I turned the ring upside-down so it was facing my palm. The thought of anyone seeing it caused a film of cold sweat to cover my skin and I prayed Jasper wouldn't be able to feel it when I held his hand during the prayer. I held Shea's hand as his father signed the words his grandmother spoke.

"Thank you Lord for bringing my family together for another Thanksgiving, healthy and humble and grateful for the joys you have bestowed upon us. Thank you for blessing us with love and the food we are about to eat. Thank you for bringing Jude into our lives and—"

"Jude! Woo!" Jasper shouted next to me, relieving some of the tension building up in my shoulders.

"Thank you for Jude, who has given Shea life and so many other things we never imagined, like the gift of music and dance. And thank you for bringing Jude's parents and Jasper's friend Tabitha to celebrate with us today. We are very blessed. Amen."

Everyone repeated, "Amen," and Zigmond began to carve the turkey. Yvonne walked around the table filling everyone's water glass as Jasper filled the small champagne flutes with his very own sparkling cider.

My mom put her hand over the glass as Jasper approached her and said, "None for us. We don't drink alcohol."

"It's sparkling cider, Mrs. Hastings," Jasper said with his charming smile. "No alcohol."

"Oh. Well okay, then."

"Oh Jasper," Yvonne gushed. "Tell the Hastings' about your wine company."

Jasper talked about his company and the idea behind it, along with the charity aspect, and I could feel my parents' eyes on me as I fixed Shea's dinner plate with a small piece of turkey, a little bit of mashed potatoes, and a buttered roll. After all the food had been passed around between the adults, Shea was looking at my plate and noticed foods he'd never seen before, which included stuffing, brown sugar glazed sweet potatoes and cranberry sauce.

"Do you want to try something?" I asked him. He nodded and I put a little bit of my stuffing and cranberry sauce on his plate for him to taste but when I tried to give him some of the sweet potatoes he shook his head violently. Obviously he didn't like the way they looked, so it was an automatic dismissal. Not surprisingly he loved the cranberry sauce but he wasn't exactly sold on the stuffing, so he didn't ask for more.

I ate quietly as Zigmond asked my dad about his job at the bank, and Aunt Sadie asked my mom what kinds of things she was interested in and what her hobbies were. My parents weren't very good at holding up their end of the conversation, giving abrupt answers and making me more and more uncomfortable as time passed like molasses.

Jasper sensed my unease and patted my leg under the table then gave my knee a gentle squeeze. I sighed with relief, knowing that I had my friend back and being surrounded by the Sullivan family was all I needed to get through the day.

Just when I thought my parents were never going to begin a conversation on their own my mom said, "This china is beautiful. Where did you get it?"

"It belonged to my mother," Zigmond answered. "My father bought it for her when they were in Italy on their honeymoon."

"Italy," my dad mused. "We spent our wedding night in a hotel and came home the next morning. No money for a honeymoon."

I shifted in my seat as my stomach churned and I looked at Sullivan, who winked at me and smiled. I gave him a nod and let go of the breath I was holding.

"So Jude," my mom began. "It appears you're working for a nice, wealthy family, but what kind of future do you see for yourself? Are you going to be a babysitter the rest of your life?"

Everyone at the table was stunned into silence. The old Jude would have spewed some expletives and told my mom where she could stick her demeaning attitude, but the Jude I'd become sat with no response, fussing over Shea as a distraction.

"Mrs. Hastings," Sullivan spoke. "Jude is far more than a babysitter for my son. Not only is she a caretaker for a child with special needs, but she's a teacher."

"A *teacher*?" my dad quizzed.

"Every day, everything she does with Shea is a lesson. He's expanding his vocabulary daily, learning new words and how to sign them. She's teaching him his numbers, how to spell, how to write."

"She's teaching him how to read lips," Jasper added. "So be careful."

"Jude doesn't have the patience to be a teacher," my mom snapped.

I could see Sullivan's nostrils flaring and wondered what was going through his head and what he might say next.

"Mom," I said. "I love Shea, and I love my job. I can't see myself doing anything else."

"Did you hear that?" she said to my dad. "She loves being a babysitter. I suppose your experience as a bartender helped—"

"Please stop," my voice quivered.

Shea could sense something was going on and that it was hurting me, staring up at me with sad eyes. I smiled at him and said, "It's okay," but I don't think he believed me. He crawled onto my lap and buried his face into my chest, stretching his arms out and patting my arms with his little hands. I wrapped my arms around him and kissed the top of his head, letting him know everything was all right. Then I looked at Sullivan and gave him a head nod; the sign he'd been waiting for.

He cleared his throat and said, "I was going to wait until dessert, but now seems as good a time as any."

All eyes were on him as Shea continued to comfort me, having no clue what was about to happen, even though we had originally agreed he'd be the first to hear our news. Since nobody was paying any attention to me, I slowly turned the ring around on my finger so it was facing the right direction.

"I have asked Jude to be my wife," he said, his face nothing but a joyous smile. "And she said yes."

There was a moment of shocked silence, then an eruption of cheers and congratulatory sentiments as Jasper kissed my cheek and smiled at me.

"Welcome to the family," he said.

"I knew you were the one!" Yvonne shouted happily. "When you walked into my birthday party with Shea, I just knew it!"

This put a genuine smile on my face until I saw my parents across from me, their faces expressionless. I had a feeling I knew exactly what they were thinking, and prayed they would keep their opinions to themselves.

"So what does our Shea think about this news?" Zigmond asked.

"We haven't told him yet," I replied.

"We'll tell him privately on our own terms," Sullivan added.

"When's the big day?" Aunt Sadie asked. "Have you set a date? Do you have a dress? Oh Jude, you'll be such a beautiful bride!"

Yvonne added, "Dear, do let us know if you'd like any help."

I began to feel overwhelmed with all the questions directed at me and Sullivan sensed my unease immediately. He quickly came to my rescue by saying, "We've made no arrangements at this time. When we do, you'll all be the first to know."

Shea crawled back into his chair and continued to eat his dinner, happily unaware of what was going on around him. My parents were stone-faced as they quietly ate their food and didn't participate in the conversation among the adults unless they were asked a specific question. Talk soon turned to publishing and I only half listened, fussing with Shea and uncomfortable with the eyes of my parents burning holes through me.

"Two weeks until Willow Kelly's new book drops," Zigmond announced, getting my attention. "Is everything in order for her book release party?"

"Everything is set," Sullivan assured him. "And Jasper insists Willow Kelly herself will be attending."

"Come hell or high water, or if I have to drag her here myself," Jasper insisted.

"Mom, you'd really like her books," I said, trying to bring my parents into the conversation.

"We're really excited about her new children's book," Sullivan inserted. "It's a story about a deaf child, and along with the actual words it will be written in braille. It's absolutely brilliant."

"She's a genius," Jasper said.

I smiled and wiped a splotch of cranberry sauce from Shea's face. "I can't wait to read it with Shea."

"Are you going to adopt this child?" my mother blurted.

"Mom, what—"

"Mrs. Hastings," Sullivan interrupted. "These are all things that will be discussed between Jude and myself privately. Not at a dinner table on Thanksgiving."

"I would think you'd have all that figured out before making such an announcement at *your* Thanksgiving dinner table," she hissed.

"Thank you for dinner," my dad said. "But it's probably time for us to go."

"But you haven't even had dessert," Yvonne told them.

"We have pie at home," he retorted.

A snakelike grin covered my mom's face as she said, "Well Jude, it looks like you finally got what you always dreamed of."

My heart dropped as I scrambled to figure out the meaning of her statement because I knew it couldn't be good.

"Mom, I love him," I said. "And I love Shea. Please don't turn this into something ugly."

My heart was hurting so terribly I didn't even notice a tear had escaped my eye until Shea crawled onto my lap.

::*Mommy cry*::

He stood on my legs and wrapped his little arms around my neck as I held him against me. "This is the best thing that ever happened to me," my voice croaked.

"Of course it is," my mom replied, a sinister smirk on her face. "You *chose* to babysit for the wealthiest couples in the area, and you *chose* to bartend at the clubs where the wealthiest men liked to flash their money. It was always your plan to snag a rich man to marry, and now you've succeeded. Congratulations."

Jasper squeezed my leg under the table as all the air in my lungs disappeared with one exhausted breath, rendering me without the ability to respond to her accusation. Hot tears burned my cheeks as I held onto Shea like a safety net, feeling every single eye around the table on me. All I could think about was Jasper accusing me of trying to scam his brother and now my mother was telling his entire family it was true.

"Do you see this?" Jasper spoke up, pointing at Shea. "Last year on Thanksgiving this kid was curled in a ball underneath the dinner table. He was locked in a silent world where nobody could reach him. He barely ate, there was no communication, and he was so broken it was gut wrenching to those of us who love him the most."

"How can you speak about your own daughter that way?" Yvonne asked softly, but sternly.

"I love Jude," Jasper continued. "She's been a great friend to me, and my brother... I've never seen him happier. Whatever scam you're trying to insinuate she's pulling here, I'm not buying it, because she's the best thing that ever happened to Ziggy."

Jasper knew if my lifelong plan was to snag a rich man to marry I could've taken advantage of him at any time, but I didn't. Since I'd confessed our hookup to Sullivan, I could only hope he saw things the same way. But he remained silent and it was only making things worse.

I stood up, still holding Shea in my arms, and said, "This may not be my house, but it's the first time I've ever felt at home. I'm not perfect but I'm loved anyway."

As I opened my mouth to continue, Sullivan said, "Jude, please sit down." I did as he asked and wondered if I'd just made a fatal flaw in our relationship. He continued, "Jude's heart is pure, and she has singlehandedly given Shea the life he deserves. Her mere presence in this house is a breath of fresh air, and I'm a better man for knowing her. Whether she's building elaborate blanket forts, helping Shea get over his fears — of which he has *many* — or teaching him how to enjoy music and dancing without being able to hear, she gives only of herself and has taught us all what true love really is. I look forward to the day I can call her my wife."

Tears burned my eyes as I watched my parents glare at Sullivan while the rest of the table was eerily silent.

"We'll see ourselves out," my dad finally said, ushering my mom out of the room by the elbow.

Jasper jumped out of his seat and followed them, and I could hear him ask, "So we'll see you at the wedding?"

I sat frozen, embarrassed that my parents would go out of their way to humiliate me but at the same time feeling more love from more people than I'd ever experienced in my life.

"Karaoke and coffee time!" Yvonne cheered. "To let our stomachs settle before dessert. Family tradition, you know."

Everybody followed Yvonne out of the room except for Sullivan as Shea's head turned on a swivel to see where everybody was going. Jasper returned saying, "Wow Jude, that was brutal."

"Can you bring Shea into the other room so I can speak with Jude?" Sullivan asked him.

Jasper held his arms out for Shea, who gladly jumped into them as they left us alone at the Thanksgiving table.

"I'm sorry you had to deal with that," Sullivan said, taking my hands in his. "Experiencing their hostility in person was quite different than hearing your horror stories."

I wasn't sure I wanted to know the answer, but my morbid curiosity got the best of me. "Did you believe what they said about me? Even for just a minute?"

He smiled and said, "No, because in the time you've been here, not once have you ever asked me for anything."

I nodded understanding and managed to put on a smile. "So karaoke?"

"You know Jasper and Mom are the karaoke King and Queen," he teased.

"Why don't you join your family and I'll clean up in here."

"I'm not leaving this room without you."

I patted his hand and said, "I could really use some time alone right now."

He watched me for a moment, then kissed me softly. "Okay, but don't be too long. Dishes can wait. Time with people you love is what matters."

After a long, emotional holiday, I said goodnight and retired to my apartment while Sullivan's family was still going strong listening to music, playing games, and recounting lots of Jasper stories for Tabitha's benefit. I soaked in a hot bubble bath until my skin began to prune, then pulled on my fluffy robe and stretched out on the couch to relax with a book before going to bed. I read one chapter before a knock on my door interrupted me. I opened the door to see Sullivan standing there, smiling and looking most handsome.

"Everything okay?" I asked.

"Dad's in bed and Shea is having a slumber party with Mom and Aunt Sadie."

"I see," I replied with a grin, inviting him inside and closing the door.

We sat on the couch and he took one of my hands in his, gently stroking it with his thumb. "I was really proud of you today," he began. "The way you always take care of Shea, how you're so gracious and loving toward my family... and how you handled yourself with your parents."

"I don't look at you as some rich guy who can make all my problems go away with money. It was never like that."

"You never struck me as that type. We were butting heads from day one... if you were trying to seduce me for my money you have a funny way of accomplishing that."

Sullivan softly touched my chin, leaning in for a long, romantic kiss that was soon interrupted by a knock on the door. I couldn't imagine who it was, as everyone else was gone or supposedly in bed.

I opened the door to find Jasper smiling in the hallway, inviting him into the living room. He stopped in his tracks when he saw his brother on the couch.

"Am I allowed to be in here?" Jasper asked.

"What do you want, little brother?" Sullivan teased him with a grin.

"I'm heading out but I just wanted to say goodbye, and thank you for making Tabitha feel at home."

"You really like this girl?" Sullivan asked.

Jasper pulled a face and shrugged, then finally eked out a response. "She's cute and she's nice and I'll see how things go."

I pulled Jasper in for a hug that we both lingered on for some time. "Thank you for sticking up for me," I told him. "I don't think my parents expected anyone to do that."

"I did what was right. You didn't deserve that, and you aren't the person they painted you to be."

"I guess I'm used to it. I'm just not used to it happening in front of a crowd."

"What is their beef anyway?"

I pulled away from Jasper and sat on the couch next to his brother. "They've always resented me," I explained. "First because I was the child who could hear, then because I was the child who lived."

Jasper blew air out of his mouth and replied, "That's messed up."

"And now you've seen it for yourself."

"Our family isn't perfect, but at least we're not crazy."

This caused all three of us to laugh and when Sullivan composed himself he said, "Jasper, I know Jude and I haven't ironed out all the details yet, but I was wondering if you would be my best man at our wedding."

Jasper was visibly shocked, then the brightest smile I'd ever seen crossed his face, revealing dimples in both cheeks and an innocent twinkle in his eyes. "Yes, Ziggy, I would love to be your best man. Thank you."

"As long as it's all right with Jude, of course."

Jasper glanced at me but I was already smiling, happy that the two of them were finally able to put aside their differences and have the brotherly relationship they deserved. Jasper gave me a hug and a kiss goodbye as Sullivan walked him to the door, where they embraced tightly and heartily patted each other on the back. As soon as he closed and locked the door, I got up and headed toward my bedroom.

"Where are you going?" he asked.

"Are you staying?" I kept walking and jumped onto my bed, trying to look sexy by loosening my robe to let him know there was nothing underneath.

"I wanted to. I thought we could discuss our plans for the wedding." He appeared in my doorway, smiling as he folded his arms and leaned against the frame.

"Sure, we can talk about that."

"Did you shave your legs?" he teased.

"Yep. Are you sure we won't be interrupted by Shea's door alarm?"

"They've got him safely locked inside the guest suite. No possible escape."

"Well then by all means, let's talk about the wedding."

Sullivan kicked off his shoes and stretched out on top of me, kissing me softly but pulling away immediately. As he smiled down at me he said, "There's only one thing I want to talk about right now, this minute."

"Okay." I couldn't imagine what was too important to wait until morning, but I obliged him with a smile.

"I knew I would never get involved with a woman unless she could connect with Shea on a spiritual level, even though the chances of that happening were slim to none. I was prepared to be alone for a very long time. I know how much you love Shea, and I know how he feels about you. You're the mother he never had, and I want that to be a reality for him. I want it to be legal. Would you consider adopting Shea as your own?"

I sucked in a breath, my mind twenty shades of blank. When I realized the enormity of what he was asking me, the emotions were almost too much to bear. Trying to keep my tears in check I asked, "What would your family think?"

"You already know the answer to that," he whispered, kissing the tip of my nose.

"Does that mean he can call me Mommy now?" my voice cracked.

"Is that a yes?"

I covered my eyes with my hand and nodded, the tears betraying me as they trickled down my face without permission. I wrapped my arms around his neck and cried as he ran his fingers up and down my leg.

He whispered, "Look at that… you did shave your legs," causing both of us to burst into laughter.

Chapter 22

The second Saturday in December was a big day for Sullivan Publishing, but more so for Sullivan himself, who nervously prepared to finally meet Willow Kelly, their most popular and lucrative author. While he would never admit how anxious he was I could see it written on his face and in his mannerisms, and I stayed out of his way as he constantly checked on the people setting up for the party.

Since it was a family party, I offered to bathe Shea while Sullivan got dressed that evening. As a special treat, Shea got to take a bath in his father's bathroom which was like being in a swimming pool for him. As I bathed him we played a game where he tried to mimic the words I was saying with his mouth while signing. This went along with teaching him how to read lips and while he struggled a lot of the time, he was doing quite well. Typically we'd do this exercise in a mirror so he could watch his own face, but I thought it might be helpful to try it in a different setting.

JoJo was the first name Shea learned to mimic with his lips, and of course, it was his favorite. He walked around with permanent pursed lips it seemed, proud that he could mime his sister's name because she was the person most beloved to him.

After washing and rinsing his hair I said, "JoJo."

Shea's face beamed.

::JoJo::

His puckered lips mimed her name over and over again as I smiled and nodded at his success. Sullivan entered the bathroom securing his tie in place, then knelt in front of the bathtub next to me.

::Daddy!::

Shea excitedly cheered not only with his hands but with his lips as well. This brought the most genuinely beautiful smile to Sullivan's handsome face.

"Who is she?" Sullivan asked Shea, pointing to me.

Shea looked confused, as if it were a trick question. He looked at his father but refused to answer.

"I love Miss J," he explained. "And she loves me. We're going to get married and then we'll be a family. What do you think of that?"

Shea's mouth curved into the tiniest of grins as he looked at his father, then at me, then back again. He then looked sideways, as if someone else were talking to him. He nodded, then turned his attention back to us.

::Mommy?::

"Yes, Shea, she's your mommy now."

His little lips moved as he tried to mimic the word he'd so desperately wanted to call me since the day we met.

::Mommy!::

::Mommy!::

::Mommy!::

He stood up and cheered with his hands as he leaned closer to my face and placed his palms on my cheeks. I watched as his tiny lips moved, and when he finally mimicked *Mommy*, Sullivan and I both clapped and cheered his success.

Shea climbed out of the bathtub and lunged at me, knocking me to the floor as he hugged me fiercely, his soaking wet body drenching my robe. I laughed at his excitement, wrapping my arms around him to return the sentiment.

Sullivan picked Shea up with a towel and began drying him off so I could get ready for the party. As I got to my feet Shea grabbed my robe and wouldn't let go.

::Mommy!::

"I have to get ready for the party. I'll see you downstairs."

::Love you, Mommy::

"I love you, too, Shea."

"I love you, Jude," Sullivan said, looking a little left out.

"I love you, too, Ziggy."

I gave him a quick kiss on the lips and as I did so, Shea placed both of his hands on his cheeks as he grinned and began to giggle. We had never shown any affection in front of Shea before that moment and it was then I think it truly sunk in as to what being a family meant.

My heart was full of love as I headed to my apartment to get ready for the party, thankful for everything I had in my life. I couldn't wait to marry Sullivan in May as we planned, and hearing Shea call me Mommy gave me a warmth I couldn't begin to describe. It was as if my life finally had purpose and I was surrounded by people who truly loved me, flaws and all.

Jasper had just arrived when I made my way downstairs, greeting him with a hug as he kissed my cheek.

"No Tabitha?" I asked, wondering why he was flying solo.

"She wasn't feeling well, so I told her it was no big deal."

Sullivan appeared as Shea ran to greet his uncle with great excitement, jumping into his arms for a hug.

"Are you sure she's coming?" Sullivan asked, wiping his brow.

"Relax, she'll be here."

"You spoke to her yourself?"

"Through her agent as always, but she'll be here."

Most people attending the party recognized Sullivan as the classy, calm businessman he always was, but Jasper and I both knew he was a nervous wreck under the smile and dazzling conversation. While Sullivan and Jasper schmoozed the guests at the party, my duty that evening was Shea, who was intrigued and frightened by all the children in attendance. He wasn't used to being around other children and I realized we had made a grave mistake in not assimilating him properly. He was going to be five years old on New Year's Eve, and it was probably time to start thinking about enrolling him in school.

One of the highlights of my evening was the way Sullivan introduced me to every guest as his fiancé, never shying away from our involvement or relationship in any way. He was always fussing over me, making sure I was all right, but I knew that was coming from his anxiety over waiting for Willow Kelly to arrive. I couldn't understand what was taking her so long when the party was already in full swing without her. I'd heard of fashionably late, but she was downright rude.

"Where is she?" Sullivan grumbled, appearing at my side.

As Shea clung to my skirt I whispered, "Jasper promised she'd be here."

"She's three hours late."

"Well let's just hope she wasn't in an accident or something." I rubbed his back and whispered, "You look very handsome."

He smiled, glancing down at Shea, then back at me. "And you're stunning. I'm so glad you're here, like this, and not under a table with your ass hanging out."

We both laughed and I replied, "Well hold onto your pants, funny guy, because Jasper could always end up passed out naked somewhere."

"That's why alcohol is limited at this party," he whispered.

Jasper joined us and said to Shea, "Having fun, buddy?"

Shea shrugged.

"Where is she, Jasper?" Sullivan asked quietly. "She's three hours late, and she was supposed to read her book to the kids. The party's almost over."

"I just got off the phone with her agent," he replied. "She's not coming."

Sullivan looked like he was going to explode. "What do you mean she's not coming?"

"I'll explain later, but these kids are getting restless. Someone should read the book, even if it's not Willow Kelly."

"Be my guest, brainiac."

"Jude, will you sign for Shea?"

"Sure."

Jasper gathered all the children to sit on the floor as I brought Shea to join them, explaining what was going to happen. He did as I asked and watched me as I signed everything Jasper said, from his sorrow over Willow Kelly not being able to attend the event as promised, to his explanation about the book. The room was silent as Jasper spoke, grabbing everyone's attention with his charisma and charm as he explained that the new book was about a deaf child, but also published in braille so blind children could read it as well. He relayed how the book was very special to him because of his deaf nephew, but did not point to Shea in order to avoid singling him out.

As Jasper read the book aloud, Shea concentrated solely on me as I told the story through sign language as his personal interpreter. He smiled and gasped at the adventures and troubles of the boy in the story, and when it was over he clapped along with the other children who appeared to enjoy it.

As the children found their way back to their parents, I sat in a comfortable wingback chair and pulled a very tired Shea onto my lap. One by one the party guests came to say goodbye and wish me well on my upcoming wedding as I cradled a sleeping Shea in my arms. When the last guest was ushered out the door, Sullivan returned to the party room loosening his tie and running a hand through his hair.

"Well that was a complete disaster," he said.

"It wasn't," I argued. "It was a nice party and the kids enjoyed the story."

"It was a book release party for an author who couldn't be bothered to show up for her own event," he hissed. "We're dropping her from the roster, Jasper. I'm not going to let her make a fool of me again. She's *gone*."

"But Ziggy—"

"I don't want to hear it. I'm *done*."

"There's something you need to know," Jasper replied cautiously.

"Was she in an accident?" I asked. "Maybe there's a good reason she didn't show tonight."

"She wasn't in an accident," Jasper answered. "She was here."

Sullivan straightened and shoved his hands in his pockets. "What do you mean she was here? Where? Is this one of your lame-brained jokes?"

"She was here," Jasper insisted. "She's me. I'm Willow Kelly."

The air in the room became so thick I almost couldn't breathe. Sullivan stood there like a statue, his face expressionless. He took a step toward Jasper then thought better of moving any closer.

"I'm sorry, what did you say?" Sullivan asked, rubbing his eyes.

Jasper ran to the other side of the food table to put something between he and his brother as Sullivan's face began to redden.

"I can explain," Jasper replied guiltily, his hands in the air to surrender.

"Then start talking!"

"About six years ago I submitted a manuscript and you, Mom and Dad all rejected it. You said I needed to hone my skills and maybe you'd give me another chance. I hired an editor to help tighten up the story then found an agent who believed in my book, and she resubmitted it under a pen name and Sullivan Publishing accepted it. So you either never read my manuscript or you just—"

"You were seventeen!"

"So what?"

"You were too young!"

"Other publishers wanted my manuscript," Jasper continued. "They were willing to pay more money than you were, but for me it wasn't about the money. It was about proving to my own family that I—"

"This was about humiliating me and making me look like a fool!" Sullivan spat. "All this time parading under my nose as Willow Kelly and knowing damn well I was never going to meet *her*."

"All those times you thought I was screwing off doing my own thing and not caring about the family business, I was home alone writing books. Books that *everybody* loves; books that *you* love. So get off your high horse and face the music, because I could easily leave *you* and go with another publisher. And I wouldn't even have to reveal my identity."

Sullivan's face was a mixture of anger and sadness as he dropped into a chair and held his head in his hands, a complete wreck. I sat there like a stone holding Shea in my arms, trying to understand why Jasper would lie to his family that way, and continue the charade when he knew he couldn't show them who Willow Kelly really was.

"I can't believe you did that," I said. "How could you let this party go on knowing you wouldn't be able to produce the author for her own event?"

"Jude, you don't understand the business."

"It doesn't matter," I protested. "You lied to your family, you lied to Ziggy, you lied to your readers."

Jasper bit his lip and stomped toward me. "Talk about lies...how about we tell good old Ziggy the truth about *us*? Tell him how I picked you up at the Cheetah Club and—"

"I told him. He already knows what happened between us."

"Well, I guess you both know each other's dirtiest secrets," Jasper chuckled. "Or maybe not."

Sullivan jumped up from his seat and grabbed the front of Jasper's shirt, slamming him down in the chair he just vacated. "It's time for you to go," he hissed.

"Come on, old man," Jasper sneered. "Jude agreed to marry you. Don't you think you need to stop lying to her?"

Every inch of my body pricked with anxiety as Jasper pulled me into the argument, behaving like a child because his elaborate scheme was uncovered.

"What are you talking about?" I asked, not sure I wanted to know the answer.

Sullivan pushed Jasper further into the cushions of the chair as he growled, "Shut your mouth."

"What's he talking about?" My stomach roiled as my hold on Shea became tighter, afraid I might lose my grip and drop him to the floor.

Ziggy Sullivan might not have been the easiest man in the world to get along with, but he was always honest, to the point of brutality at times, and I couldn't imagine him lying about anything let alone lying to me.

"What's he talking about?" I asked again.

Sullivan shoved Jasper hard in the chest one last time before standing up straight and running a hand through his hair. He shrugged off his suit coat, ripped off his dangling tie and tossed them over the back of an empty chair he slumped into. He threw his head back and covered his face with both hands, making me increasingly uncomfortable. He waved an arm in Jasper's direction, apparently giving him permission to throw him under the bus.

Jasper sat up, resting his arms on his legs and looking a bit pale, as if he were suddenly having second thoughts about his outburst and revealing potentially harmful information about his brother.

"I'm sorry," Jasper said quietly. "I should just go."

I stood up, still holding a sleeping Shea in my arms. "One of you better start talking."

Jasper looked sheepish and stared at the floor for some time before finally lifting his head to look at me. "I'm Shea's biological father."

Something in my head exploded as I lost my balance and struggled to hold onto Shea, collapsing back into my chair. I stared at him blankly, unable to comprehend the words that just came out of his mouth.

"Okay... so you're Willow Kelly *and* you're Shea's biological father. Is it April Fool's Day... I don't get the joke." Beads of sweat began to form on my face as my heart almost forgot to beat on its own. The dead silence in the room was overwhelming and the walls began to close in on me. "One of you better say something!" I shrieked.

"He's telling the truth," Sullivan finally conceded.

"I don't understand."

Jasper hung his head, suddenly afraid to say anything further after causing the uproar we were now smack dab in the middle of.

"Jasper had an affair with my wife," Sullivan spoke softly. "Shea and JoJo were the result."

Bile rose in my throat as I stared at Jasper with my mouth agape. "You slept with his *wife*? No wonder he hated you!"

Jasper raised a hand in defense and replied, "It's not exactly like that."

"Well what is it then?" I demanded.

"She seduced me," he answered, his face revealing his humiliation.

"But she was your brother's *wife*."

"I was an eighteen-year-old virgin," he argued. "He was never home, she was lonely and I was... horny. I knew it was wrong but I couldn't help myself. She was a beautiful older woman and I was—"

"Looking for revenge because he wouldn't publish your book?" I hissed.

"No, it wasn't like that, I swear."

Sullivan cleared his throat and added, "I was in London for two months trying to seal the deal on buying out a publisher there to add an international branch, but it ended up falling through. Jenny and I had been having problems before I left and hadn't been intimate in some time. When I came home she was pregnant and it was obvious I wasn't the father."

"But you raised them as your own," I said, my voice cracking.

"Jasper could barely take care of himself let alone a baby, and as much as I despised Jenny for her part in it, I couldn't abandon her. We agreed to stay married and raise the twins together and that's what we did. Unfortunately it didn't alleviate her drinking problem, and I just grew to resent her more and more."

I looked at Shea and wondered why he was trembling so, but realized I was the one in physical turmoil as I tried to wrap my head around this unexpected revelation.

"Does Shea know?" I whispered.

Jasper cleared his throat and answered, "No. I signed away my parental rights."

This punched me hard in the gut, causing me to gasp out loud. "How could you give up your children? What kind of person gives up their own children?"

The tension in the room was so thick I could chew through it with angry, gnashing teeth.

"Jude, I was eighteen. I knew Ziggy would be a good father and Shea and JoJo would be well taken care of. Can you imagine the guy who picked you up at the Cheetah Club raising two kids?"

"You're still that guy!" I shrieked. "You're immature and impulsive and *selfish*!"

"Thank you for proving his point," Sullivan interjected.

"When you bring a child into the world you're supposed to grow up and make changes and take care of them!" I continued ranting. "Not toss them to the side like a mistake you want to forget!"

Sullivan got up from his chair and knelt in front of me, placing a gentle hand on my arm, which I promptly yanked away from him.

"Jude," Sullivan said with a sigh. "Jasper knew his limitations and did what he felt was best for the twins."

I couldn't explain it, but I was behaving as though this information was an attack on me personally, when it had nothing to do with me at all. But I felt as though I'd been lied to the minute I walked into that house and no one had even thought about telling me the truth. And as Sullivan's fiancé, didn't either one of them think it mattered? And then it became a completely different ballgame for me.

I glared into Sullivan's eyes and said, "You made Jasper sign a contract?"

"Yes."

"You made your brother sign a contract giving up his rights as their father?"

"Yes, why is that so odd? I needed to make sure their future was secure and that Jasper wouldn't come along later and try to take them away from me."

"Is everything a business deal with you?" I spat. "Even your children?"

"You're being unfair. Why are you taking this so personally?"

My chest heaved as every word I wanted to say was scrambled in my head, leaving me unable to speak.

"Jude, we found a way to make it work," Jasper said. "And the twins never lacked in love where either of us were concerned. Especially Shea. Surely you've seen that with your own eyes."

I felt like someone had kidnapped me and dumped me off on another planet; a planet where I was alone, raw and naked, with no voice and no viable air to breathe. I stood up on wobbly legs as the tears welled in my eyes and gently placed Shea into Sullivan's arms before walking out of the room. I could hear both of them calling for me but I ignored them, walking up the stairs and going straight to my apartment. Once inside I fell against the door and slid to the floor, the tears pouring out of me like an uncontrollable fountain. It wasn't long before I heard tapping on my door and I slowly pulled myself up to answer it.

Sullivan was standing there with Shea still sound asleep in his arms. He looked shaken but he said nothing, waiting for me to explain my abrupt, emotional departure. But I couldn't find the words that would properly convey what I was feeling, because I didn't understand it myself.

After staring at each other for too long without speaking he finally said, "Shea is *my* son. Nothing changes that."

"Why didn't you tell me?"

"Honestly, it never crossed my mind. Once I made the decision to be their father, they were *my* children. I couldn't have a relationship with Jasper if all I did was look at him as their father. I couldn't live my life that way. Not if I wanted to save my family and raise my children."

Pain seized my heart as I choked, "But we're getting married, and this is something you should have shared with me."

"Shea is *my* son, just like *you're* his mother. It doesn't matter who his birth parents were."

"Wrong answer."

Without giving him a chance to say another word, I closed the door in his face.

"This isn't over," he shouted through the door. "After I put Shea to bed we're finishing this conversation."

I went to my bedroom and changed into my pajamas and by the time I returned to the living room he had returned. I swung the door open quickly and glared at him, but he didn't back down.

"I'd really like to be alone right now," I grumbled.

"Sorry, that's not going to happen. If we're getting married, there's no avoiding tough conversations. It's both of us, together, and we have to put in equal shares or it's never going to work."

"That whole fifty-fifty thing is bullshit if you can't tell me the truth."

"It's not fifty-fifty, Jude. Both people have to give one hundred percent, not just fifty percent. Would you be satisfied if I only gave you fifty percent of my time? Fifty percent of my attention? It's one hundred percent, or it's nothing."

"Well you one hundred percent *failed* when it came to trusting me with the truth about Shea."

"I still don't understand why you're taking this so personally. Honestly, whether you like it or not, it's none of your business. And now that Jasper opened his big mouth, the resentment I felt when I first learned he had an affair with my wife is all coming to the surface again. Feelings I buried a long time ago are eating me alive and you're angry with *me*! How can you possibly see me as the bad guy in any of this?"

I knew he was right but I was still so angry and I needed to choose my words carefully.

"Because I wasn't important enough for you to tell the truth."

"The only truth is that Shea is *my* son, and nothing else should matter," he argued.

"I'm sorry, but I can't accept that."

"Well apparently Jasper wanted you to know the truth, or he wouldn't have so blatantly gone against everything we agreed to."

"Because *he* trusts me with the truth and you obviously *don't*."

I didn't even have the chance to close the door on him again because he walked away, his hair and shoulders bouncing angrily in time with his footsteps as he disappeared down the hallway.

༄

I knew Sullivan and I were both stubborn, but the following week was brutal. I stayed in my apartment all day Sunday feigning illness, then returned to my regular duties with Shea Monday morning. We spent some time looking at the scrapbook we were creating for his father, which now included photos of the three of us together. As I looked at the happy, smiling faces of the three of us my heart melted and I realized I was being completely unreasonable. Sullivan was the unmistakable hero in this story and I had no reason to be angry with him for protecting his children.

When Sullivan arrived home from work that evening my heart swelled at the sight of him and I smiled as Shea greeted him with his daily leap into the arms, hug around the neck and kiss on the cheek.

As I opened my mouth to apologize for being a jerk, he spoke instead. "Jude, you've spent so much time helping Shea and myself, even Jasper to an extent, but you haven't received the help you need. It's obvious you have a lot of unresolved issues and I think you should talk —"

"Unresolved issues?" While I knew deep down he was giving me a compliment and trying to help me, I immediately took offense. Because that's how the old Jude operated. I was always on the defensive because I was forever on the receiving end of my parents' disappointment and disdain.

"Please just hear me out."

"Unresolved issues?" I said again. "This had nothing to do with *me*, it had everything to do with you not telling me the truth."

"Jude, I—"

"Take your unresolved issues and shove them up your ass."

I fixed myself a dinner plate and retreated to my apartment, leaving Sullivan shaking his head and Shea chasing me as far as the stairs, then turning to go back to his father.

Shea and I spent the rest of the week creating Christmas decorations to hang up around the house, which included painting ornaments, coloring pages from his giant coloring book, gluing sequins and glitter to styrofoam balls, and creating handmade picture frames out of popsicle sticks that he could give as gifts with his photograph inside. Shea loved working with his hands and was overjoyed to be creating such colorful, fun items for Christmas.

The routine once Sullivan returned home was the same; he would greet Shea and I would fix a dinner plate and disappear to my apartment. I was being unreasonable, I knew that. Years of mistrust and poor relationship skills were overwhelming everything good the Sullivan family ever showed me and I couldn't get out of my own way. Even worse, I convinced myself that Sullivan didn't really love me; he was only in love with my connection with Shea, the same way Jasper was.

I knew Sullivan Publishing shut down for three weeks during the holidays and I took advantage of that to do the unthinkable. I knew

Sullivan would be home for Shea, so on Saturday the 15th while they were outside playing in the snow, I left a note on the kitchen table saying I needed some time alone to think about my future. I placed his grandmother's ring on top and headed out the front door with my suitcase. My heart thundered in my chest as I hurriedly slid into the back of the sedan and gave Andy the address of the hotel where I'd be staying. I closed my eyes tightly as he pulled away, hoping with every fiber of my being they didn't see me leave.

As Andy pulled up to the front of the hotel he turned to face me, which is something he never did while he was working.

"Is everything okay?" he asked.

Even as I tried to talk myself into believing I was doing the right thing for everyone involved, the hot tears eked their way out of my eyes and my stomach clenched in distress.

"I would never ask you to lie," I said, barely able to speak the words.

"Ms. Hastings?"

"If he asks... just tell him the truth."

Andy helped me out of the car and set my suitcase on the sidewalk. "You don't seem okay."

"I'll never be okay," I admitted.

Chapter 23

For three days I shut myself in a boring hotel room with no amenities other than a coffeemaker and a microwave, living on whatever they had in the vending machine, but since I wasn't very hungry I didn't leave my room often.

Being so close to Christmas, I hid in the bed watching Christmas movies and blubbering like a baby, wondering if I ever truly belonged anywhere at the same time knowing I was the reason for my own despair. Things were going so well and I finally felt like my life meant something, that I had a purpose, but then I got involved with Sullivan and everything changed. I made a fatal mistake and couldn't go back and change a thing; how could I ever walk back into his home and just be Shea's nanny?

A knock on the door sent my heart racing as I jumped out of bed to peer through the peephole to see who it was. I don't know how it was possible, but I was equal parts disappointed and happy as I saw Jasper standing there. I opened the door to let him in.

"I know my brother pays you better than this," he said, entering the room. "You could have at least picked a hotel with room service."

I closed the door and replied, "I'm not here for a luxury vacation."

"Why *are* you here?"

Before I could begin to explain I burst into tears and he was soon sweeping me into his arms for a comforting embrace. Jasper said nothing, letting me weep and get it out of my system. I had to admit it was nice to see him and a relief to have someone to talk to. When I'd calmed down and stopped ugly crying, we sat crosslegged on the bed facing each other and he smiled at me.

"Come on Jude, what're you doing?"

"I told you I wasn't a good person," I cried.

"I'm tired of that bullshit excuse. You got scared and you're sabotaging everything good in your life."

"Scared? Scared of what?"

"I don't know… why are you so mad at him? *I'm* the one you should be mad at. *I'm* the bad guy in all of this. *I'm* the one who had an affair with my brother's wife and ended up getting her pregnant. *That's* why he has such issues with me, and rightly so."

I stared at my hands, tightly grasping each other as they sat motionless in my lap. "He should've told me," I said, waiting for the brow beating he was probably going to give me.

"That's where you're wrong," Jasper gently scolded.

"Wrong?" I was incensed. "Marrying him, marrying into his family, I had the right to know the truth about Shea."

"This isn't about you. This is between me and Ziggy, and the only reason I opened my big mouth was to hurt him. And I succeeded… opening up all the old wounds but even worse, you walking out on him and Shea."

"I didn't walk out on them. I needed to…." His eyes grew wide waiting for me to finish. I was rendered dumbstruck, struggling to find something to say. "I thought you wanted me to know, and that's why you said something."

"To be honest I'm glad you know, but it was never my intention to reveal our dirty family secret. Ziggy is Shea's father, and that's what matters."

"Do your parents know?"

Jasper lowered his head and was quiet for a moment before he replied, "Mom and Dad know. It nearly destroyed my family, but they chose forgiveness instead of judgment and we managed to put it past us for the kids."

I stared at my hands and thought about Shea and poor little JoJo as tears stung my eyes. "How can you give up your own children?"

Jasper grabbed my hand and said, "Look at me." He waited until I raised my head to meet his eyes and he continued, "It was *never* about giving up my own children. It was only about doing the best thing for those kids. And then after Jenny and JoJo died… I would never have been able to do what Ziggy did. I love those kids more than my own life, and that's why Ziggy is their father. He's a remarkable man, and he's dealt with more tragedy than most people can handle. And losing you would be another kick in the gut he doesn't deserve."

Guilt and self-loathing bubbled up from my toes and choked me, the ugly tears causing me to lean over and bury my face against my leg.

"But he hasn't called… he hasn't come to see me," I wailed.

"You know my brother is black and white; there's no grey. You said you needed space to think and he's giving you what you asked for. And it doesn't matter how much this is killing him, he's not going to chase you."

I wiped the tears from my face and picked at a thread on the hem of my pajama pants. "Is Shea okay?"

"No he's not, but you had to know what would happen when you left."

He was brutal, but I was thankful he chose not to sugarcoat anything because I deserved every ounce of it. I didn't deserve to be soothed for my decision because I knew exactly how it would affect Shea and chose to do it anyway.

"Look," he said with a heavy sigh. "If you're torturing yourself because you think you aren't worthy, I know my brother, and he really loves you. You need to decide what you're going to do." I sat motionless on the bed as he got up and headed toward the door. "I have to go; I have a date."

"With Tabitha?"

He grinned as his cheeks blushed. "Yes. She's a nice girl; I'm hoping I don't screw it up."

I jumped off the bed and rushed to give him a hug before he left. "Thank you," I said.

"He won't wait around forever," Jasper whispered against my face. "And once he's gone, he's gone for good. He doesn't play games."

It didn't matter how many times I picked up the phone, I couldn't dial the number. What was I so afraid of? Jasper told me that Sullivan loved me and that's what I really needed to know, wasn't it? I knew I was broken and once that switch flipped after finding out the truth about Shea, I was back in self-destruction mode and found it impossible to return. Maybe I was making it all about me, but it wasn't my intention. Betrayal was something I grew used to in my life, and this was just one more thing that, in my mind, proved I would always be the outsider looking in, even when it came to my own life.

Instead of reaching out as Jasper suggested, I withdrew further into my own self-pity and stayed in bed watching Christmas movies on cable television. The love Sullivan and his family had shown me was overshadowed by a lifetime of disdain and resentment my parents showered over me my entire life, and for a split second I found myself hating my sister. Not only for being the favorite child, but for dying on me and making everything worse.

On Thursday the 20th I took a shower, dressed, then went to the vending machine and purchased a can of soda, a bag of chips and a candy bar. I had just finished the bag of chips and bit into the candy bar when a knock on the door startled me. I opened the door with the candy bar clenched between my teeth, thinking it was Jasper returning to scold me, but there before my eyes stood Sullivan, his cheeks pink from the cold, his hands stuffed inside his coat pockets and his eyes drinking me in, sending a shiver through my entire body.

"Blanche has been worried about what you've been eating," he said. "Now I can see why." I stared at him speechless. "Are you going to make me stay in the hallway?"

I motioned him in with my hand and closed the door after he entered, promptly throwing the candy bar in the trash. I was silently thankful I took a shower, as I'd been looking pretty pathetic up until then. He pulled out the chair from the desk and sat down, never bothering to remove his coat. This told me he wasn't planning on staying very long.

I sat on the bed and asked, "How's Shea?"

"You already know the answer to that."

He was right; I knew Shea wasn't doing well and I was the one who caused it.

"What're you doing here?" I asked, my voice barely audible.

He pulled a manila envelope from inside his coat and handed it to me.

"Even if you don't want to marry me, I still want you to be Shea's mother. If you're still interested in adopting him, that is. I realize the chances of that are highly unlikely at this point, but I wanted you to know it's still an option."

I took the envelope from him and stared at it, my eyes blinded by tears.

"I'll buy you a place to live — house, condo, your choice — so we can share custody of Shea. I'll fully support you, and if you'd like to go back to school, I'll take care of that, too."

"Why would you do that?" my voice cracked.

"Because I love you. But most importantly, because Shea loves you."

I swallowed hard and asked, "What have you told him?"

"The truth."

"The truth?" I quizzed, shocked. "Why would you tell him the truth? He's only four!"

"He'll be five in eleven days," he reminded me. "What, the arbiter of truth has a problem with telling my son the truth?"

"What did you tell him?" I demanded.

"I told him you were mad at me and that you needed some time away from home."

"You *told* him that?"

"Oh I'm sorry, did you prefer me to lie to him? Make up something that turns it into flowers and butterfly kisses?"

"That's not fair."

"It's perfectly fair, Jude. You're furious with me because you think I kept the truth from you, yet you want me to keep your truth from my son. You can't have it both ways."

"That's not... I didn't mean...." Once again he was right and I had no words to contradict him.

Sullivan got to his feet and walked toward me. "Our company Christmas party is Saturday. You're still welcome to attend." He leaned over and kissed the top of my head, then headed to the door. As my eyes met his he said, "Jude, you need to figure out who you're really angry with."

I spent the rest of that evening having a throw down with myself. I locked myself in the bathroom and took a good look in the mirror, hating everything I saw. One by one I saw every single reason I was angry and addressed each one individually. I saw my hateful parents and screamed at them for treating me differently my whole life and that they had no right to love me less than my sister. I saw Prude and screamed at her for dying on me. I knew it wasn't her fault but there was a part of me that couldn't forgive her. I saw my old boyfriend Colin and screamed at him for abandoning me when I needed him most, and never truly loving me to begin with. Lastly I saw myself, the person I loathed more than anyone else. I hated her for falling into the trap my parents set, misbehaving as a child to get their attention, then self-destructing after Prude's death because it's exactly what they expected me to do. I hated her for being a drunk and a whore and for hurting Jasper, who I cared very deeply for. I hated her for pushing away Sullivan, the one person who appeared to love me despite my flaws, and then I thought about Shea, which caused me such anguish I collapsed to the floor unable to face that person in the mirror. Sweet, innocent and troubled Shea, who was suffering because I couldn't get my head out of my own ass long enough to see who I was really harming with my drastic actions.

I sobbed for the little boy I walked out on; I was no different than the mother who treated him differently because he wasn't perfect in her eyes. I was no different than my own parents who, even though I lived in their home the entire time, abandoned me in spirit because I was never good enough and could never compare to my sister.

Jasper was right. I was sabotaging everything that was good in my life because I was afraid I didn't really deserve happiness. It had been ingrained in me at such a young age that I would never be good enough that when the best things happened in my life I looked them straight in the eye and pushed them away. Sayonara good things, this girl would rather be miserable and alone than believe she was actually capable of being loved and *deserving* of that love. No matter how many hearts she crushed along her beaten path of self-loathing. The heart of a child, however... unforgivable.

I picked myself off the bathroom floor and marched to the telephone, dialing Jasper's number.

"I need your help."

⁂

I was a nervous wreck as the taxi drove through the chilly night toward Sullivan's house, trying desperately to keep my party dress from getting wrinkled. Jasper met me at the back door as planned and hurried me into the butler's pantry, closing the door behind us.

As I handed him my coat he looked me up and down and said, "Wow. Merry Christmas, Ziggy."

I wore a sleeveless red velvet dress with a floor-length skirt and matching red pumps, and I actually got a manicure and had my hair put in a French braid with red, sparkly accents to match my outfit.

Wringing my hands together I asked, "Do I look okay?"

"You look better than okay," he assured me. "You're a knockout."

"Jasper, it's not the time—"

"What? I can't compliment my future sister-in-law?"

"If I haven't completely screwed that up."

Jasper rested his hands gently on my shoulders and whispered, "He's crazy about you, trust me. You and Ziggy and Shea... you're meant to be together." His eyes began to tear up as he added, "I could never ask for a better mother for my son."

"Jasper...." I smiled as tears blurred my vision.

"Just remember everything we discussed, and you'll be fine," he said.

"Thank you."

He gave me a hug, then kissed my cheek and said, "In about ten minutes I'm going to send him for more wine. Then you can do your magic."

I smiled and nodded before he bopped my nose, gave me a wink and walked out, closing the door. Ten minutes felt like ten years waiting as I clutched the manila envelope holding Shea's adoption papers close to my chest. Jasper made it sound so easy, as if Sullivan would melt like butter in my hands, but I had my doubts. I had hurt him deeply, and the angst I caused Shea could never be forgiven.

I closed my eyes and rehearsed my speech over and over again in my head, praying I would be able to say the words that needed to be said and that Sullivan would find them honest and heartfelt. I gasped when I heard the doorknob jiggle, then held my breath as the door opened.

Sullivan appeared stunned as he stood there staring at me. I smiled and he finally collected himself, closing the door for privacy. He looked as handsome as ever in his casual suit and red Santa Claus tie.

"Jude," he greeted coolly.

"I'm sorry," I began. "I was wrong, and you were right. About everything."

"Jude, I should've—"

"No, let me finish. You were right; the truth about Jasper and Shea was none of my business. I'm sorry I got so upset with you. You did nothing wrong."

"Jude, I should've—"

"Ziggy, after you left the other night I did a lot of soul searching and you were right; I needed to figure out who I was really mad at. In the end I was angry with myself and I can't take back what I did, but I'm hoping you can forgive me."

He pointed at the envelope in my hands and asked, "Are those the adoption papers?" As I opened my mouth to speak he said, "Wait, don't answer that. I'll be right back."

He walked out of the pantry, leaving me there alone. All the courage I had mustered and he walked out, leaving me there to wonder where I stood. Where *we* stood. He rushed back in a few minutes later and closed the door.

"Are those the adoption papers?" he asked again.

"Yes, but—"

"Did you sign them? I just need to know if you signed them."

"I will sign them on one condition."

He pulled a face and let out a heavy sigh. "What's your condition?" He seemed surprised that I would have any conditions at all.

"I love Shea more than anyone else in the world," I told him. "But I want to raise him with you. As your wife."

A grin slowly crept across his face, then turned into the smile of a very happy man. He pulled his grandmother's amethyst ring out of his pocket and slid it on my finger, asking, "Jude, will you marry me?"

"Yes, Ziggy, I will marry you."

Trying not to mess up my hair, he placed his hands gently on the sides of my head and pulled me closer as he leaned down to kiss me. He showered me with soft velvety kisses and I wanted to cry because of how much I missed him.

"I should've told you about Shea," he whispered against my mouth as he continued kissing me. "Everything about Shea is your business and I'm sorry."

"Let's agree not to talk about it again."

"Deal."

"Can I come back home?"

Sullivan pulled his face away from mine and smiled. "I never asked you to leave."

Tears escaped my eyes as my voice croaked, "You're the best thing that ever happened to me. I missed you both so much."

"I'm glad you're back, and Shea will be delighted to see you."

I threw my arms around his neck and pulled him in for a kiss he wouldn't soon forget. There was a knock on the door but we both ignored it, enjoying our makeup moment to its fullest extent. The door opened and we heard Jasper say, "Santa's here."

Sullivan ignored him, waving him off with his hand as I continued to shower him with affection.

"Don't you want to see what Shea wants for Christmas?" Jasper asked.

We both stopped and I said, "I want to see Shea."

Sullivan took me by the hand as we followed Jasper out of the pantry, through the kitchen and to the party room, where Santa was pulling out small, wrapped gifts for each of the children in attendance. Yvonne was holding Shea, who wanted nothing to do with Santa Claus, nibbling his fingers with his head resting on her shoulder. He looked adorable in his little Christmas sweater covered in reindeer, and as soon as I saw him my throat dried up and I couldn't control the emotions I tried so hard to keep hidden. Sullivan led me through the crowd and when Yvonne spotted me she smiled as my shaking hand covered my mouth and tears burned my eyes. She poked Shea's belly and pointed toward me, but he ignored her. He looked so broken, and my heart shattered because I knew I was the reason. I caused it.

Sullivan ran a finger across Shea's cheek and he raised his head and held out his arms, but instead of taking the child, he pointed my way. Shea's eyes met mine and the flood of tears erupted out of me, any attempt of controlling them futile.

::Mommy!::

Shea squirmed to be released so Yvonne set him on the floor, and as soon as his feet touched down he ran at full speed until he reached me, launching himself into my waiting arms. I sat on the floor and held him against me as he bounced happily in my lap, hugging my neck and kissing my cheek. He pulled away and smiled at me, touching my mouth with his finger.

::Mommy::

::Love you::

::Mommy!::

"I missed you so much," I told him, the tears streaming down my face. "I love you."

::P told me::

"Told you what?"

::You come home::

Shea's bottom lip began to quiver as he remembered that I had been gone, and he burst into tears that tore me apart, and deservedly so. The entire party was watching the scene playing out before them, including Santa Claus, who stopped handing out gifts because the children were no longer paying attention to him. Shea wailed in quiet agony as he clung to me while I cried along with him and didn't care that my makeup was probably running down my face in black streaks.

Even though he couldn't hear me I sobbed, "I'm so sorry, Shea. I'm never leaving you again. I promise. *Never*." As I spoke his little hand was pressed against my throat, feeling the vibration of my voice.

He pulled away to look at me, his face wet with tears and his chest spasming from crying.

::Mommy::

::Voice::

"Yes, that's my voice."

He became nearly inconsolable as he watched my face mirroring his own emotions, and as he cried, a long, quiet groan escaped his mouth. I gasped and pointed to his throat as I said, "Voice! Your voice!"

He continued to cry as I held his hand against his own throat, and when another anguished groan escaped his eyes grew large and he smiled.

::Voice::

"Yes! Your voice!"

"We've been practicing this," Sullivan whispered as he placed a hand on my shoulder. "He wanted to give you something special for Christmas."

I looked away from Shea for a brief second to see Sullivan smiling at me. I immediately looked back at Shea as he took a deep breath and leaned close to my face. With his hand pressed firmly against his own throat he smiled and the entire room was silent as his little voice said, "Mommy."

THE END

"Hey Jude - The Novel" Soundtrack Available on Spotify

"Do You Believe In Love" by Huey Lewis & The News - 1981
"Here Comes The Night" by Nick Gilder - 1978
"Medicine Jar" by Wings - 1976
"Lipstick and Leather" by Y&T - 1984
"It Ain't Me Babe" by The Turtles - 1965
"Beat's So Lonely" by Charlie Sexton - 1985
"Midnight Blue" by Lou Gramm - 1987
"Young Love" by Air Supply - 1982
"Gettin' Better" by Tesla - 1986
"Hang On Sloopy" by The McCoys - 1964
"I've Had Enough" by Wings - 1978
"Gone Movin' On" by Paul Revere & The Raiders - 1970
"Speak To The Sky" by Rick Springfield - 1971
"Give It To Me Good" by Trixter - 1989
"I'd Love You To Want Me" by Lobo - 1972
"Call To The Heart" by Giuffria - 1985
"Mr. Sun Mr. Moon" by Paul Revere & The Raiders - 1969
"Any Way You Want It" by Journey - 1980
"Soul Deep" by The Box Tops - 1969
"Paperback Writer" by The Beatles - 1966
"Yummy Yummy Yummy" by Ohio Express - 1968
"I Believe In Music" by Gallery - 1972
"Bang Bang" by Danger Danger - 1989
"Just Between You And Me" by April Wine - 1981
"Hey Jude" by The Beatles - 1968
"Love Is Alright Tonight" by Rick Springfield - 1981
"Two Less Lonely People In The World" by Air Supply - 1982
"Boulevard Of Broken Dreams" by Hanoix Rocks - 1985
"I Wonder What She's Doing Tonight" by Boyce & Hart - 1967
"Makin' It" by David Naughton - 1979
"Birthday" by The Beatles - 1968
"Dancing Queen" by ABBA - 1976
"Stone In Love" by Journey - 1981

"Jailhouse Rock" by Elvis Presley - 1957
"Dancing On The Ceiling" by Lionel Richie - 1986
"Down By The Lazy River" by The Osmonds - 1972
"Oh Boy" by Buddy Holly - 1959
"Here Comes My Baby" by The Tremeloes - 1967
"My Baby Loves Lovin'" by White Plains - 1970
"Girls' School" by Wings - 1977
"Hello Mary Lou" by Ricky Nelson - 1961
"Cinderella Sunshine" by Paul Revere & The Raiders - 1968
"SOS" by ABBA - 1975
"Got To Get You Into My Life" by The Beatles - 1966
"Lost In Love" by Air Supply - 1980
"Somebody's Out There" by Triumph - 1986
"Sweet Cherry Wine" by Tommy James & The Shondells - 1969
"Gimme Gimme Good Lovin'" by Crazy Elephant - 1969
"Lay A Little Lovin' On Me" by Robin McNamara - 1970
"My Love" by Paul McCartney & Wings - 1973
"Waterloo" by ABBA - 1974
"Back On My Feet Again" by The Babys - 1979
"Let Me!" by Paul Revere & The Raiders - 1969
"Hard Luck Woman" by Kiss - 1976
"Wake Me Up Before You Go Go" by Wham! - 1984
"Take Me Home Tonight" by Eddie Money - 1986
"Inside Out" by XYZ - 1989
"Turn It On" by Danger Danger - 1989
"Everything I Own" by Bread - 1972
"Feels Like Love" by Danger Danger - 1989
"I Lost My Chance" by David Cassidy - 1972
"(Can't Live Without Your) Love And Affection" by Nelson - 1990
"I've Got The Music In Me" by The Kiki Dee Band - 1974
"Just When I Needed You Most" by Randy VanWarmer - 1979
"If She Knew What She Wants" by The Bangles - 1987
"An Everlasting Love" by Andy Gibb - 1978
"Goin' Home" by The Osmonds - 1973
"Make Your Own Kind Of Music" by Cass Elliott - 1969

ACKNOWLEDGMENTS

As always, I must thank my alpha and beta readers, for without you this would be a very lonely journey. Your extra sets of eyes, honest feedback, encouragement, late night messaging sessions and never-ending support are priceless to me. I couldn't do this without you!

There are three people in my life who, behind the scenes, give me the kick in the pants I need when I'm ready to give up, or when I need the emotional support only an author can give because they *get* it. They understand the struggle and are always there to pull me off the ledge in every aspect of my life, without question, any time of day. I am forever indebted to Amy Markstahler, Paul Salley and Barbara Avon, and I am grateful to call them my friends. They have also written some of my favorite books, and I highly encourage you to check them out.

I have to thank my family and friends, who support me unconditionally every single day. Without you, I probably wouldn't sell a single book. And last, but certainly not least, I must thank Ken, my partner in crime, for without you I would not be living the dream of a full-time writer. I am truly blessed.

www.kathleenstone.org

CHECK OUT MY THREADLESS MERCHANDISE SHOP BY USING THE CODE BELOW:

ENJOY LISTENING TO THE "HEY JUDE" SOUNDTRACK ON SPOTIFY BY USING THE CODE BELOW:

Other works by Kathleen Stone

Tell Me You Love Me

~ 2021 National Indie Excellence Awards Contemporary Fiction winner

~ 2021 Global Ebook Awards silver medal winner

~ 2021 Independent Publisher Book Awards bronze medal winner

~ 2021 Independent Press Awards Distinguished Favorite

Whispers On A String

~ 2020 IAN Book of the Year Outstanding Women's Fiction winner

~ 2020 American Fiction Awards finalist

~ 2020 National Indie Excellence Awards finalist

~ 2020 Author Shout Reader Ready Awards honorable mention

The Head Case rock novel series:

    Head Case

    Whiplash

    Haven

ANTHOLOGIES:

(Published under Kathleen Strelow)

Secrets, Fact or Fiction Volume I & II

Printed in Great Britain
by Amazon